StoneSoup

Annual 2018

Edited by Sarah Ainsworth (Blog), Jane Levi
(Annual) & Emma Wood (Print)
Cover design by Joe Ewart
Production by Sarah Ainsworth
Director: William Rubel

Published by Children's Art Foundation
–Stone Soup Inc.
126 Otis Street, Santa Cruz, CA 95060 USA

Stone Soup, founded in 1973, is a magazine
available as a single user subscription, an
institutional site license or as a print subscription
at www.Stonesoup.com.

Cover Art

"Mountain Dweller" by Eva Stoitchkova, 11,
Ontario, Canada.

Interior Art

Contents (facing page): Detail from "Orange
Landscape" by Eli Breyer Essiam, 10, Cambridge,
MA. Published in Stone Soup July/August 2018.

Preface (facing page): Detail from "My Chinese
Dream" by Li Lingfei, Shanghai, China. Published
in Stone Soup March 2018.

StoneSoup

Annual 2018

A Year of the Magazine
by and for
Creative Young People

Contents

Preface

There's something exciting and satisfying about collecting the year's work, alongside the best from our excellent young bloggers, into one fat tome. Alone, each issue seems small. Together, they are big enough to be a doorstop. You can think of the making of the *Stone Soup Annual* as being a little like making a pot of stone soup in the kitchen. Each issue, online book review, and blog post are the ingredients. It isn't until we bring all the issues and a selection of online material into the *Annual* that we can fully see what the whole year's *Stone Soup* turned out to be.

While it's exciting to hold the year's material all together in one's hands and see what a massive body of work it is, what excites us the most about this year's *Annual* is the variety and power of what our authors and artists created. There are one-page stories that evoke what we call a "sense of place," there are long stories that explore what it means to move house and to lose a friend, to bully and to be bullied. There are small poems that take on the meaning of the world, and long poems that describe a single thing. There are contemporary fairytales, and stories

that attempt to up-end our idea of the "fairytale." There are photographs, pastel drawings, paintings, collages, and watercolors. There is a screenplay, a movie review, a couple of self-por-traits. From our bloggers, there are book reviews, musical compositions, comics, and essays on a range of subjects.

We hope this book inspires all of you out there—no matter how old you are!—as each piece in it has inspired all of us at *Stone Soup* over the past year.

Thank you to all our readers and subscribers, as well as to all of our contributors, and to everyone who submitted to *Stone Soup* this year. All of you have helped to make the magazine, the website, and the book, and for that we are grateful.

Welcome to the *Stone Soup Annual 2018*.

StoneSoup

Issues

StoneSoup

JANUARY 2018   VOLUME 46 / ISSUE 1

StoneSoup

The magazine supporting creative kids around the world

Editor
Emma Wood

Director
William Rubel

Operations
Jane Levi

Education
Sarah Ainsworth

Design
Joe Ewart, Society

Production
Emma Birches

Check us out on Social Media:

Editor's Note

I write to you before a crackling fire. It is officially winter in the Santa Cruz mountains, which, for us, means rain, not snow. But I grew up in the Northeast, and so I am dreaming of snow this time of year. And these poems and stories reflect that: many of them are full of the white flakes, bitter winds, and ice. A few, however, reflect the winter we enjoy in California—crisp but still beautiful, a kind of paradise. As for the art: while there are a few wintry images, I worked to bring a splash of color to the short, dark days. Enjoy (perhaps with some hot chocolate!)

Letters: Do you have something to say about something you've read or seen in *Stone Soup*? If you do, we'd love to hear from you, and we might print your letter on our Letters to the Editor page! Post a comment on our website, or write to us at editor@Stonesoup.com.

Submissions: Our guidelines for submission are on the Submit page at Stonesoup.com, where you will also find a link to our Submittable online submissions portal.

Subscriptions: to subscribe to *Stone Soup*, please press the Subscribe button at Stonesoup.com.

On the cover:
'Night at the Lake'

**by George Tang, 9
Barrington, RI**

StoneSoup
Contents

POETRY

ART

Frozen Beauty

by Hanna Gustafson, 12
South Burlington, VT

Winter

by Sheila Northrup, 10
Madison, CT

Soft, white, flakes drift down, following the wind.
They bring a sense of happiness to the air.
The golden rays of warmth strike onto the fluffy blanket below.
The harsh cold still manages to crawl inside houses.
Heat vents roar and the windows give out a moan.
Thick clouds soon hide the sun.
Smoke floats out of the chimneys into the bitter air, while leaves and grass are out of sight.
The snow is swallowing up trees.
Hot chocolate is being slurped down at every house.
Now it is official.
Winter is finally here.

Pawprints in the Snow
Stella, the house cat, gets stuck outside in the swirling snow and freezing wind

Stella huddled against the side of the house, eyes slitted against the blowing snow. The wind whistled in the small cat's ears, slicing through her gray fur and making her tremble uncontrollably. Her teeth chattered, and her paws were numb. She let out a miserable mewl. "Why, oh why, did I ever leave home?"

Stella hadn't *meant* to run away, exactly; she'd only wanted to go outside for a little and bat at this new, entertaining white fluff that drifted out of the sky. But when Stella was done romping around and had meowed at the door, no friendly human had come to let her in. Not even when she'd yowled and raked her claws down the door!

Stella closed her eyes and pictured the door, red paint scarred with five gashes exposing raw wood. She felt like the door now, her "paint" scraped away to reveal the small, scared cat inside.

Knowing she couldn't go inside, Stella had wandered away, bored and alone. Now night was falling, the world growing darker and colder, and all Stella wanted to do was go home. *A warm fire, a comfy bed, my human's gentle hands stroking my back . . .*

Stella shook her head, trying to clear away the fantasy like it was a film of dust on her fur. *I can't sleep here*, she thought. *I've got to find a better place.* Fighting off the anxiety waging war in her mind, Stella got stiffly to her paws and raised her chin, tail high. *I am Stella. And no mere storm defeats me!*

This one sure would give her a run for her money, though. The snow was up her belly, and Stella couldn't feel a hair on her pelt after only a few heartbeats of walking. She trekked on, though, clinging to the hope that she'd somehow find a warm, cozy house to sleep in.

What felt like days later, but was probably only a couple minutes, Stella felt like giving up. No more "I can do it" mentality for this cat. But, like a vision before her, Stella saw... an area without snow? She sucked in her breath quickly, regretting it as the cold air stung her throat.

An alley lay before her, shielded from the swirling snow. Stella's green eyes stretched wide. Her tail whisked with excitement. Suddenly rejuvenated, she streaked forward, practically flying over the snow, powder flinging up behind her like a freezing mist.

In the alley now, Stella's gaze roved until it rested on a small nook behind a metal trash can, lined with shredded newspaper. Stella loped to it, kneading her paws in the newspaper, pricking it with her claws. *I couldn't have made a better bed myself*, she thought with a pleased, exhausted purr.

All of her energy spurt drained, Stella collapsed onto the newspaper, asleep almost before her eyes closed.

by Sage Young, 12
Redmond, OR

A low, rolling growl sounded through the alley. Stella's eyes popped open, glowing in the early morning darkness. Fear coursed through her, electrifying the fur on her back; it stood straight up.

A huge, gray animal stood before her. It had short, coarse fur, a bushy, ringed tail, small, round ears, and a black mask around its beady eyes. Its lips were peeled back from sharp, yellowed teeth, and its eyes had a malicious gleam.

Terror made Stella feel faint. This was a creature from nightmares, an animal that haunted even the bravest of cats.

Raccoon.

Another deafening growl erupted from the raccoon, and Stella added her own scared shriek to the clamor. The rank scent of raccoon filled her nose, and she realized it came from the newspaper as well as the creature. She must have been too tired last night to recognize the smell. "Oh no!" she wailed aloud. "I stole its home!"

The raccoon advanced on Stella, claws clicking menacingly on the concrete. Stella backed up farther and farther, until her tail lashed into the brick wall of the alley. The raccoon let out a short, sharp bark, knowing it had the cat trapped. The expression in its eyes changed from anger to a cold happiness.

Panic took over Stella's body. Her whole pelt bushed out; she looked like a ball of gray fuzz with green eyes that flickered with fear. Her mind whirled with survival instinct. Fight or flight.

Flight.

Stella's muscles tensed, and before she knew what was happening, she was leaping, soaring right over a stunned raccoon, landing neatly on light paws and sprinting out of that alley as fast as if her tail were on fire. The creature's eerie screeches still echoed in her ears, vibrating in her.

Stella was like the wind, whooshing over the snow, leaving nothing but swirling flakes in her wake. She was like a bird, riding the snowdrifts and swooping down them in great bounds. She was like an arrow, springing forward and zipping ahead. So fast . . . faster . . . faster . . . *faster . . .*

Despite herself, Stella laughed aloud, enjoying the cold air whipping around her face, fondling her ears, flattening her whiskers. She hadn't felt this free for as long as she could remember. And that thought made her skid to a sudden halt, showering snowflakes in a white cloud.

Now that she knew what it was like to be free, how could she ever go back?

Stella's mind churned like ocean waves, each idea crashing into the one before until she couldn't think straight, spraying little particles of thoughts everywhere.

Inside or out? Together or alone? Home or free?

The lure of the wild tugged at Stella. It beckoned her, waving to her with curls of wind and flurries of snow. But home called too. Warmth and comfort, a human who loved her . . . Stella's heart ached, but her decision was made. How could she abandon her human? She needed Stella . . . and Stella needed her.

As soon as she'd thought that, Stella felt a flash of something familiar. She stiffened. She could smell *home!*

Heart thumping a tattoo against her ribs, Stella breathed deeply, inhaling the scents of home, of love and welcomeness and hope. With a yowl of triumph, she raced away, tracing the smell. A few blocks away, she slowed to a trot.

There it was. Her house: gray paint, blue shutters, red door bearing her scratches. Stella approached cautiously, almost believing that if she moved too fast it all would disappear, like ripples distorting a reflection in water.

But it didn't. The door opened, and with mirroring cries of joy, the human and her cat were reunited. The human scooped Stella into her arms, hugging her close. Stella relaxed completely into the human, purrs shaking her body violently. She was home, leaving the pawprints in the snow behind forever.

Teary-eyed Giraffe

by Aevahaadya Arun, 6
Ontario, Canada

Paradise?

by **Kaya Simcoe**, 11
Cardiff, CA

As I look around me, surveying my surroundings, everything seems different. The sunlight that is spilling onto the ocean sparkles like a thousand gems, and I'm lead to wonder if there actually are a thousand gems floating on the clear surface. The palm trees sweep over me, like protectors, never tiring of providing me shade. A seagull whooshes over me, bringing freedom to my body, also. The sand softly crunches under my feet, a million grains smushed per footprint. Yet, the tide washes them away, so I'm here, but there is no proof that I ever came. My heart beats gently in my chest, like a friend. I root my feet deeper, deeper, into the sand. My eyes are closed, but the bejeweled ocean still swims in front of my focus. "Paradise", I think slowly. I open my eyes, and it's like the slow motion film has stopped. My best friend, Katy, grabs my arm and says loudly over the waves, "Melody, let's go into the water!" I smile at her, and without saying anything else, we dash in. We spend the next few hours body surfing, boogie boarding, and everything else two city girls visiting California could want to do. It was only when we returned to our hotel, late that night, stuffed with fresh sushi and organic juice, that I remembered those three seconds, standing there with my eyes closed and the wind in my hair. "Paradise" I had thought. But then I looked around the darkening hotel room, where I could see the outlines of my family, could hear their breathing, as the soft sheets wrapped around me in a perfect way, I sort of felt like that was paradise, too.

We left California a few days later, and at first, I worried that I would be losing my precious paradise. But, I had the window seat in our plane, and the clouds looked like bunnies. I also got an orange fizzy water, and some of my favorite chips, so that was pretty great, also. What I realized, sitting there on that plane, watching California fade away, is that paradise is something you carry with you. You just need to find it.

And you know what? As I sit here, writing this on the window seat of our apartment, watching the sunset over New York City, I kind of feel like this is paradise, too.

Is paradise a place... or a feeling?

Pray

by Gianna Harris, 9
Metairie, LA

I kneel down to the river
And say my prayers
As I hear the water
flowing and rolling
I think about how freedom has overgrown
The magnificent mud of the Mississippi
I hear birds skim the treetops
And remember how, when I was a little girl,
My mom walked me there, and
I saw the brown water
I feel memories drift on the surface and
See my shadow through the deep.

Ababa Wagari

by Christian W. Wagari, 11
Carlsbad, CA

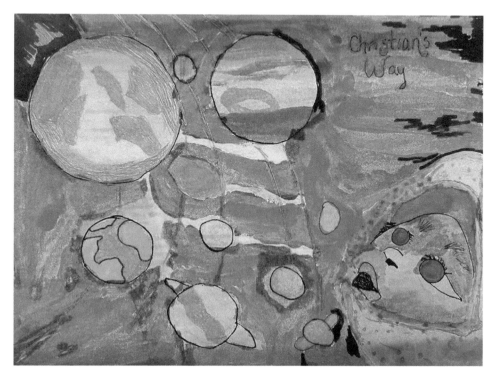

Fruits Like Heaven

Sketches

by Saenger Breen, 12
Northampton, MA

That morning at breakfast, Dylan sat perched on his usual seat at the table, sketching happily. I grabbed the milk and a spoon and sat down. I poured myself a heaping bowl of Cheerios, most of which spilled on the table. Dylan's pencil scribbled away, and he periodically blew huge breaths over his paper to get rid of the shreds of eraser. Curious about what he was working so diligently at, I leaned over to get a better view.

"Dylan!" I shouted. He was adding onto one of my drawings, and had already reshaped a good portion of it. Startled, Dylan looked up.

"What?"

"I've been working on that forever!" I snatched my notebook out of his hands. He'd made the people cartoon like and unrealistic, and shaded in all the wrong places.

"You totally screwed up the whole thing!" I yelled.

"I didn't screw up anything!" he said, defensively.

"I've told you a million times not to touch my stuff, and specifically not my sketchbook!" I flipped through the pages to see if he'd ruined any other drawings. He hadn't. I flipped back to the drawing he was working on. I examined it closely, looking for flaws to point out. The faces of the people had become less dimensional and smudgy. Dylan always drew details with tons of shading, most of which

wasn't necessary. Sometimes I'd teach him where to shade, and help him with drawing figures, but he still resorted to his box-like, over shaded style.

He'd added onto drawings before, but those were just sketches I'd whipped up in a few minutes. I'd been perfecting this one for at least a month. The paper was so worn out from my erasing, that there were shreds of it peeling off. And since Dylan pressed so hard that graphite was sprinkled all over the paper like snowflakes, I knew I wouldn't be able to fully erase what he'd done without making a hole in the paper. I also saw he smudged over the shading that had taken me forever to get right.

"God Dylan, you completely ruined it!" I said, the anger boiling out of me. "You know you suck at drawing figures. In fact, you suck at drawing, period, so why did you have screw up my sketch?"

"I didn't ruin it! And if you'd actually show me how to draw people, like you always promise, then maybe I'd be better!"

"You're so annoying! Why would I want to waste my time teaching you?"

"Oh yeah? Well then I'm glad it's ruined!"

"I hate you!" I said through my teeth. Even though he was still frowning at me, I could tell he was hurt. He started to say something, but I cut him off. "Never ask me to

*Dylan's just Zoe's annoying little brother...
until a snowstorm changes everything*

teach you anything ever again. And don't ever add onto any of my work." Not waiting for a response, I stomped out of the kitchen. I thumped into my room and tossed my sketchbook on my bed. I threw it so hard it slid off the edge and onto the floor. I just left it there. When I passed by the kitchen on my way to the front door, I didn't look in. I impatiently waited for the bus, fuming.

On the way home from school, I sat crammed into the gray leather bus seat, intensely sketching, disregarding the world around me. Frustrated that my pencil wasn't conveying the image in my mind, I flipped to a fresh page. The page I flipped to happened one of Dylan's drawings. All day had been thinking about what happened, and by the time I'd gotten on the bus to go home, I'd realized I'd been a jerk. I decided I should apologize. When I got off the bus, I was blasted with cold air and snow. The snow crept up my ankles as I trudged to the front door. When I got inside, I dropped my backpack on the floor, which made a loud thump, then slid off my boots and tossed my coat on the floor.

"Dylan?" I called. The light in the kitchen was on, but nobody was there. My bowl of dried Cheerios was still on the table from the morning. He must be in his room.

"Hey, Zoe," my Dad called up from the basement.

"Hi, Dad."

"Is it really coming down out there?"

"Yeah, there's already a solid 4 inches."

"Wow, I didn't think the storm would actually hit."

"And it looks like it's just the beginning," I added, glancing out the window. It had started piling up around noon, and there was already a thick white blanket covering everything. I went upstairs to Dylan's room. His door was closed.

"Dylan?" I called again, pushing open the door. His room was empty. His bed was unmade, and a book was propped open, face down on his bed. The phone rang. I ran downstairs to the living room, but my Dad picked it up before I got there. I looked outside again. Snow swirled around vigorously, and the wind whipped the side of the house. Where was Dylan? I was going to ask my Dad, but he didn't like it when we interrupted him when he was on the phone. I sighed. I'd just apologize later. I walked into the kitchen to look for a snack. I grabbed the Ritz crackers out of the cabinet. The wrapper crinkled as I dumped the crackers on the counter. I stood munching on them.

My Dad came running up the stairs from the basement. His face was pale, and his eyes were big and wild. "Come on Zoe, we need to go now."

"What? Why?"

"We need to go to the hospital." He grabbed his coat off the hook near the door.

"What?" I asked, shocked. I started to panic when he didn't answer.

"To see Dylan." He jammed his hat down on his head and started to tie his shoes.

"Why is Dylan in the hospital?" He didn't respond at first, but just stood there,

"Dad?" I yelled frantically.

Slowly he said, "His elementary school sent everyone home at noon, because of the snow. But then Liam's mom took Liam and Dylan to the movies. They were heading home, but then they slipped on some snow or ice or something, and they went off the road."

I blinked and shook my head in disbelief. My heart thumped in my chest like horse's hooves hitting the ground. I imagined it in my mind. Their car skidding off the road, the windows shattering as it crashed into trees. I imagined his scream, echoing over the empty roads, cutting through the silence of the falling snow. It replayed over and over. Millions of questions swirled through my head. I brushed away most of them, but one stayed, clear as the ice that covered the roads. It scared me so much, I didn't even want to think it. But I needed to get it out.

"Is he dead?" I said, my voice trembling. My words held in the silence. I bit my lip, tears welling up in my eyes. I had always assumed that my Mom and Dad had the answers to everything. I always assumed that they always knew what to do. But for

the first time, I could see the fear in his eyes. I could see the uncertainty.

"They said he was taken to the ER, but they couldn't give me any other information."

I nodded, and swallowed hard. I tried to process it. Waves of guilt flooded over me. I thought of the last thing I'd said to him. I felt like I was being broken, like I was falling into a world of pain. What if I'd lost him?

"Come on, we have to go."

My legs felt like lead as I walked to the door. I shoved myself into my coat, which was damp from melted snow. When he opened the door, my tears stung, frozen against my face. I walked to the end of the porch, but then stopped. I stared into space. The wind blew my hair around wildly.

"Zoe," My dad said. He put his hand on my shoulder and walked me over to the car. I got in the car feeling numb. Tears slid down my winter jacket.

Just as he was about to pull out of the driveway, I shouted, "Wait!" I pushed open the door and jumped out of the car.

"Zoe!" He yelled after me.

I ran to the front door, flung it open, and charged up the stairs. When I reached my door I stopped and caught my breath. I pushed the door open and ran around to the other side of my bed. It was still there, lying on the floor face down, with my name scribbled on the back. I picked it up, and grabbed a pencil from my desk. Then I ran down to the car, clutching my sketchbook to my chest.

Annie with Dogs

by Valentina Ventura, 4
Des Moines, IA

Winter

by Micah Lim, 8
Guilford, CT

The howl of the wind
The crisp air
And the crunching of boots on a bed of snow
The brightest white you will ever see
The evergreens struggle against the wind

A Surfing Tradition

by James Wilson, 11
Riverside, California

A special tradition for New Year's Day

The sun raised its head over a cold California coast. This sun was a special sun. It was the first sun of the year. There was to be a special gathering at the beach. It is what is called a "paddle-out." Cars slowly gathered at the beach. The people inside the cars exited and came to the shore. No one talked, all they did was look at the horizon, which was light red from the coming sun. The waves were so big it was hard to see the horizon at times. All of them were bundled up, trying to protect themselves from the piercing cold. Every part of their body that was not bundled up was already turning blue.

Soon an old Ford pickup truck parked with the back facing the ocean. The paint on this vehicle was chipping and there were many marks of rust on it. It was filled with wood. Three people got out of the pickup and unhitched the back, exposing the wood. The wood was twisted and knotted so bad it was terrible. Two teenagers came forward and started unloading the wood. They brought it over to a stone fireplace. The three men came into the crowd. Thankful nods went their way but still no one talked, almost as if they were in a trance. Soon a car pulled up with surfboards on the rack. The driver emerged from the car and started untying the boards. Once he was done he set the three boards by the pickup truck. The three men came forward and changed into their trunks but nothing else. They started to wax their boards, and even though they shivered and were cold to the bone they never put on anything except for their trunks. The group stood motionless, just looking at the horizon. Once the three men were done waxing their boards they walked, with their boards on their shoulder, to the shore and started whispering to each other. Then they stood motionless until the shore break calmed for a little bit and then they sprang into the water and started paddling furiously. The crowd on the beach watched them, still not talking.

When the men were outside they sat there, millions of good waves passing under them. Then one set came with three waves in it. These waves weren't good, these waves were spectacular. The waves so clear and crisp. Each one of them chose their own wave. They glided over the waves, no cutbacks, no nose-riding, nothing but gliding. They all rode in and as the last one exited the water something happened. The crowd cheered, the first sound they made all morning. Soon the festivities began. People got coffee and hot cocoa. People were yelling "Hey John" and such.

Later a spectator of the event asked one of the teenagers who started the fire, "What was the deal with that?" and the teenager said, "It's a tradition."

Book Review

Cloud and Wallfish by Anne Nesbet;
Candlewick Press, 2016; $16.99

Who knew that a regular-looking
book could have such an impact
on readers and how they view the
world? Going into *Cloud and Wallfish*,
a historical fiction novel, I was a bit
doubtful on how Anne Nesbet was
going to weave such a tragic and
complex topic like the Berlin Wall
into youth literature. However, all my
doubts were diminished after reading
this wonderfully written novel. While
this story is geared towards youth,
it still thrums with ever-important
themes of finding who you are and
remaining loyal to your friends, even
through tough times.

Set in 1989, Noah Keller, the
main protagonist, had always lead
an ordinary American life. That is,
until his parents announce that his
name is Jonah, not Noah, and that
they will be moving to East Berlin. At
the time, Germany was divided into
two countries: East Germany and
West Germany. In East Germany, the
country that Noah moves to, there are
many complications. Noah isn't free
to discuss anything in his apartment,
nor is he allowed to question his
government. Most of his days are
lonely, until he meets "Cloud" Claudia,
who lives in the same apartment with
her grandmother. The strange part?
Her parents have disappeared, and
nobody seems to know why.

This book taught me a few
moral lessons, namely about loyalty.
In the novel, Noah gets separated
from Claudia, ending up on West
Berlin with Claudia in East Berlin.
Everybody tells Noah that he will
never see his friend ever again, but
Noah perseveres, standing on the
platform in West Berlin that overlooks
East Berlin. For weeks, he holds a sign
with a message for his friend, to no
avail. Finally, right when Noah was
about to give up, he sees Claudia again
and is able to show her his message,
which is: "I have not forgotten you,
Cloud!" This shows that you should
never give up on your goal, and Noah
also demonstrates what it means to
remain loyal to your friends.

Cloud and Wallfish didn't just
teach me moral lessons—it also had
relatable characters. I personally

Reviewed by
Alexandra Reynaud, 13
Portland, OR

can identify with this situation that Noah and Claudia are in. When I was younger, my best friend moved across the country. I was scared that our friendship would drift apart on account of the distance between us, which resonates with Claudia's fear of being forgotten. As I feared, we drifted apart, due to the distance between us. However, this book inspired me to make more of an effort to keep in touch, and to show my friend that I, too, had not forgotten her.

In addition, I also related to Noah's fear of speaking in class. Noah was born with a stutter, so during school, he wouldn't express his opinions frequently in fear of being teased or laughed at. I don't have a stutter, but it can be hard sometimes to speak up in class simply because I'm afraid of what others may think. However, towards the end of the novel, Noah learns to speak up despite what others may think, which also inspired me to share my opinions more frequently in class.

Though it's juvenile fiction, I believe that everyone should read this book, even adults. It is at once a poignant novel about friendship and family, a historical fiction, and a thriller that will keep you on the edge of your seat. I know that this book changed my life—why not let it change yours, too?

Honor Roll

Welcome to the *Stone Soup* Honor Roll. Every month we receive submissions from hundreds of kids from around the world. Unfortunately, we don't have space to publish all the great work we receive. We want to commend some of these talented writers and artists and encourage them to keep creating.

Fiction

Oliver Paratore Block, 10
Sarah Baglin, 10
Bernard Elbert, 9
Evelyn Hsu, 11
Sophia Lu, 11
Laurence Manderson, 10
Derek Montes-Baffier, 11
Marwa Moustafa, 12
Stiles Fraser White, 13

Poetry

Rian Fetting, 9
Caleb Ford, 12
Nadja Goldberg, 13
Hazel Kurian, 10
Isabelle Mantecon, 6
Isabella Webb, 11

Art

Isobel Cammish, 12
Sarah Liu, 12
Vivian Wang, 10

Don't forget to visit Stonesoup.com to browse our bonus materials. There you will find

- 20 years of back issues—around 5,000 stories, poems and reviews
- Blog posts from our Young Bloggers on subjects from sports to sewing plus ecology, reading and book reviews
- Video interviews with *Stone Soup* authors
- Music, spoken word and performances

Visit the *Stone Soup* Store at Stonesoupstore.com to buy

- Books—the 2017 *Stone Soup Annual*, a bound collection of all the year's issues, as well as themed anthologies
- Art prints—high quality prints from our collection of children's art
- Journals and Sketchbooks for writing and drawing
  ... and more!

StoneSoup

FEBRUARY 2018

VOLUME 46 / ISSUE 2

StoneSoup

The magazine supporting creative kids around the world

Editor
Emma Wood

Director
William Rubel

Operations
Jane Levi

Education
Sarah Ainsworth

Design
Joe Ewart, Society

Production
Emma Birches

Stone Soup (ISSN 0094 579X) is published online eleven times a year—monthly, with a combined July/August summer issue. Copyright © 2018 by the Children's Art Foundation, a 501(c)(3) non-profit organization, located in Santa Cruz, California. All rights reserved. Thirty-five percent of our subscription price is tax-deductible. Subscribe at Stonesoup.com.

Stone Soup is available from the Library of Congress in Braille for visually handicapped readers. To request the Braille edition, call +1 800-424-8567.

Check us out on Social Media;

Editor's Note

A princess stuck in a tower. A very ill girl confined to her room. A poem that enacts the feeling of being trapped in a love/hate relationship. A young boy whose fear of heights restricts his movement. A poem that describes beauty as "suffocating." The stories and poems in this issue are about being confined, trapped, restricted, stuck, suffocated. They are about wanting to escape—either physically or mentally—from that "stuckness." This is the feeling, to me, of February: it is a time of rain, snow, cold, and wind after the novelty of that weather has worn off. It is a month for dreaming of spring, of an escape.

Letters: Do you have something to say about something you've read or seen in *Stone Soup*? If you do, we'd love to hear from you, and we might print your letter on our Letters to the Editor page! Post a comment on our website, or write to us at editor@Stonesoup.com.

Submissions: Our guidelines for submission are on the Submit page at Stonesoup.com, where you will also find a link to our Submittable online submissions portal.

Subscriptions: to subscribe to *Stone Soup*, please press the Subscribe button at our webpage, Stonesoup.com.

On the cover:
'Mist at the Lake',

**by Brian Qi, 11
Lexington, MA**

StoneSoup
Contents

STORIES

We No Longer Go Outside

Hua Hua, a young dog, reflects on life with her owner—before she got sick

Sunrays pour into the old slider window, illuminating the white-washed walls of the bedroom; posters and certificates are plastered on the opposite wall, their color faded from years of sun. A little girl is curled up in bed, clutching the blankets in fitful sleep. I sigh and gaze through the window at the pale blue sky, which is undisturbed by occasional clouds. Outside, the leaves of the cherry blossom tree slowly wave in the breeze, and the birds continue their constant chatter.

"Let's go play," I whimper as I lick Sarah's face.

"Oh, Hua Hua, you want to go play?" Sarah asks; her face reveals a solemn expression.

"Play!" I bark, wagging my tail.

"I'm sorry," she replies, and lies back down.

I rest my chin on my paws, and Sarah pulls me close to her chest as she lazily strokes my white fur. Nuzzling my nose into her arms, I breathe in the unmistakable scent of her, like daisies. Only the smell is muddled in with something else I can't quite explain; it must be from her numerous trips to the hospital. I look around Sarah's room. Her closet stands in one corner, with her clothes and walking shoes neatly sorted inside. Her homework still lies open on her desk. Usually, she would finish it before she'd take me on a walk, but it's been awhile since we've gone

outside together. The nightstand by the bed is piled high with get well cards from all her friends and neighbors, those people I like to bark at when they walk past. Her room smells like the vet's office, too spotless, not like it used to. It used to smell like sunshine—clean, fresh, crisp.

I remember when Sarah and I first met. I was a little puppy then, running around with not a thing in the world that concerned me. You could say I was very energetic, curious, and brave. I didn't care if I got hurt because I didn't know what pain felt like. In the cage at SPCA, Sarah crouched down next to me and brought me into her arms. I looked at her and smelled daisies. Her golden brown hair was like long grass growing on the hillside. Her bright smile radiated so much happiness that it was like lying in the warm sun. I took in her freckles, her dimples, and her eyes; I memorized the shape of her face and her daisy-like smell and etched them into my dog heart. Her eyes were blue like sky, and they let me see so deep into her feelings. I saw happiness, playfulness, and pleasure. I saw anything and everything I ever wanted all in a little girl.

That day, Sarah took me to my new home, and we played together in the park. She laughed at me running in circles, chasing my own tail. Sarah's laugh was so beautiful; it sounded like the wind chimes that were always

by Stella Lin, 12
San Ramon, California

tinkling lightly in backyards. That sound was so sharp and crisp, yet delicate and light at the same time.

I remember we also played with my red rubber ball that she gave me. She drew her arm back and threw it far, far into the field. I came bounding back through the grass with the ball clenched in my mouth and placed it at her feet. I yipped at her to throw it again and again until I lay panting on the grass, too tired to play.

Feeling the dryness in my throat, I heard the rushing water of the fountain nearby. I raced over to the fountain and dove in. Instantly, I realized that my paws struck only cold water, no surface. Frantically gyrating my legs, I tried to keep my head above the water splashing down from the top of the fountain. What I thought would be refreshing was suddenly like dying. Just as the water began to push me under, I felt two warm, delicate hands pull me to safety.

"Hua Hua, you're such a silly goose. Why would you jump into such a big fountain?" She dried me and hugged me close, burying her nose into my fur.

How I long to be at the park right now with Sarah. I can almost feel the wind ruffling my fur and smell the soil beneath my paws. I can feel myself soaking in the warm sunshine spilling from above, and picture myself running with my red ball in my mouth and dropping it at Sarah's feet.

With contentment, I sigh as I recall these joyous moments of our lives. I turn my head to look at Sarah now. She still has her dazzling sky-blue eyes, but she has lost her golden brown hair, and I no longer hear her beautiful laugh anymore. We no longer spend the afternoon in the park playing with my red ball, or sprawled on the grass, and we no longer go outside. Now, she just stays in bed and takes trips to the hospital.

I understand that she still loves me, but she can no longer play with me or take me on walks. I understand that things will never be like they were before. I snuggle up closer to Sarah, and she giggles. Whatever she is going through, I am her guardian and loyal friend, and I will do my best to keep her smiling. Nothing in the world can make me leave her side. Just as she saved me from the rough waters, I want to pull her to safety.

Creek Reflection

by Filomena Bertucci, 12
Quilcene, WA

Love/Hate Relationship

by Morgan Lane, 12
Longmont, CO

Magnificence!
There is no
Screeching.
The notes
Are pronounced.
Mistakes,
Nonexistent.
The beauty
Piercing the ears.
The sound
Flowing,
A river.
Unlike
Any other.
I will listen to
It all day.
Hating
When it ends.
It makes me smile.
Why me?

Why me?
It makes me smile
When it ends.
Hating
It all day.
I will listen to
Any other.
Unlike
A river
Flowing.
The sound
Piercing the ears.
The beauty,
Nonexistent.
Mistakes,
Are pronounced.
The notes,
Screeching.
There is no
Magnificence.

Untitled

by Adhav Dhanavel Kumar, 10
Coimbatore, India

Stroll at Sunset

by Nour Mokbel, 11
Springfield, VA

Rolling waves of green blue spume,
Soothe my aching feet,
Silver specks whiz by against the stone,
I look up from the shallow waters,
The sky coated in a pastel orange pink,
Seagulls soar my what beauty,
A cooling breeze whistles by,

It hums through tireless work day and night,
The painter of the skies brushes his paintbrush silently,
Tiny green creatures hidden in rough sand,
Who are brave enough to disturb the quieting day,

And now I must go before the waves whisk me off,
I watch as the remains of sunset absorb into the now starry night.

Glass Bunny

by Sarah Liu, 12
Weston, FL

The Balcony

by Una Dorr, 11
Brooklyn, NY

It was a tall, weather-beaten building with countless weather-beaten balconies jutting out of its sides. Milo, a plump and red-faced 9-year-old, had felt unsafe in the top floor drafty apartment since his grandma had sold her oceanside cottage and deposited him and his loyal and fat cat Ella into this leaning block of misery last July.

Of course, he always felt queasy in high places, afraid his usual clumsiness might send him hurtling through the air only to land as flat as a pancake on the concrete below—but there was something particularly terrifying about this place. Perhaps it was the way the ceiling fan pointed as if it might just send something—like Milo's homework—through the doors to the balcony that would swing open if the lock system malfunctioned. That thing might just land on the balcony, coaxing you to climb out to retrieve it. (Kind-hearted but pessimistic Milo always assumed the worst would happen—that his weight would make the whole balcony crack off the side of the building, as he had thought one afternoon when his math homework had sailed out there—that homework never did come back, and it caused him to get in trouble in

school for the first time the next day.)

Or maybe the scariness lay in the windows, low enough to the floor for even a boy of Milo's height to fall out of. Or perhaps it was merely the place where you would land if you did fall: an enormous gravel parking lot with stones sharp enough to cut you if angled in the correct way. Milo often stood in his apartment (as far from the windows as possible, of course) wondering if there was a reason the apartment was so cheap: the plumbing worked and there was thick carpeting in some of the rooms, even—was it cheap because it was so high, which made you more likely to—

Snap out of it, stupid! Nobody else on the top floor is scared! Grandma, with her fear of dust bunnies hasn't given its height a thought! There isn't anything to be afraid of.

But Milo's complete trust in his grandmother's protection only reassured him for a short period of time. Soon he was back to thinking of his greatest fear: the balconies. Surely three minutes of standing on one would result in it cracking off the side of the building and tumbling 20 stories down to the lot below.

The first few days of living in the

Milo confronts his greatest fear: the 20-story-high balcony

building resulted in his grandmother begging for her little boy safe at home, because he had arranged so many sleepovers with friends that he hadn't spent more than an hour in the apartment with her and Ella. Milo tried other excuses: "Can I camp out in the woods tonight, Grandma?" or "How 'bout we go to the Jersey Shore for a few nights? It's summer break after all, eh?" But it was difficult. How can a child of age nine get out of spending time in his own home?

One average afternoon when the golden summer sun was sinking down the cityscape, Milo noticed something. While stepping into the spacious kitchen, he glanced down at the checkered tiles to find that the shiny, fake gold cat food bowl was just as he had left it 3 hours ago: full. Ella, the enormous tabby cat Milo had cared for and loved as long as he could remember (and long before that too—Milo's memory was far from good), hadn't eaten her food. "Pleasingly plump" did not describe Ella. There was no doubt about it—Ella was a very fat cat, who certainly would never miss a meal. But here the bowl was: full, full, full.

When he had come home from the public outdoor swimming pool a few hours before, he had found a post-it attached to his door, decorated with his grandmother's swirly and impossibly small cursive. He hadn't bothered to read it closely—it probably said that she was at her "volleyball for old people" class at the gym, and that she would be home at 7:00. Milo found himself thinking of this note now: had Grandma gone to the vet with Ella, perhaps?

Milo fished out the note from his pocket (he had stuffed it in there on his frantic run from the bathroom—you see, Milo was afraid of the toilets at the swimming pool.) Squinting, he read what his grandmother had written:

Dear Milo,
This isn't any usual volleyball class! It's the big day, dear, my first competition! You may come if you wish (you know where the gym is, right?) but I know you have much to do. I'll be home at 8:30! I hope to see you in bed when I get home if you decide not to come!
Love,
Grandma
P.S. Don't forget to lock the doors behind you.

Silly Grandma. In their old house, they had to lock the door and Milo was always forgetting, but in this house, *all* the doors locked immediately without any help from humans, but no matter. Milo found himself forgetting small details, too. He reread the note, giving it his full attention. Nothing about Ella, but what was this! Milo hated volleyball, so despite his deep love for his grandma, he wouldn't watch her compete. That meant...8:30! It was 6:30 now, he had 2 more hours by himself! How very, very mature he was: such a long time in a terrifying top-floor apartment without Grandma! His excitement and fear set him in high spirits during his search for the cat. He closely looked in each crevice and crack that Ella's hugeness could fit into. He even ventured near the windows, with the vibrant colors of the sky illuminating the floor below him. His high spirits sunk and sunk as he went on and on inspecting the house.

"Ella! Ellllaaa!" The only response was an eerie echo, that as far as Milo could tell wasn't possible, because there was so much furniture in the house. A few minutes later, the last wisp of excitement had been suffocated by defeat, like a tiny patch of blue in a cloudy sky, gradually being covered by another gray blanket of fog.

Milo sat cross-legged on the beige velvet couch, vigorously biting his nails. He tried to think—where had Ella hidden in the old house? Under… under the bed? No. The space under there was *much* too thin for Ella. Under something, but what? The couch. The couch? The couch!

Milo moved from his position to lying on his stomach, legs dangling off the back of the couch, head dangling over the place where *feet* usually go. He squinted into the endless abyss, and relief washed over him. There she was, the big bundle of fur, probably fast asleep. He reached under and tugged gently on a roll of fat, to wake her up. To his amazement, it came loose, and loose. *Is, is … What is this? What has happened to my cat!?* Finally, Ella unraveled. The thing under the couch was a big bundle of fur—his grandmother's fur coat.

This was simply too much. Tears poured down Milo's face and snot dripped from his nose uncontrollably.

And then he heard a terrible creak, and the sound of something breaking. His tear-stained face swiveled around to face the—the—the balcony. There she was, fast asleep. Definitely her—in the last rays of daylight he could see ears, a nose and an enormous body.

Ella was at the far end of the balcony, asleep. Milo's stomach jumped up to his throat, and stuck there.

It was Ella this time, Milo told himself. Not math homework, Ella. Ella! The love of your life! In determined defiance, Milo robotically walked toward the balcony doors, knowing what the sound had been. The balcony was breaking.

Unaware of his movements, he opened the door—when it had blown shut behind Ella, it had locked. He tried to reach for Ella, call her name, but Ella was far away and totally out. *Ella*, your life. *Ella*, your only real friend. Milo took a foot off the floor that had scared him before, but now seemed as safe and sturdy as ever in comparison to the breaking balcony. *Ella.* He placed it on the concrete floor of the dangerous shelf which might take his life. *Ella.* Another foot on the balcony. *Ella.* Another step. *Ella, Ella, Ella,* another, another, *Ella, Ella, Ella!* A gust of wind. He was almost there! *Ella.* And then another gust, strong and fierce through the nighttime air. The door slammed shut behind him. He was locked out.

Flower Cow

by Cole Gibson, 8
San Rafael, CA

The Road to Williamstown

by Sophie Nerine, 12
Quincy, MA

We are in the valley between two mountains
coated in blue,
like sheep's wool.
It is suffocatingly beautiful,
and exhilarating at the same time.

A river runs by us.
White stream-water moves quickly, unreservedly
down the wooded granite peak
towards the river,
as if filled with the joy of being home.

The road we took was far too filled with cars
for any bird to call these woods their home.
We were alone
with the sky and trees,
with the mountains and river.

Succulent

by Marlena Rohde, 12
San Francisco, CA

The Waterfall

by Natalie Warnke, 12
Eden Prairie, MN

You would think that a princess's life would be amazing and magical but it's not how it seems. I sit on a bed in a tower. Every day. Always nervous. Having that one feeling where you have knots in your stomach. That something would happen. Something evil, something terrible. But every day it was the same: the same voices outside, the same hands handing me food through a slot in the wall. But then something did happen— something bad and evil. Not what I wanted. I wanted a Prince Charming like other kingdoms but I didn't get one.

I heard a scream and the castle doors shutting. People were running, voices were yelling, and I was here alone. I sat there for a while not knowing what to do. My heart started pounding. I sat patiently, knowing that sooner or later someone would remember me. But nobody did. So I started banging on the doors as hard as I could. No one heard me over the screams of terror. We were under attack, and I was stuck in a tower next to it all, hearing the whole thing. I was terrified. My hands shook like maracas. I grabbed a metal pan I had my supper on, and I thrashed it against the door. Surprisingly, a piece broke off. So

much for safe keeping.

I started peeling and chiseling the wood away. After about an hour of work, I finally had a small space to crawl out of. I slowly slipped through with a few splinters that hurt and landed on the first step of the staircase. I ran down the staircase. Then I noticed that voices were gone. Except for one hush one. "Be quiet!" I heard. I was scared. I had never had a real encounter with a human—or at least I can't remember it.

I was nervous but kept going. Quieter this time but at a fast pace. When I was almost down I saw her—a beautiful young girl. She was about three years younger.

"Who are you?" I asked.

"I'm Leda."

All the sudden I felt something I had never felt before: love. Even though I had known her for only a second, I knew she would make an amazing friend. She grabbed my hand and led me out the door.

"Where are we going?!"

"You'll see!" she said as she dragged me through the burned-down doors.

We walked until came to this place. It was amazing and so pretty. There

A princess's life is not so amazing and magical as you'd imagine

was a gorgeous waterfall. She brought me behind it.

There, behind the waterfall, was a small beaten-up mattress and a pair of old shoes. "What is this place?" I asked Leda.

"It's my home. I left the kingdom a little while after my mom passed away. About two months ago. I've been here for a while but I'm getting used to it."

It was a beautiful place. I sat down on the bed. It was kind of hard but I didn't care. We kind of just sat there. When she said I could live here, I was relieved. I would have had nowhere else to go if I couldn't stay here.

When we were done talking about me moving in, I went back to the tower to grab my clothes and maybe a couple pillows. I walked back through the castle doors and I was devastated. I hadn't really noticed how terrible it looked. There was almost nothing left.

I walked over to the tower and up the staircase slowly. When I reached my room, I grabbed a bed sheet and put my clothes on it, then wrapped it up. I grabbed the three pillows on my bed and brought them as well. The only thing left besides that was a bracelet my mom gave me. I felt tears coming up and out as I slipped it onto my hand. Then the dam broke. I sat down on my bed and sobbed. I realized the hands giving me food had belonged to my mom. My mom had been the one making the noise. My mom had protected me from whatever was out there. Now she was gone. I never said thank you when she gave me the food. It wasn't fair.

After I was done crying, I walked back down the staircase and back to the waterfall. I put my clothes down and set the pillows on the bed.

It was about ten o'clock when I fell asleep. It was hard to fall asleep with the raging waterfall in the background but I got over it. When I woke up, the sun was already rising. I saw Leda down by the water; she had something red in her hands—strawberries.

"Hey can I have some?" I asked.

She handed me one. I took a bite into it. It was sweet. I walked back up and sat on the bed. I fiddled with the bracelet around my hand. I guess this would be my life.

Gleaming Star

by Ellen Salovaara, 13
Baltimore, MD

I was young when it happened—a mere eight-years-old. Daddy had gone out one day for work . . . and hadn't come back. The funeral was impossible to bear. Mama was crying hysterically, and the grey-streaked sky pounded down fat, round tears. That night though, Mama took me outside after dinner. The sky was calm then, and a warm breeze tickled my fingers and lazily tossed my hair around. Juniper bushes swung to the breeze's song, and the flat New Mexico land stretched out around us.

"Katie, look up," Mama said as she pulled me up onto her lap. My eyes traced over the endless black sky, weaving in and out of the rooftops. "Do you see the *estrellas*, the stars?"

Even though we are not Hispanic, growing up around Spanish-speaking people had rounded out my knowledge of the language, and Mama's rich voice made the already beautiful words seem delicate and smooth, like chocolate.

I nodded, staring into the tiny stars piercing the inky night sky.

"See that one?" Mama pointed at an especially bright one, directly above me.

"That's Daddy, looking down at us."

I pressed my hands over my heart as silent tears began to roll down my cheeks.

"I love you," I whispered to him

And underneath my hands, deep down in my heart, I felt his voice. *I love you too, my little gleaming star.*

I hear a truck rumble into our gravel driveway, and I push back my chair. Papers are in a tangled mess on the deck table, and I pull my eyes away from them.

"Katie!" My mom rushes to me after she locks the doors to her truck.

"Mama!" I hug her.

"How is everything going? *Bueno*?"

"Yes," I say. "Hectic, though. It's crazy."

Mama laughs. "Been there, sweetheart, been there. I still can't believe my *hija* is getting married!!" She wraps me in another hug, and she begins to cry." Your father would have been so proud." She stands back and looks at me, a sad smile on her face. I force back tears. She had ripped apart the stitches to my time-worn wound.

"So? Where is he?"

As if on cue, Ben comes up behind me and gives me a hug. "Hi, honey. Ready for the wedding?"

I give him a fake glare. "Far from

Years after her father's death, Katie wonders who will walk her down the aisle

it."

He smiles and we all go inside. Mama places the dinner she brought for us on the table. I get up to help Ben with the table settings, but he places a gentle hand on my shoulder. "Don't worry. You've worked really hard today."

"So have you!" I protest.

He laughs. "Figuring out the seating chart is not hard."

"Yes it is! If you put my Aunt Jennie in the sun, we won't be able to hear the priest over her snoring!"

He laughs again. "You just rest, okay?"

I concede and watch their intricate dance, dodging each other as they glide around the kitchen and swirl around counters.

The dinner of chicken, rice, and broccoli is eaten quickly, and before I realize it, Mama is whisking away plates. As Ben is washing the dishes, Mama collects her purse.

"You don't have to go just yet," I try.

Mama smiles. "I wish I could stay, sweetheart. But I—"

"But Mama, the stars are lovely tonight. Just come and sit on the deck for a few minutes, please."

Mama sighs, but I can tell she is just putting on a show. She walks into the kitchen, wordlessly fills two large glasses with raspberry iced tea, and strolls out to the deck. I sit next to her on our old, rickety swing, which creaks ever so slightly when we move. It is metal, but painted white, and has little green vines encircling its arms. I lean into the old green cushion and relax a little.

"Okay, Katie, what do you want to talk about?"

My mama knows me so well. She knew I didn't just want to sit. She knew I had something on my mind.

I brush my hair out of my face and sip my raspberry iced tea. The moon is low tonight, and the night sky is covered in stars. The slight wind , whistles as it dances in and out of the wooden slats on the deck floor, and a few tumbleweeds rustle across the wide-open land.

I want to beat around the bush. I don't want to tear open my wound anymore, but I know I have to say it. So I just start talking.

"I know I should have figured this out already, given how close the wedding is. But . . . who's going to walk me down the aisle?"

Mama sits in silence for a few minutes. She places her hand on mine and stares up at the sky.

"Katie," she finally says, gazing up at the sky. "See that star?"

I nod, looking up at the bright star she is pointing at, winking amidst the sky. "Daddy," I whisper. Mama looks at me, fresh tears blossoming in her eyes. "That's right, Katie. That *estrella* is your father. He's probably listening right now. Can you hear what he's saying?"

"No," I murmur, "but I can feel it." I could. *Hey,* bonita. *I'll be at your wedding, okay? I'll walk you down the aisle if you want, but maybe you should let your Mama do it. I'll still be there, though. It's okay to let go, and know that even when you do, I will always be there. Letting go doesn't have to mean forgetting. I love you, my little gleaming star.*

"I love you, too, Daddy," I whisper

Then I turn to Mom. "He wants you to do it."

A smile spreads across her face.

"And do you want that, *mi hija?*"

Tears flow down my cheeks as I nod a yes.

She hugs me tightly, and as she does, I can feel my wound healing. Eventually, Mama stands up and heads inside. I stay out a little longer, watching the trees sway and the stars twinkle. I can still feel the echo of Daddy's voice: *Letting go doesn't have to mean forgetting.* And then, I feel my heart coming out of its cage and being free. I feel happy.

I love you, my little gleaming star.

Book Review

The Children of Exile by Margaret Peterson Haddix;
Simon & Schuster Books for Young Readers: New York, 2015; $17.99

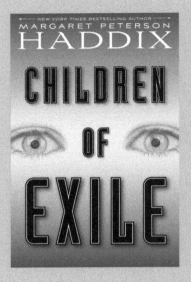

Have you ever had a hard decision deciding between two books to read? I started in the bookstore holding two precious books. My mother's eyes stared down at me expectantly, wanting me to just pick a book and leave. I looked this way and that and finally made the decision to pick the book, *The Children of Exile.* This book's back cover really intrigued me. After reading it, my mind was filled with questions: *Why were the children sent to Fredtown? What type of people were in Fredtown?* And just like that, I became absorbed in this book by Margaret Peterson Haddix. It is an amazing book about staying strong and standing up for your differences.

In this book, the protagonist is a twelve-year-old girl named Rosi.

Ever since she was born, her brother Bobo and she had been sent off to a faraway place called Fredtown. In Fredtown, there were no arguments and everything was resolved by talking it through. One day Rosi, her little brother Bobo, and all the other children of Fredtown were told that they were going to be sent back to their original homes where they would meet their birth mothers and fathers. Rosi has to take care of all the children and fight for what is right. In this action-packed story, nothing is unthinkable.

One of the important themes in this book to me is to speak up and do what is right. When Rosi comes back to her real home, she realizes the ways are different. Many things require a fight when they could be resolved calmly. For example, having lost their children for six years, the real parents want them back very badly. As soon as the plane from Fredtown lands, the parents bang on plane doors and windows making a loud racket. Rosi and the other children become even more scared. Rosi had imagined a calm line of parents waiting peacefully and welcoming their children with kindness and love. She had not expected this.

My favorite part in this book is in the middle. This is when Rosi's real parents take Bobo and her to church.

Reviewed by
Alexandra Reynaud, 13
Portland, OR

Then, when the preacher preaches, he talks about how their town had finally got all of its children back. He said that the Fred parents were evil and were thieves who stole their children. While saying this, Rosi was having a hard time keeping her mouth shut; she wanted to speak up and say how kind, loving, and caring the Fred parents were. Finally, when Rosi couldn't contain herself, she spoke up. All of the parents stared at her as if she was crazy, but she kept going. Rosi is a very brave girl and fought for what is right. I absolutely loved her character in the book.

I connected this to my piano class. In piano there is something called sight-reading. Sight-reading is when you are given a piece of music, and you have to play it without mistakes. When I tried to sight-read one of the pieces, it seemed really hard for me. One day I looked at the front cover of the sight-reading book and saw it said for level 7. I remembered I was testing for level 4, but never brought up the fact that the book was level 7. My piano teacher realized soon enough that the book wasn't the right level. Once I got the level 4 sight-reading book, it seemed much easier to me. After reading the book *The Children of Exile*, I think that if I had been brave and spoke up like Rosi, then the problem of my sight-reading book might have been resolved earlier.

I strongly recommend this book to science fiction lovers with a little bit of mystery mixed into it. This story is good for young adults. Both girls and boys will be cheering for Rosi along the way as she finds her freedom. I cannot imagine this story being written any better. Once you pick up the book *The Children of Exile* you will not be able to put it down so BEWARE!

Honor Roll

Welcome to the *Stone Soup* Honor Roll. Every month we receive submissions from hundreds of kids from around the world. Unfortunately, we don't have space to publish all the great work we receive. We want to commend some of these talented writers and artists and encourage them to keep creating.

Fiction

Beatrice Hunt, 9
Quinn Kennedy, 11
Isaac Maddock, 11
Sierra Mickelson, 13
Hannah Scheuer, 13
Malcolm Sullivan-Flynn, 9
Nasir Thompson, 7
Jessy Wallach, 10
Maya Wolfford, 13

Poetry

Vincent Anderson, 13
Gia Bharadwaj, 11
Sanja Greenawait, 11
Lila Howard, 10
Daniel Liu, 10
Emily Maremont, 11
Uma Jasmine Panwar, 11

Art

Aiza Asghar, 9
Ayaad Asghar, 5
Chloe Bowman, 8

Reviews

Roger Fan, 11
Dani Mendell, 11
Jordan Mittler, 13
Shelley Tang, 10

Don't forget to visit Stonesoup.com to browse our bonus materials. There you will find

- 20 years of back issues—around 5,000 stories, poems and reviews
- Blog posts from our Young Bloggers on subjects from sports to sewing plus ecology, reading and book reviews
- Video interviews with *Stone Soup* authors
- Music, spoken word and performances

Visit the *Stone Soup* Store at Stonesoupstore.com to buy

- Books—the 2017 *Stone Soup Annual*, a bound collection of all the year's issues, as well as themed anthologies
- Art prints—high quality prints from our collection of children's art
- Journals and Sketchbooks for writing and drawing
  ... and coming soon, single print issues of Stone Soup!

StoneSoup

MARCH 2018   VOLUME 46 / ISSUE 3

StoneSoup

*The magazine supporting
creative kids around the world*

Editor
Emma Wood

Director
William Rubel

Operations
Jane Levi

Education
Sarah Ainsworth

Design
Joe Ewart, Society

Production
Emma Birches

Stone Soup (ISSN 0094 579X)
is published online eleven
times a year—monthly, with a
combined July/August summer
issue. Copyright © 2018 by the
Children's Art Foundation, a
501(c)(3) non-profit organization,
located in Santa Cruz, California.
All rights reserved. Thirty-five
percent of our subscription price
is tax-deductible. Subscribe at
Stonesoup.com.

Stone Soup is available from the
Library of Congress in Braille for
visually handicapped readers.
To request the Braille edition, call
+1 800-424-8567.

Check us out on Social Media:

Editor's Note

Our March issue revolves around themes
of friendship, kindness, and belonging.
Kate Choi's story "Zachary, Sophie" asks,
among many questions: Why do we
often refuse to give others the benefit
of the doubt—judging them without
knowing them or their circumstances?
Meanwhile, Tristan Hui's perfectly simply
poem "Belonging" evokes the comfort and
happiness of knowing one is where one's
meant to be. I'm also particularly excited
to share Stone Soup's first issue with a
portfolio of work by an artist, Li Lingfei; I
hope her whimsical, magical watercolors,
paired with her imaginative, detailed
descriptions, will charm and delight you
as they did me!

Enjoy—

Letters: Do you have something to say
about something you've read or seen in
Stone Soup? If you do, we'd love to hear from
you, and we might print your letter on our
Letters to the Editor page! Post a comment
on our website, or write to us at editor@
Stonesoup.com.

Submissions: Our guidelines for submission
are on the Submit page at Stonesoup.
com, where you will also find a link to our
Submittable online submissions portal.

Subscriptions: to subscribe to *Stone Soup*,
please press the Subscribe button at our
webpage, Stonesoup.com.

On the cover:
'Forest Creature',

**by Eva Stoitchkova, 11
Ontario, Canada**

StoneSoup
Contents

Zachary, Sophie

The class resents Sophie, the mysterious girl who never shows up for class—and gets away with it

The first day of seventh grade our teacher, Mrs. Mahoney, took attendance. Each name was called and answered. None of them were new. We had all known each other since at least fourth grade. My name, always the last to be called, finally came.

"Whitby, Sam."

I responded, "Here!"

But unusually, she didn't stop there. One more name was called. "Zachary, Sophie."

There was silence, punctuated only by the occasional whisper or giggle. Mrs. Mahoney called, a faint frown creasing her forehead: "Sophie? Are you here?"

Still there was no response. Now we were all paying attention, and we all saw the empty desk at the very back of the room. The shadowed chair sat vacantly under our stares.

Just then there was a *ding!* from the front of the room, and everyone whirled back around to look at Mrs. Mahoney's computer on her desk. Our teacher read her message quickly, and her frown deepened.

"It seems that Sophie will not be joining us today," she told us finally. "She has . . . other matters to attend to. However, she wishes you all a wonderful day at school." Mrs. Mahoney made a mark on her clipboard, and then smiled around at us. "First on the schedule is math. Pencils out, please."

During recess we all gathered by the wall of the school to discuss the mysterious "Zachary, Sophie." John, one of my friends, spoke the loudest.

"She's *new*," he announced. "Did you hear her? She wishes us a 'wonderful day at school.'"

"She's *taunting* us, this hoity-toity Sophie," scowled Winnie Adams. "Acting all high and mighty. Being snobbish."

"And what other matters do you think she has to attend to?" John added. "Sleeping in?"

This idea was instantly seized upon by the rest of us.

"Watching television!"

"Going shopping!"

"Playing computer games!"

We hated "Zachary, Sophie" for not coming to school. We hated her for being new. We hated her for having other matters to attend to. In other words, we hated her for no reason at all.

For the next six days, "Zachary, Sophie" had no response at attendance. Every day, just after roll call, there would be another *ding!* She had other matters to attend to, she told us, and she would be unable to come to school. However, she wished us, her "fellow classmates, a wonderful day at school." Every day we hated her more; we

by Kate Choi, 11
Seoul, South Korea

would gather in the courtyard at recess and sneer at "Zachary, Sophie" and her "other matters." I was among them, but John was the unofficial leader of our group.

"Fellow classmates! As if she has the right to say that at all," he said one day. We all agreed.

"She hasn't even talked to us! Or seen us, or known us at all," I added.

"She hasn't even learned anything with us! She's not a fellow *anything*," John said indignantly, and off we were again.

"I hope *she* never comes to *this* school," Winnie said darkly. But on the seventh day, "Zachary, Sophie" showed up in the front row—in a manner of speaking.

As soon as we walked in, we could tell something was different. Mrs. Mahoney met us at the door.

"Frances, I would like you to move to the back row, to the empty seat," she said as soon as she saw Frances, who was one of Winnie's closest friends.

"I didn't do anything wrong!" cried Frances, indignant.

"I'm not punishing you," Mrs. Mahoney told her. "I just need your seat in the front."

We all looked towards Frances's desk in the front row and saw, to our surprise, Mrs. Mahoney's open computer. As we filed in and took our seats, we all glanced at the screen curiously. Finally we were all settled. We waited for Mrs. Mahoney to take up her clipboard and take attendance, but she didn't. She took up her computer instead.

The class studied the face on-screen. It was a girl's face, with brown hair. That was as much as we could tell, because the image was of extremely bad quality.

"All right." Mrs. Mahoney tilted the screen towards us. "Now, this is my class. I'm taking attendance now."

Who was she talking to? The picture on-screen?

She put the computer on her desk (screen facing us), and ran through our names.

"Whitby, Sam."

"Here," I said. There was a pause.

"Zachary, Sophie," Mrs. Mahoney said, with an air of finality. The rest of us were already whispering, taking the extra time we knew would follow to put in a few last words of conversation with our friends before math.

But then a clear voice cut through the whispers. "*Here*," it said.

All of our heads jerked up, and we all stared with shock at the face on the screen, the face of "Zachary, Sophie" at last.

Because I was the last name before "Zachary, Sophie," I was the one in charge of the computer. I was to direct the camera to whoever was speaking in class, to the board up front if Mrs. Mahoney was writing on it, to the page of my book if we were reading together as a class. I was warned severely not to break the computer, or there would be "dire consequences."

"I would also like you to bring Sophie out to recess to be part of the socialization there," Mrs. Mahoney added. "She's never been to school before, so she doesn't quite know how this works. Please include her in your conversations."

At this, everyone exchanged glances.

At recess I dutifully took Sophie out to the wall, where we all looked at each other with helpless stares. Finally John turned the computer towards him.

"My name is John," he said. "The class is going to need some privacy right now. Would you mind if I closed the lid of this computer? Just until recess is over."

"Of course!" Sophie agreed. "Absolutely. If that's how you do it."

She had barely finished before John slammed the lid closed.

That recess, we had a very heated conversation about "Zachary, Sophie." This continued every recess for the next few months.

We would complain that she was so lazy that she couldn't even drag herself to school every day. That she got to start thirty minutes after us (which she did, halfway through

math), and much more. Sophie believed everything we told her about school, and would eagerly submit to the closing of the computer for recess "privacy."

Several times during class she told us that she had "other matters to attend to for the rest of the day" and would turn off her camera to leave; it angered us that she was allowed to do this. Our hatred grew; we began taunting her at recess instead of closing the computer, and she would go along with all of it because she believed that this was what people did at school.

We would pour out all the things we had said about her to her very face (on-screen, of course) and watch her expression contort a little as she tried to pretend this was normal (because that was the only way she would fit in at school) and laugh later when the computer was closed.

We became cruel, but we didn't care; we buffeted her with insult after insult and she endured it all with a wavering, cracking smile. "Zachary, Sophie" was being revenged; we were hungry for vengeance and we did not stop.

The whole time Mrs. Mahoney believed all was well and normal. She would ask us, and Sophie, how she was doing, and we would all say she was fitting in well. Sophie said so too with total conviction, because she believed she was. Mrs. Mahoney had no reason not to believe us.

One day, at attendance, there was a *ding!* from the computer. Sophie, who was due to start the call a half-hour

The Gift of Music

by Delaney Slote, 10
Missoula, MT

after attendance, was not there yet. We all turned our heads curiously.

"Sophie has some other matters to attend to," Mrs. Mahoney informed us. "She wishes her fellow classmates —"

"A wonderful day at school," we finished.

"Zachary, Sophie" was gone again.

The next day came another *ding!* We all watched as Mrs. Mahoney read her message. She looked, to our surprise, surprised.

"Well, how wonderful!" she said at last, turning to us. "Sophie will be joining us tomorrow!"

"She finished with her 'other matters' and can call again?" Winnie asked innocently. Mrs. Mahoney beamed.

"More than that. She's coming *in person!*"

At recess we assembled with a degree of uncertainty. We did not know how to feel: should we be triumphant? Afraid? John decided for us.

"This is great. Now we can tell her everything and see the reaction in person," he announced.

"Tell her that it isn't how school really is? Tell her that it was us, acting on purpose?" asked Frances. John nodded.

"We could write a note, and put it in her desk," I suggested. John nodded again, and Winnie spoke.

"Mrs. Mahoney has ordered me to vacate my desk and move to another one," she told us. "She's going to take my desk for the day. Because it's 'closest to the door'."

"She needs her own preferred spot, does she?" But Winnie shook her head.

"That's not all. She's not going to be coming on the bus with us—and she's going to be an hour late. Can you believe it?"

John looked thoughtful. "Write the note now. I'll tell you what to write."

He did, with the rest of us chiming in. We held nothing back; we told her the truth about school and recess "privacy." We expressed our disgust at her "lazy habits": not bothering to come to school, waking up late and being late for class, going to "attend to other matters," which, let's face it (we wrote), were nothing but matters for your own pleasure. "It's not a matter of life or death. It's not even medical issues. You're just lazy. We know everything," we wrote.

And when we had finished, we each signed the note. There was no apology.

The next day we all tumbled into the room with palpable tension and excitement. At attendance, when she got to "Zachary, Sophie", Mrs. Mahoney paused and smiled.

"Let's wait for her for this one," she said.

During math we all got distracted. Mrs. Mahoney made three mistakes when teaching us a new concept, and the rest of us passed tense, excited notes behind her back as she vigorously erased the errors and rewrote them.

Halfway through, she simply gave up. "Well, since we're all so distracted anyway, why don't we make a welcome banner for Sophie?"

She took out a long sheet of paper and spread it out on the floor. We wrote, at her suggestion, 'WELCOME TO SCHOOL SOPHIE' in big letters. We drew our self-portraits (also at Mrs. Mahoney's suggestion) and labeled them with our names. We were just finished when there was a *ding!*

Mrs. Mahoney rushed to the desk. "I hope she didn't cancel," she said worriedly, but then she lit up. "She's here! Coming through the halls. Everyone, stand in front of her desk and hold up the sign. When she comes in, let's all cheer. Up now!" Excitedly she ushered us into a huddle around Sophie's desk, holding up the sign. The class exchanged eager whispers and several hushed giggles.

We waited.

Soon we heard voices, faint but clear. "It's fine! It's fine, I'll do it with these. I can do it, it's not far."

"That's her," Frances whispered. "I recognize the voice." We all did. Mrs. Mahoney grew extremely twitchy. I vaguely wondered what Sophie meant by what she had said.

There was another voice, her father's, and then silence. Well, there were footsteps. And rhythmic thuds.

"She's stomping her foot!" Winnie whispered incredulously, and we all exchanged discreet, disapproving shakes of the head.

Then the footsteps stopped, and we could all tell that she was right outside the open doorway. There was the sound of breathing.

"Okay, here I go," the voice said finally.

With that, "Zachary, Sophie" swung into the room.

Our mouths had been preparing to yell aloud in what Mrs. Mahoney would decipher as cheers, but suddenly they all collectively fell open. The banner was nearly dropped, and we all froze.

"Zachary, Sophie" was before us. Her brown hair swung around from the momentum of moving, and she was smiling at us earnestly.

Her left leg was completely nonexistent.

In a flash I—we all—understood. The reason why "Zachary, Sophie" only 'came' to school by video call was that she couldn't go to school; the reason why she 'came' thirty minutes after the rest of us (an hour today) was that she needed more time than the rest of us to prepare for the day; the reason why she had "other matters to attend to" was because she had to go to the doctor all the time.

Horror and remorse struck me like a bullet, and surged greater when I remembered the note, the cruel words we had written. "It's not a matter of life or death. It's not even medical issues. You're just lazy."

We had been *so wrong.*

"Cheer!" Mrs. Mahoney whispered behind us.

Somehow we managed to cheer weakly in our surprise. John was speechless. Winnie looked like she might cry. Frances did her best to woo-hoo and wave the banner in her hands, and the rest of us did the same.

Behind the feebly waving, cheering group, I slowly turned around. Carefully I put my hand in Sophie

Zachary's desk and removed the note.

I put my hands behind my back, tore it into shreds, and then I cheered as loud as I could.

"Zachary, Sophie!"

"*Here!*"

Artist Portfolio:
Li Lingfei, 8
Shanghai, China

"Mid-Autumn Festival," watercolor.

When the 15th day of the 8th lunar month comes, the moon becomes completely round. We would reunite with our families.

This is our ship shaped like a bird that can take us to where the moon is. Because I think the fairy Chang'e is lonely on the moon with her rabbit everyday. So I want to go to the moon by boat with my family. And watch the moon with the fairy Chang'e during the Mid-Autumn Festival.

Fairy Chang'e is very happy! She also invites us to her home.

Editor's Note: Chang'e is part of a Chinese legend, similar to our "Man on the Moon"

"My Chinese Dream," watercolor.

This painting is me boarding the ship to outer space, to see the beauty of the Milky Way. The children from that nation [of the Milky Way] are holding hands. Even the king and queen alien came out to meet us. I want to put the Chinese red flag on the top of their planet. The children of our Chinese nation on earth are singing and dancing and waiting for my good news!

"Sky City," watercolor.

If I had a time machine, I would want to fly to the future. There is a great city in space. The city is like a huge jellyfish. There is light and fresh air in it. People can walk in the transparent tubes between buildings. Every family has a flying car, and there are many shops floating in the sky. There are so many beautiful gardens where people can walk. These buildings have strange shapes. People can stop their flying cars on the rooves. The yellow building is like a cup. It has a very big trumpet that can make fresh air. The spaceship shaped like a squid is taking us to this city. I like this super city! How do you imagine a super city in your mind?

"Cat House"
——My creative journey

Who would have thought that my design was inspired by a cat sketch ? That's right! Just a cat!

CASA BATLLO was designed by Gaudi in Spain. That's an amazing building in my mind. It looks like a beautiful dragon. So, I want to design one too! My cat house!

step1 Make th the fir (The n and ima

(Cat's ears)

Do you see the little flowers in there? In fact, the two ears are unique chimneys for the house!

(The Mosaic of the roof)

they are completely made in hand! It took me a long time!

Do yo sea l

Two ears, roof and tail are all made of Mosaic collage art, I did it for a long time. There are also patterns hidden inside, only look carefully, you can see .

Cat's tail is a fun slide designed for children. Each face has a different presentation. It's very interesting.

the model and draw
irst draft
 most challenging
naginative!)

step2 Coloring and collage
(The most delicate and
busy work!)

step3 Make all the faces together!
(This is the happiest
moment!)

ou have find some interesting shapes of
life on the doors and Windows?

After two days, my "Cat House" is
finally finished! The most exciting moment
was arrived. I was very happy!

If one day this cat house can change
to be a real building, I will look forward
to...

E
X
C
I
T
E
D !

Li Lingfei
2017-9-1

The Giving Stone

by Peyton Jacobe, 12
Dallas, TX

I stared at my shoes as I walked to the 6th grade door. I sighed, and pushed some of my long, dark brown hair out of my face. It was a Monday, and on Saturday, the worst thing had happened. My parakeet Willow died. Willow was my best friend; she was always there to cheer me up when I was sad, play when I was bored, or simply make me smile. She also had the prettiest feathers that were in beautiful shades of blue. My eyes watered at the thought. I took a deep breath and tried to focus on something else, but almost everything reminded me of Willow. The black birds in the gray sky were birds, like Willow. Hearing the chirping birds in the trees didn't help either, and a thought came to mind: How could everything be as normal as last Monday for everyone else, when everything was so different for me?

I was shifting the weight of my backpack when I heard tennis shoes pounding the pavement behind me. Soon, I realized it was Ivy, who was always quiet and thoughtful. She always wore her leaf-green Nikes, and her shiny brown hair was always neatly pulled back into a braid. She caught up to me, and walked beside me, on my right. She turned and looked at me, her head cocked, and her chocolate eyes studying me. I pressed my lips together and turned away.

"You're sad, Rachel. Why?" she asked, startling me.

"My bird died," I said, voice shaking.

I had surprised myself by answering. Ivy looked like she was thinking about something. I pushed away my thoughts and looked at my shoes. Soon, she came to an abrupt stop, and reached into her pocket. She cocked her head again to look at me, her right hand forming a fist around the object from her pocket. Then, she took my left hand in her right, and pressed a small, smooth stone into my palm. She looked into my eyes and gave a small, kind smile before walking on.

Surprisingly, Ivy's stone helped me feel better about Willow. Just feeling the hard stone in my hand calmed me. After a few days, I realized that I have lots of good memories of Willow, even though she's not around anymore.

About two weeks after Ivy gave me the stone, on a Saturday, I was taking my golden retriever, Lucy, for a walk, when I came across Mrs. Hernandez. Her children are all grown up, so now she lives with her husband and cat. She was sitting on her porch chair, her orange cat in her lap. Then I noticed that she had a sorrowful look on her face. I wondered what was wrong, and I thought of Ivy, and her stone in my pocket. So, I walked up to Mrs. Hernandez and asked her what

A kind gesture helps Rachel recover from the loss of her beloved pet parakeet

was wrong.

"Kind girl, so thoughtful of you to ask. My husband passed away two weeks ago," she replied, her eyes filling with tears.

I sighed. "I'm so sorry," I said, thinking about Willow.

She shook her head.

As I shifted my weight, I felt the stone shift in my pocket. I thought about how Ivy had noticed I was sad, and she wanted to make me feel better. Much of what had helped me feel better was simply Ivy's kind gesture. I made my decision to act. I switched Lucy's leash to my left hand, then reached into my pocket with my right. I pressed my fist around the stone, and looked into Mrs. Hernandez's eyes. I pressed the stone into her palm, holding on for just a moment, and gave a small, kind smile. Then I walked back to the sidewalk. Once there, I looked back to see Mrs. Hernandez smiling, and I wondered if someone had given the stone to Ivy when she had been sad.

Hidden Moon

by Hannah Parker, 11
South Burlington, VT

Moonlight Under Water

by **Dusty Gibbon**, 12
New Haven, CT

The last look
Of the scraggly trees
Scraping their black fingernails
Across the wistful shingles
Of the buildings

The last breath of moonlight,
Whispering on the curtains
Shall forever slumber
In my iris
The last smell of sheer power,
Radiating off the skyscrapers
And the smell of the cigarette from the man with the
Rusty barbed wire hair
Who sleeps on the doorsteps of Broadway

The last blink of the artificial light of the streetlamps flickering
On and off
Like a dying firefly
Moonlight under water
Like the old man who has many ideas
But is not brave enough to present them

Oh New York, you will forever be caught
In the tangled thicket
Of past importance

Peeking Through

by Lara, Katz, 14
Weston, CT

The Runaway

by Frances Brogan, 11
Lancaster, PA

"Go to your room!" my mom shouted. "It's not all because of Rose—it just didn't work out this year!"

"Didn't work out because of her!" I said and stomped upstairs into my room. I knew I was acting like a baby. As my strict English teacher, Mrs. Hood, would say, "Grade six or age six?"

The first thing I noticed when I got to my room was the picture of my mom, Daniel, Rose, and me in the bed at the birth center. We looked so much younger, so much more carefree. I passed my hand over the glass, looking at my brother's face, forever frozen in laughter as he held the tiny bundle of newborn life that was Rose.

I flung myself onto my bed and cried for a long time. Eventually, I heard the soft, slow pitter-patter of footsteps as Rose toddled into my room. She came over to me and slobbered on my face.

"Mwuh!" she said triumphantly.

For a moment, my heart melted. Rose looked so proud of herself. Even though she was only a baby, I could see how desperate she was for closeness to me. But this tenderness was quickly overpowered by anger and resentment. "Get out of my room!" I shouted at her. She saw that I was mad at her, and she ran out of the room—awkward, precarious, baby running.

Every year since I was four-years-old, we had visited Lancaster, my grandma's hometown and like a second home to us, on the first weekend of May for the annual carnival. I remember when I was four, the carnival was overwhelming, exhilarating. There was so much to hear and see! Now that I was almost twelve, the carnival didn't give me the same kind of excitement, didn't have its old charm. The rides were really for kids my brother Daniel's age. But the previous year, my parents had taken a year off work and we had rented a house in Lancaster. Even though we only spent one year away from Annapolis, where we had lived since I was three, I had made lasting friendships there. I felt Lancaster would always be my true hometown.

Transitioning back to life in Annapolis was harder than it had been in my nightmares. For months I had been looking forward to the carnival, a chance to reunite with my friends and forget my worries, albeit only for a weekend. But because of Rose, Rose's sleep schedule, Rose's needs, we'd had

Desperate to see her old friends, Eva makes a reckless decision

to break tradition and skip the carnival this year. I was devastated. My mom had tried to console me, saying things like, "Aren't you getting too old for the carnival anyway?" But nothing she said made a difference. Even though I knew that the real reason for skipping the carnival was Daniel's soccer tournament that Saturday, I desperately wanted a reason to blame Rose.

Annapolis was lonely. A year away had been enough for my old friendships to fade. I was growing farther apart from my family, too. As a child, I had always been so close to my parents and even Daniel. What was the rift between us?

Eleven. It had been the best year yet, but still not enough. I had so much. Why did I always want more?

My emotions were like an M&M—anger the hard, colorful coating, covering up the sweet, rich sadness that lay beneath. I've always been a private person, masking my true feelings with another feeling, usually anger. My sadness and fear stays bottled up inside. I've always just convinced myself that one day, they'll explode.

When you're feeling so upset, you often act impulsive and reckless, even stupid. I so badly wanted to go to the carnival, so badly wanted to see my old friends and leave behind my lonely, friendless life for the weekend. My mom didn't understand how much it meant to me. So I decided I would run away for the weekend, go to the carnival myself. My parents would be worried sick, but they deserved it, I thought savagely.

Silently I packed a few t-shirts, a sweater, and two pairs of jeans. I stuffed them in my backpack, and left the room. Rose was waiting for me at the door, her face tear-stained. She reached her chubby arms toward me, so pathetic. I hugged her. "I'm sorry," I said, and I really was.

Daniel was in his room, my dad was at the store, my mom was on the phone. This was my chance to escape. I slipped out the door.

By the time I was at the end of the block, I realized I shouldn't have just run off. I should have come up with a ruse, a story about where I was going. My overprotective mom was probably already panicking. Without looking behind me, my heart beating at an impossibly fast rate with terror, I ran.

The wind seemed to be whispering

my name. "Eva," it echoed in my ears, "Come home, Eva, come home." I shrugged it off, running faster. I glanced at my phone. The next bus was leaving for Philadelphia in less than an hour. I silently thanked heaven for my phone. With its help, I found the bus stop, surprising myself that I had made it this far.

The bus driver, a burly, intimidating man, asked me where I was going. I hesitated, barely able to breathe.

"Oh, hurry up or we're leaving without you," he burst out.

"Philadelphia," I gulped. I handed him the transaction. I only had enough money left for the ride to Lancaster from Philadelphia; there was no turning back now.

I pushed away my guilt and felt a swoop of thrill in my stomach. I was finally on the way to Lancaster! After almost a year of waiting, I was making my dream come true!

From Philadelphia, I caught a bus to Lancaster. I felt much more comfortable on the road to Lancaster. This was my true home! I knew my way around Lancaster much better than Annapolis. With deft navigational ability, I found my way to my best friend, Annabelle's house. I didn't even bother to knock on her door, squirming with excitement.

"Annie!" I called. "I'm back!"

Annabelle's mom was home, too. She made me tell her the whole story, from the very beginning. She stood stiff and perfectly still the whole time, her lips pursed and her hands on her hips. But she didn't doubt that what I said was true.

"All right," she announced. "Get in the car. We're driving to Annapolis, now."

I was surprised she was so angry, and her decision was so sudden. I had thought she would be proud. But on the long, miserable drive back to Annapolis, I pictured the rage my mom would feel if the situation had been in reverse, and Annie had run away to our house. I realized that it's part of a mom's nature to be so protective.

Soon my reckless adventure was over, and I stood wrapped in my mother's embrace. I whispered, "I'm sorry, I'm sorry," over and over again, almost rhythmically. My mom whispered back, "I know, I know, I love you." She forgave me so readily it made me feel even more ashamed. I said goodbye to Annie, but somehow it was less painful than I anticipated.

After a long talk with my mom, I went to straight to bed, exhausted by my endeavor. My last sleepy thought before I fell asleep was: how could I have done so many things in one day?

Even though I had longed for a friend for that whole year, I wasn't ready to face my fears of judgment yet. That month I spent my lunch hour in the library, confiding in the librarian. I told myself this was practice for when I was ready to make a real friend. I started reading memoirs and diaries. I imagined a future where I wrote a memoir of my own life, and hundreds of years later it was found in the ruins of our house. This was kind of far-fetched, but it got me thinking: I could write a memoir of my life, too. I could become a writer. Maybe this was a talent that was buried within me. A few weeks after I had my adventure, I sat down at my desk, picked up a pen, and began to tell my story . . .

Rusty

by Sarah Liu, 12
Weston, FL

Belonging

by Tristan Hui, 11
Menlo Park, CA

We dig holes,

In the grainy sand

   I dig mine, like a dog, the dog I wish I'd had then,

When we ran across the sand,

        laughter surrounds us.

A small sand crab scuttles

        over my foot

   Daddy holds me

 Just over the waves

The water tickles my feet and I squeal

As he picks me up and the wave crashes down on where I was before

        he bear hugs me tight

        this is where I belong.

Book Review

The War That Saved My Life by Kimberly Brubaker Bradley;
Dial Books for Young Readers: New York, 2015; $11.89

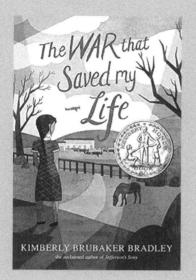

When I sat down to read the book *The War That Saved My Life* by Kimberly Brubaker Bradley, I thought it was a crummy book. But the more I got into the book, the more I couldn't put it down. Now, this book is one of my favorites!

The main character, Ada, is a girl with a clubfoot. Due to this, most people around her, such as her neighbors, hate Ada, and try to stay as far away from her as possible. This makes her feel very lonely, and she doesn't know where she belonged. As Ada thought to herself, right after a teacher wouldn't let Ada go to class because of her foot: "Why would I cry? I wanted to hit something, or throw something or scream. I wanted to gallop on butter and never stop.

I wanted to run, but not with my twisted, ugly, horrible foot." When this happened, I felt really sorry for Ada. I mean, it was just a clubfoot. Why did everybody treat her like she needed to be put in an asylum? Even her mom was not on the same side as Ada because she thought her clubfoot was an embarrassing sight. She not only hadn't taken Ada to school, but she hadn't even let Ada even step foot outside the apartment, leaving Ada not knowing about basic things.

However, Ada is a very brave and caring person. She has a lot of stress on her back, but she continued to fight forward for what was right. This is a reason I like her. Ada may look scrawny and weak, but inside, she's a good-hearted, strong person. Why, in fact, she even saves the village from a spy!

In contrast to Ada's biological mother, Susan Smith, Ada's foster mother, cares about her. Susan tries to help Ada with almost anything. She clearly showed a lot of effort into taking care of her. And when times seemed dark, she glowed, leading Ada into the right direction. Susan reminds me of my mom. My mom is also caring and supportive, and when times are dark, she helps me overcome the dark time with the light, just like Susan does for Ada.

This book takes place during World War Two. Ada sneaks out her

Reviewed by
Brian Qi, 11
Lexington, MA

apartment onto a train with many children, bound for a safe zone. Once there, she and her younger brother, Jamie, become Ms. Smith's children. After the war ends, Ada has to try to become normal and get used to the life outside of her apartment. It is hard, but she persists until she finally finds where she belongs.

In this book, Ada had to find her real home. Three years before I read this book, I had to leave my New York home and school I had lived and loved for five years, and move to a new, unfamiliar school in Massachusetts. The lonely feeling in my stomach was relatable to Ada's. But, just like her, I persisted. Three years after I moved to Massachusetts, I graduated one of the top students in the school. I had persisted, and finally fit in, just like Ada.

Another reason I like this book is that the plot is brilliant and very well thought up. I couldn't stop reading the book even when it was time for bed because I wanted to know what happened next. I would definitely recommend this book to you. After you finish it, I guarantee it will be your favorite book, too!

Honor Roll

Welcome to the *Stone Soup* Honor Roll. Every month we receive submissions from hundreds of kids from around the world. Unfortunately, we don't have space to publish all the great work we receive. We want to commend some of these talented writers and artists and encourage them to keep creating.

Don't forget to visit Stonesoup.com to browse our bonus materials. There you will find

- 20 years of back issues—around 5,000 stories, poems and reviews

- Blog posts from our Young Bloggers on subjects from sports to sewing plus ecology, reading and book reviews

- Video interviews with *Stone Soup* authors

- Music, spoken word and performances

Visit the *Stone Soup* Store at Stonesoupstore.com to buy

- Books—the 2017 *Stone Soup Annual*, a bound collection of all the year's issues, as well as themed anthologies

- Art prints—high quality prints from our collection of children's art

- Journals and Sketchbooks for writing and drawing

  ...and more!

Stone Soup

APRIL 2018

VOLUME 46 / ISSUE 4

StoneSoup

The magazine supporting creative kids around the world

Editor
Emma Wood

Director
William Rubel

Operations
Jane Levi

Education
Sarah Ainsworth

Design
Joe Ewart, Society

Production
Emma Birches

Stone Soup (ISSN 0094 579X) is published online eleven times a year—monthly, with a combined July/August summer issue. Copyright © 2018 by the Children's Art Foundation, a 501(c)(3) non-profit organization, located in Santa Cruz, California. All rights reserved. Thirty-five percent of our subscription price is tax-deductible. Subscribe at Stonesoup.com.

Stone Soup is available from the Library of Congress in Braille for visually handicapped readers. To request the Braille edition, call +1 800-424-8567. *Stone Soup* can also be heard on the telephone by persons who have trouble seeing or reading the print edition. For more information contact the National Federation of the Blind NFB-NEWSLINE® service at +1 866-504-7300 or go to www.nfbnewsline.org.

Check us out on Social Media:

Editor's Note

"April is the cruelest month," the poet T.S. Eliot famously wrote in The Wasteland. Maybe it's cruel, but it is also National Poetry Month—a month when poems appear in even the most unlikely places. To honor the celebration of poetry, I've included a portfolio of poems in this issue by five young Chinese writers, whose work I love for its weirdness and darkness, for its insight and daring. This issue also includes another rarity for us: a long story. "The Fence" is a moving portrayal of a friendship formed in spite of segregation and social taboos, while the two shorter stories, "Ride to the Fence" and "Stone Angel" both explore the edges and limits of consciousness. This is a beautiful, strange issue, and one I am very proud of.

Letters: Do you have something to say about something you've read or seen in *Stone Soup*? If you do, we'd love to hear from you, and we might print your letter on our Letters to the Editor page! Post a comment on our website, or write to us at editor@Stonesoup.com.

Submissions: Our guidelines for submission are on the Submit page at Stonesoup.com, where you will also find a link to our Submittable online submissions portal.

Subscriptions: to subscribe to *Stone Soup*, please press the Subscribe button at our webpage, Stonesoup.com.

On the cover:
'Trees and Clouds',

by Alexa Zhang, 9
 Los Altos, CA

StoneSoup
Contents

The Fence

by Lia Clark, 13
Portland, OR

In a segregated town in 1953, a secret friendship grows between Ruth, a black girl, and Donna, a white girl

Ever since I could remember, Momma and I lived alone. Just us two. She never mentioned my Poppa or any aunts or uncles or cousins, so neither did I. We were happy enough how we were.

It was 1953, and we lived on the very edge of the Black District of the town. Some thought we were much too close to the White District, because only a tall, wooden fence separated us from their houses. The Fence stretched as far as I had ever ventured, and no one could come or go through it. But that didn't make any difference; we went our own way, they went theirs.

Momma ran a business doing laundry for the neighbors. I would help her wash the clothes in big metal tubs, then hang them all to dry on the long clothesline stretched across the yard. Some days, she would send me to buy more lye soap for her washing. Other days, I would deliver the clean laundry to her customers' houses.

One day, I sat on the steps of our house braiding the long, stringy grass and wishing there was shade somewhere nearby. The hot August sun was merciless. And since Momma had a group of talkative friends over, she had strictly instructed me not to go

into the house unless of an emergency. So I was stuck outside.

After a few more minutes of this, I made up my mind. I would go exploring. Past the huge hedges behind the house was the Fence between us and the White people. I wasn't to go near the Fence under any circumstances, Momma's orders, but I was much too bored to heed that rule. She said that she didn't want me to get scratched by the prickly hedges, but I knew perfectly well that that was just an excuse. She didn't want me to see the White people on the other side.

After checking that Momma was still safely preoccupied inside with her friends, I climbed into the bushes. *So much for getting scratched up*, I thought. *They're not even prickly!* Just a few feet in, my hands found the rough wood of the Fence. I wriggled my entire body through until I was right up against it. Then I pressed my eye against a conveniently located knothole and peered through. All I could see were the leafy branches of identical hedges on the other side. Leaning forward a little too hard, the board gave way and I tumbled through, right onto the other side. Gasping with surprise, I began to

Lord of the Binder Rings

by Ula Pomian, 12
Ontario, Canada

"Do you know, exactly, why Whites and Blacks've got to live apart?"

sit up, rubbing dirt from my eyes. Until I heard a voice.

"Who's there?" it demanded.

I held my breath, trembling with fright. I didn't dare go back through. Surely whoever was speaking would notice me shaking the bushes. But if Momma found out I'd been over...

I took a quick look, not daring to even breathe. A little White girl was kneeling in front of me. She was so close that I could have reached out and touched her shining golden hair. She peered right into the branches.

I made myself as small as I could, but too late.

"I can see you in there. What are you spying on me for?"

I couldn't do anything now but answer her nice and polite, just how Momma taught me.

"I wasn't exactly spying on you," I replied. "I didn't even notice you was there at first."

"What's your name?" she asked me. She had lost her commanding voice now.

"Ruth," I replied shyly.

"I'm Donna Schultz. Nice to meet you."

"Yes," I agreed.

"Would you like to come out? We can play together, and I will show you my dolls."

I glanced back over my shoulder through the bare hole where the board had collapsed. What on earth would Momma say to see me on the other side of the Fence playing with a White girl? *Never mind*, I told myself, *She'll never find out if you don't tell her.*

"Here I come," I told the girl, tripping my way out.

Donna laughed. It was a nice sort of laugh, not mocking, but sweet and twinkly, just like her. I gave her a smile and brushed the dirt off my knees.

"So, how old are you?" she asked conversationally as she led me across the yard.

"Eight-years-old," I told her proudly.

"I'm eight and three-quarters," she responded. I had no idea what three-quarters was supposed to mean, so I kept quiet.

"This is my house. Mother and Father aren't at home, only Jonathan. But he won't play with me unless it's baseball, and Mother says baseball is unladylike, so I can't. I don't like it much anyway."

I was relieved to hear that this girl's parents weren't home because they probably wouldn't have been very happy with a Black girl like me on their side, the White side, either. Even then I didn't realize how big of a risk I was taking.

But at the time my thoughts were completely focused on Donna's beautiful dolls and playthings. I was happy just to listen to her talk, lying comfortably in the dappled shade of her yard.

Once the sun began to set, however, I told her I'd better get home. She told me that she hoped she could talk to me again soon.

"Bye!" I called to her as I scrambled

back through the poky branches a little more gracefully than before.

"Goodbye, Ruth!" she responded, waving at me.

And that was the beginning of our secret friendship.

A few weeks later, as Momma and I were completing the noontime deliveries, I asked her an innocent question.

"Momma, why do we have to live apart from the White people?"

She looked at me funny and said, "Why you asking, girl?"

"It's just that there's other girls out there just like me 'cept they have white skin. Why ain't we allowed to be friends just because of our skin?"

Momma sighed. "Many years ago, all the way back to your great-granddaddy and before him, us Blacks was slaves. The white people owned us, like property. But the government changed that so we can't be owned or bought or sold anymore, only we're not equal to them neither. It's just how it goes," she explained.

I pondered this till we reached home. It still didn't make sense. I decided to ask Donna. *She* was a White person. Maybe she could explain it to me.

Momma sent me off to play right away. "You've been helping me all day, go do something else. I'm going over to your Auntie Eveline's."

That was just fine with me. As soon as she left, I scrambled through the bushes. I tapped one, two, three times on the Fence for May I come over now?

I barely had to wait for her reply. Tap. Yes. I crawled through the hole.

"Ruth!" she exclaimed. "I've missed you so much!"

"It's only been one day!" I teased. But she didn't know how much those words meant to me.

We talked a while, her telling me all about her day at school and me just listening, as usual. The question I had meant to ask her completely slipped my mind until I had to go. But I remembered it just as I began to leave.

"Donna," I said, "I meant to ask you something."

"Yes?"

"Do you know, exactly, why Whites and Blacks've got to live apart?"

She looked at me funny just like Momma had, the smile leaving her face. She answered, "Why should it matter?" She turned away.

"It doesn't really," I said. "Because I got you and I can't ask for nothing better than that."

She smiled. "You mean, we have each other." A pause.

"Bye, Donna," I said, breaking the silence.

She turned and this time and looked me in the eye. It looked like she was crying a little.

"We wouldn't have to hide our friendship if it weren't for that horrid rule. And I don't care, because you are the best friend I've ever had."

"You are mine, too." With that, I left.

Tap, tap, tap. *Can I come over?* waited for her to respond.

Then I heard voices, two of them, coming close.

Faintly I heard Donna saying, "You wait there, I just need to check on something."

Her head appeared in the whole

through the Fence. I hoped he hedge's canopy muffled our voices.

"Ruth! Mother made a girl from school come to play today and I really don't want to, but I have to, so can we play later?" she whispered all in one breath.

"Oh," I said. "Maybe tomorrow, then?"

"Listen for my—" But she was cut off mid-sentence. Another head was emerging from the hole in the Fence.

The girl froze in her tracks when she spotted me. She gazed open-mouthed, from Donna to me to Donna again.

"Donna!" the girl exclaimed, a little too loudly. "What do you think you're—" but Donna had slapped a hand over her mouth. Her eyes were huge with terror.

"Ruth, if anyone finds out . . ." *This could be the end of our friendship forever.*

"They won't. They can't," I whispered. "Get her away, and quick!" I slipped away as Donna yanked her friend back through the hole.

And all I could do was wait.

The next day, since I hadn't heard from Donna all night and all morning, I peeked through the hole, not daring to give myself away by tapping. The yard was deserted. Nestling myself into the branches, I was invisible to the outside, but could see everything around me. I waited.

Soon, a tall, angry-looking man marched Donna by the arm outside. He must have been her father. And they were heading in my direction. I swiftly darted back through the hole and safe to the other side.

As I stood, listening intently, the sound of hammer blows rang through the air. Bang, bang, bang. Then came faint shouts which I couldn't quite make out. They subsided eventually and I crept over. The worst had finally come.

The hole, which was completely surrounded on all sides by the hedges, was now covered by two fresh planks of wood, strong and firm. I pounded my fist against it, hoping that it would fall off just as easily as before. But it was no use. It wouldn't budge.

"Donna!" I shouted, ignoring all common sense. "Donna, Donna!"

I heard the bushes rustle on the other side. "Ruth, is that you?"

"Yes!" I cried. I could say no more before I broke into tears.

I could hear her sobs, too. We cried for a long time, leaning against the Fence that separated us from each other.

"That girl ran and told Mother about you and the hole in the Fence and us talking to each other. Once Father found out about it, he forced me to show him where the hole was. And they told me to tell you that... that I'm never allowed to speak to you again."

I was devastated. And I knew I couldn't let her disobey them.

As if reading my thoughts, she said, "Ruth, promise you'll always come back. Please. I don't care what they say!"

Knowing that I would be endangering myself and Donna, I still replied, "No matter how many barriers they put between us, I will always come back."

The months passed. I didn't hear

anything from Donna, which meant that her parents were making sure that contact with me didn't continue. I had no idea what was going on on her side. Even if I did, I couldn't do anything about it.

Momma sent me to buy her some soap early one morning. The little market was packed full of people.

I grabbed the soap and handed my money to the kind old man who ran the shop.

"How are you this fine spring day?" he asked with a smile.

"Good," I replied.

"Have you heard the news? Just yesterday it was, May seventeenth. Everyone's talking 'bout it!"

"I haven't." It was best to be polite even though I wasn't really interested.

"Segregation's been overruled! Whites and Blacks are equals now!"

My mouth fell open.

The man laughed. "None of us've been expecting it, neither!"

I certainly was stunned. Wordlessly I collected my change and bar of soap.

He sensed my amazement. "Here, take a paper."

I pulled out more coins. "No, no. Free of charge, I insist," he said. I took it and walked from the shop.

I hightailed it home, where Momma was doing laundry as usual.

"Momma, you won't believe what's happened!" I cried, thrusting the newspaper at her.

Her eyes almost popped out of her head when she read the headline:

"Equality Redefined: The Supreme Court's history-making decision against racial segregation proves more than anything else that the Constitution is still a live and growing document..."

Her eyes scanned the paper hungrily. But I was too impatient.

"Momma, I need a hammer."

"Why on earth-"

"I just do!" I exclaimed.

She clearly sensed my urgency. A few minutes later, she returned, hammer in hand.

I snatched it and ran into the hedge. In only three swings I had blasted the boards right off. I dashed through the hole and was out in the middle of Donna's yard.

"Donna!" I cried loudly.

She was out the door in a moment, flinging her arms around me.

"Ruth, Ruth!" was all she could say.

We hugged for a good long time, both so overflowing with happiness we could barely speak.

"Come inside, Ruth!" she insisted, pulling me by the hand toward the door.

I froze suddenly. I had noticed what she hadn't. Donna's father was standing just inside the doorway, glaring at me.

She caught sight of him and, keeping cool as a cucumber, marched me up to the door.

"This is my friend Ruth from over the Fence, Father," she said.

He looked at Donna, scandalized. "Just what do you—"

"Segregation's been overruled! Whites and Blacks are equals now!"

But he was interrupted by Donna's mother behind him. "Michael, please." She pushed past him.

"We are pleased to meet you, Ruth. Donna speaks very highly of you," her mother said. She looked just like Donna, the same bright golden hair, the same faded gray-colored eyes, the same soft smile.

"Thank you, ma'am," I replied.

"May Ruth stay for breakfast, Mother and Father?" Donna asked hopefully.

"Of course," Mrs. Schultz said. "Just follow me."

As I passed Donna's father, he put an arm on my shoulder. "I'd like to apologize for everything," he said, bowing his head.

I didn't know how to respond; I was too surprised to even speak.

He paused, then added, "Welcome into our home."

Cedar Waxwing

by Sierra Glassman, 11
Watsonville, CA

Poetry Portfolio

The following poems were written by students in a creative writing class that took place in Shanghai, China, hosted by the Stanford University EPGY Honors Academy summer program. My students in this class wrote and read stories and poems in English, but most spoke Mandarin as well as other languages. Many of my students were totally fluent in English, while others were still practicing their English spelling and grammar.

I have noticed that students write the most original poems when they are a little bit wild and lost in their own imaginations. To do this, we read experimental poems that break the rules of English or the rules of poetry. We also read fantasy, like *The Patchwork Girl of Oz* or *The Phantom Tollbooth*. I think fantasy and ancient literature and experimental poetry do the same things for students: they challenge them to think of new structures, whether new worlds or new ways of using language.

For the same reason, I tried to make all their writing assignments weird:
1. Write a poem while sitting somewhere you have never sat before
2. Write a description of humans as if you were an alien who had never actually seen a human
3. First draw your friend without looking at the paper. Then draw your own face by putting a piece of paper on it and drawing (don't poke your eyeball). Then look at yourself in a mirror and write a poem about your eyes, nose, teeth, hair, or other part of your head
4. Write a long poem as if you were a whole bunch of fairies all speaking at once
5. Write down one of your main character's deep secrets, then fold the paper up into origami and never show anyone what you wrote

When I challenge my students with funny, scary, and strange poems and assignments, they challenge me right back, writing work that is original, spooky, heartbreaking, or just hilarious. Somebody surprises me in every class. For instance, when I told my students to write somewhere they'd never written before, one student squeezed onto a shelf of the bookshelf!

So here are some weird, wild poems that came from these assignments, or assignments like these. These poems surprise me every time I read them.

--Sophia Dahlin

Sophia Dahlin is a poet and teacher who lives in Oakland, CA. She is a teaching artist for Bay Area schools with California Poets in the Schools, and has taught creative writing in Bangkok and Shanghai for Stanford Honors Academy. She has an MFA in Poetry from the Iowa Writers' Workshop.

About the Author

by Gabriel Levy, 9

When I try my best but no words come I feel worried,
like when I drown in lava.

How does it feel like to be an author?
Great, because everyone will know
the work you wrote. It also feels like you are the most important person in the
world.

When I do not have to think more and I know what I have to write,
I feel like sleeping on a giant smooth waterfall full of bubbles.
It also feels like getting untangled from a spider web.

About the Author Poem

by Emilei Lu, 11

Before I write, I put on boots, jackets, scarfs and mittens.

"I am prepared." I tell myself.

I close my eyes and write.

For I know that if I don't prepare myself fully, I may never get out of my fantasy world.

Untitled

by Emilei Lu, 11

I hold onto the
kite of my life
I set it all free
In the winds of my childhood
It soars
high
Next to many other kites
Higher and
higher
We ascend to the
skies of reality
Listening to the
whistling sounds of
of the air
Smelling the
wafting aroma of
the viridescent garden below
The skies suddenly darken.
BAM
One lightning of frustration
A crack in my stern
You will fall
Says that melancholy voice
But be there to mend
your stern
and get back up
for at the end
your only regret will be
not taking the chance in
the first place
The purpose of my life
Is to live
A life.

tiny big valley

by Angelina Lu, 11

tiny valley big so big
grass of blue lakes of green
tiny big down-upside trees
night and day spring to spring

nothing&noone comes to tiny big valley
nothing walks the roses
&noone paints the sky with love
night and day spring to spring

nothing&noone and someone and
everyone comes to tiny big valley
nothing loves noone n roses more
night and day spring to spring

tiny valley big so big
when nothing&noone stopped to breathe
a place of beauty sky of love
night and day spring to spring

THE MOON

by Andy Wu, 10

The moon
The little moon
The lonely uncolorful moon
The only friend of earth
The moon of its only kind
There the moon stand by her only little self
The moon
The Earth's only friend
The grey boring moon
The old rusty moon

lonely boy

by Gilbert Huang, 9

Who am I, am I just a lonely boy?
When I am lonely I feel wild.
Does nobody want me?
Or do I have to stay here forever?
Well, I will be crashed by a car?
What shall I do.
I need a real life!
I am very far to become a normal boy.

A human

by Gilbert Huang, 9

A human's life is as an alien's life. This human has two feet and hairs.
It lives in a house and eats with its hair. But actually we guess that
humans eat like that. A piece of paper told us how humans are.
A human goes to work every day even Saturday and Sunday
and never gets a holiday. It grabs things with its feet.

Untitled

by Gilbert Huang, 9

The sound you can hear is the fairy's voice.
And remember the fairies are behind you.
Fairies are not same as you because they have wings and they are absolutely tiny.
And Whatever money you get it is actually your tooth.

If you have a very clean and white tooth put it under your pillow and next day
you will see money under your pillow.
because the tooth fairy will grab your tooth and exchange it with money.

Myself

by Gilbert Huang, 9

When I write I feel very soft and smooth.
I always feel nervous when the pen touches the paper.
My feelings always control myself.
When I don't know what to write I transform into a monster.

One Horse

by Lara Katz, 14
Weston, CT

The Ride of Infinity

by Raina Sawyer, 11
Santa Cruz, CA

I wrapped my jacket around me to keep out the frigid air. It was cold and drizzly and my clothes were soaked. "The tapestry of life will outlast all of us," my dad had always told me. "Everyone who has ever lived and ever will is a part of the tapestry. Sometimes a thread will come loose when the person it's connected to has given up on life. Never become one of those loose threads, Allison." But now I had become a loose thread. And I didn't think I would ever be able to weave myself back in again.

My life began to unravel when my father was diagnosed with cancer last year. He could still continue homeschooling me until he died three weeks ago. Then I was put in public school, and that was when I realized that there was no going back. That my life was changed permanently. My mom had always had a full time job, and with my dad gone, we needed the money more than ever. There was no way I could be homeschooled.

I was in the very back of the group, atop my brown and black, chomp-happy horse. The man at the front hadn't told me its name. As I watched the tour guide go on and on about some historical landmark with only the teachers engrossed, as I watched the boys have a spit fight, and as I watched the girls gossip about who liked who, I wondered if anyone would really notice if I left. If anyone would wonder why I disappeared. The more I thought about it, the more I realized they wouldn't. I was convinced no one would notice if I left.

I made up my mind. I swiftly turned my horse around and galloped in the opposite direction. And just like that, I had begun my ride of infinity.

I rode and rode until nightfall, and from sheer exhaustion, I eventually fell asleep on the horse. When I awoke, it was morning. My horse had halted. I quickly kicked it in the sides to get it moving, and then I noticed a tree line in the distance, lush and green and leafy.

Suddenly, all I wanted to do was reach the tree line. I was hypnotized by grief, and all I wanted was one small bit of hope to cling on to. I began to convince myself that if I reached the tree line, all my problems would be gone. Both my parents would be awaiting me, I could be homeschooled again, everything I valued would be within reach. My life would be back

When Allison's father dies, she begins to lose her hold on reality

to normal again. I could behold it. I could see it so clearly etched in my mind that I knew I could not turn back. I sent that horse galloping and galloping towards the tree line, without even pausing to think about what I was getting myself into.

Had I been thinking straight, this never would have happened. I never would have left the "historical tour on horseback" field trip. But I did. And I didn't have an ounce of regret. I was still so sure that I would reach the tree line, so sure that if I did, everything would be impeccable. I rode day and night, with no food or water, for so long I lost track of time. Yet the tree line never got any nearer. Never.

My absurd impulsiveness finally stopped when the horse collapsed from exhaustion, and sent me sprawling on the dew-covered grass. Determined as I was to reach the tree line, I staggered to my feet and tried to run, but I could only make it a few steps before collapsing myself. I hit my head on something hard, and in the moment between consciousness and unconsciousness, I remembered.

In that split second, I recalled so many of the times that my dad and I had had fun. Walking through the forest, the shining green canopy of trees overhead, learning the scientific names of all the mushrooms and plants. Going down the tallest slide at the water park. Jumping into the swimming hole in the river, the water sparkling like diamonds. Legions of memories swam in my mind. Then everything went dark.

I woke up to the sound of people shouting. Somebody was pulling on my leg. My eyes flew open, and I saw a crowd of people surrounding me. My class was there. Lots of unfamiliar people were there. Even an ambulance was present. My mom was there as well. *So they had noticed.*

I was told that I had hit my head on a rock and that I had passed out.

My throat was so dry I couldn't speak. But I looked into my mother's eyes, and she got the message: *get me out of here.* She had to carry me to the car because I was so weak I couldn't stand up.

Sitting in her navy blue Toyota, I realized I had not achieved anything. All I had done was made my mom think she would lose me, too. I had done it all for nothing. To this day, I am still a loose thread.

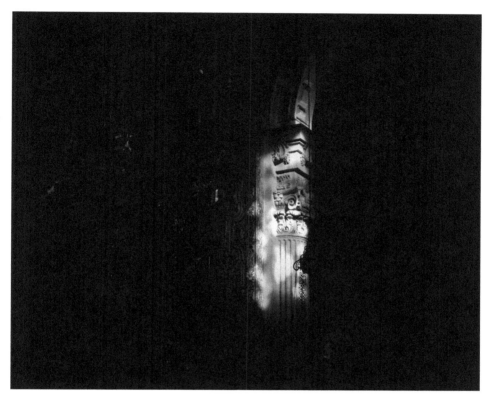

Illuminated

by Lara Katz, 14
Weston, CT

The Stone Angel

by Julia Lockwood, 12
Bellingham, WA

The pewter sky hung like a tapestry over the graveyard, dark clouds spilling across it. The clouds boomed and thundered like an angry beast, releasing torrents of water that drenched the gray headstones below. Lightning sliced through the air like a sword, illuminating the world for a second with its violet light.

Libby liked the rain. The way it left her honey hair wet and clingy, the way the droplets slid down her cheeks like cool tears. She knelt down next to her favorite grave in the furthest corner of the cemetery.

Most of her neighbors grew up in fear of the cemetery across the street, but Libby loved it. Each weekend she would place flowers on her favorite graves, and she loved calculating the ages of the people on the headstones.

Libby peered at the grave in front of her. The cool stone of the memorial was cracked and crumbling, with moss climbing up it, filling in the crevasses. A smiling angel stood atop the base of the grave, holding a harp in its chubby hands. The angel's face had been worn away by decades in the rain, giving the grave an eerie look. Engraved on the podium was the name of the girl who rested there.

Here lies Ada Lee Clemmons
1896-1907
Beloved daughter, sister.
May her soul rest in peace.

"Pretty, isn't it?" a sweet voice said from behind Libby. Startled, Libby turned quickly to see a girl standing behind her. The girl looked about Libby's age, with tawny skin and soft coils of chestnut hair. Her cheeks held a slight rosy blush, probably a result of the cold of the rain. But what struck Libby as particularly striking were the girl's eyes. They blazed blue against her darker skin, as if holding a cold fire inside them.

The girl took a step closer to Libby. "It's sad isn't it?" She asked. "She was so young. Only eleven, only as old as I am now." The girl turned to look at Libby, as if noticing her for the first time.

"You come here a lot," she said. It was not phrased as a question, but simply as a statement.

"Y-yes." Libby stammered. Something about the girl made her uncomfortable. It seemed as if the air grew cooler simply having her around. "How did you know?"

The girl shrugged.

Libby meets a mysterious girl at the cemetery

"I don't see why that matters."

She knelt down next to the grave, and patted the ground beside her as if inviting Libby to join her. Libby reluctantly obliged.

"Someone should clean the headstone," she said sadly. "But there is no one around to do it. It happened so long ago, there is no one left who remembers the name Ada Lee Clemmons."

"How do you know so much about her?" Libby asked, feeling her fear of the girl begin to be replaced by sympathy of sorts. The words that the girl spoke seemed so heavy, and as if they affected her directly.

The girl cocked her head at Libby

"I just simply know what the grave tells. Anyone could figure it out."

The girl reached out and traced the lettering on the grave with her finger.

"It's lonely I bet," she said suddenly. "Can you imagine being forgotten? Alone?"

Libby shook her head. She couldn't envision it.

The girl sighed and drew back from the grave. She stood. Libby rose with her.

"I have to go," she said. "But before I do, what is your name?"

Libby thought about lying, but the girl's eyes seemed safe and friendly as she looked her.

"Libby," she said. "Yours?"

"Ada," the girl smiled. Libby felt her eyes widen. She turned to face the headstone and its engraved letters. Ada.

"Are you . . . ?" Libby stammered, the words catching on her tongue. Ada smiled.

"Thank you," she said. "For visiting me. It's not quite so lonely when you're around."

With that, Ada faded away.

Book Review

Uprising by **Margaret Peterson Haddix**;
Simon & Schuster Books for Young Readers: New York, 2011; $11.99

Uprising. One word, but somehow this meager collection of letters presents readers with strong, vivid emotions. Some when confronted with this word would mentally tremble in fright. Some might feel a sense of rebellion brewing inside them. Others would, I dare say, laugh, regarding almost humorously the rough cards life has dealt them and their failed attempts to regain control and ultimately uprise. Such a simple word, such a simple title, such a complex concept.

In this book, Haddix creates a world so similar to our own it's hard to believe that her story is based upon historical content dating back to over one hundred years ago. It is a world we see everyday on the news, a world of division, anger, and violence. But it is also a world of hope and love. Through brilliant storytelling, the author is able to bring readers into early twentieth-century New York at the beginning of an uprising!

As 1911 progresses, the world is faced with new ideas each day. Women's rights are finally making their way into the United States, and many are hopeful that Britain's movement will sweep into America as well. While many suffragists are struggling to gain support for their cause, shirtwaist workers with very little public influence are also making their way into the headlines. Workers from around the country unite to protest peacefully for better conditions in the workplace.

Towards the beginning of the novel, we are swept into the lives of three girls, each speaking in different tongues and from different countries. However, somehow each one shares something in common, a yearning for a purpose. Timid Bella has just arrived in the land of opportunity, America, only to discover that this new land is not always paved with gold. On the other hand, headstrong Yetta is determined to change the world in some form. At the same time, elegant Jane lives in luxury, but passionately seeks more than her father's wealth can offer. As the book begins, the author focuses primarily on their

Reviewed by
Eliza Smith, 12
Church Hill, TN

separate lives, but later weaves each of these together to set a premise for a monumental conclusion.

The three girls join together about midway through the book to unite in their cause, worker's rights. Fighting peacefully each day for better working conditions in New York's crowded factories, the characters experience fear and pain in their quest for justice. However, a terrible tragedy holds the power to tear them apart forever.

Haddix keeps readers hanging on to each word throughout. I found that the many setbacks of the characters only added to the overall product and believe our modern world could learn a lot from the perseverance and hope conveyed in the book. The Shirtwaist Factory Strike is a main focus, but the author never strays away from human emotions and experiences despite the book's historical background.

Readers who enjoy the *Dear America* series will delight in this powerful portrayal of life in the twentieth-century U.S. Although intended for a young adult audience, it is my belief that anyone searching for a good historical read, regardless of age, will thoroughly enjoy this book. However, one must consider the intended age before choosing *Uprising* as their latest reading endeavor.

The story offers many historically accurate details, which pairing with the plot, create a stunning presentation. Overall I found this book entrancing, and struggled to put it down each day. It is a great representation of the power of perseverance and hope.

Honor Roll

Welcome to the *Stone Soup* Honor Roll. Every month we receive submissions from hundreds of kids from around the world. Unfortunately, we don't have space to publish all the great work we receive. We want to commend some of these talented writers and artists and encourage them to keep creating.

Fiction

Alyssa Ao, 10
Jake Henschel, 11
Tuilaepa Katoanga, 11
Gavin Lehman, 11
Tracy Li, 13
Sayana Mayeski, 11
Stella Prince, 13
Leo Zhang, 11
Sarah Zhang, 11

Poetry

Ana Carpenter, 13
Uma Coutelle, 10
Colin Davison, 9
Lily Jessen, 9
Cecilia Yang, 11

Art

Sophia Zhang, 8

Reviews

Ananda Bhaduri, 12
Nicole Qian, 13

Don't forget to visit Stonesoup.com to browse our bonus materials. There you will find

- 20 years of back issues—around 5,000 stories, poems and reviews
- Blog posts from our Young Bloggers on subjects from sports to sewing plus ecology, reading and book reviews
- Video interviews with *Stone Soup* authors
- Music, spoken word and performances

Visit the *Stone Soup* Store at Stonesoupstore.com to buy

- Books—the 2017 *Stone Soup Annual*, a bound collection of all the year's issues, as well as themed anthologies
- Art prints—high quality prints from our collection of children's art
- Journals and Sketchbooks for writing and drawing
  ...and more!

StoneSoup

MAY 2018

VOLUME 46 / ISSUE 5

StoneSoup

The magazine supporting creative kids around the world

Editor
Emma Wood

Director
William Rubel

Operations
Jane Levi

Education & Production
Sarah Ainsworth

Design
Joe Ewart, Society

Check us out Social Media:

Editor's Note

What is a self portrait? What do we learn about ourselves when take a selfie, or when we paint our draw ourselves, or even when we write a story or a poem? Any art we make, even if it seems to have nothing to do with us, comes out of our mind. This means our ideas, perspectives, and interests have played a role in its creation. In this way, you could say that any story—whether about characters who resemble us or not—is a kind of self-portrait. Same for a poem, a photograph, a painting, or a collage. What we create says something about who we are. In this issue, we have two direct self-portraits. I encourage you to think about what the two very different portraits say about the two artists, but I also encourage you to think of the other work in here as "self-portraits." What does the work tell you about its creator? What does your own work say about you?

Letters: Do you have something to say about something you've read or seen in *Stone Soup*? If you do, we'd love to hear from you, and we might print your letter on our Letters to the Editor page! Post a comment on our website, or write to us at editor@Stonesoup.com.

Submissions: Our guidelines for submission are on the Submit page at Stonesoup.com, where you will also find a link to our Submittable online submissions portal.

Subscriptions: to subscribe to *Stone Soup*, please press the Subscribe button at our webpage, Stonesoup.com.

On the cover:
'No Boundaries,' *acrylic*

by Christian Goh, 9 Dallas, TX

StoneSoup
Contents

Boxes

*Azalea tries to ignore the boxes stacked in Ronia's home,
but eventually her best friend will have to go*

Ronia's black curls bob at the edge of my vision, her toffee face connected to twisting shoulders that sweep past the bodies of sweating parents, yakking teens, and pleading children. A shiny green sign twinkles with a line of sunlight, the white text saying "Atlantic Ave" invisible where the light hits the bumpy material. Air hisses through a hole in the thick plastic material next to me, pulsing as feet make contact with its airy brilliance. The sun watches over us, its warmth touching our faces and necks and burning us with its loving gaze. The wind joins in with the chorus of voices that ride over the thumping speakers like birds chirping out a melody while floating in the clouds. I eye a dolphin balloon that floats above the crowd, blue shimmer against a blue sky. The way it shines in the sun holds my vision as if challenging me to buy a grip on its bright string. I gather some cotton from my dad's shirt in my fist and tug, gaining his attention.

"Yes, Azalea?"

I point at Ronia with one hand, and the balloon with the other. "Ronia's over there," I say, "And I want that." I watch a kid with a red shirt near the balloon stand and narrow my eyes menacingly. "I want that now," I add. Ronia's face appears next to mine, face broken into a smile.

"Azalea!" She throws her arms open.

"Ronia!" I laugh and throw my arms around her. My hand wraps around her until it reaches the opposite side of her, where it rests, on the skin between her shoulder and neck.

My hand is wrapped around the balloon, the slight tug goes up my arm and into my heart as I walk down Atlantic Avenue, hand in hand with Ronia. When we see something we like, we gallop towards it, like our hands are cemented together and never will part.

As we walk to the East River, the outline of Ronia's building becomes visible against the pale blue sky. It grows larger the more our legs burn, the more asphalt we step across, the more words we set free. It grows so large it obscures my vision, the details of the front door more than the details of the building as a whole. We enter and walk to the elevator with its old, leathery smell, like the building is a prize someone tried to wash too many times. My faded sandals cross the gap lined with metal, high-fiving the floor—thwack—a game played with Ronia's pink and my blue sandals. Her feet are golden brown criss-crossed with blue plastic; mine, a birch tree, laden with celebratory ribbons, blue as a bluebird. The white lights flash on

by Melina Ahmad, 11
Brooklyn, NY

the elevator wall: Floor 1, 2, 3, 4, 5, 6. The elevator counts with me, 6 years, 6 floors. Through the doorway, our sandals thwack.

It looks like the walls are holding negative space, like all the framed memories were forgotten. Ronia's house used to be covered with pictures; nature, us, family, memories. But now all I see are nails sticking out of white walls, empty and holding nothing. Then I notice the bumpy, wood-colored boxes, green words on the sides, clinging onto the material as if they were scared to let go. But I shake my head and ignore these things, happy to be with Ronia.

When the sun reaches its home below the horizon, we watch the streaks of light glint on the dark choppy water. We take the subway home, the vision of the boxes bumping with the train. I hold the balloon to my chest, making the ends of my hair static. I frown; my tights itch, and so do my questions. My voice comes out, light as silver, but heavy with the questions. "Why were there boxes?" I ask, looking up at my parents. They share a look.

"Azalea. We have some bad news to tell you," they say, "But we can't tell you right now." So I wait until we get off the train and into the house before they talk again. "Ronia is moving to California." They place their hands on my shoulders, but nothing can stop the flood of tears that stream down my cheeks, my blue eyes magnified with the salty water that floods my vision. The river reminds me of the time we spent frolicking in the springs upstate, allowing cool, clear water to surround our boots, laughing when it went above the rubber protection and tickled our feet. My eyes burn when I rub them, and salty water covers my face. My mind creates an image of the time when we galumphed through the snowy woods with little crackling walkie-talkies in our hands. The time we sat atop our fathers' shoulders and held hands way up high, like our heads were not only in the clouds but they were the clouds. The time I ate her birthday cupcake when she was in the bathroom, and the time she ate mine the next year. The time we ate the apples from the ground while apple-picking. The time we put on a show for our families and sang and danced and played.

I sleep with those memories floating through my head that night.

The next day, Ronia comes over with her family, and we all sit at the oak dining room table. I pout at everything, everyone. I woke up in the morning with a black cloud over my head, and my eyes raining spontaneously. Thunder booms when it wants,

Parade of Clouds, *photography*

by Asfia Jawed, 12
Portland, ME

llightning strikes as it sees fit. They explain: California offers a job that New York does not. Where Craig (Ronia's father) goes, so do they. I glower some more.

Craig looks over and says, "Azalea…"

I don't let him finish. I go to my room, but arms catch me from behind and I turn into Ronia's arms, extending my body around hers. We stand, wrapped around each other, and laugh through our tears.

The Red Balloon . . .

by Rafi Mohammed, 10
Newcastle upon Tyne, UK

When sea captains say they have sailed the seven glimmering seas, I have flown them. When climbers say they have climbed the highest peaks, including the monstrously tall Mount Everest, I have achieved higher heights. When tourists say they have travelled all over the world, I have done it more times than I can count. But I am only a vivid dark, red balloon with a loose white string.

My master was really playful, he was about 7 when I left him. One day he lost his grip and I rushed towards the blue sky like a graceful bird dancing. From that second on, it was my quest to find him.

A few years later, I navigated the winds as they talked to me and told me where to go. I crossed the golden sand beaches, crystal clear, transparent, ice-cold glaciers. I have felt the slight tickle of the lush green grass of the forever blooming countryside. I have felt the burning scars of crashing into cliffs or skyscrapers.

One morning, I smashed into a fence where a bunch of bags told me to go to the vortex in Antarctica. Soon I let go of the fence and rushed into the sea. Then I spent years trying to find it. I mastered the currents of the water as I mastered navigating the wind. Finally after a few years, I found it. I was free! No more political roars no more cars or horns. I was free! I found myself in a freezing pool surrounded by millions of other balloons. But every moment I thought of my master. Someday, somehow, sometime and somewhere I will find him...

Searching for Bows and Arrows

by Tatiana Rebecca Shrayer, 9
Brookline, MA

Because I wanted to feel like an Amazon
I asked my father to build me a bow with arrows
We went to the nearby woods that overlook
Forest Beach in the village of South Chatham.

My father, sister and I followed
A wavy uphill path to the clearing
Where we found young oak trees
With pointy strong branches,

We sawed off three branches
That looked like they would suffice.
We carved them and sanded them,
And we bent them till they could sing.

By the time we had finished tying the string
The evening chill had descended.
We shot our arrows into the darkening sky
Where the stars scampered like red foxes.

My Grandma Helen

When Maggie's grandma dies, she struggles to understand what it means to be "gone"

I walk into the cold, barren waiting room. It smells like stale peppermints and dust bunnies. My dad has his hand on my shoulder, and I feel the warmth through my jacket. It's the only thing I can feel right now.

The clerk stands behind the desk, typing loudly on her giant computer. Her lips are glistening with bright fuchsia lipstick, and the mascara is clumped on her eyelashes. She has a gigantic smile plastered on her face, and it makes bile wash into my throat.

"Hello," she sings, tossing back her streaming, golden hair.

"Good evening," my dad greets her, with cheer that comes out of nowhere.

I keep my mouth shut.

"Would you like a mint, dear?" her voice pierces the still room. She plunges her manicured hand into the giant glass jar on the desk and shoves the plastic-wrapped candy into my hand before I can say no.

"We're here to see Helen Browne," my dad continues, his words smooth and in just the right tone.

I don't know how he does that: somehow knows exactly what people want to hear and exactly how to deliver it. My mama calls him a "people person." She says that he couldn't be any more different than her. My mama gets this scratched-by-a-cat look whenever anyone says something she doesn't like. Her lips disappear inside her mouth and her eyes squeeze shut and she clenches her coffee-colored hands against her skirt.

"Oh, yes," the lady responds. Her name tag says Patty. I don't like that name. It reminds me of the cafeteria ladies at school, hairnets stretched over their giant buns, glopping food onto plastic lunch trays.

I don't know what happens next. All I know is that my dad puts his hand firmly on my shoulder again, and then we're moving down the hallway and I stare at the green and black carpeting. Dad opens the door and we enter a cold, gray room that smells like clay. A single bed sits in the middle, and there sits my grandma. My heart drops and bursts open, pouring out love. My feet move me forward.

Grandma Helen has been there for me since I was born. My whole life I felt like I had to hide my emotions everywhere except my own home. Me, Mama, Dad, Jasmine, Nathan, Grandma and me. Grandma and I would sit for hours on the porch rocking chairs, and sometimes not even say anything, just sit there thinking about the dewdrops glistening on the sharp blades of grass, and the clouds fading and the stars twinkling in the night sky. I would look over at her and her eyes would be closed and she'd just be humming to herself, and once in a while she'd nod and smile. Sunday nights were for a huge family dinner that everyone would help make.

by Sadie Perkins, 13
Madison, WI

Everyone would sit around the table, laughing and talking and eating all at the same time.

I see Grandma sitting on the bed, back propped against two white pillows. She's not who she used to be. The color has drained from her face. The wrinkles have stretched all across her skin. She's here in this cold, sad building, not home with us painting her nails and experimenting with makeup. She's not in the kitchen with flour and sugar all over her, cooking all day. She's not surprising Dad with ice cold lemonade after he'd been gardening all afternoon, or giving Mom massages after a long day of law school. She looks over at us.

"Mom!" Dad cries out. "It's me."

Grandma cocks her head and looks right at him.

"Adam?" she whispers.

"Yes, Mom," Dad whispers. "It's me."

I walk over.

"Oh, my babies," Grandma whispers. She grabs Dad's hand and pulls him close, and she wraps me in her arms. She kisses my cheek. And she lies back down on her bed.

"Mom?" Dad whispers, and then I watch as her chest slows, and then stops, and her body is still.

I run forward and grab her hand, squeezing it like I can bring it back to life, but I can't, and then Dad is wrapping me in his arms and I feel him

but I can't think, and I just know that all of a sudden it feels like someone has thrown me off a sinking ship and I smack the water, and feel a rock hit hard against my head.

My grandma had been such a big part of my life, it didn't seem right that she was just gone. She wasn't afraid to put my dad in his place around the house, but she was always so sweet to my mom. She always told her, "Aisha, you need to relax."

Whenever I came home from school, my grandma Helen was always in the kitchen. She was a cook like a lot of grandmas I knew, but she was different. She didn't just bake pies and cakes. Grandma Helen made Duck à l'Orange and Beef Wellington. Every week, she tried out a new recipe, and every day she was at the table, thumbing through her cookbook and flipping through *Taste of Home*.

The other thing she liked to do was listen to music, from Beethoven and Brahms to heavy metal. You could always hear music coming from her upstairs bedroom. Once, I peeked in her room and she had on her best purple evening gown and she appeared to be waltzing with an imaginary person. Her eyes were closed in bliss.

On Saturday nights, she would move the antique wood coffee table, leather couches, and our huge rocking chair that smelled like coffee and mothballs, so the entire living room was open. She'd put out bowls of popcorn and cups of apple juice and iced tea, which was her favorite drink in the world. We'd wrap ourselves in blankets and watch an old movie, and sometimes fall asleep spooned together on the living room floor.

Grandma always told us that she wanted us to love ourselves, and we would love others. Ever since we were babies, she told Jasmine, Nathan, and me that she loved us more than life itself. She told us that nowadays you're supposed to only care for everyone else, and not care for yourself. But that, she told us, was impossible. You can't care for others if you're not happy. You can't treat others with respect if you feel you don't owe it to yourself. She told us that if we saw ourselves as wonderful, that was how we'd see the world. She told us more times than Albert Einstein could count that we could only truly love ourselves if we were ourselves and didn't pretend to be anyone else. If you act like someone else and you love that someone else, you don't really love your true self. Everyone is different. Nobody is any more "normal" or "regular" than anybody else. That was what she told us, up until the day she died.

For a long time afterwards, I lay in my room while everyone rushed around,

preparing for the funeral: buying black clothes, calling people, and not really saying anything, making sandwiches nobody ate. I didn't know what to think. I always got annoyed when people said someone was "gone" because it was just a sugar-coated way of saying they were dead. But now I understood. Saying somebody is dead is just saying the literal fact. They are gone. They are gone from your life, gone from their life. I could feel the place in my heart where Grandma had lived. It was barren and empty and cold, just like the nursing home where she had spent her last few months. I couldn't understand how a person could just vanish, all the life gone from them.

This is why it doesn't matter how someone looks. When they die, everything about them: who they are, what they think, what they like, what they want is all gone. All that's left is a body of skin and bones. The thought sent a shiver up my spine. It seemed impossible someone that nobody could see or knew even existed could just take everything from someone whenever they felt like it. Sure, you could try to fight it, but it was just a matter of time until you surrendered.

Everyone was going about their business normally, but I knew that they were not the same either. Grandma was a huge part of our family, and now she was missing. Like the one piece that fell off the beautiful, intricate puzzle and got chewed up by the dog. I was mad at this person, whoever and wherever they were, for taking Grandma away. I buried my face in my pillow. I didn't cry. I never cried. At least that's what I was telling myself. But I could feel the tears, filling my eyes. I remembered how Grandma would always sit next to me and stroke my hair when I cried. I would feel her hands, running through my hair, not saying anything, just letting me cry, and somehow telling me without saying anything that she loved me more than life itself. I could almost feel her now. I could... I could! I jumped up and turned around. I didn't see anything but I could smell Grandma's rosemary shampoo and I could feel her hand holding mine.

"Grandma?" I whispered into the air.

Yes, it's me, Maggie.

"Are you really there?"

I know it might seem like I am gone, but I will always be here.

"That's what everyone says."

It's true. My heart may have stopped but my soul lives forever. My love for my family knows no bounds, and that includes lifespans. It will stick with you forever.

I opened my mouth to reply, but all of a sudden she had vanished. And just at that moment, the empty space in my heart filled and opened up to a flood of gold and sweet and everything that was Grandma. She was still here.

From then on, I knew that even though my grandma was dead, she could still love me, and everyone else she had always loved. She was watching over us, protecting us every second.

I love you, Grandma. And I'm going to make you proud of me.

Bubble Bee, *acrylic*

by Christian Goh, 11
Dallas, TX

Self-Portrait, *mixed media*

by Alexander McCullough, 11
Marblehead, MA

Garage Junk

by Jerry Xia, 11
Palo Alto, CA

Few things could make me enter the garage at night but thirst was one of them. Although the space was lit by a bright, automatic light on the garage door mechanism, the lighting always felt inadequate. On one side, a refrigerator stood like a steel grandfather clock next to shelves of old junk. Nearby were a couple of tool shelves and a working table. Next to the door was a shoe rack full of old shoes that looked unwearable. On the other side, a massive yellow boiler hissed next to a filing cabinet full of old papers. Everywhere were shadows that reminded me of graveyards at night.

After I stepped into the garage to get a bottle of lemonade, I noticed a huge spider slowly walking across its web above the refrigerator. It was as slow as a snail and bigger than a quarter. It was brown with a round head and an oval body. Looking at it made me feel small, as if something was wrong, as if I had my back turned to a massive beast with red eyes.

Trying to not disturb the creature, I tiptoed very slowly to the refrigerator. My thirst was more motivational than my fear, but I moved with the speed of a broken wind-up toy car. As slowly opened the refrigerator door, the spider positioned itself almost directly above my head. I could see it, and I was sure it could see me. With the care-

fulness of the snakeman who caught green mambas with his bare hands, I opened the door. Quickly but silently, I grabbed the drink and felt the coolness of the bottle. Just as I was closing the refrigerator door and carefully watching the spider, thinking I was safe, the garage light turned off.

I had forgotten that the light detected movement, and maybe my slow movements had been too slow for it to recognize my presence. But waving my arms to turn it back on would alert the spider, so I just stood there. In darkness. The spider and me. Right then, I knew that my fear was like swiss cheese, full of holes. All I had to do was face the fear and eat it. After all, what is a spider but a hairy, air-breathing arachnid with eight legs and fangs that inject venom? And how many people die each year from spider bites? Two? Five? A hundred?

The garage was absolute darkness except for the moonlight shining in through a window next to the refrigerator. I could almost feel the spider's thin legs crawling slowly across my head. For a tiny moment I thought about what I would do. I had several options: I could throw the bottle of lemonade in my hands at the spider, I could run, or I could shout for help. However, throwing the bottle of lemonade at the spider would mean dislodging it from its web, and then I wouldn't be able to locate it. It would be angry and suddenly crawling around in the mess of lemonade on the floor, somewhere near my slipper-clad feet. Shouting would only alert it of my presence. Running would mean risking crashing into things that I couldn't see in the dark.

With no options left, I nearly panicked, but I told myself that my fear of spiders was irrational. Spiders are mostly just small bugs that slowly crawl around eating flies that occasionally get trapped in their webs. A spider would have no reason to descend on my head, no reason to chase me, no reason to bite me. After all, I was a thousand times larger than the spider, and the spider was probably more afraid of me than I was of it!

Realizing this, I decided the best option was not to run, not to shout, not to throw a bottle of lemonade, but just to simply walk away. I closed the refrigerator door as silently as I could and started to exit the garage. Calmly, I avoided boxes and racks full of items that might otherwise have tripped me while I was running. As I approached the doorway of the garage, I turned on the garage light. When I looked back from the door, I saw the spider very slowly walking toward me on its web in the corner of the garage. I looked at the spider and I thought it looked at me and I thought about how spiders are their own individual selves, just like humans. They are just trying to survive and live longer. People are cruel to spiders just because they look strange, while in reality, all spiders do is keep the bugs out of our homes.

Then I shut the door and dashed into my room, thinking about what I had just done. For several minutes, I sat in the chair at my desk and considered the other spider in the bathroom, the small one that lives in the corner behind the toilet. The next day, I moved the whole package of lemonade to the refrigerator in the kitchen to let the garage spider have its space. After my encounter with the spider, I've made an effort to recognize that spiders are not the monsters they appear to be, but harmless creatures that do their own thing. I still don't like them in the same room with me, but my fear of them is a half-eaten piece of swiss cheese.

A Dream of Chaos

by Atlas William Iacobucci, 9
New Haven, CT

The sound of thunder and rain thrashing around,
clinging to the Empire State Building.
As it flails and turns, I jump
through the window.
As the small bang of me landing
gets swallowed by the sound of thunder,
I jump down the narrow stairs
just as I hear fireworks.
And then I see it.
The tiles flying in the air.
I hear a small voice.
It gets louder and louder
until I see a huge flash of light.
And then New York is all fine.
And giant whale-like things flying
are just the sound of morning doves.

The Only Life in Death Flower, *photography*

by Delaney Slote, 11
Missoula, MT

Echoes

by Bailey Curtin, 11
Ottawa, Canada

Cate struggles to come to terms with her sister's death

It's in my head. Bouncing around like a beach ball. Jade's last words to me. "Shut it, Cate, and let me die in peace." She'd smiled, squeezed my hand, and then she was gone.

I'm walking. Walking on a PEI beach in my sweatshirt and pajama pants and flip-flops with my dark hair tangled and down, with a very special something in my pocket. It sags down, far down, but no one else is here and, to be honest, I don't care.

The sun is beginning to rise and I inhale through my nose sharply. It's the same sunset, the same feeling as the first morning without my sister. It's a sinking feeling, the way I felt when we lost our pet fish. But worse, much, much worse, than that.

Jade was always strong and no one ever, ever expected her to die. She was the star centre on her competitive soccer team, the second-best on her track team, and she went to the gym every Tuesday and Thursday. But the brain tumor came so quickly that it couldn't be stopped.

I take out the tiny marble box from my pocket and finger it between gloved hands. Jade's ashes, some at least. I'd stolen it from Mom's dresser. Remembering the day that she had the tumor, I stiffen and put it back.

It started with a simple headache at school; her teacher said she was fine and her friends insisted she could stay. A migraine when she got home—Mom's aspirin didn't work. "It'll be done by morning," Dad had assured her. I could hear Jade crying from her room—then it turned to screaming and things went downhill from there.

She was throwing up, feeling dizzy, but her headache was the worst. Mom realized how bad it was and took her to the Montague hospital. I stayed home.

"Is Jade gonna be okay?" I had asked. Dad sighed and turned away from me. His phone rang and he answered it. "She's being moved to Charlottetown," he reported.

Souris to Montague, Montague to Charlottetown, Charlottetown to Halifax. In Halifax they determined she had a brain tumor, and Dad used some of the little money we had to fly us out there. The doctors assumed she would live two more weeks.

It was less than two weeks. Four days later she died.

"At least we know she's safe now," Mom had choked out.

I should have died instead of her. I was the one they were always protecting, shielding from diseases, the frail girl of the family. Jade—my strong, determined older sister—was different.

It's been a month now.

February was always Jade's favorite month. "The best time for track," she'd joke with me. In truth, she did love running in it. Jade was never delicate and once she ran half a marathon in this weather. She came back with her fingers and toes frozen and frostbitten, and Mom wanted to take her to the doctor, but Jade just laughed and went to bed until noon the next morning.

The box is getting heavier in my pocket. I plant my feet into the wet sand and grope for something, anything, that will stop the tears. Like there'll be a box of Kleenex somewhere on a beach. Now I'm crying, sobbing silently, as the orange-pink sun hovers just over the horizon and climbs the soft coral sky over me.

The water splashes quietly onto the shore and laps gently on my feet. I tear my flip-flops off and fling them away. "Why?" I scream.

I break down on a big piece of driftwood and stay silent for a moment. Then there's a sound, a disturbance in my upset tranquility. Footsteps. It's Mom.

"Hi, Cate," she says softly, and sits down beside me. "What is it?"

"I miss Jade." I'm still crying a bit, and Mom puts her arm around me, her silky blond hair brushing against my cheek.

"I know." Mom looks out to the horizon. "I miss her, too."

"Mom?" I lean against her shoulder. "Could—could she have lived?"

Mom bites her lip and takes her arm away from my shoulders. "I've

been thinking about it, and...no. We found out too late. I'm sorry, Cate. It's my fault. I should've noticed earlier."

"It's not your fault," I say in a wobbly voice. "Not at all."

She turns away. "No, Cate...Catelyn Fuller, you don't know what I know. I've spoken with the doctors. I've made sure. They said...they confirmed... that Jade would have lived if I'd gotten her there on time."

Two swift dark cormorants whoosh by, nimble as they swoop over the rocks, racing silently to the water. The wind whistles quietly. Mom's words echo in my head.

I take out Jade's ashes from my pocket and set them back on the log. Mom turns around. "Oh my goodness," she whispers hoarsely.

"You kept this?" she continues, and a tear trickles down her cheek. "I thought I'd lost it. I've searched the house for this. Cate, I am so mad at you for stealing this but god, I'm happy to see it again!"

I ignore the fact that she's never said that before and pick up the small box, cold in my hands, to press it into Mom's ice-cold palms.

Her hands automatically curl protectively around it and she smiles sadly. "Jade," she whispers, half to herself.

I stand up. "Mom?"

"Jade," she says again. "I mean—yes, Cate?"

"You should head back," I murmur, squeezing her wrist.

"I will." She blinks back tears and

Now I'm crying, sobbing silently, as the orange-pink sun hovers just over the horizon and climbs the soft coral sky over me.

squeezes back. "I will."

And she heads down the beach towards the dirt road back home.

It's quiet as she leaves. A crab scuttles towards my feet and buries itself in the sand.

I wipe my face on my sleeve. The waves ripple across the sand and I look up suddenly, startled as a slender white bird catches my eye.

Jade taught me well. We'd spent hours poring over her bird encyclopedia, memorizing each and every bird in the universe. "Chickadee," I can hear her saying in my mind. "Scientific name: Poecile atricapillus. Natural habitat: mixed evergreen forests and forest edges. Family: tit..."

I squint. It's a dove, it appears, but why is it here? Doves live in dense forests and woodlands, deserts and sometimes suburban areas in the southern U. S. But this is Souris, Prince Edward Island!

The dove starts arranging her feathers gracefully, preening its smooth white wings quietly. It rotates twice, looking for something I don't know of, then spots me. It stands stock still.

I hold my breath so it doesn't glide away, but finally exhale, my breath puffing out in the frosty air—I can see it—and the dove flutters the soft pink-white wings. To my surprise, it comes towards me on thin delicate legs, leaving a tiny imprint on the wet sand.

It emits a mournful, haunting noise like a loon, echoing in my ears. I shiver. "Hey," I breathe to it, directing my voice towards the bird, about forty meters away.

That was stupid, I think a second later, regretting my decision to try and make a friend out of it. It won't be able to hear me.

But apparently it can hear me. It doesn't hesitate to keep going farther away from the water and towards me. It finally stops beside me—is it my imagination or not? —and starts scratching something in the sand with thin black claws.

A heart. But a heart with a little loop at the bottom, our family's code for something. The one that means I'm safe.

I stare at it quizzically. How?

A train of thought runs through my head so quickly I can barely think. What? How? Am I hallucinating? I must be.

The dove calls again, the same mourning sound, and disappears with a faint popping noise.

"I'll be back," I whisper to the spot where the dove disappeared, rising from my seat on the smooth driftwood and starting the walk home.

Honor Roll

Welcome to the *Stone Soup* Honor Roll. Every month we receive submissions from hundreds of kids from around the world. Unfortunately, we don't have space to publish all the great work we receive. We want to commend some of these talented writers and artists and encourage them to keep creating.

Don't forget to visit Stonesoup.com to browse our bonus materials. There you will find

- 20 years of back issues—around 5,000 stories, poems and reviews

- Blog posts from our Young Bloggers on subjects from sports to sewing plus ecology, reading and book reviews

- Video interviews with *Stone Soup* authors

- Music, spoken word and performances

Visit the *Stone Soup* Store at Stonesoupstore.com to buy

- Books—the 2017 *Stone Soup Annual*, a bound collection of all the year's issues, as well as themed anthologies

- Art prints—high quality prints from our collection of children's art

- Journals and Sketchbooks for writing and drawing
  . . . and more!

StoneSoup

JUNE 2018

VOLUME 46 / ISSUE 6

StoneSoup

*The magazine supporting
creative kids around the world*

Editor
Emma Wood

Director
William Rubel

Operations
Jane Levi

Education & Production
Sarah Ainsworth

Design
Joe Ewart, Society

Stone Soup (ISSN 0094 579X) is
published online eleven times a year—
monthly, with a combined July/August
summer issue. Copyright © 2018 by the
Children's Art Foundation, a 501(c)(3)
non-profit organization, located in Santa
Cruz, California. All rights reserved.
Thirty-five percent of our subscription
price is tax-deductible. Make a donation
at Stonesoup.com/donate/ and support us
by choosing Children's Art Foundation as
your Amazon Smile charity.

Stone Soup is available in different formats
to persons who have trouble seeing or
reading the print or online editions.
To request the Braille edition from the
National Library of Congress, call
+1 800-424-8567. To request access
to the audio edition via the National
Federation of the Blind's NFB-
NEWSLINE®, call +1 866-504-7300 or
visit www.nfbnewsline.org.

Check us out on Social Media:

Editor's Note

Friends! "Without them," as Neel Rangan
writes in his poem "Dreamland," "we
would have the most boring sleep." Even
when they bring us pain, as in the friends
nearly broken up by political differences
in the story "Red and Blue," the other
people in our life give our life life. I hope
the stories in this issue will inspire you
to think and write about the incredible
friends in your life—human, animal, or
mineral. I also hope that when you're done
reading this issue you go to our website
and check out our new (and lively!) Book
Reviews section to help you select books
for your summer reading list!

Sincerely,

Emma Wood

Subscriptions: to subscribe to *Stone Soup*, please
press the Subscribe button at our webpage,
Stonesoup.com.

Submissions: Our guidelines for submission
are on the Submit page at Stonesoup.com, where
you will also find a link to our Submittable online
submissions portal.

Letters: Do you have something to say about
something you've read or seen in Stone Soup? If
you do, we'd love to hear from you, and we might
print your letter on our Letters to the Editor page!
Post a comment on our website, or write to us at
editor@Stonesoup.com

On the cover:
'Red Fern,' photography

**by Hannah Parker, 12
South Burlington, VT**

StoneSoup

Contents

Mother Earth

by Celeste Escobar, 9
Belmont, CA

I love my mother
My true mother
I smack my feet
Against her sandy skin
Hot or cold
I don't care
I do it every day

You do it too
Sometimes
To get exercise
But I do it for fun
To love her
To hug her
To roll around on her lap
And laugh.

Dreamland

by Neel Rangan, 9
Palo Alto, CA

There once was a land.
So far and fine,
Full of dreams and thoughts.
The place people came when they dreamed,
the place people came when they slept.
So far and so high that no one could reach.
And yet if you close your eyes, you are there!

The creator created it
So man could dream,
He is long gone but his memory still lingers,
To us he is known as god!

The people there live only to give you dreams.
Their life is a job much like in theatre,
They act out your dreams,
They make you happy,
Without them we would have the most boring sleep.

The House in the Willows

by Nicole Qian, 13
Auckland, NZ

Friends and Footprints

When Melody's brother goes missing, she's forced to venture into the creepiest house in her town

It was precisely 3:27 am, and Melody Campbell was sitting cross legged by the beach, having stealthily snuck out of the house due to insomnia. It wasn't a public beach with mobs and mobs of vacationers and gaudy umbrellas that made your eyes ache when you looked at them too long—it was more like a huge cove along the Atlantic coast, private to only Melody's family and their neighbors. In fact, Melody rarely saw anybody out there but herself, and of course the bottlenose dolphins. There was no particular reason for Melody's insomnia; it just happened some nights. But the Cove always seemed to help with that. The sound of the gentle night's waves tamed her restlessness, the humming breeze helped her to think, and the sand, cool from the shade of nighttime, was a welcome difference to the stuffiness of sharing a small room. By now, Melody's eyelids were heavy and she was struggling to keep them open. Just as she turned away from the lulling waves, she caught something in her peripheral vision. Stifling a yawn, Melody turned back and blearily took a second look. What she saw astonished her.

Footprints.

At first she thought they might be her own, but a closer inspection proved otherwise. Then she noticed the next thing. The footsteps lead right into the water-- and never back out. Scanning the ocean front, Melody didn't see any signs of a human disturbance. The churning waves crashed on smooth sand, and behind the surf, the ocean was glassy smooth. The footprints must have been fresh, the bottoms still filled with tiny pools of water.

Eventually exhaustion won her over and forced her to turn back to the house. At the front porch, Melody took one last glance at the Cove and the footprints, only to find she couldn't even see them anymore. *Maybe it was just a trick of the moonlight*, she thought doubtfully. *Or perhaps I was just dreaming the whole thing.* She went into the house, silently shutting the door behind her, and crept into the room she shared with her little brother Harmony.

by Samantha Abrishani, 12
McLean, VA

(Her parent's bad idea of a joke.) The moon shone through a crack in their curtains, forging a path onto his face. For a second, she stared at him lovingly. His shaggy blonde hair was strewn about his pillow, those plump little-kiddish cheeks were littered with golden freckles illuminated by the moonlight, and his lips were curled into a quirky smile, perfectly reflecting his sweet nature. And then she was stumbling into her bed, pulling her sheets around her, and falling asleep, dreaming of mysterious footprints leading into the ocean. . .

Melody woke up to Harmony banging out a lively (and very out of tune) song on the piano downstairs. On second thought, it probably wasn't a real song. Her little brother was indeed a... creative... composer. However, nobody in the Campbell family had the heart to tell him how he really sounded. Any headaches or earaches were carefully hidden. At first she screwed her eyes shut, trying to close off the sound and fall back asleep. And then it hit her with the force of a pummelling wave, one of the freezing ones you get when you first run into the water, one that soaks you through and makes your breath hitch up in surprise. Everything that happened last night was recalled, and suddenly she didn't feel so tired. Leaping out of bed, she dragged a comb through her honey blonde hair, changed, and rushed into the bathroom to perform the quickest brush-your-teeth-while-washing-your-face procedure mankind has ever seen.

"I'm running out, but I'll be back soon!" shouted Melody to her mom over the commotion of the piano as she scooped up a pancake and folded it into her palm. Her mom nodded and sent her a thumbs up signal, not even bothering to try raising her voice above the chaos. Slipping on her flip-flops, Melody sprinted out the door to the cute gray house and ran around to the back, stuffing the pancake into her mouth. She's always thought she must be one of the luckiest girls in the world, to have a beach for her backyard. Melody raced to the shore, golden-speckled chocolate eyes probing the sand for a trace, any trace, of the footprints she thought she had seen the night before. . . And there, to the left, a trail of faint imprints that just defined footprints leading into the water. There still weren't footprints leading out of the water. So she hadn't imagined it, she wasn't crazy. Someone or something had definitely been here last night, had definitely walked right into the water and never came back out again. Most kids would have been scared when they figured that out, but Melody wasn't like most kids. She was intrigued, curious, pulled into the mystery, the mystery of the footprints.

When she got back to the house, Melody was relieved that the piano abuse had finally stopped. Melody's mom smiled knowingly at her, one of the smiles moms can give you when they know just what you're thinking at the moment.

"Don't tell him, but I was relieved Harmony decided to go play in the back with you and got off of that poor piano." Wait. There was something wrong with that sentence, but Melody couldn't quite put her finger on it. Oh. Her eyes widened, lips parting slightly. She looked at her mom. "What, honey?"

"Harmony. He- he wasn't in the back. When did he leave the house?"

"About five minutes ago," volunteered her dad, looking up from his copy of the paper, eyebrows creased in worry. "If he went back to the Cove, you would have seen him." They all exchanged glances. They knew how quickly Harmony's little blond head moved from one thing to another-- he might have started out intending to join Melody, but by the time he left the house, had a different destination in mind. He might get hurt on the way, or get lost. There was a Campbell family rule that you didn't go anywhere other than the Cove without a buddy. Obviously, Harmony wouldn't *mean* to break this rule, but he was only five years old. There was a period of dead silence, concern shining through all of their faces. Melody was the first to act. Shoving her feet in her flip-flops again, she turned to her parents.

"I'll go and check out a couple of places for him. You two stay here in case he comes back before I reach him." Without waiting for an answer, Melody jumped out the door and began to jog away from the house, trying to tame her panic. Sure, Harmony was the annoying piano banger and always wanted her to play cars with him, (something Melody detested) he was still her little brother, and of course she loved him. Harmony wasn't at the rock, a gargantuan boulder the Campbell

siblings often went to climb and sit on the very top. He wasn't at the picnic table, a small wooden table in the middle of the woods. And he wasn't in the local supermarket, in which he liked to admire the delicately adorned fresh baked cupcakes and cookies.

"Mrs. Blake, have you seen Harmony anywhere?" asked Melody, out of breath, to one of their kind neighbors. She had older kids in high school.

"No, I haven't. Has he gone missing?" Her eyebrows lifted up to her hairline. "Poor little dear." Melody wasn't sure if Mrs. Blake was referring to her or Harmony.

"It's alright, I'll find him. Thanks." She turned and jogged away. There was no place else she could think of looking for the little boy. Melody had asked most of her neighbors if they had seen Harmony, and though their answers were sympathetic, they were all the same.

By now Melody was freaking out, ready to race back to her house and announce, breathless, that it was time to call the police. Her sweet little brother was gone.

But what was that, over there? Behind that house? She could have sworn a swatch of golden hair just whizzed by. Holding her breath in anticipation, Melody burst around the side of the old brick house and, just as she thought it must be, there was Harmony!

"Harmony!" At first, that was all Melody could get out. Her sides were heaving from her frantic dash around the neighborhood, and her knees felt weak with relief. And then she realized that he was signalling something to

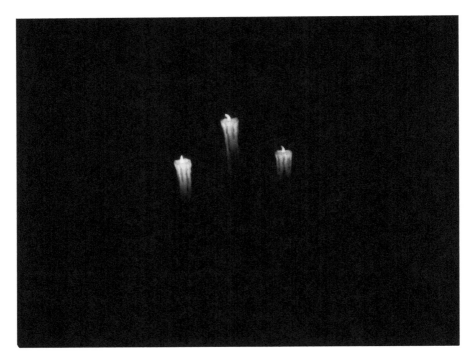

Light in the Dark

by Hannah Parker, 12
South Burlington, VT

her, smashing a finger against his lips and raising his eyebrows in a hopeful plead.

"Wha—?" Melody began to ask. Harmony jabbed a thumb towards the house.

It was, as she had noticed earlier, a brick house. The gutters, that must have once been white, were stained an ugly brown, like coffee stains on an old, musty book. It was a spider paradise; every wedge was thickly woven with glistening silver strands of cobwebs. "Ugh." Melody moved a step away from the house. Then she realized exactly whose house it was. Stifling a gasp, she stared with steadily widening eyes at Harmony. "Explain. Now." she whispered, pulling him down the side of the house to the ground. "Why are we at the crazy old—I mean, why are we at Ms. Jillian's house?"

"I was trying to see if Ms. Jillian really does eat spiders for her breakfast, like Todd from school says," Harmony whispered. "Honest, Melly, I just forgotted to go back!" Harmony called Melody 'Melly' because when he was a baby, he couldn't say her whole name.

"It's for*got*." Melody corrected sharply, still annoyed from her scare. "And that crazy—I mean, Ms. Jillian doesn't eat spiders. Honestly, Harmony, I'm really disappointed in you." Normally, this wouldn't be something the older sister tells her little brother-that's more for the parents to do. But as being the oldest and often in charge of babysitting Harmony when her parents were out, Melody had kind of stepped into the role.

"But she isn't even in there!"

"All the better." Melody snapped, taking Harmony by the hand and turning to their own house.

"No, her lights are on."

"Then she just forgot to turn them off."

"*Melly*," he said, in a voice that was beyond his age and clearly suggested she was being ridiculous. "We should go in-"

"Absolutely not." Ms. Jillian, with her wispy white hair, deep wrinkles, very pale eyes, and shaky, wizened hands had always turned Melody away.

"You are scared." He stated, matter of factly.

"I, I..." For a second, Melody stuttered and muttered, trying to find a suitable answer to this challenge. "*Fine.* Just don't be rude, don't say anything, just stand next to me and disappear." she said grumpily, taking a breath and knocking on the front door like a soldier reporting to duty.

"But, Melly, if I'm standing next to you, how can I-"

"Harmony," she said warningly. He shrugged and smiled his little dimpled grin. They waited. And waited. Melody knocked again. It seemed like nobody was home. "No one's home, Harmony." She told the little boy. But Melody's reasonable side was pushing out her fantasies of the skeletal old woman. She might be hurt in her house, needing help. Ms. Jillian lived alone. She may have fallen. Nobody knew how old she was, but by the looks of it, she was the oldest resident. "If the door's unlocked, we'll just go in and see if she's in there. You're right, it's very unusual for her to leave her lights on

If Melody had any doubt about Ms. Jillian being a little crazy, it was gone.

when she isn't home." Most times Melody ran into the old woman, Ms. Jillian gripped her wrists with her knobbly, quivering hands and informed her all about how much electricity was wasted when you left lights on. "I remembered when so many electric light bulbs in every home was a privilege," she'd tell Melody, "we never took it for granted. If only the world now thought the same thing..." She would shake her head forlornly, wisps of white falling out of her dark hood. 'Good day, child.' And like that, Ms. Jillian would be disappearing into the dreary fog. No, it would be most uncharacteristic for her to leave them on. Which meant she must be in trouble.

When Melody opened the door and pushed her way in, the first thing she did was see was Ms. Jillian, hunched on the floor in the corner. The second thing she did was think, *why in the world did I bring Harmony in with me?* Backing out the door with the little boy behind her, she turned around and faced him, trying to clear the fright from her features.

"Stay here. Don't move." She turned into the house again, shut the door, and went uncertainty for Ms. Jillian.

"M-Ms. Jillian?" She stammered, staring at the shaking old lady. She might be having a seizure, or a heart attack, or something else that was just as horrible... Think clearly, she reminded herself. "Ms. Jillian, can you

hear me?" she asked putting a hand on the back of the black coat. She went in front of Ms. Jillian and saw she was clutching a pendant around her neck.

"Campbell... you are the Campbell girl..."

"I am the Campbell girl. It's me, Melody. Are you okay? Are you hurt?" Ms. Jillian blinked, eyebrows knit up in confusion.

"Hurt...? No. He is *gone*, dear child. *Gone.* I knew it, when I found him sitting by the beach. I knew he was *magical...*" she paused, bottom lip trembling. "Yes, I should have known, I should have. It was *stormy.* Mystical things are brought up by great storms..."

"Magical? Mystical?" If Melody had any doubt about Ms. Jillian being a little crazy, it was gone. "Please, let me go get help."

"No, no, *no*," she gripped Melody's arms in a viselike way with her bony fingers that were too strong for her age. "He was huddled on the beach, gasping for water, *moaning* for water." Now it was Melody's eyebrows that were knit up in confusion. She gave a gentle tug on her arms, but Ms. Jillian gripped them fast. "So I took him to my house and put him in my bathtub."

"In your... *bathtub*?" It didn't make sense. Nothing made sense. "A boy? A human?"

"A human on the *outside*, but a beautiful *creature* on the inside." Now that both of her hands were occupied,

Melody could focus on the swinging pendant. It was glass, a sleek, gray bottlenose dolphin. But no... the crazy notion didn't make sense. Ms. Jillian's eyes seemed to be snow white and glowing in the dim, flickering lighting of her house. Those eyes probed Melody's own brown speckled eyes, trying to make her understand.

"A dolphin?" Melody breathed. Ms. Jillian's eyes were focused on something far away, and her chin barely bobbed up and down.

"Yes, he was an angel of the *sea*, never destined to live on this, this dry *land*. So he left, he *left* this earth and went to his roots, within the waves and among the other angels." Ms. Jillian's grip on Melody's wrists loosened, and she broke free of it completely. She felt like she was so close to understanding Ms. Jillian's story, she felt like there was just one puzzle piece missing. Going into the small bathroom, she saw towels strewn about the floor, all soaking wet. The tub was still sloshing full of water.

"So. . . " Melody tried to understand, walking back to Ms. Jillian. "So you found this kid a long time ago on the beach in the middle of a storm and brought him back to your house? You cared for him and put him in your bathtub because he needed water to live... and then one night he just left?" Speaking the words, she felt like she was speaking another language. This was too preposterous to believe. But Ms. Jillian nodded, a small tear making its way down her wrinkled old face. And in a way, it made sense. Ms. Jillian had already kept to herself, but when Melody was little, maybe Harmo-

ny's age, it wasn't unusual to see her walking around the town. That stormy night must have changed everything.

"Yesterday night." Yesterday night!! That was the night she saw the fresh prints, the night they went in and never came out. The mystery was slowly unfolding, the truth starting to shine. And the startling realization only seemed to prove Ms. Jillian's point.

"Well, then . . . he's where he belongs. You can't keep a . . . dolphin spirit in your tub, Ms. Jillian. Surely you know that." She put a comforting arm hesitantly on Ms. Jillian's shoulder.

"I know that." She repeated numbly, nodding slightly. "I knew it, all along. Knew that one day . . . " Her voice puttered out and eventually lapsed into a period of lengthy silence.

"Are you okay now?" As soon as she said it, Melody mentally face palmed herself. It was a bad question—she had suffered a loss, for a period of time the creaky old brick house had seemed not as creaky and old to Ms. Jillian herself, because she was sharing it with someone. Someone she had obviously loved. Apparently Ms. Jillian thought it was bad question too, because she ignored it.

"I know what people say. About me." She said. She wasn't speaking in that whispery frail voice anymore, and she almost seemed. . . well, normal. "I know they think I'm crazy. I know they think I stay in my house all day long doing nothing. . . I don't have any family anymore. I'm the last." Ms. Jillian turned to Melody with a sad smile that made Melody struggle to keep a tear or two in her tear ducts. "The folks here are nice. They bring me things sometimes, and greet me nicely when I'm out of the house. But it's not the same as having someone, of having a *friend*. And for a while, I had that friend. But not anymore."

"I don't really, either." Melody allowed herself to admit.

"But you're a beautiful, friendly little girl... surely you have a buddy from school?"

"Not really. And it's summer now. Everyone that goes to my school lives closer to it, and I live the farthest away. It's kind of like I'm an alien from another world, the places are so different."

"Then. We should get to know each other a little more." Ms. Jillian suggested hesitantly, smiling and looking decades younger. Melody smiled back, thinking that it wasn't such a bad idea.

Melody woke up early a few weeks later and clambered down the stairs, grabbing a piece of toast and waving to her mother over the thumping of piano keys and wrong notes. She ran around back to the Cove and made her way to the North side of it, where it was rocky and offered many ledges to sit down on.

"Hey, wait up!" she called to her friend who was in front of her, steadily making her way to the same spot. They had made plans the other day to meet up here. The lady turned around, grinning. Her white hair was braided loosely over her shoulder, and she was wearing a light blue shirt that brought out the pale color of her unique eyes.

"Did you wake up to Harmony's piano skills again this morning?" She asked jokingly. Melody groaned.

"I sure did!" She replied, catching up to her. As the friends sat side by side on the rocky ledge, talking, Melody smiled to herself and thought, *what a huge change one friend can make.* And she was right. And then the sun began to rise, casting beautiful colors onto the waves below, a dolphin leapt out of the ocean and slapped his tail onto the surface of the water, concentric circles spreading. The lady reached out a hand and caught a droplet that had spiraled up to them.

Ms. Jillian and Melody turned and smiled at each other.

Green Envy

by Delaney Slote, 12
Missoula, MT

What's inside my messy head?

by Tommy Swartz, 12
McLean, VA

What's inside my messy head?
Being funny
And when I'm dead.
Things I should've said
Done and said.
And always stress
About things lost
And of my actions
What will be the cost.
Was that joke
Weird or funny?
Or what I'll do outside
If tomorrow's sunny.
So what's inside my messy head?
And the day's
Shortening length.
Being a star
And messed up jokes
That I try to tell quietly
And how to escape
Authority's yoke.

A New Comfort

by Sonja ten Grotenhuis, 10
Piedmont, CA

Ding!! The school bell rings as loud as a lion would roar. I sprint out of the old crusty building, rushing along the sidewalk, leaving the chipped blue schoolhouse behind me. I only slow down when I know Patricia isn't following me.

Patricia is the star of everything she does. She executes lovely, fake smiles. She is perfect, and is the number one student in all of her classes, and every sport she does by far. She settled, after much deliberation, on making me her new best friend.

One day as I was walking home from school, the grey sidewalk beneath my feet felt bare and as soon as Patricia skipped by, I knew why.

"So did you hear the news that the school cleared the mural off of the sidewalk?" Patricia beamed expectantly.

"No. I thought that mural had been there for years." I replied.

"Yes, but that doesn't matter, they picked me to choose a team of six people to help me paint the new mural. Isn't that great!"

I shrugged and looked back down at the uncovered sidewalk.

As soon as I spot our bright new house, I rush up the stairs, through the screen door and into my room, slamming the door and locking it. I fall down on my bed, legs splayed out in front of me.

Summer is the best time of the year. The sun shines down on me as popsicles drip on my bare feet. I stroll home from the pool, still wet from swimming; my best friend Maria skips beside me and we talk and laugh together. My schedule is always free and I never have any boring camps to do, so it's just Maria and I.

"Maddy, I have a surprise for you!" I hear my mom's voice call, smooth and sweet. I slowly sit up and open my door expecting another book or baseball cap. Instead my mom is standing, smiling like a clown.

"What is it?" I ask, expecting something worse than books.

"I signed you up for bike camp! Isn't that great? Patricia will be there so you'll have a friend, and I'm sure that you'll make new ones." She said, beaming even more.

I tensed up, realizing what she'd just said. "Mom, I don't know how to ride a bike." I replied, my voice scratchy and weak.

"It starts tomorrow," she said, apparently not paying much attention

Patricia is annoyingly perfect — and she's decided to make Maddy her best friend

to me.

I close my door quietly, explaining that, "I have so much summer homework!" Instead I spend the next four hours trying to figure out how to ride a bike on the Internet.

Dinner was a depressing sight. My sister, Georgia, texting on her phone, mom planning carpools with Patricia's mom on her computer, dad tapping constantly on his iPad, trying to email his friends, and me, sitting and wondering if I'd survive the next day.

"So are you super excited? I am! I've been riding bikes since I was five!" chatters Patricia.

I sit on the neat, perfect leather seat in Patricia's minivan trying not to puke from the scent of mint tea and banana all mixed in one. Patricia stares at me expectantly, her small blue eyes like needles piercing into my skin.

"Um sure." I reply. "I've been riding since I was three," I coughed, apparently allergic to the lie.

Her mouth fell open, and I could see her perfect shiny white teeth, gleaming like diamonds.

Once at the arena, Patricia's mom waves her goodbye, not bothering to hug or kiss her. I wheel my new green bike to the starting point, where eight other people are standing. I fasten on my helmet and climb on the seat. I feel unstable and unsafe. Patricia mounts her pink bike with ease and sits on it comfortably, waiting for our instructions.

A man with spiked blue hair and bright green eyes walks up to us. He stands in front of the rainbow of bikes. "I am Sebastian." He booms, in a voice like thunder. "Let us start our camp with a little competition, shall we."

I hear whooping and hollering from a gang of boys, and I gulp nervously.

"The first person to reach the finish line," he points across the track, "will win," he finishes.

My arms are shaking and quivering so much that I can't hide it from Patricia, who looks over suspiciously at me.

"Ready . . . Set . . . Go!" Sebastian cries, waving a red flag in the air.

My legs start sweating, as I start pedaling. Instantly I'm behind everyone. Shaking I feel myself falling, then crash!! It happened. I embarrassed myself in front of everyone. I look up to see a concerned pair of brown eyes looking at me. I sit up and recognize the girl as the one sitting on her bike next to Patricia at the starting point.

"Hi. I just wanted to see if you're okay," she says.

I push myself up on my bloody elbows, trying not to cry. She was probably one of those professional bike riders who knew how to ride when she was 5.

"I'm fine," I reply, yanking my new, very damaged bike up.

The girl has short wavy brown hair and dark brown eyes. Her smile is kind and protective, the way Maria would smile at me. She grasps my hand and helps me up. "Thanks." I mumble. She nods and replies, "You're welcome." Then she mounts her bike and pedals away.

I suddenly realize that she has the same jerky movements, the same quivering legs as me. I rush toward her and say, "Wait! What's your name?"

She jumps off her brown bike and

says, "Rosie, what's yours?"

I catch my breath and say, "Maddy."

We exchange smiles before Sebastian blows his whistle, crying, "Thomas wins!"

I glance back to see one of the boys standing at the finish line, screaming, "I won! I won!" at the top of his lungs. I suck in my breath, trying not to cry from embarrassment.

Patricia walks over to me and demands, "So, you've been riding since you were three?"

I gulp and reply, "Well not really."

Patricia groans and jogs back to the starting point, her pink bike trailing behind. "As if she hasn't told any lies," I thought.

Then I silently wheel my bike back to the starting line, and sit on it, ashamed of myself. As if hearing my thoughts Rosie put a reassuring arm around my shoulder. At that moment, I knew we were friends.

Blue Heron

Ostriches

by Sierra Glassman, 12
Watsonville, CA

The Mouse Who Played Keyboard

There once was a mouse

who played the keyboard.

When he played at night

the cats came out.

The rats came out.

The owls came out!

The Lion and the House Cat

In the African sun there was a lion

and the house cat.

One day the cat told the lion

to have a race.

So the race started.

They ran so fast

a rock fell on the king of France.

The lion won the race!

by Isaiah Albro, 7
Sherman Oaks, CA

Pink

by Abhi Sukhdial, 9
Stillwater, OK

The Red and Blue Thread

The divisive 2016 election threatens to break the bond between two best friends

Stella Addle pushed through the school building door, a wave of sound hitting her. Kids yelling and laughing, smiling and scowling. The air felt weighty; the anger, the confusion, pushing down on her shoulders, feeling heavy as bricks. Stella lugged her backpack to her locker. She stared at the lime green paint, then fiddled with her lock and pulled open the locker door. She dropped her backpack on the bottom of the locker and pulled out her math books and her calculator, which was covered in leftover heart stickers from Valentine's Day. Usually seeing the stickers made her smile, but today she felt as though nothing could make her lips turn upward. This was a tragedy, an absolute tragedy. Forty five presidents and none of them had been women! Hillary Clinton should have won, she should have been the first woman president, but that stupid Donald Trump had to ruin everything! Stella thought as she slammed her locker shut with gusto. November 8th 2016 is going to be the worst day of my life! Stella walked to her homeroom, her legs feeling unsteady, her whole world feeling out of balance, broken.

Feeling dizzy, she sat down and scanned the room for Gabby while taking in the rest of the scene. Gabriella Carmann had been Stella's best friend since second grade. They did everything together; they had sleepovers and shared their deepest secrets with each other, they knew they could tease the other about their clothes and not offend them. They balanced each other out, Gabby was the flashy, stubborn, strong headed leader of the two, and Stella was the quieter, gentler one, keeping them away from heated drama. When Stella was around Gabby she felt a certain strength, a sense of courage that she didn't feel when she was alone, as if some of Gabby's confidence was magically seeping into her. For Gabby, Stella was the source of cool water that doused Gabby's flames, the flames that burned the same color as her orange hair. It was because of Stella that Gabby was starting to find some of that water in herself, way deep down, but still it was there.

Finally she saw her: Gabby walked into the classroom sporting a pair of gray hand-me-down sweatpants

by Rhianna Searle, 12
Churchville, PA

from her older sister Franny, short for Frances, and a purple t-shirt with a turquoise flower print. Her denim backpack hung over her shoulder and her long red hair was pulled into a tight ponytail. This was Gabby's usual look, so what surprised Stella was the smile that spread across Gabbys face. Stella knew Gabby and her family were Republican, but for some reason Stella never thought they would vote for Trump, or be happy if he won. Puzzled, Stella stood up and followed Gabby to her locker.

"Hey," Stella said leaning against one of the lockers.

"Morning," Gabby replied as she unpacked her backpack.

"So..." Stella said nodding slowly. Thoughts were racing through her mind; conversation usually came easy to the two of them, why was it hard now?

"What?" Gabby said. "What is it? What's wrong?"

You're happy . . . Trump's our President-Elect . . . Stella thought as she looked at the floor.

"If something's up, just tell me," Gabby slammed her locker shut and stared at her friend. "Just tell me. Please."

"It's just... you... are you glad Trump won?" Stella's face turned red with shame.

"Oh! Uh, yeah, I mean, I guess . . . I mean my parents voted for him." *She thought we voted for Hillary? She knows we're Republican*, Gabby thought.

The bell rang and the hallways were filled with noisy sixth, seventh, and eighth graders. Stella had math first period and Gabby had science.

"I got to go. See you later?" Gabby asked.

"Sure," Stella said, and she turned and walked to math, wondering what had just happened.

Stella plopped down in her chair, feeling exhausted. Family dinners were an important part of the Addle household and usually Stella enjoyed them, especially on lasagna nights like these, but not tonight. Margaret Addle, Stella's mom, placed the lasagna on the table and sat down across from her husband. Usually, though it was only the three of them, the table buzzed with conversation, a light and fluffy happiness, almost as delicious as Mrs. Addle's cooking, hanging in the air. Tonight however, the air felt heavy and cold and the conversation that usually flowed easily, had vanished.

"Well, how was everyone's day?" Mr. Addle asked. His eyes were wide and he had an awkward smile. He began scooping lasagna onto plates.

"Where do I begin!?" Mrs. Addle rolled her eyes, looking generally annoyed. "Sarah and Megan were talking about the election during our lunch break, and guess what?" She put a fork full of lasagna into her mouth. Sarah and Megan were some of Mrs. Addle's coworkers.

"What?" Mr. Addle asked.

Stella looked back and forth between her parents, she could tell this was not a good "guess what."

"They both voted for Trump! Both of them!" Mrs. Addle was yelling now. "Women! Women voted for Trump! They're uneducated women, that's what they are!" She let out a heavy sigh. "Uneducated women," she said, shaking her head.

Stella stared at her mother. She had never seen her like this: yelling, looking close to tears, yet not sad.

"Margaret, please, calm down," Mr. Addle said putting a hand on his wife's hand.

Stella kept looking at her mother. Mrs. Addle's blue eyes looked foggy and gray. Her body shook with anger, but slowly as she got back her cool, the anger lessened and a sadness settled in. Her shoulders sagged and Stella noticed something she had never seen in her mother before: helplessness.

Suddenly a frightening thought came to Stella, and her parents conversation about taxes and broken printers at work became muffled and hard to hear. Gabby said her parents voted for Trump, and that includes her mom. Her mom is a woman... "Uneducated women," that's what Mrs. Addle had said. Did Stella's parents know Gabby's parents had voted for Trump? "Uneducated women . . . "

Stella climbed the stairs to her room, pulled open the door, and flopped down on her bed. No one made lasagna better than Mrs. Addle, but tonight it had tasted like cardboard.

"It's not like we got in a fight or anything," Stella said out loud, looking up at her ceiling fan as it slowly spun around, dust mites dancing in the air. Her light was off, the room covered in a giant shadow. "We're still friends. Why am I even worried about this? I mean, it's Gabby for Pete's sake!" She lay quiet for a minute, but her mind was still

racing along with her beating heart. *It's Gabby. An unbreakable friendship.* She closed her eyes, feeling tired.

Suddenly her eyes flicked open. She reached over to her nightstand and grabbed her cell phone. She sat up and leaned against her pillows, stretching her legs out and wiggling her toes. She pressed the home button on her phone and punched in her password. Then she pulled up her texts and created a new one. She was going to make up with Gabby. But what should she say? So many things were going through her head. She started to type.

Did your mom go to college?

She stared down at what she had written. Why did I write that? She wondered as her finger moved to the backspace button. It hovered there for a minute. Two minutes. Three minutes. Stella looked up at the ceiling. Before she had been confused at why this had happened, why Trump had won. Now she was startled and confused by her own words, her own actions. *What's wrong with me?* she thought looking back down at what she had typed.

Stella closed her eyes. This was all so messed up. She hit send.

Gabby's phone made its usual "bing" sound that meant she had gotten a text. She put down her pink mechanical pencil, which she was using to solve for x, and got up to check her phone. The text was from Stella.

Did your mom go to college?

Gabby looked up, shocked and confused. *Stella had written this? Why*

Did Stella's parents know Gabby's parents had voted for Trump?

would she ask something like that? My mom owns her own company. I think you need a college degree to do that, Gabby thought.

Of course.

She sent the text and settled back into her math homework, but no sooner had she sat down than her phone "binged" again.

R u mad at me?

Again Gabby was shocked. Stella? What was up with her friend? Gabby plopped down on her bed, not sure what to write. Was she mad at Stella? She was more confused than mad. And why did Stella think Gabby was mad at her? Gabby wanted to write back, but she couldn't find the words, so instead she wrote nothing.

Stella stood in front of the school building the next morning, scanning the parking lot for Gabby. She hadn't slept well; she had been too preoccupied when Gabby hadn't written back to her last text. Finally she spotted her. She waited for Gabby to walk over, but once she got close Stella suddenly felt shy; she looked down at her Star Wars shirt, hoping to find an old stain that she could focus on. But it was too late, Gabby was already there.

"Hi," Gabby said, eyeing Stella suspiciously.

"Hi," Stella said back, blushing.

"So last night, the texts that you sent... what was that about?" Gabby asked, looking Stella straight in the eye.

"I—" Gabby's green eyes were like hound dogs, viciously searching for the truth. "Gabby, I know your mom went to college. I don't know why I said it. It's just, my mom, she said—" Stella faltered.

"She said what?" Gabby prompted. She felt a flame of anger start to burn inside her.

Guilty tears sprang into Stella's blue, unexpecting eyes; she had never cried at school before. "She said that all the women who voted for Trump were... were uneducated women."

Gabby was starting to get the picture. "So you thought my mom wasn't educated?"

"Gabby I know she's smart! I know!"

"Stella, if you didn't mean it then why did you send the text?"

"I don't know why! Okay!" Stella paused. "There's so much I don't know right now."

"I get it, I get it," Gabby said, rolling her eyes. "You're like half the country, uncertain and afraid. You think Trump is an idiot, just like you thought my mom was an idiot!"

"Gabby, I never said your mom was an idiot!"

"Just because you never said it doesn't mean you didn't think it!"

"But I didn't!" Stella insisted, she felt like she was being drowned by waves of regret.

"I always thought our political views would never alter our friendship, I guess I was wrong!" Gabby yelled.

Stella went silent. She stared at her neon orange and gray sneakers. She wanted to say that their political views didn't matter; she had been so sure about that, but now for some reason, they did seem to matter.

Gabby's chest heaved up and down, her heart pounding. "I got to go," she said, turning toward the door.

Stella stared at her friend as she walked away. Tears crawled down

Stella's cheeks; this was worse than Trump being President. She had known deep down that she could survive anything as long as she had Gabby, but now Gabby was out of reach, surrounded by her own bubble of anger. Usually when Gabby was mad, Stella could touch her shoulder, and talk to her and everything would be alright but now everything was blurred and out of place, and worst of all, Stella was alone.

Stella sat on her bed, cross legged. In front of her, fanned out, were all of her colored embroidery threads, and a tote bag. She held a safety pin in her hand. She pinned the safety pin to the tote bag as she looked down on her threads. Which colors should I use? She wondered. She knew Gabby liked purple, but her thoughts kept drifting back to the map they had looked at in social studies class before the election. The Democratic states, like California, were blue, and the Republican states, like Texas, were red. Stella picked up the bright red thread and the dark blue thread. She cut off long pieces of them and tied them to the safety pin. Then she began to make knots. Knot after knot, slowly but surely, a bracelet began to form. A friendship bracelet. Stella's mom had taught Stella how to make these friendship bracelets when she was eight, and her fingers had never forgotten. As Stella tied knots, tears of regret, and confusion slid down her face. Gabby had always been her shelter; now she was all alone, in her silent room and in the loud, jumbled-up world. Going through life was like riding a rollercoaster: Gabby and Stella sat side by side, yelling with joy and fear, Stella squeezing Gabby's arm and never wanting to let go. Now they were riding in different rollercoaster cars, Stella squeezing the handlebar, realizing how high above the ground she was. Now she was yelling solely because she was afraid.

Finally, she was done. She tied off the end and untied the top from the safety pin. Then she tied the ends together to make it a circle. She laid the bracelet down on her dresser. Now all that was left was to deliver it.

Stella walked along the tiled school floor to Gabby's locker. It was the morning and kids started to pour into the hallway, carrying backpacks to lockers and talking about funny texts that had been sent the night before in the class group chats.

Stella stood in front of Gabby's locker, suddenly feeling small. She pulled the friendship bracelet she had made the night before off her wrist and gently ran her fingers over the thread. *Please Gabby, please come back to me*, she thought. She got out a lavender colored sticky note from her backpack and, leaning it against the lockers, wrote with black sharpie:

Love, Stella.

She folded part of the bracelet into the sticky note and folded over the sticky part so that the two were attached. Then she slipped the bracelet through one of the slits in Gabby's locker. She leaned her head against the locker door and putting a hand to the door whispered, "Please."

Book Review

The Hobbit by J.R.R. Tolkien;
Houghton Mifflin Harcourt, 2012; $14.99

"In a hole in the ground, there lived a hobbit." J. R. R. Tolkien's *The Hobbit*, published in 1937, is a timeless tale of adventure worth reading over and over again. If you manage to pull open the green door that guards the cozy home inside, what do you see? Try to take the yellow brass knob placed picturesquely in the center. This door guards an adventurous tale of thirteen dwarves and a hobbit. The "unexpected party" sets off to reclaim the dwarves' treasure from Smaug "the Chiefest and Greatest of Calamities". You creep inside this door and hear faint singing; Tolkien's poetry and songs fill this story with fun rhymes and longing hopes. Down the hall, in the kitchen, is Bilbo Baggins, a clever, courageous and persistent hobbit. Farther inside the well-kept hobbit hole, you see lessons Bilbo learns along his journey. You look out the window, and in the distance you watch fourteen figures on horseback. Will the burglar and the dwarves reclaim their "long-forgotten gold"?

Whether you're on your way far over the Misty Mountains cold, chipping glasses and cracking plates, or maybe tra-la-la-lalling in the valley, Tolkien's dexterous poems and songs are sure to please for ages to come. The poems are either funny, longing or ingenious. They add an extra layer of description that makes one feel as if one is actually in Bilbo's parlor listening to the dwarves singing of the Lonely Mountain and the dragon's

Reviewed by
Catherine Gruen, 11
Chino Hills, CA

great greed that led to the destruction of Dale.

No hobbit is smarter, more stout-hearted and steadfast than Bilbo Baggins. Throughout the course of *The Hobbit*, Bilbo is clever. For example, he rescued the dwarves when they had been captured by the Wood-Elves in Mirkwood. No one would have come up with the escape plan Bilbo thought of: saving the dwarves by way of barrel. But that is only one side of the Tookish hobbit. It takes courage to go on an adventure with thirteen strange, uncouth dwarves. For instance, Bilbo was brave and bright when he bested Gollum in the riddle contest while inside the dark, damp tunnels of the Goblin King. Lastly, Bilbo is persistent. Finding the keyhole when all the others had given up shows his sense of perseverance. All in all, Bilbo is valiant, quick-witted and never quits.

The books that have withstood time's test have lessons to teach. *The Hobbit* did, and still does, just that. Along his journey, the small hobbit, Bilbo, learns many lessons. Smaug's greed for gold and jewels lead the scarlet dragon to destruction. This teaches us not to live for ourselves alone. The theme of good versus evil teaches us to fight for what is right. The company's determination to succeed in their goal is admirable. This inculcates in us to never give up. The lessons learned in this valuable book have endured.

As Bilbo said, or more rather, sang, roads do go ever on and on. Sometimes the road is made of difficult terrain, rocky and hard to climb; but sometimes the road is smooth; the sun is shining, and the sky is clear and blue. You stop short as you see your neighbor's hobbit holes—you're home! However, you notice something different. It isn't something you can hold in your hand, but something imprinted in your heart. What you find are clever songs; and an endearing character—Bilbo—who teaches you life lessons. You gently close the round door, smiling.

Honor Roll

Welcome to the *Stone Soup* Honor Roll. Every month we receive submissions from hundreds of kids from around the world. Unfortunately, we don't have space to publish all the great work we receive. We want to commend some of these talented writers and artists and encourage them to keep creating.

Fiction
Tudor Achim, 8
Rian Fetting, 9
Genevieve Gray, 10
Jasmine Li, 12
Macy Li, 12
Nicholas Taplitz, 12
Molly Tulk, 13

Poetry
Jayden Bolick, 10
Max Cummins, 13
Anna Dolan, 12
Arielle Kouyoumdjian, 9
Nandita S, 11
Sophie Yu, 10

Art
John P. Anson, 7
Jaya Shankar, 11
Audrey Tai

Don't forget to visit Stonesoup.com to browse our bonus materials. There you will find

- 20 years of back issues—around 5,000 stories, poems and reviews

- Blog posts from our Young Bloggers on subjects from sports to sewing plus ecology, reading and book reviews

- Video interviews with *Stone Soup* authors

- Music, spoken word and performances

Visit the *Stone Soup* Store at Stonesoupstore.com to buy

- Magazines—individual issues of Stone Soup, past and present

- Books—the 2017 *Stone Soup Annual*, a bound collection of all the year's issues, as well as themed anthologies

- Art prints—high quality prints from our collection of children's art

- Journals and Sketchbooks for writing and drawing
  . . . and more!

StoneSoup

JULY/AUGUST 2018   VOLUME 46 / ISSUE 7

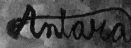

StoneSoup

The magazine supporting creative kids around the world

Editor
Emma Wood

Director
William Rubel

Operations
Jane Levi

Education & Production
Sarah Ainsworth

Design
Joe Ewart, Society

Stone Soup (ISSN 0094 579X) is published online eleven times a year—monthly, with a combined July/August summer issue. Copyright © 2018 by the Children's Art Foundation, a 501(c)(3) non-profit organization, located in Santa Cruz, California. All rights reserved. Thirty-five percent of our subscription price is tax-deductible. Make a donation at Stonesoup.com/donate/ and support us by choosing Children's Art Foundation as your Amazon Smile charity.

Stone Soup is available in different formats to persons who have trouble seeing or reading the print or online editions. To request the Braille edition from the National Library of Congress, call +1 800-424-8567. To request access to the audio edition via the National Federation of the Blind's NFB-NEWSLINE®, call +1 866-504-7300 or visit www.nfbnewsline.org.

Check us out on Social Media:

Editor's Note

Stone Soup was founded by William Rubel and a group of students at Porter College at the University of California (UCSC) in 1972, and the first issue of *Stone Soup* was published in May 1973, 45 years ago. This past semester, I got to work on this issue with a group of eight students in a Porter College classroom at UCSC. It was exciting to hear their ideas for the magazine and to discuss their reactions to submissions as we went through the difficult process of selecting pieces for the issue. I'm very proud of the result. What ties these pieces together is a spirit of experimentation and adventure, which takes us back to the excitement of that first issue four-and-a-half decades ago. I hope this issue inspires you to try new things—whether that's a screenplay, a review of a TV show, or a short poem.

Sincerely,

This issue was created with the invaluable work of a group of dedicated readers and writers from UC Santa Cruz:

Allison Finley
Gabrielle Hall
Katrina Ysabel Javiniar
Olivia Loorz
Sarah Lynn
Erin Mock
Olivia Joyce
Samantha Rozal

On the cover:
'Connected with Nature,'
by Antara Gangwal, 10
San Jose, CA

StoneSoup
Contents

Untitled, *tempera, watercolor, cellophane*

by Chloe Goodman, 7
Santa Cruz, CA

The Clock of Emotion

After being discarded, the clock of emotion sets out on a quest to find a new owner

"Blast you, too, clock!" Aunt Stephanie screamed, hurling the beautiful clock of emotion into a ditch behind her home. Her emotion rapidly changed to misery and loneliness. "I am ruined!" The clock seemed to tremble hauntingly as Aunt Stephanie dropped to her knees and wept, head in her hands. An owl hooted as the darkness of night fell over the city. The moon rose like a ballerina in the ash black sky. Shy stars peeked out of the blackness and twinkled. The clock of emotion seemed to shiver with the unpredictable tick of Aunt Stephanie's emotions. One second he ticked to misery, the next to anger, the next to loneliness, and then to sleep. There Aunt Stephanie lay, on the side of the ditch, a tear still streaming down her face.

The wind whirled, the sirens rang, and voices screeched in terror. Aunt Stephanie slept and slept. Water gushed down the ditch. As the clock was being whisked away to sea, firefighters came and pulled Aunt Stephanie up from the water, dirt, and rubble of her house. Aunt Stephanie finally woke with a jump. No one saw the clock bobbling along in the icy, harsh water, though Aunt Stephanie did seem to take one last lamenting glance at the ditch. Then, with a flick of her brown, muddy hair, she left the clock to be seized by the sea.

White gulls flew above the clock like feathery angels, occasionally swooping down and pecking at the clock, thinking it to be a fish. This was an easy mistake to make because the moon shone on the clock's ivory back, making it stand out in the dark ocean. The clock avoided the distraction, and simply sped up, leaving the gulls to find real fish. The clock felt like he had control of the sea.

The clock went down, down, down. Finally, BUMP! The clock hit the bottom of the ocean. The clock bobbled around, sand trailing behind him. At last, a fish swam over, followed by several of his friends. All of the fish— probably a grand sum of 85—seemed to be investigating the clock. Suddenly, all of the fish began to swim away in two single-file lines, about a fish length apart. They all glowed as they swam, faintly swaying with the flow

by Elisabeth Baer, 10
Atlanta, GA

5

of the water. The clock quickly picked up on what the fish were trying to say: follow us.

More fish and other creatures joined the lines, making a path going down a rocky slope and then up a seamount. On top of the huge seamount, there was a hole. The clock bobbled up the hill. Suddenly, a swift change in Aunt Stephanie's emotions threw the clock off the mound, and onto the rocks beneath it. A sharp stone left a small scratch on the clock's ivory back. With a creak, the clock righted himself and made his way up the seamount, and dropped down into the hole with very little hesitation. After all, the clock went to the bottom of the ocean. The clock could go to the bottom of a hole and have utter confidence in the fish. They knew the sea.

One of the curious fish followed the clock, watching to make sure he arrived safely at his destination. The clock just kept falling, and falling, and falling.

Finally something warm, something very warm, blew up at the clock. The fish gently pushed the clock into a passage on the side of the hole, so as not to be pushed out of the mound again by a hydrothermal vent.

The passage was narrow, dark, and stuffy. The clock of emotion had to turn sideways to get through. Then: something made out of wood

appeared. As the clock neared the object, he realized it was a scary and mysterious old shipwreck, overgrown with barnacles. It was hidden underneath the seamount that encapsulated it. One half of the ship had already decayed. The fish motioned into the shipwreck, and the clock traveled in through a splintered hole on the side of the ship.

The clock took a right, then a left, then a right, and then climbed up to the deck, as conducted by the fish. Then the clock was directed by the fish to go into what would have been the captain's quarters.

Inside, behind the captain's large desk, there sat a very small person, if you could call it that. It was more like a mermaid, except its ears were the wings of a butterfly, its eyes were entirely purple, and its hair was made out of seaweed. In the language of emotion, the being said, "Tell me, what is your emotion, clock?"

The clock responded, "Confusion."

"Tell me your story, and your purpose. There you will find what you want, and that will lead you out of confusion."

"My purpose is to regulate my owner's emotions. If my owner truly appreciates and seeks good times, then I make the happiness feel longer, and the bad times feel shorter. When Aunt Stephanie first received me, she was young and promised to always seek

"If my owner truly appreciates and seeks good times, then I make the happiness feel longer, and the bad times feel shorter."

good times. But it has been 47 years, and she is now lonely, miserable, and wretched. She no longer looks for the good times. In fact, she seeks nothing at all. I cannot regulate her emotions, so she threw me away. I have had many different owners since I was first created, and I have noticed a pattern among them. When my owner does not feel gratitude for the good times, then the bad times get longer, and the good times fly by. That is what happened to Aunt Stephanie. But in contrast, if my owner looks for good times and happiness, even when they are sad, then I can help them."

"Oh, I see . . ." the being replied. "You want to be loved and used again. And, with you, time is not constant. Whoever finds you will be lucky. Now I shall send you on your way."

The being stood with grace and began to swim out of the room, then down the stairs, and out the huge crack in the side of the ship. The clock banged on the sharp edge of the ship while exiting, and his scratch turned into a deep fracture. The clock and the fish followed the being through a nearly invisible hole in the ceiling. All of a sudden, the clock, the fish, and the being were at the surface of the water!

"Good luck, clock of emotion. By the way, I am the Empress of the sea." With that, the being and the fish disappeared.

The clock floated on the waves of the ocean. Once again, gulls came to eat him, thinking he was a fish. The rough tides swooped the clock way under the surface, and then threw the clock up in the air. Soon, the shore was in sight. The clock put all of his remaining strength into getting to the shore.

The clock washed up on shore. Children ran in the water around the clock, and parents collected shells. But there was one child, a young girl with thick, straight, black hair. She sat alone and noticed something glistening in the sand. She put down her book and walked over to see what it was. She picked it up and found it was a clock. She ran back to her seat and put it in her bag. Her parents soon walked up and said, "Let's go home, Cecilia."

At home, Cecilia marched to her room and began to examine the clock. She soon fell in love with it, and then felt a sudden comfort and control of her emotion. The clock had bonded with her, because she had loved it and gave it a home in her heart and mind.

The Moon and My Heart

The moon ate my heart.
My vision was tainted.
I staggered forward, uncertain.
I heard something disappear.
I think—
I am myself.

I taste the hole in my chest.
The moon's smile mocks me.
I know, I know
I am not myself—
I am merely a whisper
Of a husked heartbeat.

by Rebecca Beaver, 13
Tenafly, NJ

Miss-takes

Miss-takes are like tissues instead of icing on a cake.
Tying balloons to a garbage can made of aluminum.
Take a miss
Miss a take
Tiss a make
Aiss a ike
Eiss a takm
These are all . . .
Miss-takes

Dad Cut My Nails

way too short
and
now there's this feeling
you know the one
that's like scratching
sandpaper
with your teeth
or really more like
where your teeth
used to be.

by Ari Martinez, 9
Long Island City, NY

Peering Out, *photograph, Nikon D3400*

by Delaney Slote, 12
Missoula, MT

The Cryptic Crypt

by Sydney Burr, 11
Chino Hills, CA

One day, while writing about a girl lost in an Egyptian pyramid, a writer gets sucked into her own story

The river was my refuge. It was more of a stream, really, a tiny but powerful stream tucked into a corner of the Cascade Mountains. While my dad argued with my mom and my mom argued with my six brothers and sisters (and they argued with each other), I slipped out of the house and walked two miles to be at that magical place with the dozens of small waterfalls cascading into the water. I imagined some explorer discovering this place, long ago, and naming the entire mountain range after it. Cascading waterfalls . . . Cascade mountains.

I brought my journal, pen, and ink: nothing else. My "lucky rock" was a particularly large one in the center of the stream. I had to skip across stones that I had carefully placed to get to it, risking being swept away if I fell. I sat on my lucky rock and let the words rush out of my pen like one of the waterfalls around me. I wrote about everything: my pesky siblings, the beauty around me, and things I had never seen, but knew better than the real world. Some things about my writing were difficult to explain: like my use of a dip pen, or why I literally refused to write anywhere other than here. Maybe the answer to the latter question was simply that I couldn't focus in the constant noise of home or school.

One day, I was writing about a girl lost in an Egyptian pyramid:

With each tentative step forward, Kara became more and more aware that she was hopelessly lost. Although Kara understood the many hieroglyphs on the walls, they bore no information that could help her escape. The skeletons and mummies piled in the corners didn't suddenly come alive and tell her which way to go (although Kara was glad that didn't happen, because it would have been creepy). Kara tried hard not to panic, but she couldn't help it when . . .

I stopped writing. The ink on my pen dripped onto my journal, making a large blot that covered up the last line I had written, but I didn't notice. Something smelled strange. It was an underground, earthy sort of smell that filled my nostrils. When I closed my eyes, I could see an underground tunnel stretching out before me.

The source of the odd smell wasn't in sight. I looked down at my journal with the intent to keep writing, but the contents began spinning before my eyes in a tornado of words, commas, and periods. They all jumbled together, and the rushing water became inaudible.

I screamed, but my voice sounded distant and garbled, as if I were on the phone and the connection was wavering. What was happening? Was I going insane, and losing my hearing too?

I blinked, and the stream was gone. I was in a dark corridor with dust and cobwebs all around me. All I had in my hands was a torch. For a moment, I wondered where I was, but I wasn't left wondering for long once I turned to look at the wall and saw hieroglyphics there. I knew then for sure where I was, and I wasn't thrilled about it. I was inside my story, "A Cryptic Crypt."

The pyramid carried the same smell that I had caught a whiff of back in the mountains, in the real world. I never thought I would long for my siblings, or want to escape one of my own stories. It was practically my dream to be transported into one of my stories, but I never expected to feel so stuck if I was. I thought that I'd feel free, ecstatic. How I wished that I had been writing about what I usually wrote about: friendship and everyday courage and trying to make it through middle school, and those things that seemed so simple compared to this. While observing my dire predicament, I paced around the corridor and almost tripped over a cold, round object. I picked it up and dropped it with a small shriek when I realized it was a skull.

Then I felt like something was crawling up my neck. I slapped it, and it fell lifeless into my hand: it was a beetle the size of my palm, and I now noticed thousands more creeping along the walls and floor. I really started to freak out when the torch sputtered, flickered, and went out. I tried desperately to reignite it by dragging it along the floor, but I didn't produce a single spark. All the torch gathered was beetles. I was trapped in blackness with huge beetles and skeletons, armed with nothing except for what was basically a beetle-covered stick.

"Take me back!" I shouted into the darkness. My voice echoed for several seconds around the catacombs. I didn't really expect an answer, but I was panicked.

I nearly dropped the extinguished torch when the wall was suddenly emblazoned with giant, glowing hieroglyphs that weren't there before. I couldn't read hieroglyphics, but I knew someone who could. Trying not to think about the beetles that were probably all over me, I started running down the passageway with my hands out so I wouldn't run into a wall. My own shallow breathing and the pattering of my feet were the only sounds, but I hoped to hear something else—or rather, someone else. I had to find Kara.

The pyramid seemed bigger than the entire state of Washington. I wandered around through its winding passageways for hours. Once, I came to a five-way fork in the path. I listened at every corridor, one by one, for any sounds that might indicate another human's presence, but none of the corridors looked promising. I just muttered "eeny meeny miney moe" and took the path I ended up pointing at. It proved to be a mistake, because I was more lost than ever.

Here was someone that I had created on paper as a living, breathing, three-dimensional human being standing right in front of me.

I was in such a terrible situation that the sound of someone yelling a little further down the passage excited me more than it frightened me. Who could it be except Kara?

Someone almost knocked me over as they barreled past me. Whoever it was held a torch, which illuminated the passage around me. It also meant that they could see me, and so they screeched to a stop.

The stranger was a girl in faded blue jeans, a plain black T-shirt, and suspenders. This was very confusing to me, because I had never seen someone in suspenders except in photos. I lived in Washington, not Kansas. The girl also had hazel eyes, raven-black hair held up in a messy ponytail, and a tan.

"What are you doing here?" asked Kara.

I couldn't believe it. Here was someone that I had created on paper as a living, breathing, three-dimensional human being standing right in front of me. There was something else that shocked me even more, though: other than the obvious difference in what we were wearing, Kara looked exactly like me.

We stared at each other for a moment.

"Okay, whoever you are, a long-lost twin sister of mine or someone who just happens to look just like me—RUN!" Kara ended with a yell. She grabbed my hand and pulled me down the passageway behind her.

"What's going on? What are we running from?" I asked bewilderedly, trying to keep up so Kara didn't accidentally pull my arm out of its socket.

"The skeletons are alive!" she hollered. I noted that the skeletons we were now passing by seemed about as alive as my little sister's Barbie dolls, but the crashing from behind us, skeletons or not, was enough to keep me moving.

"What are you doing here, anyway?"

"I'm from Oklahoma. I had to be stupid enough to go and sneak inside the Great Pyramid. Some vacation this is shaping up to be! Say, what are you doing here?"

"I'm from Washington—" I hesitated for a moment. Should I make up a story quick, or be honest and lose the little trust that Kara had in my sanity? I probably should have thought more about it before I blurted out, "I created you!"

"What? You're crazy!"

"We're in a story I wrote." I stopped dead and wheeled around to face behind us. Kara stopped, too. I must not have been the only one to hear it: a rattling, whirring noise, different from the crashing we had been hearing. It sounded strangely like my family's washing machine.

"What's that?"

A pile of something rained on us,

and it wasn't water. It was a pile of words. I could make out the words "vacation," "Washington," "created," and "story."

"This has happened every few minutes since I got to Egypt. I don't get it at all. Is it a thing in the desert or something?" said Kara, breaking into a run again as the crashing of the skeletons grew louder, and dragging me along.

I laughed.

"What's so funny?" asked Kara. "We're being chased by skeletons here!"

"We're in a story I wrote, but we're writing more as we speak! That's why it keeps raining words!"

"Okay, fine, let's just say I believe you now and leave it at that. So you're making the skeletons chase after us?"

"Well, no..."

"But you said we're in a story that you created."

"That doesn't mean I can keep it from taking on a life of its own!"

"You can't control it anymore?"

I chuckled nervously. "Not exactly—" I was cut off yet again—this time by a slimy hand grabbing me by the ankle. "Help!" I shouted, trying to pull my ankle out of the skeleton's grip as another hand curled around my other ankle.

"Help you? I hardly know you!" said Kara, but she stopped running anyway and turned to face the skeletons. "I must be crazy," she muttered, and she pulled something out of her back pocket. It was a scroll, and I could see hieroglyphs on it as she unrolled it. She started reading the scroll, and it almost sounded like an incantation. "Arwah almawtaa . . ."

"Hurry up!" I screamed, as another bony hand closed around my throat. Struggling to breathe, I wondered what would happen if I died in the story. Whatever the answer was, I didn't want to think about it.

Kara finally finished with a fierce cry of the words "...min ayn atayt!" The skeletons crumbled to dust. Gasping for breath, I stared at Kara in awe. "How'd you do that?"

"It's ancient Egyptian magic," answered Kara, panting.

"Like in the *Kane Chronicles*?"

"What are the *Kane Chronicles*?"

"They're books by Rick Riordan... What year is it?"

"1965. Why do you ask?"

"Just curious. Say, I'd been looking for you for hours before I bumped into you. There's something I need to show you, and I think it could help us both get out of here if you can decipher it."

We set off again through the catacombs—but this time, I was leading.

Bugs are the Future!
A Screenplay

SYNOPSIS

When two boys sit down in a school cafeteria for lunch, one gets a lesson he'll never forget.

Author's note: When the topic of food stability comes up, I always point out that insects are better for us and more sustainable. I get reactions close to this every time I bring it up. This scene is an exaggerated version of that reaction.

CHARACTER LIST

BENJAMIN Male, ten years. Always the guy in the background. The guy that helps people when they're hurt. The kind of guy that doesn't like being "in the light," so to speak.

JACOB Male, nine years. Would be considered a "nerd." Is very smart, and talks very fast. Gets bullied a lot.

by Oliver Jacobs, 12
Tallahassee, FL

Among the Asparagus, *photograph, Canon Powershot Elph160*

by Ula Pomian, 12
Ontario, Canada

INT. SCHOOL CAFETERIA - DAY

TWO FRIENDS, JACOB and BENJAMIN, are sitting down to eat their lunches.
JACOB takes the meat out of his sandwich and puts it to the side with disgust.

> JACOB
>
> I wonder why the cooks always put meat in these sandwiches.

> BENJAMIN
>
> (Looking confused)
>
> Yesterday you were wondering why they didn't put more meat on the sandwiches.

> JACOB
>
> (Still looking at the sandwich, more disappointed than disgusted)
>
> I thought this school would have made the change.

> BENJAMIN
>
> (Looking even more confused)
>
> What change!
>
> (Looks around, getting more and more confused)
>
> Does this have to do with school?

JACOB looks at BENJAMIN, surprised that he didn't hear the news that everyone knows about.

> JACOB
>
> Come on! We should all reduce our carbon footprint.

> BENJAMIN
>
> Wait . . . what does meat have to do with our our carbon footprint?!

JACOB looks up as if making a list in his head.

> JACOB
>
> Well, cows, chickens, and like, sheep are causing global warming!

> BENJAMIN
>
> Has...
>
> (sighs)
>
> Has your sister told you this?

JACOB
(Looking at BENJAMIN with disbelief)
NO!
(Calmly)
I saw it on the TV.

BENJAMIN
Really? So, what did it say?

JACOB
Well...
(tilting his head)
... it said something about farts, nutrition, factory fumes ...

BENJAMIN
HOLD THE PHONE! Farts?

JACOB
(Fast-paced and excited)
Did you know that cow and sheep farts are releasing methane
into the air?! Whatever that is.

BENJAMIN
Isn't that a gas?

JACOB
I think so.

BENJAMIN
Wait! Nutrition?

JACOB
Yeah! Nutrition. It said something like ... we should stop
eating land-based backboned animals, and we should all start
eating INSECTS!
(BENJAMIN'S face sinks into horror.)
Yeah, I've been doing some research ...

BENJAMIN
WHAT! WHAT!! INSECTS!!!

JACOB
(Calmly)
OK ... So I was saying ...

BENJAMIN
WHAT IS GOING ON IN MY LIFE!?!?!

JACOB
(A little bit aggravated)
Yeah, and I was going to—

BENJAMIN
(Cutting off JACOB for the third time)
NO!!! I AIN'T GOING TO DO THAT, NO WAY, NO WAY! NO NO
NO!
(Getting faster)
NO, NO, NOOOOO!

JACOB
(Aggravated)
YEAH, and I was going to ss—

BENJAMIN
—No way I'm eating spiders!

BENJAMIN closes his eyes and takes a deep breath. A couple of beats pass.

JACOB
You're calm now, right?

BENJAMIN
(Still taking deep breaths)
Yeah. I'm still not eating spiders.

JACOB
(In a "matter of fact" voice)
Well, Spiders are ARACHNIA, not insects—

BENJAMIN
Whatever! Anyway, you get what I mean.

JACOB
No, I don't "get what you mean."

BENJAMIN
I AM NOT EATING ANY INVERTEBRATES!

JACOB
Why?

                              BENJAMIN
What do you mean, *"Why"*

                               JACOB
Why?

                              BENJAMIN
                            (Very certain)
They're spiders.

                               JACOB
                           (Exasperated)
Once again . . .
                              (sighs)
spiders are—

                              BENJAMIN
NO!
              (Aggressively but softer, softly and grumbly)
I don't care or know about any of that until now.
                             (Louder)
I don't trust this TV show.

                               JACOB
It was on National Geographic!

                              BENJAMIN
                             (Slowly)
OK, that's a little bit better.

                               JACOB
                    (SLOWLY at first, then FAST)

I've been doing some research on food sources, especially
incredibly sustainable ones, and I think I have found the
perfect spot to find the perfect food!
       (Waits a couple of seconds then says a little too loud than
                        allowed for the cafeteria)
COCKROACHES!

JACOB points off-screen. BENJAMIN'S face sinks into disbelief and horror.
BENJAMIN starts to take deep breaths, but his whole body is tightening up.

> **BENJAMIN**
> (Very softly)

Wh—wha—what—?

JACOB, completely oblivious, picks up a container with some MEALWORMS in it.

> **JACOB**

Sadly I could only find some mealworms at the pet store.
They were out of cockroaches...

> **BENJAMIN**
> (Still taking deep breaths)

B—b—bu—but ... B—b—but ...

> **JACOB**
> (Still COMPLETELY oblivious)

Mind you there are quite a lot of cockroaches in the kitchen,
but they most likely have diseases, because they're not
farmed. It wouldn't be much of a change because—

BENJAMIN holds his stomach as if almost regurgitating.

> **JACOB (CONT'D)**

We already eat about half a cockroach a day!

BENJAMIN gets more and more horrified.

> **JACOB (CONT'D)**

Through breathing!

BENJAMIN stops breathing and opening his mouth.

> **JACOB (CONT'D)**

And just opening and closing our mouths.

BENJAMIN takes both of his hands and claps them over his mouth. JACOB
shrugs then picks up his sandwich (without meat) and adds mealworms to it. As
he bites into the sandwich, BENJAMIN faints, his face falling into his food.

CUT TO BLACK

THE END

The Avocado Tree

by Sara Chebili, 13
Washington, D.C.

The chair by the avocado tree had turned a faded green from wear
For years it sat untouched behind the orange-red sunsets
Built for the old lady with the fishing hat who kept forgetting
Its purpose was to help her remember
To stay in the present of the ink-washed sand
And it stayed there till the time of her grandson
Sitting by the murky green water with his homework
Reminding them of all the beautiful sunrises and afternoon checker games played
And his days looking at the intriguing graphite numbers on bleached paper
But before then he would wonder if his grandmother would ever be the same again
If she would ever remember who he was without a lost look on her face

One day
Looking at the plants by the seaweed strewn about
He took a nearby avocado seed and buried it into the sandy ground
He began to take the wood from his backyard to build a chair
Hoping it would help her remember
He tended to them day by day
From the mornings spent on his work
To the afternoons sat with the wood
Sanding and painting it as the tree grew
And he worked right by the shore with the graphite numbers and the wood
Making progress as time went on
Eventually the chair sat next to the tree
And one day the lady with the fishing hat sat in the chair with the tree
And remembered the difference that was made

Light and Darkness

by Carly Vermillion, 10
Indianapolis, IN

I was at the pond one day, feeding the fish, under
the hot sun. When clouds have a conversation
with the sun. A cool wave of air touches my
fingers and toes. The fish swim down to the
bottom of the river.

I was at the dinner table one night, eating
the fat fish I caught, under the stars, the only
things lighting the sky. When the lights
shut off and flickered. My family rushed to their
bedrooms, scared and worried. Even me, the bravest
of the group, put down my fish liver.

I was in my bedroom one morning, staring
at my light switch. "What am I going to do
in this hatred?" I thought. So I went to my
window and spread out my curtains.
My next trip was to flip up the light switch.

I was at my desk one afternoon, thinking
about my math, when it started sprinkling.
"Anything but rain," I moaned. Suddenly,
it started to storm with thunder and
lightning partnering together. Maybe the Sun
and Moon now switch.

Untitled, *tempera, watercolor, cellophane*

by Reed Skelton, 8
Santa Cruz, CA

Swept-Up Fish

by Sabrina Feldberg, 12
Potomac, MA

Her family has just left freezing Chicago for sunny San Francisco, and Carrie is like a fish out of water in her new home

The beach was gorgeous. The glittering blue waves lapped onto the shore; they kindly slapped away small children who got too close to the foamy current. Up where I was watching the scene, the sand was lying peacefully, a tinged butter-yellow color, burned as a victim of the Sun, sifting like powder through my toes and occasionally producing a tiny crab here or there. The faint breeze carried a strong scent of sea salt from the coast, and I gazed again upon the children who had gone all the way down there, deeper to the cold, wet, sand. I thought of when I had charged my toes under it for a few seconds before (and had then quickly run up to the warm sand), watching the current make the sand appear as if it was escaping me, as if I was sliding further away, sweeping shells and fish that belonged there. If only a current could sweep me back into Chicago again, I thought. If only. But here, as if to taunt me, I saw a sign flapping in the wind by the beach gate. "Welcome to San Francisco Bay!" it read; and enough said, too. I did not need to be reminded.

As I ate my shrimp po-boy, which was also emitting a salty fume—only a stale reminder of the fact that I was here, not at home—my mother, father, and twin brothers chatted next to me with food cramped in their mouths. They didn't mind being stuffed; I think they wanted to "do as the Romans do" in Rome, except San Francisco, of course. In unison, other families were either docked under an umbrella to eat or playing at the shore, vulnerable to being swept up by a salty wave.

It was a "celebration" of our moving here, and my family posed as ordinary Californians retiring to the beach during the long summer holiday. No wonder we, former Chicagoans, blended into the crowd; there were so many people that were minding their own business here. They would never guess that we had actually moved here in the midsummer; my mom had found a new job. I clenched my teeth inside my mouth at the sight of how pleased she looked. It was all her fault; all of the moving, everything—even choosing such a breathtaking place to replace home. Nothing will make me want to replace Chicago, though. When my ears came back to their senses, I heard the chatter of my family.

"Can Henry and I go to the water?" my brother, George, asked with pleading eyes to my mother. They were both 12-years-old, but George was just a minute older. I was 15, and already considered myself (if I were to be a Californian, after all) a sit-and-sunbathe kind of teen. At least they had apparently not been in Chicago long enough to miss its long winters.

"Of course. Carrie, would you like to join?" my mom asked. She had chestnut-brown hair and eyes like me, and a sort of electric, party vibe came from her. I knew she was already loving this more than Chicago.

"No thanks," I grumbled. "This is the worst vacation ever. Take me back to Chicago!" I spat, feeling a lump of angry heat in my throat as I said it. I didn't want to take it back. My parents put on empathetic frowns and offered me ice cream, but I dismissed that as well. I'll admit, I wanted it, but I continued to glare at my parents and pretend in my head that they were the meanest people on Earth.

I bathed in the sun afterward, and the heat seemed to steam around me. It also made my skin look pinkish. Strange, I thought. Sunburn doesn't happen that quickly. Soon, I noticed my sunglasses were beside me, and my skin a scaly texture. To my horror, I saw my arms turn to tiny fins and my legs into a small tail. I was becoming a fish. And when I had transformed up to my mouth, I had trouble breathing. Water, is all I thought. Water. I need water. Flopping (literally) breathlessly around the sand, I assessed my situation. Closest water? Nowhere. This was it, and I didn't want to die a fish. I was hyperventilating, my gills opening and closing rapidly.

Just as my eyes started fluttering, and I felt a harsh feeling of restfulness and giving up, I felt a human hand squeeze me gently. Then I heard my body "plop" into a pail of salty water, and it felt amazing. My savior was a small child that looked like a toddler, and he peered into my new tank as if I were a lab specimen. For all I knew, I could have been. Then, with a giddy smile, he called his parents and showed them me. I was on display, and my fish nerves didn't like it. Unluckily, my fish nerves also wanted to skedaddle, and do so they did. I sprang out from the bucket and onto the scorching hot sand. If I had not been in a bucket of water before, I wouldn't have had enough time in consciousness to gather myself and create a somewhat plan (though, for a fish, I reflect that I couldn't have thought of anything better). First, with my fish eyes alert for finding water, I found a sandcastle moat, a watery hole someone was digging, and, for closers, the coast of the ocean. This meant a journey of hopping from water to water to get to the coast.

After taking these quick notes, I flopped up to the moat. Easily enough, I slid in. I was just swimming around to the other side when my fins froze in the action—I was having one of those tense, instinctive moments. I shivered, and my eyes darted fearfully to my left, where I had felt something alongside me. A crab, about twice the size of my fish form, had crawled its way right up next to me! My body shook, and again I sprang inconveniently out of the water.

Unfortunately, this crab could, too. And breathing. I flopped away from it quicker than ever before, in the direction of the watery hole I had seen before. The crab was too fast, and I figured I would have to use the small sense of human knowledge I still retained. I decided to flop on top of the sand just enough to get under it. By the time the crab came crawling along, I was quite covered in sand. Once he had scampered away, I flopped rapidly to the watery hole and swam peacefully for about five minutes. There were two people going to and from the coast to gather buckets rimmed with water, and I enjoyed the water the people brought to me. In the moment of relaxation, I gathered my thoughts and thought more like a human. I wondered if I would always be a fish, and if I would never see my family again this far down the beach. They might always remember me as the annoyed teen that I was before I mysteriously left. My moment of quiet did not last for long though, because the current took an unexpected sprint toward the hole, going a long way from the shore and filling up the hole with sand. I, meanwhile, had been taken and, to my delight, was now on the coast at last. I swam around the shallow bits, searching for where on the beach my family would be. All of a sudden, I saw a surfboard come toward me, and my world turned blank.

I don't know how long I was unconscious as a fish, but when I awoke I was back into a human again. But I was wet. According to my mom, I had been floating in the water knocked out, and the person who was in charge, a surfer, took me to the lifeguards who then brought me to my family. And my mom, I quote, had "just known" when she heard an unconscious teenager was found

"alone, hopelessly about to drown" that it was me. My cheeks burned slightly red when I heard the last part, and I was glad the change didn't mean turning into a fish. I smiled and thanked my family for helping me, and they accepted my change in attitude. As the waves curved around and swept up many stray fish in the ocean, I admitted how beautiful it was.

"The beach was gorgeous," I remarked, when we had returned to our new home at dusk. I was already forming a story about the day in my head that would start with just that.

The City

Stoplights reflect off the bay
The faint sound of glasses clinking and people talking is carried on the breeze
The moon is shrouded by clouds
Towering buildings blink with neon lights
A lone car drives across a scarlet bridge

Wildfire

Say one sentence
An ember sparks
Say another
Wind blows and swirls
One more
A wildfire

by Karinne Ulrey, 10
Los Gatos, CA

Orange Landscape, *watercolor and colored pencils*

by Eli Breyer Essiam, 10
Cambridge, MA

The Missing Piece

by Lucy Zanker, 11
Houston, TX

What will happen when Laika's mischievious robotic brother accidentally launches them into outer space?

"Wake up, Tommy," I said. Tommy, my thirteen-year-old robotic brother (he really is a robot—no kidding) needs to wake up! He always walks with me to school. He likes to sleep, though. And eat. And sleep some more. Oh, and get into trouble. It's not like our dad cares. He's too busy being the Big Cheese at NASA. Not that I care. He never pays a bit of attention to us. I mean come on, it's not like paying us attention costs $100.

"Laika, school was cancelled in Houston today because the Astros won the World Series last night," Tommy mumbled into his pillow. That was when I hit the roof.

"But we have our fifth grade bake sale at school today!" I groaned. "Why did the Astros have to win?" I muttered.

"Why did the Astros have to win? So I could sleep in!" Tommy pumped his fist in the air.

"You and your darn sleep," I muttered under my breath.

"Hey, I heard that!" Tommy threw a pillow at my face.

"Laika, you and Tommy are going to have to come with me to the office because there is no school today," Dad said as I stomped downstairs.

Nooooooo. I hate the office. It's so boring. Too much math and calculations.

"What about a babysitter?" I asked nervously.

"Are you kidding me? After how you two were playing hide-and-seek in the washing machine? Absolutely not," Dad said.

"Mom would have gotten us a babysitter."

"Can you not bring up Mom's death every time we argue?!" Dad huffed. Man do I wish that Mom hadn't died because Dad really just lost the ability to love and care.

As I looked out the window of our car, I thought about all the other kids in Houston who are sleeping in or watching a movie or playing video games while I have to go to the most boring office ever. Life is really annoying sometimes.

"Okay, Tommy, at the office you're not going to do anything that will get me into trouble. Go reboot or update yourself. I don't know, just don't get into trouble," I said.

"All right, sheesh. Don't get yourself in such a frenzy," Tommy huffed.

I tried to prepare myself for the

office. I brought a stack of books by James Patterson. I hoped that having the books would help with the boredom.

"We're here," Dad said.

Dad's office was big. I had to give it to him. The ceiling was a huge cupola like the churches you see in movies. The office smelled of brain power, math, and rockets. I'm not sure if a room can smell like those things, but somehow it did. I hate those smells. The room had white walls and machines everywhere. Every nanometer was covered by a machine. Oh, and coffee. There were scientists running around with coffee in plastic cups, mugs, and thermoses. Actually, it also smelled like coffee.

"Alright, kids: listen up. Stay where I can see you. NO MESSING AROUND. You hear me? I am working on a rocket that will go up into outer space in three days and we only have to install the return gear. So I need this work day. Got it?" Dad drilled.

"Chill, Dad. We get it," Tommy said.

"That's what you say every time …"

"Dad! I'm going to go read!" I called out. Two hours later, I finished my books. I looked around to make sure that Tommy was within Dad's peripheral vision. But, as usual, he wasn't there. I didn't worry. Yet. I just assumed he went to recharge at the power station. I checked there, but no robot. That's when I began to worry.

"Tommy, Tommy! This isn't funny anymore! Come out from your hiding spot right now!" I hollered. I peeked around a corner hoping that Tommy would be there. But nope. I checked around every door. Or so I thought … I popped my head around the last

corner and… Oh, wow. I saw a huge room with a rocket that almost scraped the paint off the ceiling, with a catwalk that led into it.

Then I heard a banging. I cautiously crept inside to go investigate. "Hello? Is there anybody there? I'm looking for my robotic brother," I called out. The inside was round and filled with buttons and switches and technology. There was a cockpit, a fridge, sleeping quarters, and a tube-like thing. I looked out a window, and I saw a bunch of scientists in white coats scurrying around. Then I heard the banging again and followed it. It led to . . . Tommy. He was camouflaged with all the buttons!

"Tommy, what on earth are you doing here?!" I yelled.

"I was bored. Duh. Weren't you?" Tommy shrugged. I was so mad. If we had been in one of those cartoons on television, steam would have been coming out of my ears. Actually, steam was coming out of my ears.

"Sir, you're coming with me. We're getting out of here before Dad realizes we're gone. And don't even think about touching anything," I commanded. We passed by another window that I hadn't seen earlier. As I looked out the window, my mind began to wander and think about how cool it would be to go to space.

"I wonder what this big red button does," Tommy said.

"Tommy, don't touch the launch button!" I cried out. Too late. He had pressed the button. Then I felt a deep, low, hollow rumble. The rocket was beginning to launch. We ran for the doors, but they closed just as we got there.

"Now commencing countdown. Ten, nine, eight, seven, six . . ." a female voice said over a loudspeaker.

"Tommy, what are we going to do?"

"This is awesome! We're going to fly on a real rocket!"

"Super helpful, Tommy."

The rocket rose into the sky like a giant coming out of his 200-year slumber. I looked out the window and the houses, fields, and buildings shrank and got warped as they got blasted with ignition fire. As the rocket lifted into the sky, it got darker, and darker, until it was as black as obsidian, with millions of tiny glittering diamonds flashing in space.

The next thing I knew, I couldn't feel my body. I felt weightless. I was floating! "AWESOME!" I said. After a moment, I realized how quiet it was. You could have heard a pin drop. Actually, you couldn't because there wasn't any gravity so it would just float around.

Suddenly, I thought about how worried Dad probably was. "We should try to contact Dad at NASA," I said. I floated to the cockpit to see if I could find something to contact Dad with. But there were so many buttons and latches and switches that I got dizzy. I sat down in the pilot's seat and tried to find something that could help. I found a compartment with a latch that said COMMUNICATION. I opened it and found a headset with a mic attached to it and a sheet that said who to call. Thank you universe! I put the headset on and then I heard Dad's voice.

"Laika, is that you?" Dad's voice rang in my ears.

"Yeah, Dad, it's me," I answered.

"Laika, are you and Tommy okay? I was really worried about you guys. Especially you," Dad said.

"Gee, I didn't know you would be so worried about me," I quipped.

"Laika, of course I was worried about you!" Dad exclaimed.

"Well, Tommy and I are okay. Thanks for asking."

"Let's talk about how you will get home," Dad said, moving along. "First off, I have good news and bad news. Bad news first: the rocket you are flying in has a major problem. It is missing a vital piece. The part that enables you to get home. Good news: the part is with you. Not you but with Tommy. Correction, in Tommy. You will have to dissect him, find the part, and put it in the correct spot. Then you will have to press the right button to get home. But when you dissect him, he will be gone. We won't be able to get the part back. I'm sorry that it will have to be this way," Dad affirmed. I fell back against the seat, stunned. I looked up at Tommy. I felt a medley of stunned, angry, melancholy, and shocked.

"Laika, are you okay?"

"Yeah, I'm fine," I said. I didn't notice it but I was crying, silently. Quiet tears ran down my cheeks, as if they wanted to escape my eyes.

"Laika, are you sure you're okay?" Dad asked again.

"No, I'm not okay! I am about to lose my big brother and you expect me to be okay? You're a heartless father!" I yelled.

"I'm sorry, Laika, I—"

Was that crying I heard from Dad? I didn't mean for him to cry. I know Dad was sensitive since Mom's death. I didn't realize he was that sensitive. But I guess I am the one who was insensitive about Dad. I should have known that he would get upset. I also should not have kept all those feelings bottled up inside.

"Dad, please. I'm really, really sorry."

"Laika, it just hurts me so to hear how you think of me. I try so hard to be a good father," Dad sniffled. I was so remorseful at that moment. I felt so bad!

"Dad, can we get back to the whole getting-back-home thing?" I asked.

"All right, let's get to that," Dad said. "You unfortunately have to disassemble your brother. Fortunately, it will not be bloody. It will just be very metallic."

"Haha. So funny, Dad," I said sarcastically. "Tommy, come here!" I called. Tommy sauntered in with this I-am-so-cool kind of attitude. "Tommy, I'm going to have to do something very unpleasant. But if I don't do this, we will both die. I'm going to have to take you apart," I cried.

"I understand this is very important. I just want you to know that, as your brother, I'll always be there for you. Even if I'm not there physically, I'll be there mentally," Tommy acknowledged.

"Thank you for understanding, Tommy."

"Laika, there's a little button that says POWER. Press that."

"I'll miss you, Tommy," I sobbed.

"Same here," Tommy answered. I threw my arms around his neck and pressed the button. His eyes went dark, his arms stopped mid-hug, his eyes closed shut, his body slumped forward. He was gone.

"Did you do it?" Dad asked.

"Yes," I whispered.

"Now get a screwdriver to undo Tommy's screws," Dad directed. I found one in a compartment and began to undo all the screws.

"Are you done?" Dad asked.

"Yeah, what's next?"

"Well, the piece you're looking for looks like a cylinder and it's about as big as your hand," Dad instructed.

"Got it."

"Good. Now, do you see the part on the control panel that says DESCENT with a little hole?" Dad said.

"Yes," I replied.

"Put the piece there," Dad responded.

"Okay. Next?"

"Check the computer screen to see if something pops up," Dad said.

"It says DESCENT ENABLED," I confirmed.

"Now, when the ship turns around, you will go through the atmosphere and the parachute will deploy. It will be a water landing," Dad said.

"What should I do?"

"Just follow the instructions on the manual. I will come pick you up in the water."

The ship began to ever-so-gently turn itself around. We started heading back home. Suddenly, I fell to the ground. I was okay, but I realized that the rocket had already gone through the Earth's atmosphere. I rushed to the pilot seat and buckled up. We began to pick up a bit of speed. The rocket began to shake and heat up. I was worried that I may be reunited with Tommy sooner than I thought. I mean, sure, I read what to do. But I was still scared. I saw out the window that we were approaching the Earth. I felt myself being pulled towards my seat. It felt like somebody had put an elephant on my body. The rocket was tumbling and rolling this way and that, while being tossed around like a hot potato. It felt like the Roller Coaster Ride of Death. Then I felt something jerk me upward and realized that the parachute had deployed.

"Prepare to make a splash landing," a robotic female voice said.

As the rocket drifted toward the ocean, I was relieved to be finally getting back home. I had really missed my dad. I never really thought I would miss him as much as I did. The Earth got closer and closer until . . . BAM! We hit the water. The impact knocked me out cold.

The next thing I remembered was waking up in my bed. I looked up and saw Dad. I hugged him tight.

"I missed you. I was worried that I wouldn't see you again."

"I missed you, too. You took a pretty hard fall last night," Dad joked lamely.

"Yeah. I miss Tommy, Dad. I want him to be here but that's impossible because he's at the bottom of the Gulf of Mexico."

"Look, I'm sorry about what happened to Tommy. I really am." Dad said, "I miss him, too." This was a surprise. I never really knew that Dad cared a lot about Tommy. I mean, sure, he was his kid (sort of). "I'm also sorry about not being a very attentive father. I guess that after Mom's death, I sort of closed up feelings-wise," Dad confessed.

"I'm sorry I wasn't the nicest, too. I had a lot of feelings bottled up inside and when I let them out, I don't think I did it in the best of ways," I conceded.

"You think so?" Dad tried, yet failed, to be funny.

"Can I have a hug?" I blurted. That's just what he did. He gave me one of the best hugs of my life.

After breakfast, Dad walked in with this big, long sort of metal rod with a magnet attached to it. "What's that Dad?" I asked.

"We're going fishing in the Gulf of Mexico," Dad said with a wink. I smiled.

Dedicated to Laika, the real hero. May you live forever in the sky.

Church at Sunset, *photograph*

by Cordelia Athas, 10
San Jose, CA

Queen of the World

by Ana Carpenter, 10
Chicago, IL

Sometimes I pretend I am the queen of the world
Gliding in a silver sleigh of dreams
My dress is made of ripped up clouds
And my crown is woven with moonlight
I float above the sun each day
Watching over my empire
I can feel every triumph and every
Disappointment ripple through me like a
Stone cast into a deep crystal pond
But as time steals by it is not so wonderful
To hold the weight of the world
And I would much rather be a normal girl
Bound to life and nothing more
So I raise my lips to the velvet sky
And gently kiss each star in the Milky Way farewell
I suppose that even the queen of the world
Grows weary of her place in the universe

Review

A Gritty but Triumphant Return to Avonlea:
A review of the Netflix Original *Anne with an "E"*

I remember reading *Anne of Green Gables* when I was younger. I would sprawl across the couch and slowly flip through the delicate pages, savoring the words like candy. This is why when I noticed Netflix's 2017 adaptation, entitled *Anne with an "E,"* I had to watch! Set in Avonlea, a fictional town on Prince Edward Island, *Anne with an "E"* tells the heartwarming story of a 13-year-old orphan. After bouncing between orphanages and foster homes, Anne is sent to elderly siblings Matthew and Marilla Cuthbert to assist on their farm. Here, throughout seven 45-minute episodes, Anne navigates the road of adolescence and learns what it feels like to belong to a family and a place.

The coastal and rural setting is gorgeous, but the show's true beauty lies with the emotion and passion of the actors. One especially moving scene occurred mid-first episode when Marilla (Geraldine James) relays to Matthew (R.H. Thomson) that skinny and loquacious Anne would be no help and should be returned to the orphanage. Matthew's face, partially lit by candlelight, strains as he looks down at his hands. After a few seconds of silence he responds, "Well, we might be of some good to her." These words were so passionately put that, paired with his emotive expressions, I found myself fighting back tears.

Additionally, *Anne with an "E"* explores valuable themes, like acceptance, that are as meaningful today as they were in the late 19th century. At first, Anne, like many of us, doesn't fit in at school; she's

Reviewed by
Neena Dzur, 13
Toledo, OH

ridiculed and excluded because she's an orphan with raggedy clothing and conspicuous red hair. Then she meets and befriends Diana, a girl her age who consistently makes an effort to include her. Whether it's sitting next to her in class or making room for her at the lunch table, Diana's acceptance helps Anne hold her head high.

Still, despite the uplifting messages, some critics argue that *Anne with an "E"* is too negative for the usually younger *Anne of Green Gables* fans. Anne often has violent flashbacks about being beaten by a foster parent and tormented by other kids at the orphanage before living with the Cuthberts. While it's true the novel doesn't depict these barbaric acts, the television version uses them to develop Anne into a complex, compelling, and resilient character. Anne may be haunted by her past, but she perseveres and maintains a vivacious, imaginative personality— one I grew to side with during the series.

All in all, I thoroughly enjoyed *Anne with an "E."* Sure it's gritty, but the talented cast, realistic writing, and multifaceted characters prove that it is, without a doubt, a worthwhile show to watch.

Honor Roll

Welcome to the *Stone Soup* Honor Roll. Every month we receive submissions from hundreds of kids from around the world. Unfortunately, we don't have space to publish all the great work we receive, so we want to recognize some of these talented writers and artists.

Fiction

Alyssa Ao, 11
Sophia Cossitt-Levy, 12
Taylor Fujihara, 13
Mercer Goldmann, 10
Emily Hou, 13
Claire Klein-Borgert, 7
Renatka Maria Kozlowska, 12
Ethan Li, 11
Jeffrey Liang, 13
Fannie Liu, 11
Olivia Luyando, 12
Hannah Rubin, 12
Gabe Rini, 10
Cassidy White, 13
Ashley Xu, 13

Poetry

Annabel Cooley, 11
Aashi Chowdhury, 8
Vanessa Gonzalez-Rychener, 12
Gavin Jarvis, 12
Lysandre Marot, 9
Surya Odom, 10
Sophia Schaffer, 11
Brooks Robinson, 12
Cristiano Alvarado Ramos, 8
Shiva Rahel Swaminathan Strickland, 10
Heysam Sufi, 9
Whitney Turner, 11
Nicholas Taplitz, 12

Art

Alexis Forman, 11
Chuiyee Kong, 11
Sreenika Perumalla, 9
Nevaeh Santiago, 9
Udit Vaishnav, 7

Don't forget to visit Stonesoup.com to browse our bonus materials. There you will find

- 20 years of back issues—around 5,000 stories, poems and reviews
- Blog posts from our Young Bloggers on subjects from sports to sewing plus ecology, reading and book reviews
- Video interviews with *Stone Soup* authors
- Music, spoken word and performances

Visit the *Stone Soup* Store at Stonesoupstore.com to buy

- Magazines—individual issues of Stone Soup, past and present
- Books—the 2017 *Stone Soup Annual*, a bound collection of all the year's issues, as well as themed anthologies
- Art prints—high quality prints from our collection of children's art
- Journals and Sketchbooks for writing and drawing
   ...and more!

StoneSoup

The magazine supporting creative kids around the world

Editor
Emma Wood

Director
William Rubel

Operations
Jane Levi

Education & Production
Sarah Ainsworth

Design
Joe Ewart, Society

Editor's Note

I'm thrilled to finally share the winners of our Science Fiction Contest with you, in this special Science Issue of the magazine. Each story is inventive, strange, suspenseful, and "scientific" in its own way. "Middlenames," the winning story, imagines a society that assigns you a middle name—which determines your identity for life—at birth. "Young Eyes" explores the dangers of technology, while "Mystical Creatures of Blue Spout Bay" and "Sunk" take on the environment. This issue also features nonfiction writing on scientific topics—from the solar eclipse to organ transplants—as well as three poems that engage with scientific topics and ways of thinking. I hope this issue serves as a reminder that writing and literature don't happen in vacuum; they aren't separate from other subjects like algebra, physics, or biology. As you read, I want you to think about your largest, non-literary passion. How can you engage it in your own writing? As always, send the results of your experiment to Stone Soup! Enjoy—

Submissions: Our guidelines for submission are on the Submit page at Stonesoup.com where you will also find a link to our Submittable online submissions portal.

Subscriptions: to subscribe to *Stone Soup*, please press the Subscribe button at our webpage, Stonesoup.com.

On the cover:
'Parker,'
**by Kate Duplantis, 13
Houma, LA**

StoneSoup
Contents

How the Universe Came to Be

by Yutia Li, 9
Houston, TX

Once,
In the middle of nowhere
There hid a
Tiny speck of dust
Smaller than
The smallest microbe.
With all the playful energy
The miniscule pinprick contained,
It couldn't wait
A single moment longer
To meet the world
And make new friends.
So
The tiny speck of dust
Exploded,
Launching a shower
Of vibrant reds,
Oranges,
And yellows
Into the swirl of gloom above.
And that was how
The universe began.

Glamorous stars
Blinked at each other
In the inky night sky.
Bits of cast off rock,
Large and small,
Sped around the stars
Like race cars.

More and more rocks joined;
The racetrack became too packed
And the charging rocks collided
Until gradually,

Planet Earth
Emerged from the chaos.

Back then,
Our home planet
Was a totally different world.
Infuriated asteroids and meteorites
Crashed into the
Simmering surface.

But planet Earth
Tired of its intense workout,
Finally settled down,
Falling into rhythm
Around the sizzling sun.

All of a sudden,
A stray ball of rock
Came hurling through outer space,
A furious untamed lion
Ready to devour all in its path.

But our newborn planet
Fought back,
Cracking the foreigner into pieces,
Sending a spurt
Of dusty stone
Into the air.

But the fight was not over yet—
Some of the stone
Was squashed into a ball,
Forming our
Now dearest companion,
The moon.

Sights of life
Finally appeared on Earth.
Molecules linked together,
And as more joined,
Began to make
Replicas of themselves.
Membranes formed
Around these molecules

By fatty by-products.
And humans finally made
Their first appearance
As invisible
Single-celled organisms.

This,
Reader,
Is how our dazzling universe,
Full of all its stunning wonders,
Came to be.

I Wonder

by Sterling Waterfield, 11
Fort Wayne, IN

I wonder why we call bats "bats"—
why do we call them that?
I wonder why little kids burp
and crickets chirp
and why snow is in the winter.
Speaking of snow,
why is it called snow and not sand?
Why is music sometimes called a band?
And
why do people walk on land?
And why do they die
or cry
or get mad
or sad?
Why are we the ones that can talk
and the ones that have technology?

Why aren't hedgehogs a sophisticated species?
Why do spiders give you the creepies?
It doesn't seem right to me,
why the world is this way.
I think the world should be different
but I can't make hedgehogs talk
or fish walk.
So I think that I will just
burrow under the earth
inspect the workings of the world
and see what makes
the world this messed-up way.
But I kind of like the world this way—
just a little.
So I will stay
here where I am
and watch the flow.

The Absence of Opposites

Many things are true,
I know this is, too:

there is no cold,

there is only
the absence of heat.

Heat is a
fluid thing

that has no form

except
for life-saving warmth.

Cold only happens
when heat is
not there.

Cold is not a
thing.

It is a
happening

that makes the body
shiver and shake.

Heat relieves that pain,
makes you sweat
(and sweat can be a nuisance)

but

by Kieran O'Donnell, 11
Philadelphia, PA

it is just heat
reassuring you
that it
will always
be
there.

"The night after the concert I dreamt I was dancing across the surface of a viola dressed in ballet clothes, desperately trying to keep up with the flawless music. It ended with me falling off the edge into the dark abyss."

Graphite pencil, Copic fineliner pens, Prismacolor pencils, and an ink brush pen

by Avery Multer, 12
Chicago, CA

Middlenames

Winner of the 2018 Science Fiction Contest
by Thomas Faulhaber, 13
Seattle, WA

Robin lives in a religious society where her identity is set at birth

In his book *Meaning*, Galer wrote, "God created the human race as an experiment; He wanted to see if life was capable of creating for Him. Ultimately, He wanted us to produce beauty." I felt that I had failed Him. I had been practicing from a young age, yet my music remained mostly devoid of beauty. And despite that fact, I continued to practice.

"It's for my family," I would always tell myself when I listened to myself play.

I wasn't referring to my mother or father, but to my mid-family, the Burkes. The Burkes have been famed for their music for the past 60 years (before that, they weren't really famous for anything). The most well-known singer's name was John Burke Raymond. The best composer was Sophia Burke Kasparov. Burkes weren't just everywhere in the music world. They entirely comprised it.

Even my music teacher, Ms. Tilson, was a Burke. She was very good at being a Burke. She didn't just play well; she played with a captivating, eccentric style. She would be famous if only her personality didn't reflect that to quite the extreme that it did. She was almost crazy.

I have never felt like a Burke. My music was bitter to the ears. People sometimes asked me if my viola was broken. The pastor who gave me my middlename at baptism continued to insist that he had given me the correct one. The pastor was a Follower of Galer who had converted from an older religion after being "shown the way" by older Followers. As a result, he had no middlename. He went by Papa Chris, and everyone in town going back two generations loved him.

One night, after a particularly bad concert for the town's Winter Festival, when I was eleven, I asked Papa Chris if he was sure that he hadn't made a mistake in choosing my middlename.

"Of course not! I can see you improving every day!" he said. He was lying. I'm not sure why he lied, but the forced smile on his face made the lie clear.

"Even my mom winced!" I said in protest, as if I had a point to prove.

He went on to assure me that I would get better over time. Even Burkes weren't always prodigies, after all. Despite his reassurance, my viola still sounds like its voice is cracking whenever I try to play.

The night after the concert I dreamt I was dancing across the surface of a viola dressed in ballet clothes, desperately trying to keep up with the flawless music. It ended with me falling off the edge into the dark abyss.

These midnight terrors continue to this day: the most recent example involved me playing music for a party of fiery demons who would cook me alive if I failed. *Unreality*, Galer's book on dreams, says that dreams of this sort (dreams in which the subject is forced to do something for a party of festive demons) usually represent a need for flight. *Unreality* is not his most religious work.

My best friend then was Jonah Rosedale Beatty. The Rosedales were known for being aristocratic. They were envied by most, and they had formed a tight alliance among themselves over time. Rosedales often came to resent their status as much as it was envied by others.

Jonah, who hardly believed that he would become rich because of his Rosedale name, often joked about his place in society. When I would desperately attempt to play my music, he would cheer me on by saying, "When I become rich, I'll make you my head musician!" This made us both laugh, but I secretly wished that it would come true. I would daydream about conducting an orchestra in Jonah's mansion, being applauded by the nation's most powerful. It was one of the few things motivating me to continue.

Jonah had to leave last year. The riots in our city were getting especially bad, and Rosedales were the main target. As a result, Rosedale leaders started paying for their fellow Rosedales, whom they saw as their nieces and nephews, to leave the rioting cities. We lived in one of the safest parts of town, in a very open space where almost everybody was contented, but Jonah's paranoid parents took the money anyway.

A few months ago, I received this letter from Jonah:

Dear Head Musician,

The country is very boring. I can't tell my parents because that would be ungrateful, so I decided to send you a letter.

A lot of the kids here are Rosedales like me. It's the only thing we can really bond over. One of them, Mason, is from our school in the city. Do you remember Mason? I didn't until he approached me. I never even knew that he was a Rosedale!

The people in the countryside are excited to have us all here. They seem to be under the false impression that we'll draw people out into their towns. They think that wherever Rosedales go, everyone else will follow. Given how much people seem to hate us, I wouldn't agree.

The weather out here is usually very sunny and dry. In the winter, there was no snow. My parents say that I'll be able to visit them this winter. I guess we'll be able to see each other again! I'll be excited to see how much my chief musician has improved!

Please write back!

Yours truly,
Jonah

"When I become rich, I'll make you my head musician!"

It took me a month to write back. I wrote a very short letter because I honestly couldn't think of much to say. I was especially reluctant because I didn't want to admit that I had not improved at all. Here is my letter:

Dear Jonah,

If you were hoping for improvement, you will probably be disappointed. It will be a while before I'm prepared to be your Head Musician.

It is good to hear that you are making new friends. I am looking forward to your visit.

From your friend,
Robin

He never wrote back again, probably because of my letter's disappointing detail in comparison to his. It is almost winter now, so I suppose I'll have to meet him soon.

This brings us to the beginning of the story that needs to be told—to the point at which things began to change for the first time in almost a century. I was at the center of this change. I might say that I even played my own small role in it.

The whole thing started when Ms. Tilson asked me to speak to her after a certain class, on November 24, exactly a month before our Winter Festival concert.

The conversation began when Ms. Tilson asked me to come to her desk.

"Robin, will you please come over here?"

Once I had reached her desk, she said, "Would you like to play a piece in the Winter Festival concert, on behalf of the school?"

For a minute I seriously considered refusing. Then, after nearly a full minute of dazed, pointless contemplation, I realized that Ms. Tilson would not take "no" for an answer. She was the reason I played that solo in sixth grade. I had refused twice, to no avail.

"Okay," I said meekly, in a voice barely above a whisper.

Ms. Tilson's keen musician's ear picked up the sound. Her face immediately brightened with an eccentric smile, which was characteristic of her. She told me that I could play any song I wanted. Any at all. I ended up picking a song called "Katyusha." It was a simple song that I had seen Sophia Burke Kasparov play a few years ago, in tribute to her country, Russia. Despite its simplicity, she had made it sound so beautiful. I wanted to do the same. I had to.

The first thing I did when I got home was tell my mom about the offer. "I can't wait to hear you play, sweetie!" she said with a genuine smile, unlike the lie that Papa Chris had given me. "What song are you going to play?" "I'm playing "Katyusha." You know, that song that Sophia Burke Kasparov played at that concert last year?" "That's a good choice. I remember it being very Christmas-y," she said slowly, trying to remember that concert. I left abruptly to go to my room to practice.

I reached my room and sat down at my desk. I had the sheet music out and my instrument at the ready, and I began to interpret the notes on the page.

I tried playing it slowly first, allowing the bow to quietly whine as I pulled it across the strings. I played faster, and I imagined the lyrics as I played.

I placed the bow on the strings and began to play the song in my head. "*Rastsvetali yabloni i grushi*," and I made the first mistake. A terrible noise was produced as my bow slipped onto the wrong string. Despite my mistake, I continued.

"*Poplyli tumany nad rekoy*
Vykhodila na bereg Katyusha
Na vysokiy bereg, na krutoy."

I figured that this was enough for self-evaluation, as the rest of the song was a simple repetition of the notes in this verse with different words. Despite the short span of time, I had still made more mistakes than I wanted to count. My instrument sounded more like it was weeping then singing.

I continued to practice for over an hour. No matter how hard I tried, the music refused to sound like it was supposed to. Soon the hour became two hours, with little progress made. I practiced every day. Sooner than I thought they would, days became weeks, and then those weeks transformed into a month. After just six weeks, four of which had turned themselves into a month, my performance was one day away.

Coincidentally, a mass riot was supposed to happen on the same day as the concert, led by a man who thought that middlenames were the root of all suffering. The neighborhood that I lived in was very unlikely to be affected, though. It was so unlikely, in fact, that Jonah was going to be able to come to my performance. Here is the letter that he sent:

Robin,

Despite the rumors that my parents heard, about the rioting, I will still be able to come back for the planned week in the winter. See you then!

Sincerely,
Jonah

I was not as happy about this as Jonah was.

The last day slipped by as I desperately tried to get the music to come out right.

"*Poplyli tumany nad rekoy...*"

Under the stress, the lyrics played incorrectly in my head. This did not help things in the slightest. I still felt that I had improved over the course of these six weeks, even if it wasn't perfect. It would at least be satisfactory, I thought.

My sleep that night was very restless. I could see myself playing onstage, and I was overwhelmed by a mix of excitement, dread, and terror. That night, I had the dream with the demons again.

During breakfast the next morning, my lack of sleep caused my head to ache, like a weight pulling me down. I ate my breakfast in silence, preoccupied with my own thoughts. I barely noticed my foot tapping the tune of "Katyusha." The minutes crawled by, and I practiced for an hour or so before lunch. Then I practiced for an hour or so after lunch.

Finally, night came. My mother had

dressed me formally for the occasion. We walked to the church, where the ceremonies would take place.

The Winter Festival was a holiday right before the holiest of holidays. It was a very festive occasion, full of music, dance, and other entertainment. However, it was also almost as important as the holiday it preceded. I could not afford to mess up.

When we got to the church, I was immediately brought to the corner of the room for a brief bit of practice. Ms. Tilson told me that my music sounded alright and that I should be ready to perform, which was honestly more than I expected. Mine was the second performance. I sat and waited through the first performance.

The first performance was supposed to be very long. A half-hour long, in fact. It was interrupted after 28 minutes by the sounds of breaking glass outside. Soon, the light of fire came through the windows. The church doors were broken down. A band of thugs participating in the riot had broken in.

One of the men who had broken in marched up to the stage. He was wearing dark clothes and dark glasses, like a criminal from a movie, and he was holding a torch in one hand and a piece of paper in the other. The paper seemed to be some sort of manifesto. He paused for breath, read the manifesto, and yelled: "This Festival is a celebration of the system of middlenames! The system that decides who should be rich, who should be famous, and who should be trodden upon! It is the superstitious system that has governed the lives of everyone for over 100 years! We will end its tyranny!"

Papa Chris stepped up to the stage. The girl who had been playing her music before the disruption had already fled. Papa Chris raised his hand, and the room went silent. It was as if the approaching inferno had been put on pause. He said, "Here, my son. I will prove to you that middlenames are real. Robin here is a Burke, a family well known for their music. Robin's music will certainly show you that the prophetic nature of the middlenames ritual is not mere superstition."

He beckoned for me to come to the stage, and I obliged. I looked into the crowd. It was full of men in dark clothes with torches. I prepared to play my song. I raised my bow to the strings of the viola.

What came next was the single noise that caused the avalanche to fall. Scra-a-a-tch-ch.

The man leading the rebellion laughed. The rioters began to burn the church, and we all fled. After running outside, I looked back. There was light visible inside of the church, but all that came out was smoke.

Apparently, these thugs had a point. The next day, the Eldest Brother, who was the greatest leader of Galer's religion, wrote to every parish in the country. His letter was read by every pastor. It was read by Papa Chris among the ruins of the church.

*To the People who want my decisive
answer to this chaos, and to the future
Scholars who want to see what it was all
about,*

*Galer said in his final letter to his
Eldest Sons, "This religion is an experiment
with many parts, each devised by God,
and each designed to bring peace, love,
and tolerance to the newer generations of
mankind." The middlenames system was
clearly a failed piece. It forced many of
you, my children, into situations that you
never asked for. I am sorry.*

*With Love to Everyone,
The Eldest Son of Galer called Michael*

Within months, no one had a
middlename anymore. Jonah moved
back into the city now that there were
no more Rosedales, and people were
slightly more pleasant to each other
for the time being. We still loved Galer,
and I still love Galer as I write this.

But, to the future scholars who
want to see what it was all about: this
was my perspective.

Young Eyes

2nd Place in the 2018 Science Fiction Contest

by Allie Aguila, 13
Miami Springs, FL

A pair of illegal goggles have the power to return you to the imagination of childhood

Douglas Wamboldt stared at the scrap of paper in his hand, careful not to crumple it. The words "Noodle Palace" were inked onto the paper in his associate's flowing handwriting. The cool night wind blew steadily, sending discarded newspapers and flyers down the deserted street. He stood in front of his destination hesitantly. The sign flickered, illuminating the words "Noodle Palace" for just a few seconds before flickering off. This was the place.

Douglas hurried toward the door, desperate to get away from the biting chill of the evening. He pushed open the door to be assaulted with different aromas of food. The restaurant was steamy and surprisingly nearly empty. Five booths lined the far wall and a few small tables were squeezed into the space. He approached the woman behind the counter nervously. Her eyes were sunken, and hard and grey like stone. Her dark hair escaped her bun in coarse, thin strands that hung limply around her face. An old scar lined the skin above her right eyebrow. Douglas fidgeted with his tie and the scrap of paper.

She watched him impatiently before Douglas leaned forward and whispered to her, "I'm here for the goggles? The imagination goggles, I mean. The ones that let you—"

"Shut up," she snapped at him. "Follow me."

She swung herself over the counter with ease and latched onto Douglas's wrist, her fingernails digging into his skin. She led him to the back of the store, past the bathrooms and through a door. This door opened up to a stairwell, which she dragged Douglas down quickly. At the bottom of the stairs, a man at a desk sat waiting.

The woman shoved Douglas toward the desk and hurried back up the stairs.

Douglas rubbed his sore wrist and neared the man at the desk, so far confused with his treatment as a customer.

The man sported a buzz cut, dark skin, and an intimidating stature. "Name?" the man inquired.

Douglas stood up straighter, collecting any pride and resolve he had left. "Douglas Wamboldt."

"You wouldn't happen to know a Celia Spencer, would you?" Douglas added.

"Unlikely." The man shook his head.

"To Douglas's amazement, the moon loomed before him."

Watercolor

by Lingfei Li, 12
Shanghai, China

"But, you see, she's been here before. She told me about it."

"Most of our customers tend to feel unsafe leaving their real names with us."

"Oh," Douglas responded. "Is there anything for me to sign?"

"Regarding the legality of this business, no. However, going into this, you should know that these goggles are not toys. They are basically untested technology and can be dangerous."

Douglas stiffened, beginning to feel very apprehensive and regretful. "I see."

Still, Celia had recommended it as a way to get out of his head and escape his many anxieties, for a change. "That being said, loosen up. Have some fun, Wamboldt. Youth is precious. Not everyone gets a second go at being a kid."

Douglas nodded.

"Ready?"

He nodded again.

"Right this way, then," the man guided him.

They walked down a dimly lit hallway and paused in front of the fourth door on the left. The man pulled out a ring of keys from his pocket and searched for the right one. "You'll be going into Kitchen 2. It looks like your basic kitchen, but with these..." He produced a pair of thick-lensed goggles equipped with dials and gears installed in the frame. "It'll look like a whole new world."

Douglas swallowed his fear and delicately grabbed hold of the goggles. "How long do I get?"

"As your friend, I'd recommend under 20 minutes for your first try, but as a businessman, I'd recommend 45 minutes," the man answered honestly.

"Can't I do any longer?"

"We don't know what'll happen after an hour. We want to keep you somewhat safe."

Douglas cocked his head in confusion. "What could be so bad about the innocence of imagination?"

Ignoring his question, the man unlocked the door. "Remember, we've enhanced the overactive imagination of a child, so time will also feel exaggerated. We'll give you a stopwatch. When it beeps, your time's up. To turn them on, just say 'activate' and say 'deactivate' once you've finished." The man set the stopwatch and placed it on Douglas's wrist.

Douglas nodded, beginning to tense up in anticipation. "How much is it?"

"$450."

Douglas placed the folded bills into the man's palm.

"Best of luck, Wamboldt." The man began to count the money. "The door will lock automatically once you're inside to keep you safe."

Douglas gulped and placed the goggles on his nose. He took tentative steps into Kitchen 2 and took in his surroundings. The kitchen had a traditional white tile floor, along with a pantry, a microwave, an oven, a counter, several cabinets, and a table with four seats.

"A-activate," Douglas stammered. He cleared his throat before trying again. "Activate."

The goggles flickered, startling Douglas. The click of the lock sounded with finality. The experience had begun.

Before him, the kitchen seemed the same, but his eyes felt different. They were supercharged with excitement and playful energy. He felt the youth coursing through his body, all the way down to his fingertips and toes. His eyes sought out entertainment in the room. They were almost hungry for it. It didn't take him very long before the young eyes latched onto a broomstick that was leaning up against the floral wallpaper. His mouth stretched to form a rare smile and his legs were ordered by his eyes to move. He gripped its plastic handle, and just like magic, he was no longer standing in Kitchen 2. The setting of his adventure had switched like a slideshow. A dense and hilly forest now surrounded him. His suit had transformed into an explorer's uniform. In his hand was a sleek rifle, waiting to be fired.

Through the brush, Douglas spotted a fluffy hare a few feet away. He lifted the gun and fired, catching his target right in the chest. A brisk wind swept through the woods and Douglas let out a triumphant yell. He began to run, unable to bottle in his energy any longer. He whooped and hollered as he raced up the steep path ahead of him. Douglas paused as he came to a break in the trees—a hill that overlooked much of the forest. An instinct overcame Douglas. He was compelled to bend his knees and spring up into the air. The wind caught him with sturdy arms and he flew. His fingertips

brushed the tops of trees. The rifle had vanished and his digits seemed to be morphing into fine, gold feathers. Douglas flew so fast that his breath seemed to be sucked away by the air around him. He laughed gleefully as he continued ascending, breaking through the cotton clouds. The atmosphere did not deter his climb and he was soon soaring above Earth and into the depths of space. He was invincible, and he never wanted to leave this dream that he was living.

To Douglas's amazement, the moon loomed before him. The slide in the slideshow changed once again, placing Douglas in an astronaut suit and in a rocket on course for the cratered surface of the moon. The distant lights of stars twinkled cheerfully; the sun smiled at him. Douglas soaked in the feeling of being alive almost greedily, frightened that he might never feel it again.

As the rocket touched down on the moon, Douglas eagerly climbed out of the spacecraft and began to leap. He rose higher with every bounce and even attempted flips in mid-air. Once he was finished jumping, he noticed something strange about the rock he was standing on: it wasn't rock at all! Instead, slices of Swiss cheese coated the moon in generous layers. Douglas smiled and then began to laugh like he had never laughed before. The laugh was a stomach-shaking, side-aching, breath-stealing, chest-heaving, all-around-hearty belly laugh that he

He was invincible, and he never wanted to leave this dream that he was living

really needed. It was as simple as that. Douglas needed to laugh (at cheese moons of all things).

And then there was beeping. Loud, incessant beeping that penetrated his astronaut helmet and rang in his ears. *Beep!*

Douglas didn't know why he was so sure, but he told himself that the sound could only have one source: an alarm clock.

"Just five more minutes!" he called out.

However, the beeping didn't stop. On and on it went, stubbornly insisting that it was time to go.

"I don't want to go!" Douglas whined.

The man from the desk was waiting outside Kitchen 2. He was almost certain that 45 minutes had passed. Why was Mr. Douglas Wamboldt taking so long? He heard the beeping, didn't he? Another few seconds passed before the man grew anxious. He called for his business partner, "Jia! I need you down here!"

She was downstairs in an instant, clamping her hand over his mouth. "What did I tell you about lowering your voice?" she hissed.

"It's been 46 minutes," he whispered in panic.

Jia's tired eyes widened. "Control room, now."

The pair dashed down the hallway and flung themselves into the control room. The man hurried from panel to panel, flipping switches nervously. Each switch was labeled with a four-digit number that Jia couldn't decode. "They're not working," the man informed her.

"Let me try," Jia reached out for the panel in front of her.

The man held her hand back. "No. They won't work."

Jia's fingers twitched, aching for control over the situation. "When do the nightmares set in?"

The man's frantic eyes didn't leave his watch for a second. "After 53 minutes. We have—"

"Seven minutes," Jia finished grimly. "We have to break the lock."

"I'll get the tools," the man agreed.

Douglas sat in his rocket, trying to ignore the incessant beeping. "Shut up!" He screamed desperately.

To his great surprise, the beeping listened to his command. It was now silent on the moon. Douglas stepped out of the ship cautiously and looked around for any indication of what had just happened. At first, the moon seemed the same as it had been while the noise had been torturing Douglas. He squinted at the barren landscape. He saw nothing but miles and miles of craters...and a shadow. The shadow was so faint and distant he could almost have imagined it, but it was there nonetheless. It could've been an oddly-shaped crater, but as it drew closer, it became evident that it was something else. Perhaps, even a sentient entity.

The shadow sucked away the juvenile liveliness from moments before and Douglas's knees threatened to buckle. He hurriedly sealed himself inside the rocket and shut his eyes, repeatedly murmuring, "Leave me alone."

The shadow only drew closer. It didn't listen to him like the beeping had. He couldn't control it.

After a few seconds, Douglas dared to open an eye. Thick darkness had enveloped the rocket completely. The clear windshield of the craft was covered in layers and layers of shadow. He searched for an opening, a slit of hope in the shadows, but found none. The darkness seemed alive and almost triumphant. It had caught him. Douglas felt his throat close up. The darkness was so thick that there was no longer air. It was suffocating him with fear.

"Help!" he gasped. He lifted his hands to his throat, but it didn't stop his attacker.

"Deactivate!" a female voice hollered.

The scene flickered and died. There was only the light of Kitchen 2. The woman from upstairs, and the man from the desk were watching him worriedly, waiting for his next few words.

"I want my old eyes back," Douglas decided.

The Mystical Creatures of Blue Spout Bay

3rd Place in the 2018 Science Fiction Contest

by Marlena Rohde, 12
San Francisco, CA

Viola discovers a mysterious golden seaweed that has the potential to change the world

Viola, clad in her tight scuba mask and with the weight of her oxygen tank pulling her towards the water, leaned over the edge of her small boat, and fell through the soft, smooth surface of the bay. Viola adjusted her eyes to the pale sunlight streaking the sands and oriented herself as she did every day. A fish, a common Gray Spout, swished by her face, narrowly missing. *That's funny*, she thought, *Gray Spouts are usually predators, but this one seems to be running away from something.*

Just as she finished her thought, Viola saw a streak of glittering orange fly by her eyes. She looked after it and saw a fish that looked to be made of solid gold, unlike anything she had seen during her life by the sea. Viola had come by plenty of goldfish in her day, but nothing quite so massive. The girl immediately kicked off from a bit of coral, rocketing after the fish. Because the creature was going at a breakneck pace, it was quite a challenge for Viola to catch up to it, and the Gray Spout was long gone by the time she did. Viola watched the golden beauty retire into a home in a rock and disappear from sight before she realized what was living around it. Beautiful glittering seaweed towered above her, as far as the eye could see. It shimmered like nothing the girl had ever seen, and continued on in every direction. It was like a forest bathed in bright, full sunlight, the same color as that fish. Daisy would love this, she thought, thinking of her sister lying in her bed, yearning for the waves they had so loved in their childhood.

Viola snapped out of her awe and cut a small piece of the plant to inspect later, tucking it into a pocket in her wetsuit for further examination. She swam up, finally surfaced, and saw her boat nearly a mile away. Viola began the long journey home.

Viola arrived home, hair damp and very exhausted as she did every day.

"Daisy, I'm home," she shouted.

"I'm up here, right where I always am," a soft voice called back.

Viola leapt up the stairs, the seaweed in hand. It had a lovely odor, not one of salt water, but one of warm sunny mornings, a breath of fresh air.

"Look what I found," Viola exclaimed as she entered her sister's room. Daisy lay in her bed, very weak and pale from having been sick for one year. Viola showed her the plant, and the girl's face lit up.

"It's incredible," she gasped. "Where did you find it?"

"Out on the reef," Viola explained, telling Daisy of her adventures.

"I wish I could go with you," said Daisy. "I miss the days when we went diving together. But that plant, it smells fantastic! I wonder. . . Could you perhaps make a wonderful tea with it?" Viola figured that it couldn't hurt to try, and the seaweed seemed so magical.

If there was anything that could help her sister heal, it was the mysterious plant. She boiled some water and steeped the plant in it, then gave it to Daisy. To Viola's relief, her sister didn't die, but nothing else happened either. She called Max and in the meantime she began to inspect the plant.

"Mornin'," Max called as he stepped into the lab that Viola had made from the basement; he could always count on finding her there.

"Max, you'll never guess what I found!" Viola exclaimed, stepping aside so he could look through the microscope the plant lay under.

"It's beautiful," he murmured as he peered through the glass.

"I found it out on the reef," she explained.

Suddenly, she heard a shout from above.

Viola sprinted up to Daisy's room where she stood, overwhelmed with joy, staring at her reflection in a small hand-mirror.

"Are you alright, Daisy?"

"Look at me," she said, trembling. "I look like I did before. . ." Her voice trailed off.

"Before you were sick," Viola finished, noticing for the first time that Daisy's cheeks were rosier, her thin face and limbs were no longer thin. She felt happiness that she hadn't felt since a year ago.

"Daisy, you're not sick anymore!" she exclaimed, hugging her sister closely.

At a floorboard creak, Viola turned and saw Max, stunned.

"Imagine how much money you could make from this," he said, but in a tone Viola had never heard from him before. He sounded as though he had a horrible idea.

Viola suddenly regretted telling Max of the seaweed, remembering what he had done a year ago, when Viola had discovered a new sort of fish. Max had taken it and sold it to a marine biology center, which named the fish after him. Max told her he needed the money to help his dad recover from a broken leg, but his expensive car and the fact that she had seen his father up and walking the next day said otherwise.

Before she went to bed, Viola took the seaweed and laid it in her bedside table, where no one could get to it.

Maybe I'm overreacting, she

"Beautiful glistening seaweed towered above her, as far as the eye could see."
Watercolor

by Nicole Qian, 13
Auckland, NZ

thought. Max had been a good friend to her when her parents left them, when she had studied to become a marine biologist and turned her basement into a lab, when her sister fell ill. He had apologized extensively for the mix-up and said he had gone back to try and change the name of the fish, but why then had it stayed the same?

Viola expected to sleep that night like she never had before, without worry over her sister or what was to come, but she was roughly awakened by a cacophony of crashes and bangs, then her sister's scream. Viola jolted up, leapt out of bed, and dashed to her sister's room. The girl tiptoed quietly up the stairs, listening to the sounds grow louder and louder. Viola heard another muffled shout, which drowned out a creak she had made from stepping down on one of the wooden steps. The girl heard a gruff voice speaking indistinctly when she reached her sister's room. As noiselessly as she could, Viola opened the door. She saw a dark figure against the light of Daisy's fish tank; whoever it was was ransacking drawers while holding Daisy in a headlock.

"Who are you?" Viola said, trying to sound unafraid even though her hands were shaking.

"Where is the plant?" the man shouted at her as Daisy looked up, and

Viola realized with a pang of fear that the voice belonged to her best friend. Max.

"Don't do this, Max," Viola tried to reason.

"Tell me where the plant is," he continued, as if Viola hadn't said a thing.

"Why are you doing this, Max?"

"Imagine how much this thing would sell for. Think of it, a plant that cures all disease. We could be rich," Max said, and Viola began to realize how obsessed he was. "We could be immune. Now just show me to the plant; don't make me hurt someone you love."

He pulled her sister even tighter.

"I will show you, but only if you promise to stay away from me and my sister," Viola conceded, afraid for her sister, and hoping that she knew what she was doing.

They dressed in their scuba gear and in the dark, still night, a boat could be seen, very faintly, passing along the dark waters. The three dove into the bay, and in the harsh beam of the flashlight, Viola tried to find the coral she had pushed off from and the direction she had gone. The sisters held tightly onto each other, Daisy trusting Viola to save them both.

All of a sudden, a glow appeared, a golden one, the color of the fish Viola had seen and the seaweed she had taken. Viola swam towards it, and Max and Daisy followed. Soon, they were just in range of the glow, and they were stunned by what they saw. Hundreds of creatures swam in the golden lights, dancing beneath the illuminated seaweed that bent majestically with the waves. The light, they realized, came from the creatures, all of which were glowing gloriously. Viola and Daisy stared in awe, and Max tried to calculate the riches he would accumulate from the ecosystem.

Suddenly, from the corner of her eye, Viola saw something hit Max's oxygen tank. She looked in his direction and saw that a small hole had appeared in the tank. Max gasped as he breathed in a mouthful of saltwater, and Viola saw an illuminated swordfish go by. It was what the creatures wanted, Viola realized. The fish that she had followed earlier that morning circled around her and Daisy then swam over to the other creatures, beckoning her.

Viola looked at Max, who was trying to remove his mask, then Daisy, who was looking, wide-eyed and longingly, at the creatures. She looked at the glowing light. It was so tempting . . . Simultaneously, the girls drifted toward the glow, leaving Max, who was desperate for air, then joined the dancing sea animals in the amazing glow. As they swirled around in the beings, Viola noticed her sister's skin, bluish from the light of the ocean, slowly beginning to glow. She looked down and saw that her own hands were illuminating. Viola laughed and hugged her sister closely, and soon the magical marine life had become people, though not losing their shimmer. They were people the girls had never encountered and ones that had mysteriously disappeared from their town in the past. The sisters saw their parents in the distance, and soon Max appeared, smiling a normal, friendly smile.

Any lucky outsider who went diving in the early hours of dawn and happened to come by a festival of mystical golden creatures, would have seen two animals, a dolphin and a turtle, in the center of a glowing whirlwind. They would have smiled at the sight of the animals, like old friends, swirling around each other in euphoria, and then perhaps the outsider would take a small leaf of the golden seaweed beside them, and share its wonder with the world.

Sunk

4th Place in the 2018 Science Fiction Contest

by Benjamin Mitchell, 13
Davis, CA

*After rising sea levels and global temperatures
render the world uninhabitable, self-sustaining
"Communities" are formed*

Oswald awoke, as he did every day, to the grating sounds of his alarm clock buzzing insistently, until he swatted the off button with his hand. He really would have rather slept in, and, as he frequently found himself doing, he wished he could whack his ten-hours-younger self for setting the infernal alarm the previous night. But he knew that today he couldn't sleep in, no matter how much he wanted to.

Today was The Day of Waters, the annual festival within his isolated Community. It was repeated each year as celebration of all that they had accomplished since the founding of the Community six years ago, although why their current state was worth celebrating was too difficult for Oswald to fathom.

Although he didn't feel like attending, the festival was a city-wide holiday, and attendance at the big ceremony was mandatory for all citizens. So what choice did he have, really? Plus, there was free, quality food, a rare luxury in modern society.

He kicked off the thin sheet he had lain under, sweating voluminously. He sat up, and walked to the bathroom to get a towel. He despised the weather, which had grown increasingly hotter since the ice caps had melted and started this whole nightmare. He glowered, remembering a vacation he had once taken, travelling to Hawaii for a week. Nobody could ever do that again, though, since all of the islands were underwater.

He pulled on a pair of light grey shorts and a thin short sleeve shirt. Even how people dressed had changed. Although the seasons' names didn't change, not for any reason other than nostalgia, they became fundamentally different from how they used to be. As the atmosphere trapped more heat, the hotter it became, no matter what season. Snow doesn't fall on the vast majority of the world, and in some places it is too hot for all but those with nowhere else to go, barely clinging to humanity, and their life.

Tapping his thumb against the pad to the left of the doorframe, Oswald trudged outside into the austere hallways of the Community. Many factors lent themselves to the feeling of cold emptiness that seemingly clung to the walls of the Community. There was the lack of plants, due to how inhospitable the hot environment had become to most plants. There were also very few windows showing outside the Community, but this was because there was nothing to look at. The extreme heat had dried out all of the plants in the vicinity, and the only source of water, a landlocked lake, was isolated from the terrain by the technology of the Community, which periodically siphoned some of the lake's pure water. The lack of plant life had severe effects on the ecosystem. Much of the flora died due to lack of things to eat, and without plants to hold it down, dust swirled around the barren landscape like the souls of the dead plants and animals. Not that it mattered—after all, because the Community was located in rural Nevada, crisis or no, there would still be nothing but dirt and sand to look at.

Oswald reached the end of the stark hallway and pressed a button, signaling for an elevator. This wasn't actually the worst it could get, he begrudgingly accepted. The Community, a safe house for people displaced by the disaster that had gripped the Earth in its hand, was one of the most well-equipped communities in the world. It housed over 10,000 refugees inside its shining walls and had stockpiles of food to last for ten years. Not that it needed it, though; the Community was self-sustaining. It grew crops beneath the compound, and collected rain water as well as purified the water from the nearby lake. And besides, it would all be over in about five years anyways.

The elevator beeped, and the doors slid open, letting Oswald step inside. The elevator was already full of members of the Community, most of whom were dressed more elegantly than Oswald. The stainless steel doors slid closed, and the elevator rocketed up, fast approaching the Parlor. With another resolute ding, the elevator stopped, and the elegantly dressed party-goers disembarked.

The Parlor was the fanciest section of the Community, which is to say that there was no stainless steel in sight. Today it was filled with cushy red folding chairs, each facing the stage, where a classical orchestra was playing. Later in the day, the High Chancellor of the Nevada Community would be giving his Day of Waters address there. For the time being, though, the seats were empty, and all of the guests were bustling around, talking and eating. Oswald waded his way through the crowd of people, grabbing a cheesy potato gratin from a passing server as he walked. Or rather, it was a substitute for potato, since most of the potatoes had been submerged when the ice caps melted, raising the water level more than 200 feet over what it had been previously.

Oswald's stomach growled hungrily as he neared the food table. The table was covered with an assortment of foods, as exotic as they came these days. Although the Community couldn't serve any fish, sushi, or shrimp, as a result of the toxicity of the water, they made up for it by training skilled chefs to create top of the line pastries and elegant meals. But that didn't stop Oswald from craving sushi. He swiped a bear claw from the table and contemplated all the foods he couldn't eat anymore. Seafood was an impossibility, more trouble than it was worth; when the climate grew warmer, the permafrost in Alaska melted, revealing a nasty surprise for the people of Earth: there were about 800 million kilograms of mercury hiding there. That, coupled with rising waters, proved to be a disaster. Countries scrambled to contain the mercury, but they were too late, and it leached into the water, killing almost all ocean life in a span of a few months. At the same time, water rose, spreading the deadly waters inland, killing some people and destroying many crops and animals to the point of extinction. One such casualty was Northern California's wine country; although it was left mostly high and dry, the mercury in the water managed to leach into the ground and kill all of the crops.

Oswald scowled as he bit into his bear claw, chewing aggressively. The world was an astronomically different place now; many coastal countries, mostly in Europe, were unable to maintain their governments in the face of the disaster, and their lands had dissolved into anarchy. Larger countries, like America and Russia had been forced to retreat within their borders and build compounds like the Community. Only when people banded together could they survive the intense heat, toxic seas, mass extinctions, and lack of water. If the world wasn't at the brink of destruction, perhaps it could have been viewed as poetic. On that note, Oswald seized a chocolate-covered profiterole from the table and bit into it, feeling immensely better with each bite.

Loading a handful of truffles onto a plate, Oswald made his way to the seating area and sank into one of the cushy chairs. Taking a truffle in hand, Oswald proceeded to deposit it in his mouth, as the orchestra stopped playing, prompted by the appearance of the High Chancellor of the Community. He was smartly dressed in a simple suit and tie so dark they looked like a void in which everything had been devoured by some hungry creature.

He smiled crisply to the now seated members of the Community. Oswald ate another truffle.

"Hello, good people of the Community. I will try to keep this short so you may return to the festivities. I bid you good health on this auspicious day; six years ago today I founded this Community, to give the people of a downtrodden Earth a place to live while the effects of the melting ice caps persisted," said the High Chancellor. Oswald found it remarkable that the Chancellor could keep smiling this long.

"And today, I have some especially splendid news to impart on you. Now, before I tell you, let me explain. The world was in a precarious position prior to the disaster that brought you all here. It looked to many people like the world was going to end. They needed assurance that should humanity be pushed to the limits they feared, they could still survive, and even thrive in an apocalyptic landscape. And so the Community was created as a peacekeeping initiative, a way to keep the people at ease."

"We built the Community in an isolated area of Nevada and called it a top-secret government base. It drew a lot of suspicion, but ultimately that was effective in keeping people from guessing the truth. You probably know of it as Area 51. We then set up water siphons in Lake Groom, the lake encompassed by Area 51. We created an artificial habitat here, a place that could trick its occupants into thinking that they really were trapped in a nightmare come true. Because it wasn't enough to show people that they could survive; people needed to know that they could survive. And so, a world-altering event was staged. One so terrible that nobody would question its believability. We sent a disaster warning to the surrounding counties, calling for a mandatory evacuation to the Community, where they'd be safe. You were called to live a lie so the rest of the world would know that, in the event of a disaster, they would still be safe."

He paused to let that sink in.

"But what I am trying to get at here is that it's over. The people around the world are reassured. And so: you can all go home now! The Apocalypse wasn't real! Isn't that great?"

The room was dead silent. The mixture of anger and happiness that radiated in the room was so palpable that even the High Chancellor's enduring smile faltered.

"Anyways, rejoice! Party away! Tomorrow you go home!"
Still quiet. The High Chancellor looked a bit frightened of the mob at this point.

"You're all probably pretty shocked. I'll send some more drinks around, to lighten the mood." It was still as quiet as the grave.

"Well, I'd love to join you all, but I've really got to go; there's a lot of paperwork to be done, and I've got to cash in my paycheck. Enjoy the party!"

Saguaros at Sunset, *watercolor*

by Evelyn Yao, 11
San Gabriel, CA

Saguaros: Amazing Plants

by Marco Lu, 11
Champaign, IL

During my visit to Tucson, Arizona during the winter break, I had many close encounters with cacti on the hiking trail, including getting pricked by a jumping cholla cactus. However, I decided to research possibly the most iconic cactus in the world: the massive saguaro cactus.

The saguaro cactus is not very common; it is only found in Arizona and parts of northern Mexico. The Sonoran Desert in Arizona is one of the few places with naturally growing saguaro cacti. Saguaro cacti are amazing plants. For one thing, large saguaro cacti are incredibly valuable. This is because it takes a saguaro cactus several hundred years to grow to that size. In fact, the signature "arms" of the saguaro actually don't grow until the cactus is at least 60-years-old.

The saguaro cactus has a unique, accordion-like skin texture that can expand to gather more water in wet weather. Amazingly, some can expand up to 16 inches during a rainy season. Yet another adaptation that the saguaro and some other desert plants have developed is a thin web of roots just below the surface. This allows them to capture rainwater even if deeper soil is not very saturated. Weather significantly affects the growth of a cactus's arms. If a winter is unusually cold, the cold could weaken an arm and make it sag. If the damage is not too severe, the arm will continue growing in its new direction.

The saguaro flower, the state flower of Arizona, is typically only open for one day. When it is open in the day, it is pollinated by various birds and insects, including bees and white-winged doves. At night, it is pollinated by lesser long-nosed or Mexican long-tongued bats.

The spines of a saguaro are very unique adaptations. While they resemble, say, a hedgehog's spines, they are actually modified leaves. Their first purpose of the spines of a saguaro is fairly obvious—to protect them from predators. But this does not deter all predators. For example, javelinas (a type of wild pig), tortoises, and pack rats are unfazed by the painful spines. The main reason that the leaves of a saguaro have evolved into spines is that spines lower the transpiration rate, or the rate at which water is lost via water vapor. Stomata are minute pores on leaves, which allow water vapor to escape. Since saguaro spines have no stomata, the transpiration rate is reduced. The third purpose of a saguaro's spines, surprisingly, is to provide shade for the cactus. While a single spine does not seem to provide much shade, multiply that spine by one hundred or one thousand, and you will realize how much help these spines provide. The shade these spines provide helps lower the surface temperature of a cactus, which lowers the amount of water lost to the atmosphere.

The way a cactus has evolved to life in the desert is quite amazing. I can never forget the sight of hundreds of towering saguaros standing in the Sabino Canyon near Tucson. Despite their daunting appearances, they provide shelters to little birds and reach their arms out as if to welcome people to the Sonoran Desert.

Author's note: various sources were consulted to put together this article, in particular:

James, Mark. "The Giant Saguaros of America's Southwest" (Video, August 2014). Youtube, http://www.youtube.com/watch?v=YncseaXQUsc.

Smart Learning for All. "Transpiration— Why do cacti have spines?" (Video, September 2017). Youtube, https://www.youtube.com/watch?v=DfO-65MGQTsU.

The Eclipse

by Kyle Wu, 9
New York, NY

I walked out onto the balcony. I was barefoot and the balcony was hot, so I was jumping around. We were in South Carolina to see the eclipse. My dad put a blanket on the floor so I didn't burn my feet. I swiftly jumped onto it to save my poor feet from being burned by the intense heat. I then put on my special eclipse glasses. Now I could carelessly look at the sun without blinding myself. I saw the moon hovering over the bright sun, one quarter of the way to totality. I ducked down, and my mom handed me some cold, refreshing iced tea we had gotten just for this occasion.

I learned about the stages of a total solar eclipse on a NASA website.

P1 is called first contact. The moon looks like it is touching the sun but it's actually not covering it at all.

When it was halfway to totality, I ducked down again, took off my glasses and gazed at the ground, wondering what totality would be like. Maybe an explosion of blinding light? A dark light? I imagined in my head what would happen.

Now, at three-fourths the way to totality, it was much colder and much darker, like sitting under an umbrella. I slurped my iced tea and put on my special glasses, then I stared at the eclipse in amazement. For some reason, my mouth was wide open. I ducked down, removed my glass-es, and pretended to be a tour guide. "Shade break. A beautiful experience," I said to my sister. She laughed.

P2 is second contact. It looks like the moon is covering the sun and there are more sun rays than the sun, but the sun still shows. It is the last instant before totality. It usually looks like a diamond ring!

I drank some iced tea and gurgled it in my mouth. Racing the clock, I put my glasses back on and looked up right in time to see . . .

TOTALITY!

In an explosion of light, the sun and moon seemed to pop out, then arranged themselves into a beautiful, shimmering, ghostly ring. Everyone around me cheered. My dad took pictures by putting his glasses onto his camera lens. I could not believe it.

Totality is the point when the moon covers the sun completely so you can only see the sun rays. Totality can only be seen in a path of totality, which is less than ten miles wide but some-times more than 10,000 miles long. Totality only occurs because the sun's radius is approximately 400 times the radius of the moon, and the moon is approximately 400 times closer to the earth than the sun. This makes the sun seem smaller than the moon, so the moon can "cover the sun."

Afterwards, when the moon start-ed to show the sun again, sunglasses were not needed anymore. Totality was really fun.

P3 is third contact. It looks like a mirror image of the diamond ring. It is the moment right after totality ends.

P4 is fourth contact. It looks like a mirror image of First Contact. It is the first moment after totality where the sun is not being covered by the moon, but some of the sun rays are.

Later on, I thought more about eclipses. I was amazed at the sun's brightness in the beginning and the darkness during totality. I would like to see an eclipse again and share my experience with others. I wondered what others thought of the eclipse and if they liked it as much as I did.

Pigs to the Rescue

by Taryn Morlock, 11
Chicago, IL

There is a need for organ donors all over the world. Many people lie in hospital beds hoping for a replacement organ. There just aren't enough available, and no wonder. To get just a few, someone young and healthy would have to die in a way that doesn't affect their organs. In the U.S. alone, an average of 10 people die every day because there weren't organs for them.

Scientists have worked with this problem for a while. First, they turned to animals like the monkey as donors. But most of these experiments failed. In 1984, scientists transplanted a baboon heart into a newborn. The heart seemed to work at first, but baby Fae lived for only 20 days. Two more men with livers transplanted from monkeys only lived a little longer, one living for 70 days and the other for 26. These experiments failed because our immune systems recognize the transplanted organs as foreign and attack them.

Recently, however, scientists have had a breakthrough, not with apes, but with . . . pigs! Pigs have organs of similar size to ours, and they have the same functions. But, as with the ape organs, there are problems. The two main issues are that pig cells are coated with a distinctive sugar that alerts our immune system that there's an intruder, and that the pig genome carries dormant viruses that could hurt humans. These viruses are called Porcine Endogenous Retroviruses, or PERVs.

For this problem, scientists use a gene-editing technique called CRISPR. They are now able to knock out the gene for the sugars on the cells, and some groups are identifying and trying to cut out some of the PERVs.

It's a huge task. But progress has been made. One team of scientists identified 45 genes that need to be removed. On August 10th, 2017, 37 piglets lacking some PERVs were born in China. 15 survived. Another big step forward was the creation of a pig lacking 3 PERV genes. 30% of patients should be able to host those organs.

Even though the technology has leapt forward, I wouldn't count on a porcine organ anytime soon. Scientists have only gotten to testing the pig organs on apes, and those experiments have had mixed results. And even if they could identify all the PERVS and remove them and successfully create a litter of pigs missing the PERVS, there's no guarantee hospitals and doctors would accept replacement organs from pigs. The scientists definitely have a long battle ahead of them.

Honor Roll

Welcome to the *Stone Soup* Honor Roll. Every month we receive submissions from hundreds of kids from around the world. Unfortunately, we don't have space to publish all the great work we receive. We want to commend some of these talented writers and artists and encourage them to keep creating.

Honorable Mention in the 2018 Science Fiction Contest

"The Transmitter," Sabrina Guo, 12
"Holding On," by Macy Li, 12
"Shhh" by Harper Miller, 11

Fiction

Riley Brodie, 12
Ella Butterfield, 8
Makayla Doyle, 10
Melody Falcone, 11
Sri Koneru, 11
MJ Lyon, 10
Madaline Moren, 9
Anya Nasveschuk, 10
Emma Russell-Trione, 13

Poetry

Esme Barker, 10
Kaia Hutson, 11
Helena Kondak, 13
Rose Olshan, 9
Alyssa Schofield, 12

Art

Nicole Qian, 13

Don't forget to visit Stonesoup.com to browse our bonus materials. There you will find

- 20 years of back issues—around 5,000 stories, poems and reviews
- Blog posts from our Young Bloggers on subjects from sports to sewing plus ecology, reading and book reviews
- Video interviews with *Stone Soup* authors
- Music, spoken word and performances

Visit the *Stone Soup* Store at Stonesoupstore.com to buy

- Magazines—individual issues of Stone Soup, past and present
- Books—the 2017 *Stone Soup Annual*, a bound collection of all the year's issues, as well as themed anthologies
- Art prints—high quality prints from our collection of children's art
- Journals and Sketchbooks for writing and drawing
  . . . and more!

StoneSoup

StoneSoup

The magazine supporting creative kids around the world

Editor
Emma Wood

Director
William Rubel

Operations
Jane Levi

Education & Production
Sarah Ainsworth

Design
Joe Ewart, Society

Stone Soup (ISSN 0094 579X) is published online eleven times a year—monthly, with a combined July/August summer issue. Copyright © 2018 by the Children's Art Foundation, a 501(c)(3) non-profit organization, located in Santa Cruz, California. All rights reserved. Thirty-five percent of our subscription price is tax-deductible. Make a donation at Stonesoup.com/donate/ and support us by choosing Children's Art Foundation as your Amazon Smile charity.

Stone Soup is available in different formats to persons who have trouble seeing or reading the print or online editions. To request the Braille edition from the National Library of Congress, call +1 800-424-8567. To request access to the audio edition via the National Federation of the Blind's NFB-NEWSLINE®, call +1 866-504-7300 or visit www.nfbnewsline.org

Check us out on Social Media:

Editor's Note

I remember the first time I sat down in a room different from the room where I'd grown up, in my parents' house, and said, "This is home." I was in college, and it was a strange feeling—to feel at home away from home. What is home anyway? Is it a planet, a city, a feeling, a person, a piece of furniture? Each of the pieces in this issue wrangles with the idea of "home" in an interesting, exciting way. I hope they will inspire you to write about your own home as well!

Sincerely,

Letters: Do you have something to say about something you've read or seen in *Stone Soup*? If you do, we'd love to hear from you, and we might print your letter on our Letters to the Editor page! Post a comment on our website, or write to us at editor@Stonesoup.com.

Submissions: Our guidelines for submission are on the Submit page at Stonesoup.com, where you will also find a link to our Submittable online submissions portal.

Subscriptions: to subscribe to *Stone Soup*, please press the Subscribe button at our webpage, Stonesoup.com.

On the cover:
'Window to Another World',
Nikon Coolpix L830

**by Hannah Parker, 13
Burlington, VT**

StoneSoup
Contents

A Great Community

Zach's family is immigrating from Poland to the U.S.—and he's scared: what if America smells bad or is too hot or too expensive?

We were at the airport. We were there for a good reason. To go to America.

My dad had stayed in America for two years. The reason for this was to get a job and be able to take me and Grandma Nicole there to live. But while he was there, the stock markets crashed and Dad lost a lot of money. But he did find a job eventually, so we are moving there now.

The reason we were moving is because my dad had little money, and, before staying in America for two years, he got fired from his job. Grandma, Grandpa, and I had to work at great-uncle Bill's sausage factory to get the money for our family while Dad was away. In the sausage factory, it was hot and the pay was not quite enough to sustain four people. While I worked there, I always felt the sweat cling to my face after only one hour of work. We had to carefully place the sausages into the boxes, then tape the boxes shut. It doesn't sound like much work, but doing it nonstop for long amounts of time is tiring. We were so grateful when Dad returned from America! But, as soon as he got home, we had to get ready for our trip.

We were at the airport security desk, getting our passports checked.

"Hello!" my dad said in Polish. "This is the Berkes family. I'm Jim, and this is Nicole and Zach. We are here for our flight to America."

My legs were bouncy, and I was biting at the sides of my fingernails, which I do when I'm nervous. And I was. I didn't know if America would be a good place to live or not. And even if it was, there might be other dangers waiting. Actually, I was probably getting too nervous.

We were apparently moving to a place called Miami. The temperature there is always hot or hotter. Here in Poland, it's usually cold, so I wasn't sure if we were going to be able to stand the heat—especially because we were moving in spring, the second hottest season.

We were taking clothes, money, and a plastic sword I got when my dad started his two-year staying period in America. When Dad went to America for his job finding period, I was worried that he would stay forever, not get a job, and not be able to come back. My friend Tim got the plastic sword for me to keep me from thinking about Dad. I have always admired the sword from then on. I wished Tim could go to America with me. I wished everyone could come.

The security person checked our passports, wished us good luck in America, and we were on our way to the other security, like the scanners and the bag checks. At the bag checks,

by Charlie Kubica, 11
Chapel Hill, NC

the worker reluctantly informed us that we would have to wait so that they could make sure the plastic sword was safe. It took half an hour, and we almost missed our plane, but we made it. I hoped everything won't be that challenging in America.

We had never been on a plane before. We had to look around and figure out where the bathroom was. Another downside of this plane was the disgusting smell of rotten peanuts. I found a pretzel wedged into the crack of the seat that looked like it was two-years-old. These things would have made me gag, but working in a sausage factory that can't afford fresh meat most of the time drastically raises the strength of your gag reflex.

After a little while, the plane started moving. The unsettling sound of the wheels on the runway tortured me. Luckily, a safety video started playing, so I could listen to that instead. The video talked about what would happen if a plane crashed in the water. The video ended when we were in the air. I was afraid that the plane would fall out of the sky. How does a giant metal tube support itself in the air and not fall?

When the plane was flying straight forward, the flight attendant came down the aisle and handed out peanuts. I heard him mumbling about how he hates his job.

"Do you even want peanuts?" asked the attendant very rudely.

"Yes please," I responded. "Do you have them salted?"

"If you want them salted, put salt on them."

"I've heard that planes offer a choice between salted and unsalted peanuts."

"Uuugh. *Fine.* We have them in the back," he finally admitted.

He was *extremely* rude. I felt my fists clenching, and I even bared my teeth a little bit. I hoped people wouldn't be this rude in America.

It had been two hours on the plane. I really needed to use the bathroom. I tried to walk over to it, but I couldn't remember where it was. I eventually found it, but somebody was in it. My legs were crossed, and there was sweat beneath my eyes. But it finally opened! Huzzah! I walked in and...

All my senses except for my sense of smell momentarily stopped working. I can't describe the stench that invaded my nose. It was foul. What I smelled was a mix of basically everything that smells disgusting in the entirety of Poland. I gagged, and I kneeled to the ground. I also almost threw up directly onto the floor, which would have made the stench even worse. Yes, even with my enhanced gag reflex. I hoped it wouldn't smell that bad in all of America.

After I was done, I went back to my seat and ate more of my peanuts. The bag said the peanuts were "salted to the finest degree," but what it actually tasted like was a bag of salt with peanuts dropped into it. If all food in America was like this, I wouldn't be able to survive.

Sometime in the middle of the ride, Grandpa Skyped us on Dad's phone.

"Hello, Jim!" Grandpa exclaimed excitedly. "How's the ride on the flying tube of death?"

Out of all my family members, Grandpa was, no doubt, my favorite. He's funny and always kind. I wished he could come, but he wasn't allowed to because he had head lice.

"It's going alright," Dad replied, obviously lying.

Grandpa gave us a face like he does when he knows we're not being truthful.

"Hey, Zach, how's that sword of yours?" asked Grandpa.

I was glad somebody finally asked about the sword. It showed how much Grandpa cared about me.

"Good," I replied. We talked a little more, and then he hung up. I was feeling more positive about America now.

The ride had gone overnight, but it was finally finished! We landed at a very well-air-conditioned airport in Miami. I say it's well air conditioned because it had to work very hard to battle against the Miami heat. I was not looking forward to checking the weather. It might be too hot outside for me to stand. Well, now was the time to test.

But first we had to go through tons of airport immigration security. We waited in line for 90 minutes. My feet were aching, and my mind was racing with bad possibilities for what things could happen in America. When the security was at last done, we ventured outside.

I almost fell where I stood. It felt like it was a thousand degrees outside! I was dizzy, and I was sweating like a person from Antarctica wearing a fur coat in a garment factory in summer with no air-conditioning. I was definitely right to be worried about the weather.

"Oh my goodness!" Grandma Nicole exclaimed weakly. "It's hotter out here than it was in the sausage factory when the machine broke the third time!"

But weather was only one of our problems. We were low on money after the plane ride here. I wondered how small our house would be.

We carried our bags to the place where our house apparently was. I saw a huge building with tons of windows and doors. "Is that our house?" I asked happily, my confidence starting to rise a little bit.

"No, Zach. Well, some of it is," Dad replied.

I was confused. I had no idea what he meant. We started walking up the stairs of the giant building. Part of the building? That did not clear anything up for me. Dad revealed a key that was in his work bag and put it into the keyhole in one of the doors. When we opened the door, it was a tiny room with two beds, a nightstand, a bathroom, and a little closet.

"This is our new house! What do you think of it?" asked Dad.

But weather was only one of our problems. We were low on money after the plane ride here.

"It's good." I replied. But what I was really thinking was: *What!?! How is this even considered a house!?! We're all going to live in this thing!?!*

"Thank you for being optimistic, Zach," said Grandma Nicole. "It's the best we could do with how little money we have."

Well, I guess it was time to put on my brave face and get some rest, because the next day I was going to school.

On the walk to school, I took in the scenery around me. The trees were beautiful, and the ocean glimmered like freshly-cut diamonds. This was one thing about Miami that I didn't hate. What I do hate is:

The weather

The apartments

Wait. What am I doing? I'll hate Miami more if I think about the things I do hate. The things I like are:

The scenery

And I haven't come up with anything else. But at least I'm staying positive.

When I finally reached the school, I appreciated basically all the scenery in Miami. Even the school itself. The large bell tower in the middle made the whole rest of the school look good as well. But I had no idea what was coming my way.

I made my way to the classroom I was apparently assigned to. Room 344. I found a desk in the back of the room because I didn't want to get called on in class too much. Then class started.

"Hello, class!" exclaimed the teacher excitedly. "We have a new student with us today! Please welcome Zach Berkes!"

I didn't want anyone to welcome me. I just wanted to stay as quiet as possible. I couldn't say anything. I didn't know the words to. I couldn't speak their language. After a long wait, my teacher finally saved me from having to speak in Polish.

"Maybe he's too nervous right now. Let's try again later," the teacher replied to her own comment.

After awhile, we had a break. In America, they call it "recess," which is probably an English word for "przerwa." I went outside and saw all the swings, slides, and jungle gyms we had in our old school. It was the first thing at the school that made me feel at home. But, just then, some kid who looked like he was very overweight walked up to me. I started biting at the sides of my nails, and I felt my sweat start to stick my clothes onto me. He was also saying a bunch of English words I didn't understand. The kids around me let out gasps and "ooooOOOOhs," so I'm assuming they weren't good words.

"Nie lubimy imigrantów," said the kid, his posse surrounding him.

That meant "we don't like im

migrants" in Polish. I'm guessing he learned to say that in almost every language.

"We don't want you here," added the kid, in English.

Then he pushed me. My eyes were wide, and I was sweating basically everywhere. This kid was not nice. I landed on the concrete and one of my baby teeth broke out. The sting felt like three bees had just stabbed the bottom of my gums at once. The hole was bleeding. Badly. No adult saw me. And that's the last thing I remember before I blacked out.

I woke on a very uncomfortable cot in the nurse's office.

"Don't worry," said a lady I thought was the nurse. "He won't hurt you again. We suspended him."

I wanted to ask how she knew who hurt me, but I didn't know the words.

When I got back outside, the kid was gone. But, just then, I heard a "Witaj! Czy wszystko w porządku?" That means "Hello! Are you alright?" in Polish.

Then I turned, and a boy was standing right behind me.

"Słyszałem, że Joshua cię popycha," he said, which means "I heard about Joshua pushing you."

THIS KID SPEAKS POLISH! I thought excitedly to myself. Maybe there are other immigrants in the school, immigrants that speak all different languages.

"Tak, wszystko w porządku," I replied, or "Yeah, I'm okay."

"Hey. My name's Greg. Greg McAllister," he told me, as we spoke Polish.

"Nice to meet you! I'm Zach. Zach Berkes," I informed him back. "Do you know a place where I could learn English?"

"If you want to learn English, there's a class called ESL that you can take, where a bunch of immigrants learn English," Greg replied.

My mind was made up. I was going to take that class.

The next day, I went through a bunch of classes in English like math and reading. But, close to the end of the day, I walked into a room that had a big sign on the door that read "ESL." Of course, Greg was there, but there were so many other people that spoke so many different languages, too! A boy named Jav spoke Spanish, someone named Brenda spoke French, and a girl named Yutong spoke Chinese! Those are just a few examples. There were so many of them!

At the end of the class, I went out into the hall and bumped into Jav by the lockers.

"Hey, Zach," Jav greeted me, in English.

"Hello," I replied, saying my first ever out-of-ESL English word.

I was actually very calm for the first time in a while.

Maybe all my worry was for nothing. What was I thinking? America is pretty cool. I would give a lot of things to not go back to Poland. The jobs there were horrible, and our family probably wouldn't do so well. It's hard to enjoy a place like that. Eventually, I thought, my worry would most likely die down a little, and I would have a great time. I can definitely settle in a place that has all these immigrants. If Greg can do it, I can do, too!

A Field at Sunset, *Nikon Coolpix L830*

by Hannah Parker, 13
Burlington, VT

Home

by Pauline McAndrew, 9
Larchmont, NY

"Cousins!" I hear a little voice call. Two small, sticky hands wrap themselves around my legs. I see two shining blue eyes beaming up at me.

"Pauline!" I turn around to see Uncle Brendan and Aunt Kathy striding toward me, warm smiles spread across their faces. I hug my uncle, and immediately I inhale the sweet, piercing fragrance of pine trees, a whole forest of them. He makes me want to go deep into the forest brush and take a sip from a cool, fresh stream. I bury my face into Aunt Kathy, and the warm, homey aroma of fresh hot cookies draws me in. But I am pulled away from them all too soon and led out by another pair of sticky hands to where the grass is up to my thigh. I then see the old, ragged tire swing I've known for more than half of my life. I run toward it and slide on, for even though it appears as if the slightest tap will cause it to collapse to the ground, it can be trusted.

The tree begins to sway and creak slightly as I glide serenely from side to side. I slip off, and jog over to the wooden fence out where the cows graze. I lean over to stroke their bristly coat and fish around in my pocket for my leftover apple slices to feed them.

"Come on, Pauline!" more laughing cousins shout. "We're collecting wood for the fire!"

My cousins are all sorts of ages, sizes, shapes, and hues, but to us that matters no more than the types of clothes we wear. The soles of our shoes have walked the same ground, so we always play together as one.

I hurry to catch up with my cousins and we set off, a little wagon rumbling behind us. We find all sorts of wood around old barns so frail no one had the heart to knock them down. Driftwood, bark, pine cones, wood chips, even a long, slender black leg from a piano with missing keys. We bring it all back to Uncle Brendan, and we watch him whittle away on the sticks as we savor the captivating sunset. Any northern sunset can be beautiful, but a North Carolina sunset is really something special. The fading sunlight leaks through the trees like water through a strainer.

Uncle Brendan adds the shavings to the mountain of wood, which erupts into flames. We gather in a circle around the fire, shoulder to shoulder, sitting on logs, chuckling with each other in the firelight. There are grandparents, parents, aunts and uncles, brothers and sisters, cousins and more cousins. Everybody. Sparks dance in the air, like little lanterns held by invisible hands as we begin toasting the marshmallows and popcorn. The smoke rising up through the curls of flame gives off a wondrous scent. It smells of Uncle Brendan's pine trees and Aunt Kathy's cookies. It smells of sticky hands and old rundown barns. It smells of almost-burnt marshmallows and popcorn. It smells of home. Home sweet home.

A Child's Memoir

by Alejandro Lugo Saavedra, 13
Lithia, FL

The sky's vibrant gray was an embodiment of metallic hues colliding. Smothering the arid landscape like a hazy hand. The shrill, choppy thrilling of the desert songbirds forewarned of night's arrival. It would soon engulf the soothing ash-stricken contour in its obsidian abyss. A boy treaded through the sandy asphalt of the neighborhood, shoes clomping steadily in a monotonous rhythm. He wore an apparent trait, weariness. His cheeks were pinched in a nostalgist manner. His wiry silhouette was accompanied by a downcast shadow. Willow-worn and sallow, his facial complexion was pleasant and provided an atmosphere of easy-goingness not displayed in his current state. Even his rounded, melodious, Tuscan-brown eyes, were glassy and non-talkative. Taut palo verde trees shimmied their decumbent leaves in the brisk breeze, waving at the youth, clearly unaware of the flora. The boy's fervent forehead glistened with beads of sweat, which threatened to cascade in a trickle of perspiration. The malicious heat was exhausting him. He trembled back home; the impulse of a phantom burden suddenly seized him.

"Gabriel!"

A gasp of distress from afar jarred him. His puffy, crusty eyes unfurled a minuscule sliver. The comfort that pulsated from his body relieved him like a tight fist blooming into a hand.

He sighed.

"Yes Mom?" Gabriel skimmed his bronze-skin hands across bedhead eyes. Wiping the discomfort away.

"It's time to go to school, son."

Gabriel groaned in displeasure. In a relieved-but-sleepy-and-grumpy manner. He was a forthwith Pennsylvania native, after living six years in a cramped, but comfortable apartment. He hailed from Phoenix, Arizona however, and his childhood was a bustle. He had lived in Caborca and Chiapas, Mexico. His lucid flashback as a flourishing five-year-old living in the Sonoran Desert seemed all too genuine. *Real? Not real? Somewhere in between?* Answers to questions lost in the dusty catacombs of time.

Hawkins Middle School of Lebanon, Pennsylvania. Gusty, frost-heaved riptides of a draft wavered across strikingly lofty oak trees. Crisp, autumn leaves crunched into multicolored ash under Gabriel's feet. Steam-like figurines spatially billowed from his mouth. The suggestively glacial weather exposed the middle schoolers to a seductive quantity of indoor time. No recess. Gabriel felt enclosed and captive; his school's vicinity was restricting to him. He was accustomed to swaying freely with the frisky undergrowth caressing his liberated feet in a tender embrace.

Gabriel was heartfelt about nature and its conundrum. He was captivated preeminently by insects and akin. Abounding ubiquitously, he was obsessed with every nook and cranny of their existence and strived to unearth their every secluded perplexity. Winter was agonizing to him. A full six-month period without a trace of an insect. Eradicated. Vanished. Like a potent existence switch, winter blanked them. Mrs. Roseté, his superb science teacher, comprehended. She was a captivating reliance to him. Their prominent similarities encompassed them. His vision fazed and sputtered. Daydream. Gabriel gasped: A hollow sound that momentarily resonated against the dingy cut-rate aluminum lockers. He remarked grainy rubber gaits on the azure and cyan filamented tiles of hallway 300. He bolted to homeroom. He roughly gripped the doorknob in his right hand, gingerly turned, and winced as the bulky, birch-wood door chirred.

"Take a seat, Gabriel. Glad you're on time."

Gabriel's mind churned as Mrs. Young, the mathematics teacher, coursed through algebra "…And so, the domain of a parabola . . . " Boredom beckoned with succulence. Its enticement held affiance. Gabriel endured, aggravation vexing to reign. Despite struggling to stay on task, he felt satisfied in school for the most part. But all this would corrode to an abrupt halt.

A pace from bus 40's stationing was their corrivated home. A rusky apartment with crude clay-mound bricks as the structure. He clutched the hand-polished bronze handle on their door and jerked. His dad's concern radiated as he talked to his mom from the meager living room, a formal silence of speech that barricaded any suggestive normality element. This altered him, although he blundered mentally to comprehend. He noisily trampled inside, hoping for his parents to perceive him. To no avail.

"Hello Mom!"

He was answered with a concerned smile. A phony, concealed grin. Dinner was eaten in the quietness of secludedness. Gabriel merely an eyewitness account of an unprovoked speech. He felt his parents' selectivity of words. As though they strained their words. The exchange of words, or the lack of it, left him on edge. Stress overwhelmed him in a void of isolation.

A discussion took place that night. A finalizing, executive meet. They took in consideration their social position, their experiences, and especially Hawkins Middle. The stale bitterness of Lebanon's wind rimmed the fleur-white stalks of their windows with coincidental gloominess. A crest-fallen Gabriel contemplated the memories he constructed. Snow, friends, school. Fuzzy brightness flooded him. Ghosts, reaching their tinge of liveliness in limbs of animation. Things. Gained, earned, made. Fairytales of whimsical aspects. Summarized as his memories.

"Son, it's final. We're moving to Florida."

Gabriel managed a faint nod. In
time, the rhythm of tempo paved
weeks beyond seeming. May brought
a floral boutique of daisies, cherry
blossoms, and cul-de-sac poppies.
Gabriel felt equilibrated and integrated
with the time he had left. He chased
and tumbled around the foliaged hills
he had come to know. The earthy
soil a hearty perfume. Walnut trees
loomed atop. Their ridged trunks a
nutty brown. June fletched into view,
the vastness of May dominated by its
upheld viewpoint of expectations.

An act of kindness was shared by
Mrs. Roseté and her alumnus. A beautiful necklace of enlaced golden hoops
and a hug were exchanged between
the two. The last day of school cur-
tailed. Gabriel and his parents snugly
lodged their possessions into the truck
and drove into the amber dusk.

Farewell Lebanon.

Wheat in Heaven, *Nikon D3400*

by Delaney Slote, 12
Missoula, MT

Raking the River

by **Charlotte Tigchelaar**, 11
Huntington, WV

Jeff Kovatch Memorial Ohio River Cleanup,
Harris Riverside Park, Huntington, WV

My father
reaches out with the rake
and pulls the bottle toward us.
I pick it up with my litter-getter and
drop it into our big green plastic bag.
"I'm raking the river," he says.
We both laugh.
I think that would be a good idea for a poem.

No one knew

by Jada Kovatch, 11
Huntington, WV

The rain pounded the windows. No one knew
what to do . . . What would happen to everyone? The baby started to cry. He had been
born in a happy, sunny place.

Mysterious Moon, *Nikon Coolpix L830*

by Hannah Parker, 13
Burlington, VT

The Blue Planet

by Arabella McClendon, 13
Racine, WI

Captain Vistyz Stausk is on a mission to find and destroy malicious planets in the universe

Captain Vistyz Stausk paced the command center of her ship. It had been her father's ship, but he had passed onto the next multiverse a Sastorian year ago. Captain Stausk missed Sastorus, but she missed her father more, and thus stayed with his ship.

She had been given a commission to either find and destroy or rehabilitate particularly malignant species. Sastorus and its brother planet, Castea, had been attacked by an unknown entity that left as quickly as it destroyed. This was one of the more far-reaching and broader missions to stop both their attackers and the general malice in the universe. So far, they hadn't disintegrated anyone, but they also hadn't found any civilization that didn't need serious help. The crew's morale was low and what they needed just then was to come across a kind and loving race that they could ally with. They seemed to be in luck, as Captain Stausk's co-captain, Naeq, came in with a report: "Smallish blue planet off the starboard side. Looks to be inhabited. Should I organize a scouting party?"

Captain Stausk thought for a minute before replying.

"No, just set up gear and a landing pod for us two."

~20 minutes later~

Vistyz and Naeq unboxed the high-tech, to-be-reserved-for-special-missions, highly-adaptable camouflage suits for the seventh time that voyage. They lamented their one-size-fits-all label as they squeezed their six limbs inside and climbed into a two-person landing pod. As they sat in the dark interior of the white, bubble-shaped contraption, hurtling towards the little blue planet, they both thought about how wonderful it would be if the inhabitants were nice. How perfectly lovely it would be if they could negotiate an alliance. How highly likely it was, based on the laws of statistics. Sadly, they were wrong.

The first thing the two noticed was that the planet was divided up into nations, each with a different language and different customs. Of course, though they would be much stronger united as a whole planet, they had to be forgiven for this fault because of the language barrier. Yet another thing they noticed within their first "week" (a term used to describe seven days on that planet) was that most of the world's leaders were power-hungry and corrupt. They didn't work together peacefully, as would have been best for all on the planet; instead, they squabbled among themselves childishly. Many of the humanoid inhabitants were without basic necessities, while others had an almost disgusting surplus of material wealth and currency. The planet itself was polluted and littered, which took its toll upon the flora and fauna, which had done nothing wrong. Even worse, some beings were considered less than or more than other beings simply because of trivial surface traits! And when Vistyz and Naeq began to perform experiments of moral character and look into the minds and psychologies of many, they found irresponsibility, avarice, malice, and many more things. Captain and co-captain were saddened by the fact that so many vibrant cultural traditions and kind, loving people were overshadowed by the much larger amount of bad.

Back aboard the ship, Vistyz called a meeting with all of her advisors, counselors, friends, and trusted allies. They argued about the fate of the planet for many earth days, talking in turns, sitting in reflection, screaming at each other, and then laughing about it afterwards. Finally, they came to the conclusion that they could neither destroy, nor heal, this planet. There was too much wrong and sadness to be fixed by an outside force, but the goodness and kindness was enough that it could not be destroyed. So, they isolated it: they placed a special barrier around it, preventing interaction with any other planets or societies until the good in this planet became enough to destroy the barrier. They had a chance to change.

And so Captain Vistyz and her ship went on its way, but this violent little planet, violently good and bad, had left its impression on many. Some were significantly saddened by the wrong and the dirty, but others were uplifted by the good and clean and pure they had seen there. Many were confused, others convinced that they had done the right thing.

All would remember it.

Found

by Maya Wolfford, 13
Cincinnati, OH

The fire-colored butterflies
Flying drunkenly
Silently sipping on the budding milkweeds.
Snowflakes delicately falling
Landing on open mouths of youth.
The lake, calm and tranquil
Silently discovering the ocean.
The smallest trail of smoke
Making its way to the sky.
Fate isn't sealed
Like an envelope,
Instead it guides
Like the rails on a cliff
To prevent falling
Into a never ending
Darkness.
Or the stars
Dotting the sky like freckles
To prevent the sailors
From stumbling into a whistling whirlpool.
Not all maps
Must be followed.

To Contradict

The waterfall, thought as brave,
Viewed as unwearable, unstoppable, ablaze,
Secretly cowers and hopes to end its days
But continues to roar and never strays.
The brambles, viewed as fierce and tough,
Ignorant, guarded, as if they've had enough
And stay like that until they wither,
Pretending to be cool and tastelessly blither.
The garden, swaying with the wind
Seen as vulnerable, flimsy, weak, and thin
But only leans with this harsh blow
Because it has learned to go with the flow.
The ocean, scrubbing away at the sand,
Knows it could do something much more grand
But still tries to reach for the land
With a watery, frothy, desperate hand.
The dirt, seen as filthy and rotted,
With jewels and gems its depths are dotted
But still it chooses to follow the dark way
For it's afraid to be seen with a happy day.
The pebble, smoothed down by the stream,
Seen as solitary, so hadn't tried to join a team
And as it tried to let out a scream
Beneath the waters, it was held, serene.
But the rose, viewed as superficial behind thorns
Was expected to laugh with pity and scorn
At the ugly weeds as they were promptly picked
But instead it didn't, thoughtful to contradict.
And until this very significant moment
It had been waiting for the bestowment
Of the gift it had long ago earned:
The petals it has, since young age, yearned.
And this is how the rose gained its beauty,
For performing a kind act, a necessity, a duty,
And now you look at the rose and think pretty
Instead of low, arrogant, and gritty.

The Standing Mountains

by Cora Gelman, 8
Washington, D.C.

They are frozen

but not yet gone

They feel so sad but cold

I can't

Oh I can't feel my body

when I stare at them

for they're so great

and I'm so small

Fog on the Mountains, *Nikon Coolpix L830*

by Hannah Parker, 13
Burlington, VT

The Hut on the Hill

by Linden Grace Koshland, 11
Berkeley, CA

The ferocious waves slapped against the shoreline, spitting mist and bits of white foam into the crisp air. The gray clouds conquering the sky like a vast cotton blanket of darkness responded with the occasional crack of thunder. Rain beat down hard onto the backs of seagulls desperately searching for cover. The gloom was a plague that reached the toes of everything in the vicinity. Everything, that is, except a small wooden hut daintily perched atop a towering hill rising from the ocean. It observed the storm with a sort of wisdom and knowledge that pleased it, because it had lived a long life and knew many secrets. Its small form looked ready to be swept away by the wind like a miniscule piece of dust, but it sat firmly on the hill, proud of its resistance. A large oak tree curved over it, partially shading it from the merciless rain pelting from the heavens.

Inside the hut, a crackling fire burned merrily in the hearth, and a large, cushioned armchair stood invitingly before it. There was a cozy-looking four-poster bed in the corner of the single room, its colorful quilt pulled back and the mattress still warm. A kettle dangled before the fire, the hot water inside bubbling and boiling like children frolicking on a warm summer's day, the pot whistling along, too. Over on the corner opposite the bed, a little table was placed with two sides against the wall, with windows bearing cheerful, yellow-flowered curtains directly above them. A single three-legged stool was beside the table, and the remains of a berry pie was on a china plate beside it. Near the table was a wooden cupboard, the door ajar. The door on the other side of the room swung open as if a ghost had entered, and, from outside, the pleasantly fresh smell of petrichor wafted in, signaling that the rain had lessened. Emerging from the clouds, the sun shone, a bright light illuminating all the earth. Out the window of the hut, a gorgeous rainbow arched across the sky, basking in the glory of both sun and rain. The little hut sighed and creaked slightly at the wonderful sight. *What a great view,* thought the hut. *I hope another storm comes one day.* And, with that, the hut gave a huge yawn and fell fast asleep. The floral curtains slid closed, the fire lessened to glowing embers, the kettle was still, and the covers of the bed slowly were pulled over the mattress.

And although the hut was empty, it would always be full to the brim with memories of Home.

Wild Wyoming Horses

by Gwen Deutsch, 12
Dubuque, IA

As the horses ran down the mountain like a raging
sand storm, I knew I was in Wyoming.
The swift, creek water was mint in my mouth.
I felt sandpaper as I touched the horse's hair.

I turned around to see the trees of the forest swaying as if
they were rocking their leaves to sleep.
Everywhere I walked I could smell the scent of the
flowers like the perfume of a beautiful women.

I found myself crying as I watched the beautiful
horses run across the plains beating
their hooves to a strong, clear beat.

Honor Roll

Welcome to the *Stone Soup* Honor Roll. Every month we receive submissions from hundreds of kids from around the world. Unfortunately, we don't have space to publish all the great work we receive. We want to commend some of these talented writers and artists and encourage them to keep creating.

Fiction

Isabel Angle, 10
Beatrice Cappuccio, 8
Wyatt Goeckner, 9
Vivian G. Hoffman, 11
Avery McPherson, 12
Caleb Meyaard, 11
Maggie Tan, 11

Poetry

Maya Kalbach, 11
Emily Maremont, 11

Art

Natalie Dougan, 13
Coco Wu, 12

Don't forget to visit Stonesoup.com to browse our bonus materials. There you will find

- 20 years of back issues—around 5,000 stories, poems and reviews

- Blog posts from our Young Bloggers on subjects from sports to sewing plus ecology, reading and book reviews

- Video interviews with *Stone Soup* authors

- Music, spoken word and performances

Visit the *Stone Soup* Store at Stonesoupstore.com to buy

- Magazines—individual issues of Stone Soup, past and present

- Books—the 2017 *Stone Soup Annual*, a bound collection of all the year's issues, as well as themed anthologies

- Art prints—high quality prints from our collection of children's art

- Journals and Sketchbooks for writing and drawing
  . . . and more!

Soup

NOVEMBER   VOLUME 46 / ISSUE 10

StoneSoup

The magazine supporting creative kids around the world

Editor
Emma Wood

Director
William Rubel

Operations
Jane Levi

Education & Production
Sarah Ainsworth

Design
Joe Ewart

Stone Soup (ISSN 0094 579X) is published online eleven times a year—monthly, with a combined July/August summer issue. Copyright © 2018 by the Children's Art Foundation, a 501(c)(3) non-profit organization, located in Santa Cruz, California. All rights reserved. Thirty-five percent of our subscription price is tax-deductible. Make a donation at Stonesoup.com/donate/ and support us by choosing Children's Art Foundation as your Amazon Smile charity.

Stone Soup is available in different formats to persons who have trouble seeing or reading the print or online editions. To request the Braille edition from the National Library of Congress, call +1 800-424-8567. To request access to the audio edition via the National Federation of the Blind's NFB-NEWSLINE®, call +1 866-504-7300 or visit www.nfbnewsline.org

Check us out on Social Media:

Editor's Note

Imagine if animals could talk: what we would learn, and how we might be different, and how much chatter we'd hear every time we entered a forest! In the fantastical stories in this issue, there is a talking, magical butterfly and a shape-shifting goddess of the forest. There are gods at war with humans over leaves. And there is a lovingly reared pig, who must be sold at auction. In the poems, there is nature in its real—and ever-strange and unknowable—state. In the art, fantasy and reality meet. I hope you will enjoy the magical, the animal, and the natural in this issue!

Best,
Emma

Submissions: our guidelines for submission are on the Submit page at Stonesoup.com, where you will also find a link to our Submittable online submissions portal.

Subscriptions: to subscribe to *Stone Soup*, please press the Subscribe button at our webpage, Stonesoup.com.

On the cover:
'Mighty Exquisite Parrot'

by Nicole Qian, 13 Auckland, New Zealand

StoneSoup
Contents

FICTION

POETRY

ART

The Legend of the Leaves

The gods gave people the greatest gift of all—leaves—but the humans kept demanding more and more

Long, long ago, in the days when dinosaurs roamed, and the Earth was filled with lush, green grass, the first people were born.

The gods shaped them from the mud of the Earth, dropping them on the soft ground and giving them shelter from harsh weather.

In the time before humans, the gods were lonely. They would eat and sleep and occasionally play bingo at the top of a volcano. But they never experienced joy or happiness like we do today.

So they created humans.

The gods would make houses and villages for the people to live in. They would give food to the people when they were in need.

The gods were so generous they gave the people the most valuable resource of all.

Leaves.

Now, when you first think about it, doesn't it sound a little silly?

But, back then, they didn't have the same animals as we do today. They wouldn't be able to make clothes or blankets without the soft animal skins we have now.

The gods saw the humans in distress. They were cold at night and made clothes out of tough alligator hides. So they took action. The gods thought up something that would solve the problem. Something common, that could be found everywhere.

And so they created leaves.

Lots and lots of leaves.

The people used the leaves right away. They made soft clothing to wear that was a million times better than the scaly lizard skin. They stuffed pillows with them. They even used sticky tree sap to glue them together and make roofs.

The gods gave them everything.

But, the problem was, the humans were still not satisfied. They demanded more from the gods. Better food. Nicer homes. More recipes for Italian beef stew.

The gods were astounded.

"They must be put under control. They want more, and they are greedy. If we give them more, the people will only want more. What can we do?" said Civerous, the most powerful of the gods.

"We must take away their things," replied Nethran, Civerous's son. "Maybe then they will realize that to survive they must do things for themselves."

Meanwhile, the people were gazing at the palace of the gods, perched at the top of the tallest volcano.

The palace shone with gold and bronze statues, depicting the gods themselves.

"We must have that palace to our-

by Marcus R. Bosley, 10
Amery, WI

selves," said the human leader, Sarah. "We will drive the gods out of the palace and live in it. We shall climb the volcano. Assemble the Warriors!"

People rushed off to gather the Warriors, the strongest men and women in the colony.

Sarah and the Warriors climbed the steep volcano to the gods' palace.

Sheggera, the eldest god, spotted them coming before they were even halfway up the volcano.

She shouted to the other gods: "The humans are coming to attack us!"

The gods rushed into the room.

"You are right, Sheggera. They have come to attack us. My son was right. We must take away what we have given them," Civerous spoke up. "If they attack us, we will fight back."

And the humans did attack.

And the gods did fight back.

A great war began, gods on one side, humans on the other.

It waged on for many years until the gods came to a decision.

"We shall use the last of our strength to drive them down the volcano. At whatever costs," Allegro, the wisest of the gods, said in a set tone.

"Aye!" said all the gods in unity.

"It is decided then," said Sheggera. "We will drive them down the volcano!"

And so the gods used the last of their strength. They piled it together and strained and sweat.

The volcano shuddered with power as hot lava started to come together into a big glob.

The human army stopped and stared at the lava spilling over the side of the volcano, heading straight for them. They screamed, dropped their weapons, and bolted down the volcano.

Civerous yelled after them: "Because of your ignorance, we shall take away what we have given to you. Once a year, we will take away your greatest resource—leaves! And in that time, you will be without clothes, without shelter! This was caused by you!"

The humans retreated down the volcano and never set foot there again.

The gods, however, died at the top of the volcano that day, having used up all of their remaining strength.

And so it is that every year, in the coldest days, trees lose their leaves. And so it is that the gods are no more.

Night and Day

by Hannah Parker, 12
Burlington, VT

Night is dark and mysterious.
Every soul is asleep.
Even the tiny baby birds don't make a sound
for we know the moon is quite big,
its falling, glowing gaze from up above.

The stars are bright.
The fairies dance under the twinkling lights.
In the moonlight, God casts a spell on the glowing Earth
to make the sun peek out from behind the clouds
again and again.

After the darkness has gone,
a big yellow ball of fire emerges from the sky.
Everybody is awake except the owls
who sleep and don't make a hoot.

Birds fly everywhere and tweet their melodies.
Butterflies flutter with excitement and dance along.
The sky is painted blue
like a canvas.
The sidewalks are warm under my feet.
It is time to shout and play!

As evening approaches,
God casts a spell to make the starry night appear
again and again.

Space Travel: Goh to Van Gogh, *acrylic on canvas*

by Caitlin Goh, 8
Dallas, TX

The Teacher

by **Charlie McDermott, 13**
Vienna, VA

The wind teaches
the bare trees
how to dance

The trees try but
they are not agile and thrash
like a beached fish

I wonder why
the wind does not
just give up

Its next lesson may
be more fruitful

The green leaves
flutter in the wind
against the bare tree

I wish that the
wind would teach
me how to dance

I wonder if
I would ever be
the wind's great pupil

Violet Break

by Georgia Marshall, 9
Marblehead, MA

Up, out of the Spree!
(of the city) he said
We should get out of town!
(in the meadow)

Do you know how breakneck it is?
to be alone (on a dusty bridge)
when you have a violet break?

Dancing in the sunshine
(bare feet) you see!
He was right all along

(Maybe I should propose)
in a violet break!
(and I did!)

Cherry Blossom Visitor, *Nikon Coolpix L830*

by Hannah Parker, 12
Burlington, VT

The Magic Female Butterfly

by Seven Guo, 6
London, UK

Long, long ago, in a scorching, wet rainforest, where the leaves of trees were covered in sweat, lived a poor family. They had: a sister called Vigo, a boy called Cancy, and a mother, but the father was killed by a crocodile.

One day, when Vigo was exploring the jungle, a vivid spark fluttered past. It was a butterfly but not an ordinary one because it was speaking. It sang: "Hi, girl, I'm The Magic Butterfly and poor people can make a wish!"

"Are you joking?!"

"No," the butterfly said while gliding. Vigo waddled towards the insect.

Then, as expected, the girl said: "I wish my family were the richest in the world!"

When Vigo got home, she found her house was loaded with gold as heavy as an elephant.

Then, ruthlessly, they started spending their wealth and bought a fabulous house. Soon the money ran out!

The End

George's Dream

by Yanni Yohannes, 9
Alpharetta, GA

A brilliant scientist invents a potion that allows people to live forever

My name is George. I'm a six-year-old boy. I have a nose-picking brother who annoys me constantly. I want to be a scientist. Specifically, I want to make a drink that will make people live forever. My mom and dad tell me that I have a good imagination. I tell my parents that I have 100 in science, and in every other subject, my grade is an 80. Also, I have won four science fair projects.

Like my parents, my teacher also says that I have a good imagination. My teacher says that I could be in the fifth grade science class, but my parents say that I am good where I am. It is not fair, but people in fifth grade may pick on me, so I agree with my parents.

I'm in college now; I skipped middle school and high school. I attend Harvard University, and I still want to be a scientist. I told Mr. Johnson that I want to make a potion product that will make people live forever. He almost expelled me because he said it was impossible. I decided to quit Harvard and begin working.

I use very complex math and science. After many years of challenging work, I knew that I did not have one material. For two decades, I have been looking for the right material. I have tried everything—sticks, rubber, liquid, fruits, rocks, and more. The weather reporter stated, "There will be a meteor crash on the border of Georgia and Florida." I live 25 miles from the border of Georgia and Florida.

The following week, the meteor crashed in the morning, and I went outside to see. I picked up a bluish red rock. When I returned to my house, I tripped, and the rock fell into the drink that I almost finished. When I looked at the drink, it looked and smelled like it was supposed to when finished.

I took a sip, and it tasted as it was supposed to according to my calculations. I knew that this was the last ingredient. I gathered all the bluish red rock I could.

A year later, I went on television and showed my product. Ten minutes later, companies gave me billions of dollars for my product. My parents called and asked if they could have some of my product. I refused because they hadn't believed in me.

Within an hour, I received trillions of dollars from Bill Gates and Warren Buffett because they asked for some product. One person said they would trade their baby for my product. I am very rich.

Over the next two years, I got married, and we had two children. The children are twins. They once switched their classes, and no one knew until I saw their handwriting. My children have millions of dollars, and they spend their money on candy and mansions.

Two-thirds of the Earth's population has purchased my product. I have everything I need: a hot pool, a house as big as Minnesota, limousines, a puppy, and even a McDonald's in my house. The problem is that I have too much paperwork. I also have complaints that my product doesn't work for cancer.

I wish I could just discontinue my product and create something else. I asked the president to discontinue my product, so I can have my normal life back again. However, I did not receive an answer. The next morning, my family was robbed. I lost billions of dollars. I asked the president to close my product again, and the answer was finally "yes."

I'm now a normal man with trillions of dollars who will live forever because I drank my own product.

Meeting of the Minds, *pencil and copic marker*

by Avery Multer, 11
Chicago, IL

The Emperor and the Animals

by Natalie McGee, 13
Pittsburgh, PA

The animals in the forest rebel when the emperor attempts to destroy their land with a new palace

Ra-ra-ra. Raurau-ra . . . An extraordinary barking cry shattered the frosty air. A huge black eagle settled itself on an icy birch limb. Ruffling his feath-ers against the chill, he stretched his enormous wings one last time before settling them comfortably on his back. Respectfully, he cocked his head to meet the calm stare of the small copper animal before him, her sleek hide spotted like earth dappled with sunlight.

Dea had taken the form of a rare Amur leopard and was reclining in the peeling branches of a birch nearby. The Protectress's draping tail swayed hypnotically as the sea eagle began his narration of the day's events. Through a series of harsh barks and calls, he told Dea of an emperor from the neighboring land who had come to build a palace in the birch forest. He explained that all of the creatures would be forced to move into the barren tundra surrounding the tiny woods and would have to live like reindeer, serving humans forever. The entire time, Dea sat with her tail twitching, showing no emotion on her severe face. When the sea eagle was finished,

the goddess sat up.

"I will take care of it," she stated peacefully. "It will all work out in the end."

The eagle cocked his head, preparing a question, but, when he blinked, the leopard was gone.

The emperor posed with his advisors on the barren hill outside the birch forest, surveying the wintry land which would soon be his.

"Your Highness?" a melodious voice echoed from behind the troop. The men turned slowly. Before them stood a petite young woman swallowed in a spotted fur parka. "I heard you have plans to build a palace in these woods, am I wrong?"

Surprised by the girl's audacity, the emperor responded affirmatively.

"And who might you be?" he asked.

"I am called Dea," the girl responded. "I have something to ask of you. Before you build in these woods, you must solve one riddle to prove your worth. As soon as you bring me the creature it is describing, you shall be free to do as you wish . . ."

The emperor glanced at his advisors, speechless.

"If you fail to do this, your palace shall never stand. Would you like to hear the riddle?" The trio of men started to speak, but were swiftly interrupted.

"All right! 'Legs and nose both long and red, night-sky hands and snowy head.' Would you like to hear it again?"

When no one answered, she repeated the riddle: "Legs and nose both long and red, night-sky hands and snowy head." And, with that, Dea skipped down the glittering hill, the end of her spotted sash fluttering like a tail.

Still bewildered by the girl's speech, the emperor watched the retreating figure curiously until she disappeared among the frozen birches.

Suddenly, both of his advisors burst out into cacophonous laughter, rolling in the frost-laced grass, and doubling over, slapping their knees. The emperor whipped around, his heavy furs slashing the bitter wind. He barked at his men to stop and ordered them to fetch him a plane back to the village, as it was too cold to walk. Though the rest of his fellow travelers laughed off the incident lightheartedly, the emperor remained in a sour mood, unable to push Dea's riddle out of his mind.

The next morning dawned blinding white, a thin layer of fresh snow blanketing the birches.

Bang . . . bang . . . bang . . .

The emperor shouted for the visitor to enter. The heavy oak door creaked open, revealing three of the royal architects, panting and ruddy-cheeked from the cold. The emperor scowled, extremely annoyed at being interrupted.

"Well, what is it?" he barked. "This had better be important!"

The man in front stepped inside, backed by his shivering comrades. "Well, sire . . . you see . . ."

"GET ON WITH IT!"

"It's the palace! Your Highness, we have been working with our entire team for a day and a night, but not a stick or a stone will remain where we have placed it. It's as if the land is enchanted or—"

"ENCHANTED?" the emperor yelled, ignoring the voice in his head reminding him of Dea's warning. "Of course it's not enchanted! The forest is as plain as you are, you lazy, cheating fools! Off with you! Away! I have no more need for you . . . GENERAL? GENERAL! Come and take these filthy malingerers out of my sight, and hire me some new architects while you're at it!"

"But sir—"

"SILENCE! I will deal with you when you return!"

The four men stumbled out of the house, the heavy door slamming behind them. Inside, the emperor paced the frigid floorboards anxiously. After this report, he had no doubts about the strange girl's message. If all was as it seemed, the only way to break the curse was to solve the riddle . . .

That night, after the generals in the neighboring cottages were asleep, the emperor himself emerged onto the moonlit snow, pockmarked by the smudged footprints of the morning's scuffle. Enveloped in layers of heavy fur, he made his way into the shadows among the birch trees.

Each crack of the ice-laced snow caused him to jump and glance around the shadowed forest. Every hoot from an owl or scuttle of a small animal sent a shiver down his spine. Over and over these noises haunted him, until he began to grow exhausted from the stress. The woods seemed innocent enough, and nothing bigger than a dormouse had scurried across his path. The emperor decided to sit against a tree and wait for his answers to arrive. After all, he couldn't see much in the dark...

Click ... Clickclick ...

The emperor woke with a start. The dawn was just breaking in the frosty forest, and a strange humming sound was resonating very close to his head. Slowly, he sat up and looked around, his back and neck creaking from a night on the ground.

Clickclickclickclick ...

"AHH!" the emperor whipped around and came face-to-face with a huge swarm of beetles. They were crawling from beneath the birch bark, swarming all over his parka, his trousers, his pouch of food! More and more of them, forming a shimmering wave with thousands of long, clicking, jointed legs.

Unable to move, he let out a quiet whimper. How could he, the king of all

he knew, be so disgraced by insects? Meanwhile, the beetles continued swarming from the tree. His fine fur coat was crawling with them. The emperor closed his eyes, swallowed hard, and did something he had never done before—he called for help.

"Someone, over here! I'm being attacked!

Mmrraaaa ... MrrraaAAAH ...

A strange, whining bleat resonated from behind the tree. The beetles all froze, then began scuttling away as fast as they could.

A large, furry animal lumbered out from the leaves and started snapping up insects with a short, tapered muzzle. Within seconds, the bugs were gone, and the emperor leapt up to leave.

As soon as he snatched his food sack, however, he stopped and turned slowly. Before him stood a medium-sized animal with long, gray fur and little, rounded ears. It looked a bit like a cross between a bear and a raccoon. The emperor cleared his throat.

"Well... um, I suppose I should... uh... thank you for that. It was very ... very kind of you to ... assist me. I shall forever be indebted to you and—"

"Oh, well, that's fabulous! You know, that is exactly what I need right now!"

The emperor stared at the creature in shock, his mouth hanging open.

"What?" the animal asked. "Oh,

Unable to move, he let out a quiet whimper. How could he, the king of all he knew, be so disgraced by insects?

of course! I am so sorry . . . I forgot to introduce myself! I am Raccoon Dog, and I need help. Since you are forever indebted to me, you can solve my problem! After all, no one ever helps Raccoon Dog. I was trying to fish in the river, but I can never catch any good fish. I heard your kind is good at this sort of thing, so . . . will you help me?"

The emperor had really no other choice than to assent.

On the way to the river, the pair passed many exotic animals. They all spoke very politely to the emperor and Raccoon Dog, like friendly passersby on a street. The emperor wondered how it was that he was all of a sudden able to understand them.

Suddenly, before them was a great stretch of frozen land, split by an icy-blue swath which was the river. Raccoon Dog and the emperor sat on a large pile of sticks by the river to fish.

Clack, clack . . . Clakclakclak . . . Clack . . .

A loud clattering sound came from nearby. A large white bird with gangly red legs and inky-tipped wings was clacking its beak impatiently. Apparently, it seemed to consider the pile of sticks its nest. Just as Raccoon Dog was suggesting they both move over, the emperor recalled Dea's riddle.

"Legs and nose both long and red, night-sky hands and snowy head."

Of course! This bird had to be the answer to the riddle! It boasted long, red legs and a long, red beak, as well as wingtips black like the night sky and a strikingly white head. The emperor leaped up and, much to the shock of the stork, lifted it off the ground and danced along the river.

"Aha! Aha! I have found the an-swer to my riddle! I can now build my palace here and all will be well . . ." He stopped. All of the other animals along the river had abandoned their jobs and were now backing away slowly, murmuring amongst themselves in strange barks, hisses, and growls.

"What is it? What's wrong?" The emperor looked around and finally located Raccoon Dog. "What are they saying, Raccoon Dog? What's wrong with them?"

His new friend only let out a cautious bleat and bolted into the forest. The others followed him in a cloud of foliage, leaving only the emperor and the stork.

The emperor stood shocked for a second, then his eyes widened. Instantly, his kingly brain put together his recent past like a jigsaw puzzle. If he built his palace among the birches, he would lose the bond he felt with its resident animals. After all, he would be kicking them out of their home. He set down the bird. "I'm sorry, Stork. Will you forgive me? I promise no one will ever hurt another animal as long as I live." The stork looked at him sadly, then darted away into the forest.

The emperor made his way back through the frigid birches. The sounds of construction resonated from the middle of the trees, and he plowed forward, determined to stop it at once. As soon as he reached the clearing, however, no one even looked up. Abandoned by all of his followers, he was instantaneously filled with aggression.

"STOP!" he bellowed. Very, very slowly, the work ground to a halt, and the emperor's people turned to face him. For the first time, he felt uncomfortable standing before them. "You must cease all work immediately." Shocked and angry protests rippled around the crowd, and the emperor could feel his influence quickly slipping away. He tried again. "If any of you threaten to harm another animal or clear any habitat. . . you. . . I shall. . ."

"He's crazy!" called a voice from the crowd.

"Yeah! What's wrong with him?"
RRROOOAARR!!!

All protests ceased as a huge menagerie of forest animals, led by the stork and Raccoon Dog, burst into the clearing and took their place behind the emperor.

"Way to go!" whispered Raccoon Dog.

"If anyone knowingly threatens an endangered animal, they shall be banished from the earth! Now, run, RUN and NEVER RETURN!!"

Completely startled by this, the people at the scene dropped their tools and dashed across the snowy ground as fast as their legs could carry them, chased by the horde of animals.

Finally alone in the clearing, the emperor looked up. Among the ice-laced branches, he thought he caught a glimpse of a spotted tail disappearing into the foliage.

Blue Leopard, *pastel chalk*

by Quinn Kammer, 13
Madison, WI

Alive

by Katie Turk, 11
Palo Alto, CA

Bright moonlight fills
the rainy forest.
Trees' leaves glisten with rain.
The shadow of a wolf
slices the white glow.
His paws softly touch the damp mud.
He has a place to go.

The moon flickers,
appears again
in a crack
between two treetops,
{the light shining like fire.}
The wolf opens his jaws,
throws his head back,

howls.

The sound echoes through the woods.

He ceases his noise.
His job is finished.

All around him
the forest awakens.
Owls' wings beat.
Rats scurry, bats squeak,
foxes growl.

He runs back across the mud,
paced by the rhythm of his feet against the ground,
and watches the black shapes of animals travel from tree to tree.
He has nothing more to do.
The night has come alive.

What the End Is

When Freya signed up for the 4-H hog project she knew she would have to say goodbye—but that didn't stop her from getting attached

I knew how it would end. I knew from that first spring day when my dad and I took the old green pickup over to Big Sky High School's Future Farmers of America (FFA) building and came back with the 25-pound piglet I called Ash. From that night when I carried an old sleeping bag out to the pen and snuggled up in the straw alongside him. I knew every morning, when I woke up at seven to make sure his feed and water were full. Every day when I let him out in the yard to teach him how to walk for the fair, when he taught me to do what sounds fun in the moment and that happiness is more important than checking items off my to-do list. I knew when I brought letters to local Missoula businesses asking if they would bid on my pig at the Western Montana Fair on August 11, 2017. It couldn't last. It would be smarter not to become attached, but I couldn't help loving him anyway.

I lie in the sawdust of the pen, arms wrapped tightly around Ash. Tears slide down my face and onto his warm side. I feel every breath he takes. Every heartbeat. But it's only days now until that beat grows quiet. He sleeps so contentedly. *Does he know what comes next?*

This was my third year in the 4-H hog project, so I had a decent idea of what I was doing, but it was still a challenge to train my pig. I would release him from his pen and out into the yard, and he would immediately run off to eat something. Pigs like to stick their snouts in the ground and dig up the grass, which is not exactly desirable for my family's suburban lawn. I would rub his belly, and he would flop over on his side and stick his legs out like a puppy. If I was upset about something, I would go out and sit in the pen with him, and I would feel better because he reminded me how good my life was. Of how lucky I was to be in 4-H and to get to raise pigs. Sometimes, on hot days, I would turn on the pump in the middle of the yard. No matter where he was, Ash would come running and drink as much as he could, standing directly under the spigot as the stream of water gushed over him. He was so smart that after a while he figured out that if he put his nose under the handle and pushed up, the water would turn on.

I hold Ash close, whisper his name, over and over, telling him I love him, telling him I'm sorry. I don't say it will

by Freya Jones, 13
Missoula, MT

be okay. It's hard to imagine that it ever will be. *How many times can I do this? Will there be a day when the pain finally pulls me apart, the pieces left to drift like shadows on the wind?*

Outside, children still roam the fairgrounds, dragging their parents from one ride to the next, screaming at the moment of weightlessness, suspended upside-down at the top of the Kamikaze, then careening in wild circles on the Tilt-A-Whirl. Teenagers laugh as they try to knock over a tower of bottles, spending more money than they can afford on something they never had a chance of winning. The world still spins; somewhere a man wins the lottery while another begs on the sidewalk. So much like me, that day I got my pig, and now as I let him go. People are born, entering reality at the same moment as others leave. I know this, yet it feels like life has been put on pause. The world slows its rotation, people hold their breath to see what comes next.

I close my eyes and lean my head against Ash's side. I think of the day I got him, so full of joy. My dad and I piled into the 1994 Chevy pickup, old stickers saying things like *flammable, do not play on or around* plastered onto the driver's side door. We pulled into the parking lot of the FFA building. The second I was out of the truck, I ran across the pavement and went to look for my 4-H friends and the piglets the FFA students would soon be auctioning.

This room, usually as bare and colorless as a black-and-white photo in an old magazine, had transformed into a bustling action movie. Full of sound and motion, adrenaline pulsing, an invisible electricity running through us all. The cold, concrete floor was mostly covered by makeshift pens and illuminated by metal heat lamps. We crowded around the pigs, commenting on which ones had the best muscle tone and build.

After half an hour, we moved into an adjacent room, and the auction began. The top 15 pigs would be sold to the highest bidder, at a minimum price of $250. A tall boy stepped out into the ring with a small, white pig, speckled with black spots. The auctioneer called out numbers, and I saw an arm raise. Suddenly my dad lifted his bidding card, and a quick scan of the audience showed that no one else was going to pay for the first animal. Just like that, I had a pig.

Though I didn't admit it then, I felt a pang of anger. This was supposed to be my decision. The price was amazing, only $25 dollars over what the non-auction pigs cost, so I didn't complain, but it took me longer to love him than it had ever taken me to love a pig before. The fact that he had not been my choice led me to believe that he was not the right one. Now, clinging to Ash like it was *my* life ending, not his, I can't imagine how I could have pushed him away. We only had four months together, much too short a time to waste on anything but unconditional love.

Ash stretches his legs and snorts, a small motion, but it's all it takes to push through my thoughts, bringing with it the realization that this really is the end. My tears slow, and I hang on tighter. He weighs almost 300 pounds now, but, unlike most people, I still see him as cute. I love the way his curly-cue tail wags when he trots around the yard. The way he always looks like he's smiling. He's only six months old, a baby really. I feel Ash's warmth, send my love. This is the last time I will get to hold him, I want to remember every perfect second.

"Time to go," my mom gently prompts.

I give Ash one last hug and whisper, "I love you." Slowly, I climb over the gate of his pen and walk away. I made a commitment when I signed up for this project and now I have to follow through. The air feels heavy, suffocating, like the force of the entire universe is pressing down on me, but I take another step.

I wake in the morning to a slow throbbing, deep in my chest. I can't even try to heal; every time I smile, I feel guilty, as if I'm betraying Ash by not completely breaking. I collapse in bed at night where sobs shake my body— rational thinking abandoned. Mechanics have taken down the Kamikaze at our fairgrounds, but I'm still spinning along on this wild ride.

Somehow, I manage to go back-to-school shopping and run to get ready for the cross-country season. My family squeezes in one last trip, and I meet my new eighth grade teachers. I wear a locket with Ash's picture in it, but, gradually, I need it less and less.

Mid-September, I climb off the bus and walk down my street. I look up and notice that the maple trees have changed color. Crimson and gold frame the sky. Leaves decorate the yards and crunch merrily under my feet. I know fall is the time when plants die, decomposing back into the ground, but to me it feels like a fresh start. I think of Ash and close my eyes. It hurts so much, but I am making money to support my future, and in doing so I'm also supporting the future of farming. There

Now, clinging to Ash like it was my life ending, not his, I can't imagine how I could have pushed him away.

are so many feedlots that treat animals cruelly, but with 4-H they have good lives. I gave Ash healthy food, my companionship, belly rubs, and his own water spigot.

The pain that comes with remembering is sharp, but this time there is something else, too. A spark of warmth, because, in less than a year, there will be a new creature digging up my yard. I'll take care of it, and then I'll sell it. I will never forget Ash, but that doesn't mean I can't move on. I take a deep breath, close my eyes, and let my pig go.

Dozing in the Sun, *iPhone 5*

by Estella E. J. Howard, 11
Alberta, Canada

Camping with Bears

by Rose Zimmerman, 7
Oakland, CA

The trees are like people running a marathon. The noise that's coming from them I imagine to be the sound of the crowd cheering.

I was in the car. My older sister Chanah and younger sister Sarah are fighting.

"We're here," my father shouts over the noise. Here at the campsite.

"How many more camping stops until Oregon?" I ask.

"This is the last stop," my mother replies. Yes! I cheer silently. It's not that I don't like camping, it's just going to be nice to sleep in a real bed.

We enter the forest which we are camping in. It's breathtaking. The sun hits the trees like a wave of light. It's magical. We check in at the wooden booth and we also find out there are bears. We all cross our fingers for good luck and head for the actual campsite.

That night, as we're climbing into our sleeping bags, I hear a soft rustle coming from outside the tent. What's that?" I ask my parents.

We all are quiet listening for other sounds. It comes again except this time it's a little squeak like a baby bear. My mother peeks out of the tent and gasps with surprise. We all peek out and see a family of bears eating our leftovers. It's an amazing sight. The stars are twinkling underneath the midnight sky and over a family of bears. I hear a sudden click of a camera. We all turn around in surprise. It's Chanah. She smiles sheepishly. "Sorry," she says, "it's just too much of an amazing sight not to take a picture," she protests. We all smile and laugh. Chanah smiles. We all crawl back into our sleeping bags and go to sleep.

Autumn Leaves

by Eva Bandy, 9
Quarryville, PA

I stand here,
still in the
open air,
paused in
a lawn of
crisp, crackly
leaves. I feel
sorry they
had to die.
I'd feel bad
to crunch.
I stand
still in a
strangely
deep
sorrow.

Letters to the Editor

Here are two letters we received from readers during the summer of 2018.

Dear Emma Wood, *Stone Soup* Editor,

I really appreciate all of the creativity and talent that is exemplified within the originality of *Stone Soup*. From my personal opinion as a reader, I am truly grateful for all of the work that you publish. Your magazine is the rare link between the youth of this country and literacy, which can inspire them as writers and artists. Because of its reliability and character, *Stone Soup* is definitely an essential resource for students, parents, and teachers alike. I am so grateful for all of the stories that this magazine has shared and which I carry with me. It was such a gift to take in the words other young authors wrote. I am also grateful that this magazine continually produces artwork that continues to inspire and push me to become a more creative and motivated version of myself. You continually show children different perspectives of the world, which is such a difficult thing to do, and your grasp and influence is so far.

Thank you for continuing to promote young creators; it is such a gift.

Sincerely,
Kendall Vanderwouw, 13
Nevada City, CA

Dear *Stone Soup*,

Recently, my teacher introduced my class to *Stone Soup*. After reading the book reviews, I submitted one. Sadly, it was not accepted. Now I think I will write a letter to you guys about *Stone Soup*.

I really like your website. I am on it at least five times a week. I love reading book reviews and poems. My classmate's book review on *Moo* caught my eye. After a while, you guys published it. I am almost done with 5th grade. I think you guys should add a section for adults because I love to read adult work, too! I can tell your website is extremely popular because of all the great work on *Stone Soup*. Personally, if I were to choose one of your awesome poems to include on another website, it would be "What's inside my messy head?" by Tommy Swartz. Your website is absolutely amazing, all the work you publish. I hope *Stone Soup* carries on forever!!

Sincerely,
Vincent Liu, 11
Manlius, NY

Do you have something to say about something you've read or seen in Stone Soup? If you do, we'd love to hear from you, and we might print your letter on our Letters to the Editor page! You can write us a letter via our Submittable page (choose 'submit' on our website menu and follow the link), or leave a comment on our website. Tell us what you think!

Honor Roll

Welcome to the *Stone Soup* Honor Roll. Every month we receive submissions from hundreds of kids from around the world. Unfortunately, we don't have space to publish all the great work we receive. We want to commend some of these talented writers and artists and encourage them to keep creating.

Fiction
Elise Dilci, 11
Elizabeth Li, 13
Anaya Shri, 12
Ella Thompson, 13
Kathleen Werth, 9
Jacky Xue, 11

Poetry
Alyssa Chow, 13
Zoe Roettger, 13
Oscar Samelson, 8
Shiva Swaminathan Strickland, 10
Lin Lynn Tao, 13

Art
Enoch Farnham, 11
Joshua Garza, 9
Emily Mao, 13
Kaitlyn Rose Sheman, 9

Science Writing
Aaron Du, 10
Jahnvi Mundra, 12
Allison Webber, 12

Don't forget to visit Stonesoup.com to browse our bonus materials. There you will find:

- 20 years of back issues—around 5,000 stories, poems and reviews
- Blog posts from our Young Bloggers on subjects from sports to sewing— plus ecology, reading, and book reviews
- Video interviews with *Stone Soup* authors
- Music, spoken word, and performances

Visit the *Stone Soup* store at Stonesoupstore.com to buy:

- Magazines—individual issues of *Stone Soup*, past and present
- Books—the 2018 *Stone Soup Annual*, a bound collection of all the year's issues, as well as themed anthologies
- Art prints—high quality prints from our collection of children's art
- Journals and sketchbooks for writing and drawing
  ... and more!

StoneSoup

DECEMBER 2018   VOLUME 46 / ISSUE 11

StoneSoup

The magazine supporting creative kids around the world

Editor
Emma Wood

Director
William Rubel

Operations
Jane Levi

Education & Production
Sarah Ainsworth

Design
Joe Ewart

Stone Soup (ISSN 0094 579X) is published online eleven times per year—monthly, with a combined July/August summer issue. Copyright © 2018 by the Children's Art Foundation, a 501(c)(3) nonprofit organization, located in Santa Cruz, California. All rights reserved. Thirty-five percent of our subscription price is tax-deductible. Make a donation at stonesoup.com/donate/ and support us by choosing Children's Art Foundation as your Amazon Smile charity.

Stone Soup is available in different formats to persons who have trouble seeing or reading the print or online editions. To request the Braille edition from the National Library of Congress, call +1 800-424-8567. To request access to the audio edition via the National Federation of the Blind's NFB-NEWSLINE®, call +1 866-504-7300 or visit www.nfbnewsline.org.

Check us out on social media:

Editor's Note

During the holidays, when cookies, cake, and hot chocolate seem to be everywhere, we tend to think of food as a comfort and as a delight. We don't often talk publicly about the many anxieties surrounding food, about the allergies, intolerances, and religious or ethical dietary choices that can make it difficult to enjoy a meal with one's friends and family. In this year's food issue, some of our young writers explore this darker side of eating, alongside its joys. We also have six delicious recipes to share with you, and hope you will enjoy sharing your kitchen with each other and with Stone Soup this holiday!

Submissions: our guidelines for submission are on the Submit page at Stonesoup.com, where you will also find a link to our Submittable online submissions portal.

Subscriptions: to subscribe to *Stone Soup*, please press the Subscribe button on our webpage, Stonesoup.com.

On the cover:
"Snow in Clouds"
Nikon Coolpix L830

by **Hannah Parker, 13**
South Burlington, VT

StoneSoup
Contents

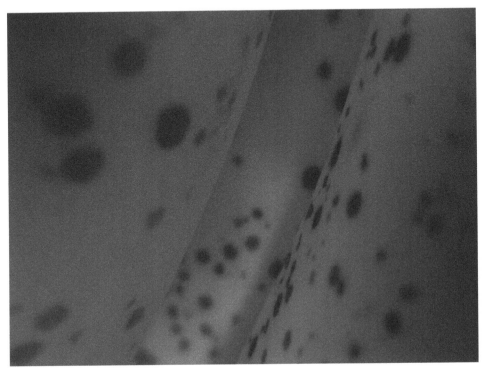

In the Land of Bananas, *photograph*

by Ula Pomian, 12
Windsor, ON, Canada

Composition o

by Sabrina Guo, 11
Oyster Bay, NY

An orphaned painter is given a daunting task—to paint her childhood

When my father first saw my mother on stage, he was amazed by how the words flew out of her mouth so naturally. I've never seen my mother perform, but in old photographs, she always appears angelic. She had luscious blonde curls and stormy grey eyes. She didn't have my frizzy brown hair or my big feet. I only have her grey eyes. In these photographs, my father looked like a young prince, with cool brown hair and soft green eyes. It was truly a miracle that they met—they would always look so perfect together no matter what.

I am an artist myself, in the studio art program at Yale. Throughout my life, I've been told I can paint anything, as long as I use my senses. If I hear a bird's song, for example, I can paint what it sounds like. I'll add a bit of yellow for happiness or brightness here, a bit of white and black for sadness or loneliness there. If I taste berries, I can paint bursts of sweetness in red, purple, and pink; if I smell oranges, I can express it as clouds of sunshine and gold filling the canvas.

My professor's name is Dr. Richards. Up until now, I've been allowed to paint the present world of sounds, sights, smells, and tastes, but Professor Richards wants me to do something different for my next project. He wants me to remember what my childhood was like and paint it. He gave an example of enjoying a good time with my parents, like a picnic. As if my childhood had been as predictable as that. But the problem is I have very few memories of my real parents. Of my mother especially.

My art studio is an abandoned classroom, a tranquil place that comforts me whenever I get stuck. There is a beautiful view through the window, looking over a small garden with pansies, chrysanthemums, and violets in the summer. You can also see the Yale flag up high, waving, and a perfect reflection pool by the main library. Sometimes I end up staring at it for hours, trying to imagine the different images cast into the pool or create pictures out of the sound of water trickling.

For weeks, I haven't known where to start with my painting. Professor Richards is insistent that if I try hard enough, my memory will tell me what to do, but I can't seem to get it across to him that it is impossible to find a single memory capable of capturing what I can't know about that memory. I guess it's just that I keep going back to how my parents met, wishing I could have been there.

When I try to think on my own

childhood, inevitably my mind wanders back to my parents at Juilliard, and that moment my mother first walked by the music room, not expecting the sound of my father playing the piano. My father had already been struck by my mother's voice on stage, so the fact she walked by, noticing him too, was the closest thing to fate there is, I think. And I guess I want to tell Professor Richards that this is the only memory I need to recreate, even though it isn't mine, but in a way, I want to tell him it is—because the simultaneity of these two moments is what allowed me to be born. I shudder to think of this miracle, that I am somehow here, *alive*—even though my parents aren't here to bear witness to that fact. Yet somehow, I think that if I can try to make my longing real on the canvas, my parents might be able to know that I live on through them and their first memory of one another.

I want to tell him that I'm stuck trying to envision the bright smile of my father and the warm eyes of my mother, the light on the stage, and my father's piano—he once told me his piano was the only way for him to understand anything, especially his love for my mother.

My mother died at the age of 30, when I was just four, and my father left just a week after she died, unable to bear his grief. I was raised by two adoptive parents, and though they have both been very loving and supportive, encouraging me to pursue my dreams as an artist, I still feel think about my birth parents, wondering if they also like to smell soap before they use it, or if they had to set their alarm clock in the same corner of the room, perfectly

aligned against the wall, or if they liked the light buttery taste of corn on the cob or toast as much as I do. I wonder if I would have needed these things as much, too, if my mother hadn't gotten sick and my father was still here to confirm my odd habits.

The repetitions circle my brain like a plague as I try to picture the room in Juilliard where my mother first discovered him playing. I imagine my mother in a pale green dress, walking past the door as "Somewhere Over the Rainbow" from *The Wizard of Oz* seeps through the door.

I imagine my mother pausing by it, ear pressed, devouring the sound of fingers gliding smoothly over the keys.

These repetitions should be enough I think, and I want to tell Professor Richards this, as I pick up a colored pencil and begin to sketch the outlines of my parents over the canvas. A pale green dress for my mother, like the stem of a violet. I hum "Somewhere Over the Rainbow" as my lines grow thicker. My humming is rudimentary, yet I can hear a whole orchestra in my father's single piano that leads to foggy streaks of blue and purple skies, the color of bluebells and soothing lavender.

I sketch a picnic scene and imagine a picnic basket we might have shared if they could visit me: creamed corn, corn on the cob, Greek egg salad, and, of course, sandwiches packed with lettuce, mayonnaise, and tomato, the kind my mother might have made if she'd never turned ill and could visit me here in New Haven, where the buildings are gray and shimmery in the rain and you can see all of the city at the top of East Rock. As I work, I think about how maybe memories don't always have to be figments from the past, but dream moments, hypothetical scenarios I might have had with the people who brought me into this world.

I draw sponge-like holes in the picnic sandwich bread as if the crusts were more important than the taste of fresh cucumbers my senses want to remind me of. I wish I could smell the variety of mayonnaise my mother liked best or know if she still made my father's with honey mustard even though she hated it. I envy my friends who take their memories for granted, the dozens of traditions and stories by which they can so easily recall their loved ones.

I am still trying to remember my fourth birthday, the last I would have had with my parents. I picture a bright and cozy living room with strings of lights bursting with color, illuminating everyone's happy face. I am sitting in my mother's warm lap, and she strokes my head. My father smiles and plops a perfectly wrapped box in front of me: flashing green paper, like the Emerald City, and a red ribbon for Dorothy's slippers. *Happy Birthday, my dear Lily*, his card said. *May you blossom with life.* I picture my father's meticulous handwriting.

But, as much as I want to paint with bright colors, I am overcome with this same feeling that the colors will never be vivid enough to match the sounds, tastes, and smells of the moment. I decide to swirl the sky with thick whites and grays like the tornado that sends Dorothy far from home— and, as I paint, I think of my mother's stormy eyes, how she might even be the eye of this storm, my memories

spinning around me in pieces: this mixture of my fourth birthday, my parents' meeting, the picnic sandwiches on East Rock.

It is as if my imagination is a tornado, and as I paint in a stanza from "Somewhere Over the Rainbow," the part that expresses "where skies are blue," I imagine fuzzy green grass, illuminated by a twinge of sunshine seeping through the clouds, as if my mother was walking towards my father in the piano room, somewhere outside of the frame. Into the beyond, somewhere my father met her, by fate, or by chance, I think, wishing for the music that might guide my brush.

Move forward, I think suddenly, imagining my mother getting closer and closer to my father, the start of their story, my story, converging at that moment.

I step back and look at the different layers of color, adding more gray and shadow to the clouds, but not so heavy as to cover the sun, and not too windy that the light would be extinguished, because only in leaving that glow and sensing my brush as it continues to stir, can I preserve time as a moment, let our love move on.

I AM Poem

by Kathleen Werth, 8
Silver Spring, MD

I am a singer and a vet
I wonder how people develop personalities
I hear flowers singing
I see a magic carpet
I want my dog to talk
I am a singer and a vet

I pretend I'm my favorite character in my book
I would feel great if I lived in nature
I touch a bird's soft silky feathers
I worry I will die too soon
I cry when something goes wrong
I am a singer and a vet

I understand I need to wear clothes
I say what you believe is what's correct
I dream I will meet a unicorn
I try to make a good first impression
I hope it will snow
I am a singer and a vet

A Trip to the Hospital

by Sophia Fu, 9
Belmont, CA

In the middle of Ms. Imura's lectures on geometry, I rested my head on my palms, with my elbows on the desk, and tried not to fall asleep. My eyelids felt like elephants. I got home from school and curled up on the couch. The room was spinning. My vision was double. And then I fell asleep.

"Do you feel okay?" my mother asked.

"Are you getting enough sleep?" my father wanted to know.

At school the next day, I threw up on my clothes. The teacher stopped class and said, "Sophia, you should go to the nurse."

Shortly after that, the nurse asked me, "How do you feel?"

"Not well," I told her, so she sent me home. That day, I climbed the stairs and curled up in my bed again and slept through the whole day.

On Saturday, I took more naps. My parents looked at me as if I were going to die at any moment and suddenly decided to speed me off to the hospital, where doctors and nurses put me in a bed and gave me a little, white teddy bear. It was a decently big room with giant machines and tubes and computers. There was a small table beside the bed where I put my stuff. There was even a TV in the room, so I could watch *Bunk'd* and *Mickey Mouse*. Also, there was a bathroom with a shower in the room. Out the window, I could see trees and the Stanford Shopping Mall. I had a needle poked in my skin and a tube connecting it to the IV. When I went to the bathroom, the nurse had to roll the "little metal tower" with me.

Finally, the doctor said, "You have type 1 diabetes." That meant my pancreas didn't make enough insulin to let the sugar go to the cells and make energy. She explained that I would have to check my blood sugar before every meal and take shots. When I heard that I had to take shots, I felt frustrated. I didn't want to take three or four shots every day before I ate! I imagined myself covered with dots. And even more, needles pricking my fingers just so I would know if my blood sugar was stable.

Three weeks later, I have gotten used to pricking my fingers to check my blood sugar and counting carbs, so I'll know how much insulin I need. At lunch, I miss sharing snacks with my friends, like potato chips and fruit roll-ups. Now I just eat rice, vegetables, fruit, and milk. Ten minutes before I eat, I have to check my blood sugar to make sure that my insulin is at the right level.

If I could go back and change anything, I would not have diabetes. However, I can't change that. Instead, I just have to get used to it and pay more attention to my health.

Storing Up, *Canon SX600HS*

by Sage Millen, 10
Vancouver, BC, Canada

The Girl Who Is Allergic to Everything

by Kyra Yip, 11
New York, NY

Allergies

A lot of people have allergies. Allergies to gluten, nuts, and eggs. I have allergies to a lot of things like nuts, seafood, eggs, and gluten. The list goes on and on. You're probably thinking how I can survive or if I'm lying, but I'm not. I'm alive. I deal with the consequences of being an allergic person. I've never tasted a gooey chocolate fudge cake with gluten in it on my birthday. I've never had scrambled eggs on a Saturday morning, as the sun shines through my window. I deal with it. This is my life. I can't grieve about how sad it is that I cannot eat certain foods. It's a weight that I've carried on my back for years. It's a barrier to enjoying things in life. It holds me back like a parent holds their child back from danger. In my life, having allergies is like a black stain on a white shirt that you can't wash off. It can stay there for an eternity.

EpiPen

Click. The sound the practice EpiPen makes as my mom plunges it into her thigh. For days, I've been dreading doing this. An EpiPen is a hero who saves people from allergic reactions. This is what the stories of kids being saved by their EpiPens have made me think. In the back of my mind, I know it is a shot that you have to plunge into your thigh.

My mom speaks, and it snaps me out of my thoughts.

"Now that I showed you how to do this, you can try. It has no needle, so it won't hurt," she says to me.

I take the EpiPen in my hand. The green color is inviting and almost seems friendly, but that won't fool me. The part of my thigh throbs, as I think about how much it would hurt if this was a real shot. *Deep breaths*, I tell myself. *This will save your life someday.* It shakes in my hand. *Ten seconds. Just ten seconds. Hold it only for ten seconds. It doesn't have a needle, so it won't hurt. It will be fine.* My thoughts go through my head as fast as a jet plane.

I drop the fake shot. I can't do it.

Even though it will save me, even though it is fake, I will not stab this shot in my leg for ten seconds. I will have to, or I might die.

"I will, I will, I will, I will," I mumble, as I fall asleep.

I will.

Birthdays

"Ooh! What did you bring?" says a classmate.

The birthday boy walks to the back

of the room with a bag. He holds it close to him. It's as if there is a priceless artifact sitting in a display case inside of it. People crowd around him trying to get a peek at what's in the bag.

"Cupcakes!" someone yells and is immediately scolded by the teacher.

The birthday boy chooses people to pass out the treats. In my head, I picture the creamy frosting covered with rainbow sprinkles and soft cake underneath.

No. I can't eat that. Can I? Nope. It contains wheat. Darn it!

"Hi! What flavor would you like?" says a boy who is handing out the treats.

"Oh. I'm okay. I'm allergic to that. I brought my own treat though," I answer.

"Oh. Okay," he mumbles, looking disappointed. Wait, it's pity.

"What are you allergic to?" he asks.

As I go down the list, his eyes go wide.

"Wow," he says. "You're allergic to everything!"

I look for some tone of a joke, but instead, I find that it is a statement. My cheeks burn, and I clench my fists so hard, it hurts. He walks away, leaving me to sulk about this for the whole party. Everything. The way he said it made my anger flare out. If I was allergic to everything, I would be dead. Nobody has ever said that to me before. I'm allergic to everything. I bet I'll be on the news. "The Girl Who is Allergic to Everything."

Twizzler Twist

"Hey. Do you want a Twizzler?" asks a teacher.

I look at the shiny twist of red color. I can smell the sweet aroma coming from the package of Twizzlers. I hesitate a little. *Am I allergic to this? No. The teacher wouldn't give it to me if I was allergic.* It calls to me, and I slowly inch towards the smell.

"Sure!" I exclaim.

I can't wait to try one! I unwrap the packaging and take a giant bite out of the sweet candy. A burst of flavor burns its way down my throat. It tastes delectable. After I finish my treat, I go back to play. After a while, my throat starts itching. My mind races, and I start to panic. This has never happened before! I shrug it off, and I figure it will go away. A few minutes later, my skin starts itching. It's like a million ants crawled under my clothes and started biting me. I need a teacher. I stand up, but I stumble because a wave of dizziness hits me. I feel as though I've been on a roller coaster that goes in a loop-de-loop for hours. I slowly make my way to where the teachers are standing.

"What's wrong?" one asks.

"I don't know," I say, panicked.

In a few minutes, my mom comes bursting into the room like a madwoman. Worry is present on her features, and I immediately feel sympathy. She must be so worried. I spill the beans.

"I'm so itchy, and I don't know what's happening!" I exclaim.

I start to tear up, and then I begin to cry. My mom hands me a medicine cup with pink liquid in it that I identify as Benadryl. I curl up into a ball, and I sob.

Why does this happen to *me*?

Cake Mistake

Before bed, my mom baked me a cake from a mix.

"Can I please eat one tiny piece?" I plead.

"Ok. Fine! Only one tiny piece," she says, smiling.

She hands me the piece of cake, and I gobble it up in one bite. My taste buds yell in excitement and pleasure.

"Thank you, Mommy!" I exclaim. I crawl into bed and drift off into a deep sleep.

All I remember is the itchy, scratchy, red hives that cover my skin, a towel on the floor picking up the dinner and dessert I had that now went up the other way, and a pink liquid that slides down my throat. Blackness creeps up on me, as I slowly fall asleep with my itchy, scratchy hives, as I am surrounded by the lingering sour smell of throw up that has just been cleaned up.

Epilogue

Allergies are not my burden. They are not my enemy. They have made me stronger as a person. I deal with rude comments and pity looks, but I don't care. I don't care if I'm allergic to everything. I don't care that you can eat some foods, and I can't. My life is not your life.

I wrote this memoir so that I could share my thoughts and struggles of being an allergic person with you, the reader. This is a small part that is neither good nor bad. Even though this has been something I hated earlier in my life, I won't ever let anything get in the way of me and others being happy. I will live my life to the fullest. I am me. I refuse to worry, and I will not let something like allergies bring me down. When I go out to a store with my friends looking for snacks or go out with my family, I laugh it off when someone makes a rude comment. I take this as a lesson, a challenge that I will face over the course of my life. I want to be those people who walk down the sidewalks, laughing, joking, being themselves, without a care in the world.

I have learned that when life gets hard, you can't just sit there and cry. Push through it when life gets hard. I know my friends and family will always be there and will support me, so I stand strong. I hope everyone does. Be happy. My mom always says, "You have one life. Make it count."

Ode to Flowers

by Irene Surprenant, 8
Santa Clara, CA

Oh, flowers, smelling like nothing else

Your colors shining in the sun

Sitting on the ground and grass

And swishing in the trees

Your petals blowing everywhere

So very beautiful

Red or green or yellow

And all the other colors

Oh, flowers,

I'm happy to be seeing you every day

Vase on a Stand, *acrylic paint, oil pastels, and tempera paint*

by Pearl Lee, 10
Greenwich, CT

Wave

by Irene Surprenant, 8
Santa Clara, CA

I am a wave

I splash on soft shore

I feel the yellow sand

Fishes gliding in me

All windy days

I am so big

sometimes

So big

called

a tsunami

On sunny days

I am so small

Sometimes

not even there

Birds chirping above me

I am salty

The sky above me

making me blue

Without it I'd be clear

People throwing trash in me

I hope it would stop soon

Because the fishes

eating it

dying

I can't feel

so many

tiny

scaly bodies

rubbing against

me anymore

But then more fish

get born

I feel them once again

I am so happy

Rainy Day, *Painter Essentials 5 on a Wacom tablet and computer*

by Mia Fang, 13
West Lafayette, IN

The Barista

by Thomas Jones, 13
Bradbury, CA

The barista in the LAX airport got to his shop at 5:00 a.m. and opened at 6:00. He did this so he could catch the early tide of people that usually came in at that hour. He would smile and give coffee to all of the tired, angry travelers that came through terminal seven. Their baggy eyes and solemn expressions spoke more than their halting words of thanks. He was the only barista who came at that hour and it usually paid off (along with the fact that his was the only coffee shop at terminal seven). His cafe was usually the first place people went when they arrived or were picking up people from a flight. He usually walked away with $200 in his pocket.

At the end of the day, he would have to walk through the entire airport. Because he started off as a pickpocket himself, he knew how to avoid them. They were usually the people who slunk in the back or to the sides of the walkway, and they usually preyed on the tired passengers changing planes when all they could do is try to bully their brains into thinking straight.

From his coffee shop, the barista could see everything. He saw a tired father watching his sons with tired eyes and a wife sleeping on the man's shoulder. He saw nervous, impatient people with bags, waiting in a security line for their bags to be checked, their minds rapidly going through all the things they had packed. A security guard was telling a young boy, "This three-cell flashlight is too big. You can check it or throw it away." The boy looked sullen as his father got the flashlight checked. Flight attendants looking like packs of wolves on the prowl clustered as they were. The barista was the benevolent watcher, seeing all, but not affected by all, the one who served with a smile and who walked through the airport like it was his own personal castle.

One evening leaving work, the barista's watching eyes saw a little boy no more than six, his tiny fist clenched on a small teddy bear until a hurried yank from an oblivious father made him drop it. The barista rushed over and tried to get the father's attention, but the man kept walking, powering through the crowd with long strides. As he searched the walkway he realized he had no chance of catching him. The barista walked backed to his little coffee shop, the little boy's distraught face still etched in his mind.

A month later, the barista arrived at his shop one day at exactly six o'clock. He opened the door and saw the little toy bear. He didn't know why he didn't throw it away. He picked it up and stared at the little brown body that had held such relevance to that little boy. He opened the trash can and was about to throw it away when he heard the counter bell ring and a muffled "Hey." He turned around to see the boy's father whose eyes were fixed on the bear.

"That is my son's," the man said.

The barista quickly handed over the bear and heard a happy scream of delight. He looked over the counter and saw the little boy hug the bear tightly to his chest.

"We've found Baloo," the boy said in a voice of shrill excitement.

The boy's father, obviously relieved, turned and shook the barista's hand. He said, "Thank you. We have looked everywhere since we got back." He turned back to the boy and said, "Do you want a hot chocolate?" The boy, still ecstatic, nodded eagerly. The father ordered two hot chocolates, paid the barista, and clasping his son's hand tightly, walked away into the tide of people. The boy held his bear tighter than ever. They were both happy.

The barista watched them walk away then wiped down the empty counter. They had forgotten to leave a tip.

Recipes

Basil-Asiago-Garlic-Olive Oil Tortillas

by Catherine Gruen, 11
Chino Hills, CA

Have you heard of the stinking rose? On nearly every dish that comes from our kitchen, the stinking rose is the star. So much are the garlic-filled dishes loved, it is common to say wholeheartedly, "Don't eat it all!" Once, my dad even ate a raw garlic clove, just to see what it tasted like. While I would never do that, I still love garlic.

Seven years ago, on April 16th, a cool breeze blew our neighbor's tree in front of the window that faced the street. I watched each passing car intently, wondering if it would be the one that carried my baby brother. In the wee hours of the morning, he had been born, and I couldn't wait to see him. My grandparents had bought my sister and me teal jelly beans, so I chewed them nervously as I waited. Just as the clock chimed 11:00, the garage door opened and I heard the small wails of a newborn baby. My sister and I made such a fuss over our new little plaything that we worked up an appetite. After a while of baby tears, my little brother fell asleep and Mama rested with him. Then Daddy cooked his forever-to-be-remembered Basil-Asiago-Garlic-Olive Oil Tortillas. My dad rarely cooks, but when he does, he adds too much cheese or too much garlic, which is awesome. The Italian-style tortillas became legendary.

My little baby brother loves these Italian-style tortillas and has grown to cherish the stinking rose, too. He now joins in the chorus of, "Don't eat it all!"

Taken in the Stone Soup *Test Kitchen*

Serves 1
Takes 7-10 minutes

Ingredients

2oz / 60g asiago cheese, shredded or thinly sliced (you can substitute with
parmesan, pecorino or other hard, melting cheese)
1½ teaspoons olive oil
6 leaves of fresh basil
1 small garlic clove (or half of a medium one)
2 flour tortillas (10-inch / 25.5cm)
1 tomato, diced

Method

1. Pour the olive oil onto a nonstick pan. Set the stove to medium heat.

2. Crush the garlic over the pan and sautée. Do not let it brown.

3. When the garlic is sautéed, transfer it to one tortilla. Place the tortilla, garlic side
up, in the pan.

4. Sprinkle the cheese over the tortilla.

5. Tear 5 of the basil leaves and put them on the cheese. Top with the second
tortilla.

6. Let it cook for one and a half minutes on each side.

7. Top with freshly diced tomatoes and the last leaf of basil.

Enjoy as an afternoon snack, appetizer, or a quick lunch.

Cream of Tomato Soup

by Lina Martinez Nocito, 13
Sunderland, MA

First of all, I love tomato soup. And knitting. (It turns out that these two things can be a very dangerous combination; strange, I know, but trust me.) Last Hallowe'en, I had almost finished a pair of knitted slippers, which I had been working on for a while—all that remained was to add grippy treads to the soles. But I didn't have time to add them immediately, and I was excited to finally try them on, so I was wearing them when my mom called me in for lunch. Tomato soup and toast with fresh goat cheese. Yum.

And so I, in my very slippery slippers, ran across the very slippery wood floor, and (you guessed it) I slipped. Not just slipped! My feet shot out from under me and I crashed to the ground, landing on my arm. My concerned mother, in an attempt to discern the extent of my injuries, asked if I could wiggle my fingers. Since I could, she was confident that I hadn't broken anything (it turns out that that is not a good test for broken bones). And it wasn't until the doctor insisted that I get an X-ray that we realized that there was anything wrong.

My arm healed quickly, though, and tomato soup is still one of my favorite foods. I've experimented with several recipes, and this one's my favorite. Enjoy—and please walk carefully when you smell its delicious aroma. . .

Photo by the author

Makes four servings

Ingredients

2 tablespoons extra-virgin olive oil
1 red pepper, seeded and sliced, or roasted peppers from a jar (the latter adds a particularly nice flavor)
1 large onion, sliced
1 carrot, peeled and diced
1 to 2 cloves garlic, chopped
4 cups / 800g chopped tomatoes (canned tomatoes work well, too—include their juice)
1 teaspoon fresh thyme leaves or ½ tsp. dried thyme
1 cup / 250ml chicken/vegetable stock
Salt and freshly ground black pepper to taste
13 oz / 400g cooked / canned cannellini beans (optional)
1 cup / 250ml cream (optional)

Method

1. Place the oil in a 3-quart saucepan and turn the heat to medium. Add the onion, pepper, carrot, and garlic. Season with salt and pepper and cook, stirring, until the onion begins to soften, about 5 minutes.

2. Add the tomatoes, beans (if using), thyme, and stock, bring to a simmer and cook for 10 minutes. You can proceed with the next step now, or simmer for up to 60 minutes longer for a deeper flavor. The beans will give a creamier, thicker, texture to the soup, so you may wish to add more liquid at the end.

3. Allow the soup to cool to room temperature. (You can refrigerate it for up to two days at this point before continuing.) When the soup is cool, add the cream and purée in a blender or food processor. Then, adjust seasonings and reheat before serving.

Honey Beach Bars

by Arielle Kouyoumdjian, 11
Fairfax, VA

Every year, my family and I harvest the honey from our beehives. We scrape off the thin lacing of wax capping, and honey glistens on the frame. It comes in a variety of colors, such as yellow-gold, a deep rust-colored gold, and dark brown. It is rich with flavor, a hint of flowers and clover. We spin the frames with honey in a special contraption that shakes all of the honey off, then filter it three times. I made a dessert with this honey and entered it into the 4-H fair, where it won the grand champion prize. Enjoy the dessert I created.

Photo from the Stone Soup test kitchen

Makes approximately 18 bars

Ingredients

Bottom layer:
½ cup / 115g butter
½ cup packed / 75g light brown sugar
1¼ cup / 160g all-purpose (plain) flour

Top layer:
2 eggs
½ cup packed / 110g light brown sugar
½ cup / 170g honey
⅓ cup / 45g all-purpose (plain) flour
1½ cup / 180g dried tart cherries
¼ teaspoon salt
½ cup / 30g shredded coconut

Method

1. Heat the oven to 350°F / 180°C.

2. Crumble the first three ingredients together until there are very few lumps, either by rubbing with your fingers or with a quick blast in a food processor. Make sure that there are no huge balls of butter. Gently press the mixture into a 9 x 9"/ 23 x 23cm pan. Bake for 10 minutes. While it is baking, start on the top layer.

3. Beat together the eggs, sugar, and honey, until the mixture is light and thick. Stir in the other dry ingredients and use a spoon to spread it evenly over the baked bottom layer. Bake for 25-30 minutes, until the top is golden. Stick a toothpick into the middle of the pan when you think they are ready, and make sure that no batter comes off on the toothpick.

4. Remove from the oven, allow to cool, and cut the bars into equal rectangles.

Matcha Crepe Cake

by Alicia Xin, 13
Scardsale, NY

When I think of a crepe cake, I think of the dainty mounds of crepes stealing the spotlight in a bakery window, the creamy sensation that explodes in my mouth after I take a bite. My family and I often go to a little bakery by my home to buy a slice of matcha crepe cake. One day, I thought, why not make one in my own kitchen? I decided to try with my friend Olivia. It seemed a bit intimidating, but how hard could it be?

On Saturday, we met at my house. We blended the crepe ingredients together to make a liquid green mixture, and then put it in the fridge to settle. When mixing the cream to go between the layers of crepes, we accidentally flung heavy cream everywhere. That attracted my dog, Archie. He made a beeline for any cream he saw, and we laughed as he smudged cream all over his snout. After three minutes, the cream hardened into an airy, white fluff, stiff enough to form firm peaks as we pulled the mixer out of the bowl.

Two hours later, we oiled the pan to cook a crepe. It wasn't until we spread the batter that we realized neither of us knew how to flip it. In the end, we managed a maneuver with forks and a spatula, and ended up flipping, but also ripping, the crepe. We called it our "tester", gobbled it up, and then made another one using that spatula operation. Our crepes looked better and better, and in the end, we had a beautiful stack of 20 matcha crepes. We spread the cream with a knife and layered them one by one. Finally, we sprinkled matcha powder on top with a sieve, and then gathered some mint leaves from outside to position on the cake. The end product looked surprisingly like a store-bought crepe cake.

As we were devouring our masterpiece, the combination of the delicate crepes and the sweet cream made every bite melt on my tongue and ooze with flavor. I was surprised that it was such a success, and I learned never to underestimate the power of a good recipe, quality ingredients, and some determination.

Photo by the author

Makes approximately 8 servings

Ingredients

For the crepe batter:
1 ½ cups / 350ml milk
3 eggs
1 teaspoon sugar
1 tablespoon matcha powder
1 cup / 130g all-purpose flour
2 tbsp / 30g melted butter
1 teaspoon baking powder

For the cream:
2¼ cups / 540ml heavy whipping cream
2 teaspoons sugar

Method

1. Mix all the crepe batter ingredients together. You should have a liquid green mixture with a consistency similar to a thoroughly blended smoothie.

2. Put the batter through a sieve, pushing through any lumps, and let it sit in the refrigerator for two hours.

3. In a separate bowl, add the sugar to the heavy whipping cream, and whisk it until it is thick, but easily spreadable. Put it in the refrigerator.

4. Butter a 10" / 25cm pan lightly and pour enough batter in the pan to thinly cover the bottom of the pan. Cook both sides of the crepe. To do this effectively, let the first side cook for a little while and then when the center is firm and the edges are starting to look cooked, try scooping up the edges of the crepe with a thin, metal spatula. Then shake the pan a little to free the rest, and flip the crepe with the help of some utensils. You may need to practice a few times! Do this with the rest of the batter, ending up with 20-25 crepes.

5. Let your crepes cool down, then stack them one on top of the other spreading a thin layer of cream in between each layer.

6. You may want to sprinkle some matcha powder on top of the cake, but this is optional. To make it look more professional, try sprinkling it with your sieve.

7. I put mint leaves on my cake, but feel free to put what you want on yours, such as raspberries or strawberries.

Enjoy!

Apple Rose Tarts

by **Mia Widrow, 11**
Olympia, WA

When I think of fall, I feel leaves crunching under my boots, globules of rain sliding down the window, and our big tall apple tree. It stands proudly in our yard, brown bark slick with rain. By the time school starts, the tree is drooping under the weight of sweet red apples. We pick hundreds of apples, giving away loads to neighbors and friends. My mom cooks applesauce in the big red pot, and I help my dad juice some to make cider. I think food should look, as well as taste, amazing. But applesauce and cider don't showcase the beautiful crimson of apples.

So I decided to make these delicate apple rose tarts. Since apples are a universal fruit, I think that everyone will enjoy this recipe. The roses are actually fairly easy to make, just make sure to slice the apples thinly. These make a perfect sweet snack or dessert. Enjoy!

Photo by the author

Makes about 14 apple tarts

Ingredients

1 sheet thawed puff pastry (if using ready-rolled, enough to make a total size of 14 x 10" / 35 x 25.5cm)
2 Gala, McIntosh, Fuji, Red Delicious, or other red-skinned apples
½ teaspoon ground cinnamon
¼ tsp. ground nutmeg
⅛ tsp. ground cardamom
¼ tsp. ground cloves
1½ tsp. lemon juice
2 tablespoons brown sugar

Method

1. Slice the apples thinly, about 1/16 of an inch / 2 mm. Do not peel them! If they are a little thicker, that's all right. Toss sliced apples in big non-metallic bowl and add in cinnamon, nutmeg, cloves, lemon juice, and brown sugar.

2. Roll the puff pastry into a 14 x 10" / 35 x 25.5 cm rectangle. Then, cut it into 1 x 10" / 2.5 x 25.5 cm strips.

3. Microwave the apple slices for 35 seconds, so they are flexible enough to roll.

4. Lay the apple slices on top of the dough strips, overlapping the edges.

5. Carefully roll up the strips. Lay the tarts rose side up—the prettiest cut edge up—in a buttered muffin tin.

6. Bake at 350°F / 180°C for about 40 minutes, or until the edges begin to brown.

7. Remove from the oven, allow to cool slightly, and carefully remove from the pan.

I like to serve these warm with a sprinkle of cinnamon on top. You could also try them with honey or powdered sugar.

Dairy-Free Apple Pie

by Maya Viswanathan, 12
Champaign, IL

The aroma of cinnamon and freshly baked dough. The taste of juicy fruit and a crisp crust. Lattice neatly placed over the filling. What could be more perfect than pie?

Pie always stood out to me, whether displayed in cafes or mentioned in books. It stands for a homey treat that is an American classic. Yet, as much as I wanted to, we never made pie at home. Don't get me wrong, we do bake a lot. We've made all kinds of breads, cookies, cakes, and tarts, yet never pie. Part of the reason is that nearly all pie recipes call for butter, and I am allergic to dairy. My efforts to convince my parents to find a solution never worked.

"Let's make a pie and substitute oil for butter," I'd suggest.

"The dough won't be the right consistency for the lattice. Let me look into recipes," my dad replies.

"You don't have the time for it. Let's just make a tart-it's the same thing," my mom put in.

But it isn't! A pie has lattice. And lattice is what makes pie a pie.

The curtain to the Broadway show Waitress *inspired me. It was designed to look like the top of a pie with a cherry filling and a golden-brown lattice. The show was about a waitress who had a hard life. She made scrumptious pies, through which she remembered her mother, and that cheered her up. Later, it helped her create a better life for herself. When the curtain closed at the end, again I saw the lattice and bright filling. Right then and there, I made up my mind that when I got home, I'd make a pie.*

The recipe I used was originally meant for Linzertorte. I made a few small changes: oil instead of butter and oat bran instead of nuts because of my allergies. And a dash of maple syrup, which my grandmother does to give the dough a nutty flavor. You can use any filling for the pie. It was summer when I made my first pie, so I made a blueberry-peach pie. Plain peach is sour, and the blueberries make it sweeter. I'm making this pie in the fall, so I am using apples. I think apple pie is a very wintery and autumn thing. I hope you enjoy making this pie and experimenting with flavors for different seasons.

Photo by the author

Ingredients

For the crust:
1 cup / 95g oat bran
1¼ cups / 160g all purpose/plain flour
1 egg, beaten
1 tablespoon of cold water
½ cup / 120ml olive oil (or sunflower oil)
1 tablespoon cinnamon (or to taste)
¼ cup / 50g white/caster sugar
1 teaspoon maple syrup

For the filling:
5 medium to large apples
½ cup / 100g white/caster sugar
1 teaspoon maple syrup
1 teaspoon cinnamon

Method

Prepare the filling:

1. Peel the apples and cut them into half inch cubes. Mix them with the sugar and cinnamon in a pot. Then add the maple syrup and cook on low heat for 20-25 minutes until the apples are soft. Stir as needed.

2. Preheat your oven to 400°F / 200°C.

Make the dough:

3. Mix the oat bran, flour, sugar, and cinnamon. Add the oil.

4. Beat the egg with the water.

5. Add the egg and water to the dough and then mix it with a spoon.

6. Mix it with your hands and then bring it into a ball. The dough might appear dry and lumpy, but that's okay. (If you can't bring it into a ball, then you can add a tablespoon of water.)

7. Divide the dough into two halves and put one half in a round pie pan, 8-9" / 23cm diameter. Push it with your fingertips so that the entire pan is covered with dough, including 1½" up the sides.

8. Put the apple mixture on top of the dough.

9. On a cutting board make a rectangle that is approximately 9 x 4" / 23 x 10cm with the other half of the dough by pressing the dough with your fingertips until it is evenly thick. Then cut it into 9" / 23cm strips, each ½ " wide (1.25cm), ending up with 8 long strips. Now use a knife to pick up the strips and lay them over the apples, 4 in one direction, 4 in the other, evenly spaced. Then weave the strips. If a strip breaks, you can stick it back together with your hands when it is already on the apples, or make sure the join is underneath another strip.

10. Bake the pie at 400°F / 200°C for 20 minutes, and then reduce the heat to 350°F / 180°C and bake for another 25 minutes.

Serve and enjoy!

Honor Roll

Welcome to the *Stone Soup* Honor Roll. Every month we receive submissions from hundreds of kids from around the world. Unfortunately, we don't have space to publish all the great work we receive. We want to commend some of these talented writers and artists and encourage them to keep creating.

Fiction

Kayla Bjorn, 13
Aditi Chowdhary, 10
Julia Marcus, 11
Martha Mayes, 10
Luna Castro Mjoica, 11
Addison R. Vallier, 13

Poetry

Vandana Ravi, 12
Ivy Segal, 13
Ezra White, 6
Cecilia Yang, 12
Caitlyn Zhu, 10

Art

Joshua Garza, 9
Madeline Nelson, 12
Gabi Park, 13
Mary Rothermel, 10

Comics and Graphic Writing

Kathleen Werth, 9

Don't forget to visit stonesoup.com to browse our bonus materials. There you will find:

- 20 years of back issues—around 5,000 stories, poems and reviews

- Blog posts from our Young Bloggers on subjects from sports to sewing—plus ecology, reading and book reviews

- Video interviews with *Stone Soup* authors

- Music, spoken word, and performances

 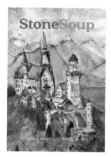

Visit the *Stone Soup* store at Stonesoupstore.com to buy:

- Magazines—individual issues of *Stone Soup*, past and present

- Books—the 2017 *Stone Soup Annual*, a bound collection of all the year's issues, as well as themed anthologies

- Art prints—high quality prints from our collection of children's art

- Journals and sketchbooks for writing and drawing
  ... and more!

This Year on the Blog

Have you checked out the Stone Soup blog? We publish excellent work by young bloggers every week on every topic under the sun—nature, sports, knitting, and everything in between—as well as opinion pieces, reviews and graphic art. Here's a selection of our favorites from this year, including some from our new Book Review section.

Young Bloggers

NBA Tanking
by Leo T. Smith
Posted April 9, 2018

When the Chicago Bulls announced that Cristiano Felício and David Nwaba would start in place of Robin Lopez and Justin Holiday, it was not so that they would win more games. It was exactly the opposite. In the NBA, every bad team tanks. Tanking is losing games intentionally so that you get a higher draft pick. When you get a better draft pick, you get a better player. When you get a better player, you have a better team. When you have a better team, you win a championship. When you win a championship, more fans come. When more fans come, the owner gets more money. Basically, tanking is for billionaire owners to get even richer.

Tanking is supposed to be illegal, but the NBA doesn't enforce the rule. During prohibition, law enforcement knew that speakeasies existed and didn't do anything. When Mavericks owner Mark Cuban said that his team should lose games, Adam Silver, the NBA commissioner, fined him $600,000. That may seem like a lot, but Cuban has a projected net worth of $3.7 billion.

If you want to know why the NBA does not punish teams for breaking the no-tanking rule, you must know why the rule was created. In other leagues, like the NFL, there are power-houses (like the Eagles) and teams like the Browns (0-16 last season). If the Browns play the Eagles, it will most likely not be competitive. The reason that the NBA established the no-tanking rule is that they hope that more fans come to games, thinking it will be too über-competitive. Again, when more fans come, the owner gets more money.

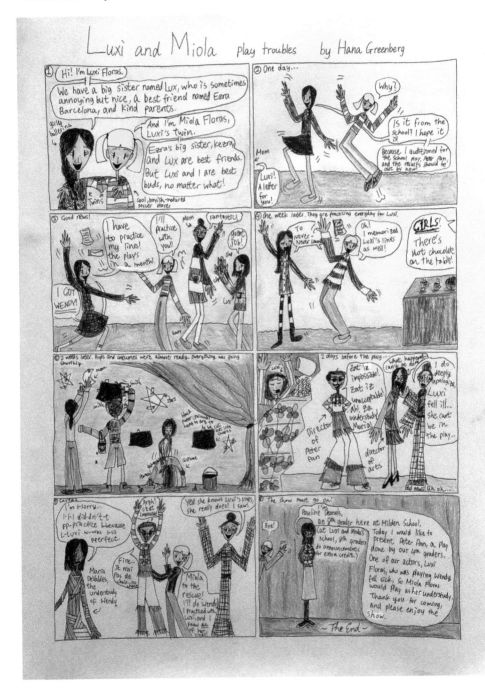

Luxi & Miola—The New Girl
by Hana Greenberg
Posted July 27, 2018

Get Started with Birdwatching
by Rebecca Moberly
Posted February 28, 2018

If you're interested in birds or you read my last post, you might want to bird-watch. It's pretty easy to get started, but here are a few tips if you get stuck:

- Just watch. There are birds every-where. You just have to look out-side. There will probably be some birds. If you want to know what kind of birds they are, you can just look it up on the computer or your phone.
- Some more advanced things to do are using a field guide and note-book. A field guide can be useful if you just want a physical book to read to identify birds instead of a website or app. A notebook can be fun if you want to write down the birds you see.
- Bird feeders, houses, and baths help you attract birds to your yard. Bird feeders are also fun because lots of birds can come to them, especially in winter when there is less food. Buy some wild bird food, and then make or buy a feeder, or just spread out the food on the ground and wait for the birds! Bird houses are cool and sometimes work. Make sure to get a good one. It's really fun to see the parents going in and out of it, and you might even see the babies' first flights! Bird baths are also nice because you can see the birds bathing and it's really funny, but make sure you clean out the leaves every once in a while.
- Binoculars are nice to have and help you see close up. It helps for identifying birds in a flock at a feeder, or just birds that are far away.

I hope this helps you get started. Good luck and happy birdwatching!

---

5 Ways Children Can Make a Difference
by Lucy Regnier Kline
Posted March 5, 2018

By now, we all know about the school shooting in Parkland, Florida. Seven-teen students and teachers are now dead, and many more are injured. I, for one, am tired of hearing about so many children that are dying, in addition to other mass shootings in our nation.

However, for those like me, it is diffi-cult to support the fight for gun con-trol. As a kid, I cannot do much—one of the major things being voting. Another problem is that sometimes adults do not take children seriously. I find it hard to speak up and raise my voice. I know that this is true for many kids with strong opinions. It can be scary

Detail from illustration by Erik Zou, 10, for "The Radiant Melody."
Published in *Stone Soup*, March/April 2011.

381

to fight the standard, especially when your elders belittle you or weaken your voice.

I've compiled a list of things you, as a younger person, can do—not only for gun control, but for any political topic.

1. Social Media
I know that many of the younger children reading this may not have social media or even phones, but if you are a bit older, this can be really important. So many people are on social media, such as Instagram, Twitter, and others. If you really want to spread your opinions, social media can be a great place to start. Not only is there a lot of publicity, but you can keep as much of your identity as you want secret. People may take you more seriously, and might even listen to you.

2. Write to Politicians
In our society, politicians have all the power. They write the laws and approve them. They are the ones that can make a difference. By writing to senators, congressmen, even the president, you can change a vote. By knowing what the people think—what the future people will think—politicians can work to fulfill the ideas so many citizens are behind.

3. Write to Magazines and/or Newspapers
Although most publications want more professional writing, there are plenty that do accept submissions from children. There are also many that will take letters to the editor. You can always find out how to submit letters on the magazine's website. As for writing

sources written by kids, you can find a list of good publications at this link: https://www.authorspublish.com/15-magazines-that-publish-writing-by-children-and-teens/. Some of them have age limits or writing guidelines, so make sure to read those before submitting anything.

4. Express Your Opinions Through Art Forms (Including Dance, Drama, and Singing)
If you are not into writing, or you are into artistic expression, this can be a great way to show a story or point of view. Many artists create work that showcases the political environment of the world at present. For inspiration, look at pieces created by artists. This can include fine art, photography, and plays.

5. Talk About It
Talking to people in power can be really useful. Even if it is just your parents or someone else in your family, discussing your opinions can make a difference. Giving older people new ideas can help them spread the word. They might also give you new ideas to think about, and therefore expand your political insight. In addition to talking to authority, you can also strike up a conversation with other kids. Children have more flexible minds, so they might be less stubborn and be willing to listen to you. Who knows, you might even have them question their ideas, and change for the better.

I have an African proverb on the calendar in my room that says, "If you think you are too small to make a difference, try sleeping in a closed room with a mosquito..." You are never too young to change the world. Remember to keep on fighting for what is right, and don't ever back down from it.

The Winds of Change
by Lukas Cooke
Posted April 8, 2018

Photo by the author.

As I stepped into the morning sun, I found that it was not as cold out as it had been these past few months. I went back inside to quickly change out of my jeans and sweater into shorts and a t-shirt. My boots felt unusually hot as I pulled them on and walked out the door into my yard. And there I felt the wind. But I realized it was no regular wind, but rather the Winds of Change. And upon them rode Spring.

I walked towards the barn, breathing in the fresh air. A smell mingled with the oxygen, the smell of new blossoms on a tree, a little pungent, but not altogether unpleasant. Reaching the barn, I opened a stall door, for in the stall was a small chicken house, and within the chicken house, month-old chicks.

It was that season. Chicks could only be bought in spring, where I lived, and to our family, they were one of those cute little miracles that are one of the things in life that makes us happy. They were gifts of the season, just for us.

A little while later, I was watching our burn pile crackle and pop as it burnt up old logs we didn't need. My dog Lucy was sniffing around in the grass next to me, and suddenly I heard a squeak. At first I thought it was one of the many birds that were singing their hearts out around me. But then it became obvious that it was close—and right behind me. I turned and saw Lucy pawing at a small hole in the ground.

I bent down for a closer look. To my astonishment, I found a mole frantically digging to get away from her. It disappeared, and I turned away. But then I noticed that Lucy was still nosing around, and at a nest of woven grasses. What I saw melted my heart

Two small mole babies, who hadn't even yet opened their eyes, were nestled comfortably into the dried grasses. I shooed my dog away, and picked the nest up. I was astounded to find two more mole babies nestled in a different part of the grass. I gently picked them out of the spots they were in, for otherwise they would have fallen to the ground, and put them with their siblings.

I looked to the ground, searching for any other mole pups who might have fallen from the refuge of the grasses. And I found two more. I hurriedly put them with the rest of their family, and began to study the way they looked.

Their paws were definitely a digger's paws, sharp claws at the tips of tiny toes. The moles' small heads had rounded noses with multiple tiny whiskers protruding from them. No ears poked out from the heads; I couldn't detect any earholes either. Their fur was a dark brown color, and was very soft to the touch. All in all, they were hardly as big as my thumb.

And, hard as it is for me to admit, I found them very, very cute.

An hour later, I found their mother. She was in the same hole. I gently set her offspring down into the hole, and watched as she took them one by one to wherever she lived. I was sad to see them go, but luckily I had made a couple of pictures.

As the mole mother took the last of her babies away, I thought to myself, The Winds of Change are here, and they are bringing much new life, among other things. Goodbye, little moles. I will miss you.

The Winds of Change truly are here, Mother Nature slowly rebuilding what was lost in the past year. And when the Winds leave, they will have left a better Earth.

Knitting Socks and Learning from Someone Younger Than You
by Sarah Cymrot
Posted July 15, 2018

Zoe kindly–like always–helping me with my sock on a ferry. Photo by the author.

My fingers crept along, slowly following the pattern—wrapping the yarn, twisting, poking, prodding. My sister's fingers flew. "You are still there?" she would say, teasingly, every few minutes. By the time I had finished the first row, she was at the fifth, by the time I was at the fifth, she was at the fifteenth. How embarrassing. What was I doing letting my younger sister tell me what to do, act like she is better than me?! And yet, here she was. Carefully guiding me, experimenting, correcting, laughing with me, at me. Who was I to pretend that I wasn't having fun or that she wasn't doing a perfect job?

There is usually a bizarre discomfort that older siblings have when their younger sibling—or any younger person—starts teaching them something. I feel this discomfort sometimes and try my best to fight it. My sister, Zoe, and I have a wonderful relationship. We homeschooled together for 6 years and my parents mostly decided to pull me out of school so that we could spend more time together, resulting in a close relationship between us. However, children grow up these days with a strong distinction between ages. When we start school, we are separated by age into grades, almost never crossing in between. We are led to believe that older kids learn more complicated stuff, so they must clearly be more advanced, and therefore do not need the help of younger kids.

In the homeschooling world, ages interlap often. My close friend group for most of my homeschooling time was made up of kids both four years older and younger than me. We were a group of varying ages, personalities, and experiences. The differences in our ages didn't separate us, instead it enriched our friendships. Now that I am in school, I can feel myself slipping back into the mindset that I should not hang out with kids that are a different age than me and it impacts my opportunities for friendships at school and at home. When I push myself to break the barrier of age, the different stages that the kids I meet are in and the interests that come with them push me to think harder and be more compassionate, resulting in my greater happiness.

When I think of Zoe as an equal, someone who I can learn from and grow with, I find myself growing in ways that I wouldn't normally. Our personalities and interests overlap and twist together, like knitting, making something special.

I finished my sock a couple of weeks ago. It is a little crooked in some places, has holes in others, and is in no way comparable to Zoe's pairs of socks, but it carries the air of a new skill. It has reminded me that I am not stuck to people only my age, but am able to learn from everyone.

My finished sock! Photo by the author.

This summer, reach out to someone younger than you and let yourself learn from them. Whether it be your younger sibling or someone else that you know, try to push yourself out of your comfort zone. Happy learning!

Tara Abraham's Reflections on the Syrian Refugee Crisis
by Sabrina Guo
Posted August 30, 2018

Tara Abraham is the Executive Director of Glamour Magazine's The Girl Project, which promotes education for girls around the world who are not in school due to war, poverty, child marriage, and gender-based violence. Ms. Abraham traveled to Jordan in January 2018, to the Za'atari and Azraq refugee camps, as a part of the UNICEF USA delegation. I recently had the chance to listen to her speak when she gave a talk through Harvard's Alumni Global Women's Empowerment group called "Reflections on the Syrian Refugee Crisis." It's estimated that 1.4 million refugees have fled to Jordan since the Syrian war began. Ms. Abraham interviewed refugee girls at the camps about their daily lives, how they were affected by leaving Syria, and what educational opportunities were available to them.

Za'atari Camp was the first refugee camp to be founded in Jordan. The number of buildings there can seem endless, for they stretch to the horizon as far as you can see. It is home to almost 80,000 people and is considered Jordan's fourth largest city. However, Za'atari was not planned—as people leaving Syria crossed the border into Jordan, they stopped almost as soon as they entered safe territory. Za'atari camp sprang up where they stopped, just twelve miles from the border. Shelters were hastily built in clusters without any kind of planned infrastructure to support the community. Because of this, the camp faces logistical challenges when it comes to things like security and delivering water to the people who live there.

Due to its close proximity to Syria, Ms. Abraham said the sounds of ammunition and explosions are audible within the camp; even though the refugees had escaped from the war, the sounds of battle still followed them. Along with the trauma of having left their homes in Syria, the people in the camp face practical challenges as well. For example, they only receive twenty-eight dollars per week for food, which is not nearly enough. Also, there are extremely few formal job opportunities for refugees in Jordan.

Despite all of this, Ms. Abraham explained the resourcefulness and resilience of the community. To make ends meet, some refugees travel to Amman, a city in Jordan, to buy goods that they can then resell at a profit to others in the camp. Also, because Za'atari grew organically, Ms. Abraham said it felt more like 'life' than other camps she visited, which were planned. In Za'atari, people plant vegetable gardens between the jumble of shelters— life springs up here and there. There's even a main market street, complete with barber shops and food carts, nicknamed the Champs-Elysees, after the famous street in Paris, France.

According to statistics, families can spend an average of up to 10-18 years in the camp. In other words, an entire generation can grow up within the camp. For example, while Ms. Abraham was there, she met refugee children who were as old as 5 or 6 who had been born at Za'atari and knew no other life besides it. She described seeing girls and boys playing on the side of the road, just running around 'being kids.' It struck her as strangely carefree given the circumstances. UNICEF has set up Makani ("my space") centers to provide some educational and recreational outlets for young girls and boys. At the centers, kids do things like compete in soccer games, paint, and play with building blocks.

After a few days of being in the camp, Ms. Abraham noticed something unusual. She began to realize that she rarely saw any adolescent girls outside of their houses. As she explained it, once girls hit puberty, they began to be more exposed to the companionship of men and all of the real and perceived risks that come with that. The parents, seeing their daughters' vulnerability, restrict the girls' movements to keep them safe and protect their virtue. Parents don't want older girls to travel around the camp alone or even in small groups. Often, the older girls only leave the house with their mother or another older family member to go grocery shopping or visit people in their homes. The rest of the time, the girls are doing 'women's work': cooking, cleaning, collecting water and caring for younger siblings, which is all incredibly important work for the family. However, Ms. Abraham couldn't shake the feeling that as the girls retreated inside their homes, which she described as 'aluminum boxes,' they disappeared from other parts of their lives, including school.

Luckily, the coordinators that work in the Makani Center are often young refugees themselves and can provide some support for the girls because they understand what they have to go through every day. But sometimes they meet resistance from the families, who worry about sending the girls alone to the Center, so the coordinators do everything they can to build trust with the families. For example, if the families are worried about their daughters walking alone to the center, they arrange transportation for the girls. Ms. Abraham spoke to two coordinators at the center, both young and married, who described their efforts to develop a pathway for the girls to keep attending school, and also help give them guidance and emotional support for life skills. They like to encourage openness in topics like boys, relationships, or wearing a bra for the first time. The girls look up to the coordinators as role models who aren't a mother or sister, but rather a trusted mentor outside of the family who can give advice. The girls need extra support when they reach adolescence, because life is harder and more complicated at that point—they are entering the age when they might have to marry.

According to statistics, many Syrian girls as young as twelve are discontinuing their education and getting married to much older men. Parents struggling to feed their families sometimes choose to marry their young daughters to other households to ensure economic security. UNICEF staff told Ms. Abraham that just a few years ago 8% of children under the age of 18 were married. Today, that number has risen to 38%. It may appear to an outside viewer that these families must not care about their daughters. Ms. Abraham stressed that this was far from the truth—families are desperate to figure out a way to help their daughters survive and have domestic security. The parents are in what Ms. Abraham described as "an impossible position," having no good options from which to choose. When daughters are presented with an opportunity to marry, families sometimes feel that the girls must accept the proposal since it's uncertain whether there will be similar opportunities later to ensure their safe economic future. Despite the challenges that families face, Ms. Abraham saw hope. For example, while some families' older daughters are married off at a young age, the parents hope that with more time and economic stability their younger daughters can marry later, at 19 or 20, and continue their education until then.

Thanks to Tara Abraham's talk, I learned so much more about how much refugees truly struggle and what they must go through in their day-to-day lives. I was struck by Ms. Abraham's passionate, well-informed, and determined voice. She is truly an inspiring role model!

Special Feature: Kids React to Gun Violence
Posted May 18, 2018

Sometimes at Stone Soup we receive several submissions that have to do with the same topic. In the spring, we received several related to gun violence, most notably school shootings and police brutality. In light of the shooting in Santa Fe, Texas

on Friday, May 18, 2018, we decided to publish a selection of these sadly relevant pieces online.

There is a lockdown on October 23, 2015.
by Aidan McClure, 7

It was very scary! We had to hide in the coatroom for an hour and a half. Everybody was freaking out except for me, you know, because I am writing this. The police needed to give us an emergency early dismissal but not the good kind. Some people hid under their desks. We didn't get to have lunch at school. The people who are working on the track left early. Mrs. Fitzgerald turned on Johnny Appleseed. Someone named Madison is writing about this to remember. I said I wasn't afraid. Well now I am. Hu hu hu hu. That's me breathing loud. I do that when I'm scared. I'm pretty sure everybody is terrified, even our fish is terrified. I will never forget this day. They'll probably make my mom leave early too. I can't wait until I get home and by the way I am still hu hu hu huing. They are starting to call the buses now thankfully. Some people think that they are going to die.

Illustration by William Drewes, 13, for "The Bullet." Published in *Stone Soup*, January/February 2000.

Lullaby
by Rebecca Beaver, 13

This little boy
Shot dead—
17
Got into an "altercation"
His killer claimed self defense
And got away free
Florida 2012
That's where it went down

This little boy
Hood pulled up
Iced tea in hand
Skittle in back pocket
A figure, observing from inside a van
Zimmerman—
I'm not even sure he was a man

Called the police
Said he was afraid
Of the little boy
Was ordered
"Stay put. Keep away."
Wait.
Soon the world would know their fate

He didn't
Slowly slithered out of his van
Stalked the little boy's way
Stared
In his eyes
So bright, so full of life
Suddenly, the "man"

Reached for his gun—the bullets . . .

BANG.

BANG.
BANG.

BANG.

Tore through him
Dressed in red—
Alone, the little boy died
Hood pulled up
Bright eyes dull
Light; gone
No one seems to care
He's gone, his killer free
He becomes a symbol
Of injustice
Gun violence
Police brutality
But when all is said
And all is done
He was just a little boy
Loved by a mother
Who doesn't want a symbol
She wants her son
Here, safe, alive
She wishes with all her heart
She had been able to tell him she loves him
Say goodbye
And sing her son
Her poor, sweet baby
A lullaby.

Seventeen Graves
by Kate Kuan, 11

A terrible loss on Valentine's day
Students and teachers dead in the fray
How did so many lives end this way
Because no one saw the signs
He aspired to murder and told others so
Through an Instagram profile that showed he was a foe
But no one noticed and no one would know

No one saw the signs

Cruz was nineteen, and passed a background check
Nobody knew he would take a trek
To a school where his expulsion was put into effect

Nobody saw the signs

Seventeen gravestones ringed with wreaths
Because bullets were shot from their metal sheaves
Each grave for a person who no longer breathes
Because no one saw the signs

Author Interview:
Patricia Newman, author of *Plastic,*
Ahoy!: Investigating the Great Pacific
Garbage Patch **talks to Lukas Cooke,**
Stonesoup.com blogger
Posted September 14, 2018

Lukas Cooke, our young blogger
interested in nature and the environment,
had the opportunity to read Patricia
Newman's book, and then talk to the
author about her books, her writing
process and being a published author.

Lukas Cooke: What inspired you to
become an author, specifically to write
about saving the natural world?

Patricia Newman: My husband's
mother first suggested I try writing.
I remember the exact moment. I was
reading picture books to my one-year-
old son and four-year-old daughter on
the sofa. Before that I'd never considered writing as a job.

My first books had nothing to do
with the natural world. I wrote about
railroading slang in *Jingle the Brass*
and fighter pilot slang in *Nugget on*
the Flight Deck. I also wrote several
books that editors asked me to write.
Through all that writing and researching, I hiked, visited nature centers and
zoos, recycled, composted, and saved

water, and yet it never occurred to me to write about our environment.

An article in my local newspaper planted the initial seed. I read about a group of young scientists who set sail for the North Pacific to study plastic. I was hooked!

LC: Did you always dream of becoming a writer? If not, what did you originally plan to be your career?

PN: Not at all! I knew I wanted to work with kids and I taught math for a while. Then I wrote computer code for a software company. I also worked for Cornell University, my alma mater, raising money, talking to high school students, and meeting alumni. Although my various jobs required that I communicate through writing, I'd never thought of it as a career. I think I was afraid to share. You see in fifth grade I was bullied. At the time, sharing stories seemed like painting a target on my back.

Something about becoming an adult and a parent made the bullies of my childhood powerless. I'm glad I changed my mind, but I'm sorry it took me so long to figure it out.

LC: What is your favorite tip for new or aspiring writers?

PN: Read. All writers are readers. It's how we soak up the elements of good dialogue or a page-turning plot. It's how we discover what annoys us about certain stories. (Have you ever read a book where you disagreed with how the character acted?) Reading improves our vocabulary so we can describe settings. It helps us understand that people are complicated so we create characters with complex emotions. Reading stimulates ideas and exercises the imagination. We uncover fascinating aspects of the world. I read because I'm curious. There's no limit on knowing. Pack it in and let it shape who you will become.

LC: It seems like a lot of research went into writing your books. Can you describe the process of how you do the research for a book you're writing?

PN: My books start with a kernel, such as the article about scientists sailing to the North Pacific to study plastic (*Plastic, Ahoy!*); my daughter's job as an undergraduate with the Elephant Listening Project at Cornell University (*Eavesdropping on Elephants*); or a group of girls in a Kenyan village who can't go to school (*Neema's Reason to Smile*).

From there I read—online, books, magazines, newspapers—anything my library or the Internet spits out on my topic of choice. I watch videos. I listen to speeches about my topic. I want to be sure the idea is book-worthy and will appeal to kids. I also look atpublished children's books to see if anyone else has already written about my topic.

Next, I contact the people I'd like to interview. In the case of *Neema's Reason to Smile*, I interviewed two women closely involved with a school similar to the one in the book. In the case of my science nonfiction, I interview scientists.

These people have jobs to do so they don't have an unlimited amount of time to spend with me. If they don't have the time or the interest in working with me, the idea dies. I know that sounds sad, but believe me, there are plenty more ideas to take its place!

For *Neema's Reason to Smile* I conducted several hours of interviews and watched video of real life kids who go to the school I was writing about. I also reread my travel diary from my long-ago trip to Kenya to remind myself of the smells and colors and light of Africa. I wrote the entire picture book before submitting to publishers.

But my environmental science nonfiction is longer. Instead of writing the entire book, I write a proposal to sell my idea to an editor. The proposal includes an overview of my idea, a chapter outline with a brief explanation of what I plan to include in each chapter, and a section on the competition— what's already out there on the subject and how my book will be different.

Once I receive an editor's go-ahead, I begin researching in earnest. Sometimes I travel, sometimes I don't. For *Sea Otter Heroes* my daughter, Elise, and I went to the Elkhorn Slough near Monterey Bay in California. Brent Hughes, the scientist I interviewed, took us on an amazing boat trip down the slough. We saw a lot of marine life, including sea otters, seals, pelicans, herons, jellies, and crabs. I interviewed Brent and some of his colleagues. Elise took photos and asked her own questions.

For *Zoo Scientists to the Rescue* photographer Annie Crawley and I visited three zoos in the US. We interviewed the scientists and took behind-the-scenes tours with them. We touched a rhino and watched an orangutan baby climb all over her mother.

Traveling is a blast AND hard work. Scientists are extremely busy and can generally only speak to me for a day, so I have to be organized. I've read enough about their story to be able to prepare detailed questions. When I work with Annie, we also set up specific shots because half of every book is visual.

Back at home, I listen to many hours of recorded interviews and ask follow-up questions via email. I also pore over scientific studies to understand the smallest details, for instance, how to construct a sea otter-proof cage or how to measure if a rhino is sleeping. Then I write many, many drafts before sending the manuscript to my editor. She reads it and returns it with comments. A lot of comments. I reorganize and rewrite at least three different drafts before we're ready to talk about the photos or illustrations.

LC: In reading your book *Plastic, Ahoy!*, it appears you had a lot of input from scientists. Can you describe the process, and what you felt like being able to work with them?

PN: When I interview scientists, I definitely feel star-struck. These people are amazing thinkers, doers, achievers, and I get to spend time with them! They make a difference in the health of our world. I want to know how they do it, and I want to share that know-how with readers. Science is about people asking questions and discovering answers. Kids do that every day. Doing what comes naturally can be a launching pad for a career in science

Scientists often talk and write using words I don't understand. They have a specialized vocabulary that comes with their training. I need to do some homework before I visit or chat with them on the phone. I don't want them to feel as if I'm wasting their time and I want to use the time I have with them as efficiently as possible.

So, I read. A lot. Not only to understand the basic terms, but to ask questions that go deeper than the surface. Questions that get to the heart of what's going through their minds as they solve a scientific mystery. Questions that get to the heart of their passion for science.

As an author, it's my job to translate difficult scientific concepts into language that kids can understand. I ask detailed questions, such as how long did that take? How many times did you fail? What materials did you use? My favorite question for every scientist is, "How would you explain what you do to a 4th grader?"

LC: Also while reading *Plastic, Ahoy!*, it seemed a lot like a firsthand account of the ship *New Horizon*'s trip to the Great Pacific Garbage Patch. The research that Miriam, Darcy, and Chelsea did also seemed to come from a witness. Were you aboard *New Horizon* during the voyage? If so, what did it feel like?

PN: I love that you noticed this detail. I was not aboard *New Horizon*, but Annie Crawley was the official photographer for the expedition. I interviewed Annie as well as the scientists to understand specifics of the journey, such as the ship's layout, how long they worked, what a typical day was like. I asked for weather reports, wildlife they spotted, how much it cost to charter the research vessel, and a lot more.

I combined these notes with the many time I've been at sea. I remembered the way the sun rose on the water, how the swells sounded, the wind, the smell of the salty water. Nothing ever goes to waste for authors. We somehow manage to use our life experiences in many of the books we write.

LC: What is your favorite part about being an author?

PN: The creative process is one of my favorite parts. It's hard work that requires a lot of research and deep think ing about how to distill a mountain of material into the truth that I want to tell. The creative process also involves failure. Although I never (repeat that, never) get it right the first time, it's rewarding because I end up with a book that only I could write.

With all that said, my absolute favorite part is the day my book arrives on my doorstep. I open it like a long-awaited birthday present and do a little happy dance when I hold it in my hands for the first time!

Check out Patricia's website to read more about her books, and watch videos about them.

Book Reviews

The One and Only Ivan
Reviewed by Phoebe Eckstein, 13
Posted May 25, 2018

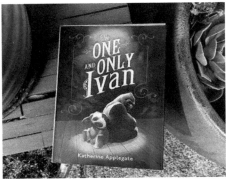

@stonesoupbykids

This story is about promises kept, selflessness, and friendship. It's about Ivan keeping his promise to his friend, Stella, and trying to get Ruby to a better place.

Ivan is a silverback gorilla. For twenty-seven years, Ivan has lived in the mall. Every day, Ivan is in his domain watching the people outside as they go about their lives. Ivan hardly ever thinks about his old life when he was living in the jungle. Instead, he watches television, draws, and paints. Ivan's life is not sad. Sometimes he's happy, especially when he's painting. But Ivan doesn't seem to realize what he doesn't have. He doesn't realize that his cage is small and he insists on calling it a domain and not a cage.

There's a part where Ivan says "I know what most humans think. They think gorillas don't have imaginations. They think we don't remember our pasts or ponder our futures. Come to think of it, I suppose they have a point. Mostly I think about what is, not what could be." This suggests that Ivan might not have any hope. I think it's more that Ivan doesn't hope for anything because he doesn't know what to hope for. So when Stella tells him about a zoo, a place where she says humans try to make amends to the animals, he begins to have something to hope for.

Ivan's best friends are Stella and Bob. Stella is an older, wise elephant who remembers much of her old life in the jungle, and knows many stories. Stella and Ivan have a very strong friendship that compels Ivan to make a special promise to her. His other friend, Bob, is a crafty stray dog who stays at the mall, but doesn't want an actual home. Bob would rather find his own food than be fed by someone else. At one point in the story, when he is asked why he doesn't want a home, he answers, "Everywhere is my home, I am a wild beast, my friend: untamed and undaunted."

The other main character is Ruby. Ruby comes into the story when business at the mall slows down, and fewer people come to see the animals. Mack decides to get a small baby elephant (Ruby) for the circus. Ruby is young and naïve and asks lots of questions. When Ivan sees her in her small cage, and when he sees how Mack makes her practice her circus routine even when she's very tired, Ivan decides he must make some changes.

The story is narrated by Ivan. But as Ivan says, gorillas don't waste words. I think the author did a great job incorporating that concept—short sentences and descriptions without wasting words—into the way the book was written, but without making the story too simple.

This is a wonderful story for anyone ages 8-13.

The One and Only Ivan by Katherine Applegate. Harper Collins, 2012.

Holes
Reviewed by Abhi Sukhdial, 10
Posted May 27, 2018

@stonesoupbykids

Have you thought that nothing could be worse than jail? Well you would be totally wrong because in the book *Holes*, the prison is about as bad as it can get — so bad that in this prison, you spend hours digging holes in the ground to find treasure for the warden. This prison is called Camp Green Lake.

Stanley Yelnats is an ordinary kid going about his everyday normal life. Until one day, he is taken to court for stealing a pair of shoes (which he actually didn't steal!). The court doesn't believe him, and they take him to Camp Green Lake. In CGL (Camp Green Lake) Stanley meets a few friends named Zero, X-ray and more!

CGL was once a nice lake in Texas EVERYONE came to, and then one day, all the water dried up. Now CGL is a dry, hot desert prison. Stanley stays at CGL for eighteen months until he finally leaves. The thing that makes *Holes* so interesting is how the plot develops over the course of the book. There are many scenes that are intense, leaving you in suspense and making you scared so badly. Like

...ple, when Stanley survives ...f poisonous lizards after he ...lly falls into a hole. Or when Zero (one of Stanley's friends) hits one of the assistants working for the Warden with a shovel and runs away to a mountain called The Big Thumb. The scenes in the story are pretty violent, but are okay for kids 10 years old and up. The thing that I don't like about the story is how sad the ending is. I don't want to be a spoiler, but even after Stanley returns to his home, his life (although better than it was at CGL) is still not at all great.

I empathized with Stanley because he was very brave and helpful to other prisoners in CGL despite it being a harsh place. I wish that when I sometimes face difficulties at school (like tough projects or homework), that I could stay more positive and not give up.

Holes was published in 1998 and won the 1999 Newberry Medal. At first the book was very popular and became a classic, but as other young adult books like *Harry Potter* and *Percy Jackson* have gained appeal, less recognition has been given to *Holes*. Which I think is unfair.

I highly recommend *Holes* for kids in 5th grade and up; 3rd and 4th graders might find the scenes of violence, guns and explosions too scary. If you are able to be patient and get through the first 50 pages, the story picks up its pace tremendously, especially when Stanley develops closer relationships with his prison mates. I am disappointed about three aspects of this book that I wish could have been changed. One, I wish the story had less of a scary beginning. Two, I wish the ending was changed to include more action and suspense as Stanley finds Zero hiding in the mountain and brings him back to CGL. Finally, the story has a few flashbacks, like telling us about how life was before CGL became a prison. However, these chapters are full of violent bloody scenes of destruction and death and reading them made me feel very sad.

Holes is a challenging and fun book to read. But once you complete it, you'll be so happy and exhausted!!

Holes by Louis Sachar. Yearling, 1998.

The Adventures of a Girl Called Bicycle
Reviewed by Nina Vigil, 11
Posted August 8, 2018

@stonesoupbykids

During the summer, I'm sure you are all looking for new summer reads. May I suggest *The Adventures of a Girl Called Bicycle* by Christina Uss, a unique book that will keep you reading for hours straight. It sure did for me!

The book is about a girl (as you may have guessed) named Bicycle. She has lived at the Mostly Silent Monastery for most of her life, a place where near-silence is the norm. Bicycle has no friends because she isn't used to how loud other kids are. Sister Wanda, Bicycle's official guardian, decides to send her to The Friendship Factory, a camp in Nevada that guarantees she'll make three friends. But Bicycle has other ideas. On her bike, Clunk, she sets out across the country to cover the 4,000 miles from Washington D.C. to California in order to meet her idol, a famous bicyclist she's hoping will become her friend. Along the way, Bicycle will encounter a bike burglar, a Civil War ghost, a French restaurateur, a ghost town, a bike-crazy horse and 838 pigs.

A central theme of *The Adventures of a Girl Called Bicycle* is perseverance. Even when she's faced with difficulties and problems and exhausting miles, Bicycle keeps working towards her goal. In Virginia, she rides up hill after hill after enormous hill. She bikes through the Rocky Mountains. She even treks for hours and hours through a sunflower field. Bicycle stays on a strict 50-mile-a-day schedule for weeks on end, for thousands of miles. You have to work hard to in order to reach your goals, and this book is an excellent reminder of that.

Another theme is the importance of friendship. Bicycle sets out on her epic quest in the hopes of making one single friend, but along the way, she makes a lot more friends than she expected, like Griffin, Estrella, Jeremiah, Chef Marie, the Cookie Lady . . . I could go on and on. Bicycle's life is made so much better because of the friendships she develops. Another point the book makes is that friendship can't be forced. You can make friends unexpectedly and in the unlikeliest of places.

I loved all the zany adventures Bicycle has on her trip across the U.S. Few of us have been run over by a parade of pigs, or biked over the Rockies, or won a missile-launching bike at an auction, or accidentally wandered into the Kentucky Derby. Reading this book made me want to take a road trip, and any book that makes you want to go have an adventure is a good book! You will definitely love *The Adventures of a Girl Called Bicycle*, so ride your bike to the library immediately!

The Adventures of a Girl Called Bicycle by Christina Uss. Margaret Ferguson Books, 2018.

Harry Potter and the Sorcerer's Stone
Reviewed by Kaya Simcoe, 13
Posted July 23, 2018

Reviewing *Harry Potter* is kind of like reviewing Taco Bell or vanilla ice cream. Most everyone has read it, but sometimes just knowing that a book is famous or has won awards won't make you read it, especially if you are a careful reader, like me. Yes, *Harry Potter* is

@stonesoupbykids

scary. And it is also inspirational, amazing, spellbinding, and deeply profound.

I had never read it on my own, because I knew it has some very scary moments (and it does). Scary books just aren't worth it to me. But, one day my grandma persuaded me to read one chapter on the phone. Just one chapter. How hard could it be?

HARD! But not the book. Needing to put the book down! From the first page I was hooked. I never knew Harry Potter was funny, but I think it's hilarious. The characters are strong, well thought out, and multi-dimensional. They are real to me, and that's one of the magical things about Harry Potter. ("Of course it's happening inside your head!" Dumbledore exclaims in book seven, "But why on Earth should that mean it's not real?")

I love Hermione, one of Harry's best friends, immensely. She is strong, independent, and brave, but I really appreciate that author J.K. Rowling sometimes lets her break or be real. "We could have been killed!" Hermione says in book one, "Or worse, expelled." By book seven though, "We're coming with you. That was decided months ago—years really." Though not well known, that is one of my favorite Hermione quotes.

I think J.K. Rowling is very brave. As a writer myself, I know how hard it is to put your characters in difficult situations, or make bad things happen to them. You love your characters like friends (at least, I do) and often you can tell something about the author by what he or she makes happen to theirs. *Harry Potter* IS sad, and scary, but it revolves around love. "You are protected, in short, by your ability to love!" Dumbledore tells Harry in book six. These books have many layers, which makes it interesting for me to read, and you get to decide if it's worth it to you to see them all.

I see the books differently now at thirteen, rather than eight. I really value the beautiful and dynamic characters J.K. Rowling adds to her books. The realness of it all is one of the reasons that I love *Harry Potter*. No, you probably can't make someone's wand shoot out of their hands when you yell "expelliarmus!" in this world, and mail is delivered by postman, not owl. But you CAN stand up, fight back, break down, laugh, cry, and LOVE each other in this world. This is the kind of magic we can all perform. We all have this magic inside of us. Will we use it? Do we even know it's there?

I love *Harry Potter* because it is its own world. I am a part of it every time I open a thoroughly well-loved book, where dragons exist and broomsticks can fly. My collection of the hardcover books have a million pages folded down, and every funny scenario is highlighted. Some may argue that this isn't the way to treat good books—but I think, it's the best way. *Harry Potter* inspires me to enjoy smarts, love, and use MY wizard powers. What are they? How will they help?

What are YOUR wizard powers? Maybe you'll find some you didn't know were there... when you read my favorite book.

Harry Potter and the Sorcerer's Stone by J.K. Rowling. Arthur A. Levine Books, Reissue 2018.

To Kill A Mockingbird
Reviewed by Maya Viswanathan, 12
Posted September 5, 2018

@stonesoupbykids

To Kill A Mockingbird is about Scout, a girl growing up in Alabama with her brother Jem, a daring adventurous boy, her friend Dill, Calpurnia, a

mother-like figure who watches over her, and Atticus, her father, a kind and caring person who stands up for what is right. When Tom Robinson, a black man, is wrongly accused of committing a crime, the Judge knows that Atticus is the right person to be Tom Robinson's lawyer. In Alabama, blacks had different churches and had their own section of the courtroom. They didn't mix with whites. When a black man was accused by a white man, he was nearly sure to lose. Society was clearly very different then. But despite the differences in society, I can relate to Scout as well as if she was growing up in the 21st century.

One thing that helps me relate to Scout is that the book is written from her point of view. Although the story is about Tom Robinson's case, it also talks about Scout's daily troubles from Jem ignoring her to her teacher reprimanding her. These details about her daily life are what make the book hard to put down. Tom Robinson's case causes problems for Scout. People were angry with her father and it infuriated her because she felt that people have no right to be angry. At the same time it scared her. She worried that their anger would lead to actions against her father. Although I never felt such feelings, I can easily understand the way Scout thinks.

Every other character in *To Kill A Mockingbird* is just as vibrant and realistic. Another example is Calpurnia. At the beginning of the book, Scout does not like Calpurnia because she is too strict.

However, as the book goes on, Scout grows fonder of Calpurnia. Calpurnia stays as strict as she always was but in other ways, she proves that she cares. When Atticus was out of town, she took Jem and Scout to church with her. When Miss Lula May, another woman who went to Calpurnia's church, said that Jem and Scout should not be at the church because they were white, Calpurnia defended them. I can relate to this because my mother is strict with me. She wants me to work hard on math and music. Recently, she told me to start playing a song that my violin teacher had not assigned yet. I was very annoyed by this. I was already working hard and didn't need to add this extra work to my practice. Reading about Calpurnia and Scout reminded me that my mom is strict with me because she cares about me and wants me to excel. Like my mother, Calpurnia really cared about Jem and Scout. She was like a mother to them, and by the end of the book they wouldn't think of letting her leave. Through Calpurnia and other characters, *To Kill A Mockingbird* shows that nobody is perfect and everyone is good in some way.

Tom Robinson was not perfect, but he was innocent. He was convicted because he was black. We have come a long way, but today African Americans are still treated unfairly and we should do our best to prevent it. *To Kill A Mockingbird* shows us how wrong prejudice is and reminds us to try to be fair and just. We also learn from Atticus to stand up for what we believe in and to never give up. There is a lot to learn from this book and you should read it to discover plenty of wise thoughts and ideas.

To Kill a Mockingbird by Harper Lee. Harper Perennial Modern Classics, 1962.

The Westing Game
Reviewed by Ananda Bhaduri, 13
Posted August 27, 2018

@stonesoupbykids

"And now, dear friends, relatives, and enemies, the Westing game begins."

The inhabitants of Sunset Towers are in for a surprise. Samuel Westing, the eccentric millionaire, is dead and they have been named the official benefactors of the Westing estate. But wait—there's a catch. In his will, which is as eccentric as the man himself, he states that his life was taken by one of his heirs. The heirs have been divided into eight pairs and asked to find the guilty. The team which succeeds wins the inheritance. The heirs soon find out that the Westing game is much more than an old man's idiosyncrasies. It's a game designed to test them in every possible way.

This book was also hilarious. This is not something you would associate with murder mysteries. Nevertheless, I enjoyed the comedy. Seeing a bunch of plain and simple people trying to defeat the most cunning man on Earth at his own game was extremely funny. There were no complex deductions made, no fancy detectives, no "Elementary, my dear Watson"s. In fact, the heirs' attempts at finding the murderer were so feeble, I doubted that anyone would be able to win the inheritance. However, I was proven wrong in the end. There were some who were quite intelligent even though they were not on Westing's level.

This is one of those books where you feel the presence of a mastermind controlling everything from behind the scenes. Sam Westing might be dead, but he is able to perform feats from the grave which are beyond the ability of any living man. It seems, from the beginning of the book, that almost every action taken by the heirs has been predicted or is being controlled by Sam Westing. You cannot help but appreciate the old man's tricks and subtleties. Even though he was not present physically, his presence could definitely be felt by the heirs as well.

My favorite part was the last few chapters. The heirs were trapped in a room in the Westing manor and had five minutes to produce an answer. Those five minutes were more eventful than the rest of the book. A lot of things happened which made them think and reflect. They were desperate and needed an answer to explain the bizarre events that had just occurred. And in those crucial moments, a solution was found. And what a solution it was!! Never in my wildest dreams would I have been able to think of it.

Reading this book was like watching two grandmasters play chess. When you see a queen sacrifice, you know that the move must have a deep meaning and you try to figure out the reason. When I finished this book, I still didn't know the answers to a lot of questions. I read the book again and tried to decipher all of Westing's moves. And this was perhaps the most enjoyable part of the book. This book will make you think, make you laugh and it won't let you get up until you've finished it. I would recommend this to anyone who is bored and would like to exercise their grey cells. It doesn't matter whether you're eight or eighty-eight. If you're strong of heart, try and have a go at *The Westing Game*.

The Westing Game by Ellen Raskin. Dutton Books, 1978.

Music

GLOCKEN DER FANTASIE
by Justin Park, 13
Posted August 13, 2018

I started to compose when I was about 9 years old and wrote about 5 pieces of music. Back then I had played the piano for about 5 years already. I started to play the oboe when I was about 12 years old and still play both instruments today.

What inspired me to write this piece was another composition that had a rhythm as the bass and a violin that was playing out the melody much louder and unique. I decided to create a piece for the oboe and piano because I am familiar with them. It was to represent a melody that related to the calmness and the subtleness of Beethoven's Moonlight Sonata left hand, which consists of the melody, and the right hand, which plays a simple yet iconic rhythm over and over again while the left hand plays different chords and keys.

The piece is something that sort of questions and answers the melody (as you might be able to tell), and also has one instrument play most of the melody in the first section. My teacher helped me with what to do and the rules when doing this kind of piece. We decided to split up the piece into multiple sections and that is how we got the piano solo at the end.

You can listen to Justin playing his piece, and print out additional copies of the music, at Stonesoup.com. Try playing it yourself with a friend, and send us a recording, or leave a comment on our blog.

Glocken Der Fantasie

for Oboe and Piano

Justin Park

Copyright @ Justin Park 2018

STONE SOUP

MISTED
by Abe Effress, 11
Posted September 11, 2018

I have been playing saxophone since I moved to Los Angeles from the mountains of Colorado four years ago. This year, I wrote a piece for piano and submitted it to the Composers Today program for young composers. I became very interested in making music, and have started to realize it is a passion that I want to pursue.

I decided to really challenge myself with this new song, "Misted." This is the first time I have composed music for two instruments, piano and saxophone. The saxophone that you hear was inspired by a spider that has been living outside of my windowsill in the room I share with my brother. This song is in a minor key because for one day the spider was not there and it made me sad when I thought my new friend had gone away. Many of my creations, especially my writing, are dark and gnarled, like the branches of my mind.

In this song, I also included my love for music production in the form of a beat, which I added in GarageBand. When I started making songs on GarageBand this summer, my parents decided that I could get an Instagram account for my music, fiction stories, drawings, and any other art created by me. The positive response I have been receiving from real professionals in the music production industry has motivated me to work even harder.

I really hope you enjoy "Misted." I did my best to write down the notes for both instruments even though the piano is naturally in a different key than the alto sax. Thank you for taking the time to check out my work!

You can listen to Abe playing his piece, and print out additional copies of the music, at Stonesoup.com. Try playing it yourself, and send us a recording, or leave a comment on our blog.

Misted

Slowly and Soulfully

Abe Effress

STONE SOUP

Contests

It's been a great year for *Stone Soup* contests. So far, we've awarded prizes in three contests, described below. And, as this year's Annual goes to print, our last contest of the year—the Secret Kids Contest, in partnership with Mackenzie Press—is still open. If you are reading this in 2018, you could enter to win a book publishing deal! Visit the Contests page at Stonesoup.com for all the details.

SCIENCE FICTION CONTEST

We held this contest in the spring and we have to admit: when we put out the call, we were nervous. But, once we started reading your entries, we realized what a good reminder this contest was—a reminder of the fact that a good story is a good story, regardless of genre. The winning stories used exciting language, created realistic worlds, kept us engaged, created suspense, and ultimately led us to a deeper understanding of ourselves and our world.

First Place ($80)
"Middlenames" by Thomas Faulhaber, 13

Second Place ($40)
"Young Eyes" by Allie Aguila, 12

Third Place ($20)
"The Mystical Creatures of Blue Spout Bay" by Marlena Rohde, 12

Fourth Place ($10)
"Sunk" by Benjamin Mitchell, 13

Honorable Mentions
"The Transmitter" by Sabrina Guo, 12
"Holding On" by Macy Li, 12
"Shhh" by Harper Miller, 11

Flip back to the September 2018 issue to read the winning stories.

FLASH FICTION CONTEST

For this contest, which ran from April to mid-June, we asked for tiny, short short stories (300 words or less) that told a big story or captured a big idea—or maybe just described a single moment or a single thing in extreme and unusual detail.

We were amazed, reading the submissions, at how much can fit into 300 words. Some entries chose to focus on describing a moment or scene in sparkling, clear prose. Others chose to tell an action-packed narrative. Both types worked, and both felt much longer than the word limit. Flash fiction reminded us of a clown car: each story managed to pack in so much more than we thought possible.

First Place ($50)
"The Pendulum" by Sabrina Guo, 12

Second Place ($25)
"The Sycamore Tree" by Mira Johnson, 8

Third Place ($10)
"A Dinner Party" by Anyi Sharma, 10

Fourth Place ($5)
"The Hummingbird" by Clare McDermott, 12

Honorable Mentions:
"Symbiotic" by Madeline Pass, 13
"Potato Diaries" by Christian Goh, 10
"The Mystical Trees" by Hannah Lee, 10

Look out for the winning short short stories in the magazine in January 2019.

CONCRETE POETRY CONTEST

A concrete poem is a piece of art to which both the visual and the written element are essential. With just the image (no words), you lose something, just as with only the words (no image), you lose something. A concrete poem is one you need to see as well as hear! We asked for a piece of visual art made with words for this contest that ran from July to September.

The pieces that ended up standing out to us were the ones that not only showed us the writer had a clear understanding of the concrete poem but that used the shape of the poem to emphasize and illustrate the text.

First Place ($50)
"Steam" by Sabrina Guo, 12

Second Place ($25)
"Moonlight" by Ashley Xu, 13

Third Place ($10)
"Octopus" by Marco Lu, 12

Honorable Mentions
"Snowflake" by Emma Almaguer, 13
"A Tree" by Andrew Lin, 8
"The Cloud" and "Disappearing" by Madeline Nelson, 12
"Seeing the Sea" Maya Viswanathan, 12

Look out for the winning concrete poems in the magazine in March 2019.

STONE SOUP

Donations

Stone Soup is produced by the Children's Art Foundation, a 501(c)(3) educational non-profit organization registered in California. While most of what we do is funded by subscriptions, we are also the grateful recipients of donations, which help us expand our work. Our suggested donation levels are each named for a well-known author or artist who, like our *Stone Soup* contributors, did remarkable work as children, before going on to adult greatness.

Since the publication of last year's *Stone Soup Annual*, we have received donations from the following kind individuals. We thank all of them sincerely for their generosity.

Daisy Ashford (up to $25)

Joan Lee Holdefer
Debbie Mason
Theresa Wallinger

Margaret Atwood (up to $50)

Sarah Bilston
Peter Clark
Yael Gertner
Vrinda Khanna
Aparna Ramachandran
Rachel Thornton

Charlotte Brontë (up to $100)

Bridget Brett
Sabrina Guo
Rachel Thornton

Albrecht Dürer (up to $250)

Roger Forman

Edith Wharton (up to $500)

Spencer Guo

Jane Austen (up to $1,000)

-

LIFETIME GIFTS

We also gratefully acknowledge the significant support of our founders, friends, and other major donors throughout the lifetime of *Stone Soup*:

Michael Axelrod
Mr Alvin Baum
Joanna Hamburg
Mr & Mrs Lowell Christy
Gerry Mandel, Editor Emerita
Lillian McMullen
Mrs Harry Rubel
John & Dorothy Rubel
Mrs Mildred Rosencranz
Garth Sheldon

CPSIA information can be obtained
at www.ICGtesting.com
Printed in the USA
BVHW051017171118
533152BV00002BA/2/P